THE CHUCKWAGON TRAIL

THE CHUCKWAGON TRAIL

WILLIAM W. JOHNSTONE
with J. A. Johnstone

PINNACLE BOOKS
Kensington Publishing Corp.
www.kensingtonbooks.com

CHAPTER 1

Dewey Mackenzie shivered as he pressed against the wet stone wall and blinked moisture from his eyes. Whether it came from the chilly rain that had fallen in New Orleans earlier this evening or from his own fear-fueled sweat—or both—he didn't know. He supposed it didn't matter.

Right now, he just wanted to avoid the two men standing guard across the street. Both were twice his size, and one had the battered look of a boxer. Even in the dim light cast by the gas lamp far down Royal Street, Mac saw the flattened nose, the cauliflower ears, and the way the man continually ducked and dodged imaginary punches.

At some time in the past, those punches hadn't been imaginary, and there had been a lot of them.

A medium-sized young man with longish dark hair and what had been described by more than one young woman as a roguish smile, Mac rubbed his hands against the sides of his fancy dress trousers and settled his Sunday go-to-meeting coat around his shoulders.

Carrying a gun on an errand like this was out of the question, but he missed the comforting feel of his Smith & Wesson Model 3 resting on his hip. He closed his eyes, licked his lips, and then sidled back along the wall until he reached the cross street. Like a cat, he slid around the corner to safety and heaved a huge sigh.

Getting in to see Evangeline Holdstock was always a chore, but after her pa had threatened him with death—or worse—if he caught him nosing around their mansion again, Mac had come to the only possible conclusion. He had been seeing Evangeline on the sly for more than two months, reveling in the stolen moments they shared. Even, if he cared to admit it to himself, enjoying the risks he was running.

He was little more than a drifter in the eyes of Micah Holdstock, owner of the second biggest bank in New Orleans. Holdstock measured his wealth in millions. The best the twenty-one-year-old could come up with was a bright, shiny silver cartwheel and a sweat-stained wad of Union greenbacks, but he had earned the money honestly at a restaurant in the French Quarter.

Mac held his hands in front of him and balled them into fists. He had worked as a farmhand and a half dozen jobs on riverboats before he washed ashore in the Crescent City three months earlier. Every bit of that work was honest, even if it didn't pay as well as sitting behind a bank desk and denying people loans.

He tried to erase such thoughts from his mind. Hold-stock's bank served a purpose, and the man made his money honestly, too. It just wasn't the way Mac earned his. It wasn't the way anyone else he'd ever known in his young life had earned their money, either.

If he wanted to carry out his mission tonight, he had to concentrate on that. He had gotten himself cleaned up for a simple reason.

Looking his best was a necessity when he asked Evie to marry him.

"Mrs. Dewey Mackenzie," he said softly. He liked the sound of that. "My wife. Mrs. Evangeline Mackenzie."

A quick peek around the corner down Royal Street dampened his spirits a mite. The two guards still stood in front of the door leading into the Hold-stock house. Shifting his eyes from the street to the second story revealed a better way to get in without being caught and given a thrashing.

More than likely, Evie's pa had told those bruisers they could toss him into the river if they caught him snooping around. This time of year, the Mississippi River roiled with undertow and mysterious currents known only to the best of the riverboat pilots. It wasn't safe to swim anywhere near the port.

"Besides," he said softly to himself, "I don't want to muddy up my fancy duds." He smoothed wrinkles out of his coat, then boldly walked across the street without so much as a glance in the guards' direction.

He stopped and looked up when he was hidden by the wall. A black iron decoration drooped down from the railing around the second-story veranda just enough for him to grab. He stepped back a couple paces, got a running start, and made a grand leap. His fingers closed on the ornate wrought iron. With a powerful heave, he pulled himself up and got a leg over the railing.

Moving carefully to keep from tearing his trousers or getting his coat dirty, he dropped to the balcony floor and looked down to see if he had drawn any unwanted attention. Mac caught his breath when the guard who must have been a boxer came around the corner, scratched his head, and looked down the street. Moving quickly, Mac leaned back out of sight before the man looked up.

Senses acute with fear, he heard the guard shuffle away, heading back toward the door where his partner waited. Mac sank into a chair and used a handkerchief to wipe sweat from his forehead.

If this had been a couple of months later, he would have been drenched in sweat and for a good reason. Summer in New Orleans wore a man down with stifling heat and oppressive humidity, but now, late April, the sweat came from a different cause.

"Buck up," he whispered to himself. "Her pa can't stop you. You're going to marry the most wonderful girl in all New Orleans, and tonight's the night you ask for her hand."

Mac knew he had things backward, but considering how Mr. Holdstock acted, he wanted to be sure Evie loved him as much as he did her. Best to find out if she would marry him, *then* ask her pa for her hand in marriage. If Evie agreed, then to hell with whatever her pa thought.

He took a deep breath, reflecting on what she would be giving up. She claimed not to like the social whirl of a young debutante, but he had to wonder if some part of her didn't enjoy the endless attention, the fancy clothing, the rush of a cotillion followed by a soirée and whatever else they called a good old hoedown in New Orleans society.

A quick look over the railing convinced him the guard had returned to his post. Stepping carefully, knowing from prior experience where every creaky board was, he made his way along the balcony to a closed window. The curtains had been pulled. He pressed his hand against the window pane, then peered into Evie's bedroom. Squinting, he tried to make out if she stood in the shadows. The coal-oil lamp had been extinguished, but if she was expecting him, she wouldn't advertise her presence.

He tried the door handle. Locked. Using his knife blade, he slipped it between the French doors and lifted slowly. When he felt resistance, he applied a bit more pressure. The latch opened to him, as it had so many times before. Evie liked to playact that he was a burglar come to rob her of her jewels, then ravish her.

The thought of that made him blush because he enjoyed it as much as she did. More than once, he had sneaked into her room and gone through the elaborate ritual of demanding her jewels, then forcing her to disrobe slowly to prove she had not hidden anything on her body. Both of them got too excited to ever carry on with the charade for more than a few minutes. He went to the bed now and pressed down on it with his fingers, remembering the times they had made love here.

Mac swung around and sat, wondering how long he should wait before he went hunting for her.

For all he knew, her ma and pa were out for the night. Their social life mingled with Holdstock's banking business and caused them to attend parties and meetings throughout the week to maintain their standing in the community. Mac got antsy after less than a minute and went to the bedroom door. Carefully opening it, he looked down the hallway. Evie's room was at the back of the house, while her parents had the room at the front, at the far end of the hallway lined with fancy paintings and marble sculptures. The Persian rug muffled his footfalls as he made his way to the head of the stairs.

The broad fan of steps swept down to the foyer. He ducked back when he heard Holdstock speaking with someone at the door. From the guest's accent, he was French. That meant little in a town filled with Frenchmen and Acadians. French Creole was almost as widely spoken as English or Spanish.

"I am glad we could meet, Monsieur Leclerc. Come into the study. I have a fine cigar from Cuba that you will find delightful."

"*Bon*, good, Mr. Holdstock. And brandy?"

"Only the finest French brandy."

The two laughed and disappeared from sight. Mac cursed his bad luck. It would have been better if Holdstock were out of the house rather than entertaining—or conducting business, judging by the formality the two showed one another. Some high-powered deal was being struck not fifty feet away. That deal would undoubtedly make the banker rich. Or richer than he already was.

But Mac didn't care about that. His riches were wrapped in crinoline and lace, with flowing blond hair and eyes as green as jade. He stepped back and wondered where she might be.

Then he heard her soft voice below as she greeted Monsieur Leclerc and exchanged a few mumbled pleasantries. The sound of her slippers moving against the foyer floor set his heart racing. He hastily retreated to her bedroom and closed the door behind him. From past times here, he knew the exact spot to stand.

Beside her wardrobe, hidden in shadow when she lit the oil lamp, he could cherish her for a few seconds before she realized she was not alone. Mac pressed into the niche just as the door opened. He closed his eyes and took a deep whiff. Jasmine perfume made his nostrils flare. This was her favorite perfume, but he told her often she did not need it, not with him. Just being around her intoxicated his senses more than enough.

He opened his eyes and squinted as he stared directly into the burning wick of Evie's bedside lamp. She bent over slightly, hands on the bed, her bustle wiggling delightfully.

"I have never seen any woman so lovely," he said. "If I live to be a thousand, I never will forget this moment, this sight, this beautiful—"

She straightened and spun. Her eyes went wide. His heart almost skipped a beat when he realized it wasn't surprise that caused her face to contort. It was fear.

"What's wrong, my dear?" He went to her, but she pushed him back.

"Go, Mac. Get out of here now. Please. Don't slow down. He knows we've been seeing each other."

"I don't care. I love you. Do you love me?"

"Yes, yes," she said, flustered. She brushed back a wayward strand of lustrous, honey blond hair and looked up at him. True fear twisted her face. "I love you with all my heart and soul, Mac. That's why you have to leave."

"Then let's go together. Let's elope. We can find a justice of the peace. We don't have to get married in the St. Louis Basilica."

"Mac, you don't understand. I—"

"I can't give you a fancy house or fine clothing or jewelry like this." He touched the pearl necklace around her slender throat, then moved to caress her cheek. "Not now. Someday I will. Together we can—"

"You have to go before he catches you!"

"I'll go down and beard the old lion in his den. We'll have it out, man to man. I won't let him chase me off from the love of my life." He moved her around so he could go to the door.

Before he could get there, the door slammed open, reverberating as it smashed into the wall. Silhouetted against the light from downstairs, Micah Holdstock filled the frame.

"I should have known you would come, especially on a night like this!"

Mac began, "Mr. Holdstock, I—"

"Papa, please, you can't do this. Don't hurt him." Evie tried to interpose herself between the men, but Mac wouldn't have it. No woman he loved sacrificed herself for him, especially with her father.

"Evie and I love each other, sir. We're getting married!"

Micah Holdstock let out a roar like a charging

bull. The attack took Mac by surprise. Strong arms encircled his body and lifted him off his feet. He tried to get his arms free but couldn't with them pinned at his sides. Still roaring, Holdstock went directly for the French doors and smashed through them. Shards of glass sprayed in the air and tumbled to the balcony as he used Mac as a battering ram.

The collision robbed Mac of breath. He went limp in the man's death grip. This saved him from being driven against the iron railing and having his back broken. He dropped to his knees as Holdstock crashed into the wrought-iron railing and fought to keep from tumbling into the street below.

"Papa," he heard Evie pleading, trying to stop the attack.

Mac got to shaky feet to face her pa.

"This is no way for future in-laws to act," he gasped out. "My intentions are honorable."

"She's betrothed. As of this very evening!" Again Holdstock charged.

Mac saw the expression of resignation on Evie's face an instant before her father's hard fist caught him on the side of the head and sent him reeling. He grabbed the iron railing and went over, dangled a moment, then fell heavily to the cobblestone street and sprawled onto his back. He stared up to see Evie sobbing bitterly as her father grabbed her by the arm and pulled her out of sight.

"You can't do this. I won't let you!" He got to his feet in time to see the two guards round the corner. From the way they were hurrying, he knew what they had been ordered to do.

Shameful though it might be, he turned and ran.

The guards' bulk meant they were slower on their feet than Mac was. Three blocks later, he finally evaded them by ducking into a saloon in Pirate's Alley. He leaned against the wall for a moment, catching his breath. The smoke in the dive formed a fog so thick it wasn't possible to see more than a few feet. He coughed, then went to the bar and collapsed against it.

"I say this to damned near ever'body what comes into this place," the barkeep said, "but in your case I mean it. You look like you could use a drink."

CHAPTER 2

The bartender poured a shot of whiskey.

Mac knocked it back, and it almost knocked him down. He wasn't much of a drinker, but this had to be the most potent popskull he had ever encountered. He choked, swallowed, then said, "Another."

"The first was on the house. The next one you pay for."

"I just had a run-in with my lady friend's pa." He sucked in a breath and endured the pain in his ribs. Micah Holdstock had a grip like a bear. The powerful liquor went a ways toward easing the pain. He fumbled out a greenback for another drink. He needed all the deadening he could pour down his gullet.

The bartender picked up the bill, examined it, and tucked it away. "Don't usually take Yankee bills, but seeing's as how you're in pain, I will this time." He splashed more whiskey into Mac's empty glass.

Mac started to protest at not getting change. As the second shot hit his gut and set his head spinning, he forgot about it. What difference did it make anyway? He had to find a way to sneak Evie out of the house and get her to a judge for a proper marrying.

"Do tell."

Mac blinked and frowned. He hadn't realized he had been talking out loud, but obviously the bartender knew what he'd been thinking. He ran a shaky finger around the rim of his empty shot glass and captured the last amber drop. He licked it off his fingertip. The astringent burn on his tongue warned him that another drink might make him pass out.

"I'll find a way," he said, with more assurance than he felt. He needed both hands on the bar to support himself.

As he considered a third drink, he noticed how the sound in the saloon went away. All he heard was the pounding of his pulse in his ears. Thinking the drink had turned him deaf, he started to shout out for another, then saw the frightened expression on the barkeep's face. Looking over his shoulder, he saw the reason.

The two guards who had been stationed outside Micah Holdstock's front door now stood just inside the saloon, arms crossed over their chests. Those arms bulged with muscles. The men fixed steely gazes on him. Out of habit—or maybe desperation—Mac patted his right hip but found no revolver hanging there. He had dressed up for the occasion of asking Evie to marry him. There hadn't been any call for him to go armed.

He knew now that was a big mistake. He turned and had to brace himself against the bar with both elbows. He blinked hard, as much from the smoke as the tarantula juice he had swilled. Hoping he saw double and only one guard faced him, he quickly realized how wrong that was. There were two of them, and they had blood in their eyes.

"You gonna stand there all night or you gonna come for me?" He tried to hold back the taunt but failed. The liquor had loosened his tongue and done away with his common sense. Somewhere deep down in his brain, he knew he was inviting them to kill him, but he couldn't stop himself. "Well? Come on!" He balanced precariously, one foot in front of the other, fists balled and raised.

The one who looked like a boxer stirred, but the other held him back.

"Waiting for the bell to ring? Come on. Let's mix it up." He took a couple of tentative punches at thin air.

"Mister, that's Hiram Higgins," the bartender said, reaching across the bar to tug at his sleeve. "He lost to Gypsy Jem Mace over in Kennerville."

"So that just means he can lose to me just east of Jackson Square."

"Mister, Gypsy Jem whupped Tom Allen the next day for the heavyweight championship."

"So? You said this man Higgins lost."

"He lost after eighteen rounds. Ain't nobody stayed with the Gypsy longer 'n that. The man's a killer with those fists."

Mac wasn't drunk enough to tangle with Holdstock's guard, not after hearing that. But the boxer stepped away deferentially when a nattily dressed man stepped into the saloon. The newcomer carefully pulled off gloves and clutched them in his right hand. He took off a tall top hat and disdainfully tossed it to the boxer. Walking slowly, the man advanced on Mac.

"You are the one? *You?*" He stopped two paces away from Mac, slapping the gloves he held in his right hand across his left palm.

"I'm your worst nightmare, mister." Still emboldened by the booze, Mac flipped the frilled front of the man's bleached white shirt. A diamond stud popped free. The man made no effort to retrieve it from the sawdust on the floor. He stared hard at Mac.

"You are drunk. But of course you are. Do you know who I am?"

"Not a clue. Some rich snake in the grass from the cut of your clothes." Mac tried to flip his finger against the man's prominent nose this time. A small turn of the man's head prevented him from delivering the insulting gesture.

"I am Pierre Leclerc, the son of Antoine Leclerc."

"I've heard the name. Somewhere." Mac tried to work out why the name was familiar. His head buzzed with a million bees inside it, and he was definitely seeing double now. Two of the annoying men filled his field of vision. He tried to decide which one to punch.

"He owns the largest shipping company in New Orleans. It is one of the largest in North America."

"So? You're rich. What of it?"

"You will leave Miss Evangeline Holdstock alone. You will never try to see her again. She wants nothing to do with you."

"Why's that, Mister Fancy Pants?"

"Because she and I are to be married. This very

night my father arranged for her hand in marriage to unite her father's bank and our shipping company."

"Your pa's gonna marry her?"

"You fool!" Leclerc exploded. "You imbecile. *I* am to marry Miss Holdstock. You have given me the last insult that will ever cross your lips." He reared back and slapped Mac with the gloves. A gunshot would have been quieter as cloth struck flesh.

Mac stumbled and caught himself against the bar. He rubbed his burning cheek.

"Why you—"

"You may choose your weapons. At the Dueling Oaks, tomorrow at sunrise. Be there promptly or show the world—and Miss Holdstock—the true depth of your cowardice." Leclerc slapped his gloves across his left palm for emphasis, spun and walked from the saloon. The two guards followed him.

"What happened?" Mac said into the hollow silence that hung in the air when Leclerc was gone. He was stunned into sobriety.

"You're going to duel for this hussy's favor at sunrise," the bartender said.

"With guns?"

"You'd be wise to choose pistols. Leclerc is a champion fencer. He can cut a man to ribbons with a saber and walk away untouched."

"Heard tell he's a crack shot, too," piped up someone across the saloon.

"Eight men he's kilt in duels," another man said. "The fella's a fightin' machine—a killin' machine. I don't envy you, boy. Not at all."

Mac found himself pushed away from the bar by

men rooting around in the sawdust looking for the diamond stud that had popped off Leclerc's shirt. He watched numbly, wondering if he ought to join the hunt. That tiny gemstone could pay for passage up the river.

Then he worked through what that meant. Evie would call him a coward for the rest of her life. And running would show how little her love meant to him. He loved her with all his heart and soul.

If it meant he laid down his life for her, so be it. He would be north of town at the Dueling Oaks at dawn.

After another drink.

Or two.

CHAPTER 3

"You sober?"

Dewey Mackenzie made an attempt to force away the hand shaking his shoulder. He tried to roll over but got tangled in a threadbare blanket. He sneezed as he pressed his face down into sawdust—and then everything crashed into his head, crystal clear and as sharp as if he hadn't drunk himself into a stupor.

"Glad to see you're awake. It'll be dawn in another half hour. Time for you to be on your way to destiny."

He stared at the smirking barkeep, wondering what he meant. Then that, too, came rushing back.

"Duel," he said, his voice hoarse.

"You were challenged. You got to show up or ain't nobody in town'll have anything to do with a coward."

"Leclerc. I remember." Mac sat up and threw back the blanket. He had spent the night pressed against the front of the bar, using the sawdust on the saloon floor as a mattress. With every bone in his body aching, he pulled himself to his feet and stretched. He regretted it immediately.

The bartender sounded almost eager as he said, "You want me to get you a buggy to take you out there?"

Mac patted his pockets. Empty. He tried to remember if he had spent it all on whiskey or if he had passed out and been robbed. It hardly mattered. He was stone broke, and he was in a world of trouble.

"Evie."

"That the girl's name? She must be special for you to tangle with a killer like Pierre Leclerc."

"Eight men killed in duels," Mac croaked out. His voice sounded rougher than sandpaper. That matched the way his brain began to feel. The instant of clarity faded against a surging tide of hangover.

"Well, no, me and the boys got to discussin' that number and decided it's not true."

"What? He hasn't killed that many men?"

"Nope. It's only seven. You'll be the eighth."

Again thoughts of hightailing it raced through his brain, but he knew that wasn't possible. What would Evie think of him? He would give his life for her. She was that special. If Leclerc had told the truth and their parents had arranged a marriage between her and Pierre, he had to prevent it. He had to save her from what would be a terrible life. One look at the younger Leclerc told even a casual observer that he would cheat on her and treat her badly.

"I have to get my gun."

"As the one what got challenged, you get to choose the weapon. Usually, you get a choice between two matched pistols. I don't reckon Leclerc will give a fig what you use."

"Got to hurry. It's going to be dawn soon." Mac stumbled to the doorway and saw the faint traces of false dawn slipping from the sky. He didn't have much time.

On increasingly steady feet, he made his way to the stable where he kept his horse and often slept because he lacked money for a hotel. He made sure the horse was fed as he pawed through his saddlebags for the Smith & Wesson Model 3 he carried. He slung his gun belt around his middle and strapped it on. The heavy .44-caliber pistol weighed him down. A few steps around the stable settled the gun into place.

He hadn't worn it much in town while he was courting Evie. The bosses at the few odd jobs he'd held frowned on janitors and cooks' assistants packing iron while they worked. He had considered getting a job as a bouncer at one of the Storyville brothels or even at a saloon like the one where he'd spent the night, but jobs that didn't require him fighting it out with the customers appealed more to him.

"All right, boy. We're going to settle a score." He saddled his stallion, led it outside, stepped up, and rode out to Market Street before heading north.

The whole time he had been in New Orleans, he had never been to the Dueling Oaks, two massive trees in a park outside town. There hadn't been any reason for him to stray in this direction. Now he wished he had at least ridden past to get the lay of the land.

He had never fought a duel before. He'd never even shot a man, but he'd heard stories. Check for sun in the eyes. Keep the light to your back and turn to the side to reduce the other gunman's target. A dozen thoughts like that crashed through his head, confusing him.

One thing he remembered on the way was to draw his gun and break it open. He looked down at the cylinder filled with .44-caliber brass cartridges, except the chamber where the hammer rested. Would Leclerc agree to a duel using five rounds, or was he honor bound to demand only one? There were too many things Mac didn't know about dueling.

He entered the meadow and saw the two oaks against the faint light of dawn. He took a deep breath, hoping it would settle his nerves. It didn't. He rode to the trees and looked around. He was alone.

It hadn't occurred to him that Leclerc might not show up. Here he had been worrying about not having a second or how many paces to take before turning and firing. With a slight shift in the saddle, he grabbed for his iron and drew it. Face to face suited him better. He wasn't any fancy gunslick, but he was quick enough. Maybe Leclerc wouldn't want to face a cowboy who dueled like that.

"Show your true colors, Pierre Leclerc," he said, enjoying the sound of his voice in the early-morning air. "Let Evie know what she's getting in the way of a husband."

He rode around between the trees as the dawn turned to pink and finally cast the first real light of day across the meadow. The shadows from the trees lengthened, then began to shrink as the sun rose. As the light filtered through the leaves, he felt better by the minute.

Mac dismounted and paced around, beginning to feel his oats. He practiced his draw a few more times, aiming at first one tree trunk and then the other.

"Yes, sir, I ran him off. He's too lily-livered to face me." His horse reared and tried to bolt. Mac pouched the iron he was holding and said, "Whoa, boy. Settle down. What's spooking you?"

It took a few minutes to gentle the horse. He secured the reins to a sapling growing several yards away from the two oaks. Curious as to what had frightened his horse, he went to one of the thick-boled trees and glanced around it.

Mac stopped dead in his tracks. "My God!"

He turned away from the horrific sight, then stopped. Every instinct in his body told him to flee. Only a considerable effort of will allowed him to return to the dead man tied spread-eagle on the far side of the giant oak tree.

His stomach churned and threatened to empty whatever remained in it when he saw that Micah Holdstock's throat had been slashed with such savagery that he had almost been decapitated. Whether he had been tied to the tree and killed or murdered and then strung up was a question that Mac couldn't answer as he felt utter shock setting in.

Not that it mattered. Holdstock was very, very dead.

Mac inched closer and saw that the bloody knife used to sever the older man's throat had been stuck into the tree trunk.

"No, no, no!" Hand shaking, he gripped the knife's handle and pulled hard to free the blade. He stared at the murder weapon.

It was his knife, beyond doubt. The last time he re-membered having it was when he had used the thin blade to open the French doors leading into Evie's bedroom. He reached behind him to the sheath at the small of his back, hoping against hope that his knife still rested there and this was a duplicate.

The sheath was empty.

This was his knife. The murder weapon that had slashed his would-be father-in-law's throat was his.

When he thought things could not get worse, he heard hoofbeats in the distance, approaching at a gallop.

"Leclerc," he breathed. Not knowing what else to do, he slid the knife into his sheath and went to his horse, taking the reins and pulling it around. The horse shied from the coppery smell of fresh blood. "I've got to deal with Leclerc, and then—"

His eyes went wide in surprise when he saw not Pierre Leclerc and his seconds riding to the Dueling Oaks but rather a half dozen New Orleans police-men. There was no question as to their destination, nor that they had spotted him. The one riding in the lead pointed and called out for him to stop; then they all raced toward him.

Mac looked around in panic. A coldness settled over him when he realized he had been framed. Someone had taken his knife and killed Micah Hold-stock, then rousted the police to come out to arrest him. He touched the gun at his hip, then knew shooting it out with the officers coming after him would solve nothing—and likely make his situation worse even if he prevailed. Kill Micah Holdstock, the police would hunt him down. Kill four policemen and he would be dogged to the ends of the earth for the New Orleans police to extract revenge.

With a speed he didn't realize he possessed, he drew and fired four times. At least one slug hit the leading policeman's horse and brought it down. That pained him, but it was his only chance. The horse collapsed and forced the others to veer away. This gave Mac a few precious seconds to mount and gallop away into the woods.

The lawmen shouted and fired at him. He kept his head down and reached the stand of trees at the edge of the meadow, then cut off at an angle. He had to lose any pursuit. Mac didn't know that much about hiding his trail, but what he did know, he used. Keeping to the fallen leaves helped eliminate hoofprints on the spongy earth. He avoided low-hanging limbs and tried not to break branches or twigs. As he zigzagged through the trees, he came to a stream and splashed down in it a hundred yards, then left it in favor of a road leading back into town. Once he reached New Orleans, there wouldn't be any need to cover his tracks.

The hunt for him there would take a different tack.

Any clues to his identity started with the Holdstock household. He had to reach Evie and talk to her. Getting her to come with him might be harder now, but they could still leave the city, maybe head into Texas and settle down there. She hadn't been schooled in ways to survive on a ranch or farm, but she was smart. She could learn. She could learn, and they'd be together.

Back in the city, he twisted through the maze of

narrow streets and drew rein in front of the Holdstock house on Royal Street. His heart pounded
when he realized he would be the one bringing the
bad news of Micah Holdstock's murder to Evie and
her ma.

With a quick kick, he got his leg back and over the
horse to drop to the street. His legs were shaky, as
much from fear of the police as from knowing his
presence inside the house wasn't likely to be well re-
ceived. He took a deep breath that did nothing to
settle his nerves. Hands out in front, he saw how they
shook just a little.

Knowing time mattered and he had little of it before the police came to this very door, he stepped
forward and lifted the brass knocker. Deep in the
house, echoes died away. He knocked again, shifting
from one foot to the other and looking around. He
expected the law to show up at any instant.

Before he could knock again, the door opened.
The butler looked down his nose at him.

"Sir, you are not welcome here. The master has ordered the entire staff to keep you away from Miss
Evangeline."

"Can you give her a message for me? I—"

The butler tried to close the door. Mac moved too
fast, shoving his foot out to stop it. He had to add his
shoulder to the door to force it open. The butler
staggered back and stared at him, not believing anyone would violate etiquette in such a boorish manner.

"I need to talk to Evie. There's been a terrible accident."

"There has, sir. You entered."

Mac didn't see how the butler signaled, but the bodyguard who had watched the door the night before and then accompanied Pierre Leclerc lumbered from the rear of the house. He cracked his knuckles and smirked. The misplaced nose and scars on his face turned him into a juggernaut of pure evil.

"Remove him. Don't get any blood on the floor. It is difficult to clean off." The butler stood back to let the bruiser tear Mac apart.

With a feint to the right, Mac got the mountain of gristle and meat to commit. Smaller, quicker, he darted left and ran into the parlor where he startled Mrs. Holdstock. The woman looked up at him with bloodshot eyes. She had been crying.

"Ma'am, I need to talk to Evie."

"H-he sent her away," she said. "After he fought with you, he sent her away."

"Where? Where is she?" He saw his death coming through the door. The guard opened and closed his hands, anticipating wrapping them around a scrawny neck and squeezing all the life out.

"The convent. He—I shouldn't tell you. Micah wants to kill you."

"Convent? Which one?"

"Please leave," she said. Her hands fluttered like upset birds. "You are intruding. Evangeline is marrying Mr. Leclerc's son. It's all decided."

"She loves me! You can't agree to an arranged marriage with a man she doesn't even know, much less love." Mac dodged the guard's groping hands and scurried around to the far side of the settee where Mrs. Holdstock perched. She looked around, confused and distraught.

But she made no move to call off the bulldog of a guard. He began circling, arms outstretched to grab the intruder.

"She and Pierre will be married the first week of October in the basilica."

"That's hardly a month off!" Mac protested.

"So much preparation is required. I know it will be hard, but Micah is adamant about the marriage being consummated quickly. Something about shipping contracts and—"

Mrs. Holdstock let out a yelp as the guard lunged over her and seized Mac. The powerful grip pulled him toward sure death as the guard cocked back a fist, ready to deliver a punch capable of knocking out a bull.

Mac threw up his arms and protected his face. His forearms took the blow. From the shock of pain, he thought both arms had been broken. As the guard drew back for another punch, Mac twisted hard and kicked the settee away from him. The furniture, carrying Mrs. Holdstock, smashed into the man's knees and toppled him over her. With squeals of outrage from the woman and angry shouts from the butler and others of the staff in the foyer, confusion gave Mac the chance to pull free.

He made one last attempt to learn what he needed to know. "Where, Mrs. Holdstock? Where is Evie?"

He got nothing coherent from her. He darted from the parlor and into the dining room. The bruiser had gotten untangled from Mrs. Holdstock and came after him.

Dodging around the table already set for dinner, Mac reached the kitchen. He had two escape routes.

Out the kitchen door took him into an alley and safety. From there he could easily circle the house and retrieve his horse. The other was a staircase used by the staff to reach the second floor.

"Evie," he muttered as he took the steps three at a time. He couldn't make himself believe she was really gone. Reaching the landing, he twisted into the up-stairs hallway lined with the ugly paintings and peculiar sculpture he had always joked about before. He pounded down the carpeted corridor to her bed-room door.

He started to knock, then heard pursuit coming up the main staircase from the foyer. Ignoring polite-ness, he opened the door and burst into her bed-room.

"Evie, I—"

He stared in disbelief. Her wardrobe door stood open. Half the clothing inside had been removed, leaving only the fancy ball dresses and other clothing better suited for social occasions. Her jewelry re-mained on a dresser, and several pairs of shoes had been lined up along the far wall, only to be aban-doned. Her trunks and carpetbags were gone.

Mrs. Holdstock hadn't lied. Evie's father had shipped her off to a convent until her marriage to Pierre Leclerc.

Despairing, he turned to leave, only to face a police-man. In the hall behind him stood another. Of the boxer-guard he saw nothing. Whether the butler had summoned the police or these were the ones who had chased him from the Dueling Oaks hardly mat-tered. The copper reached for him.

Mac grabbed the door, put his shoulder to the

paneling, and slammed it hard on the man's hand. The loud shriek and snapping sound told of a broken wrist. That wouldn't set well with the police. They would want to arrest him even more now.

As the copper pulled his hand back, Mac closed and locked the door. Spinning, he retreated through the French doors. He couldn't help himself. He looked down at the latch he had slipped open using the knife the night before, the knife that had murdered Micah Holdstock. He slammed through the doors and never stopped when he got to the railing. A quick vault took him over and down to the street. Landing heavily, he paused an instant to recover his breath and looked around.

The police hadn't blocked off this street. He stood and walked to the corner. Two officers stood outside the front door, rapping their night sticks against their palms. A shudder passed through him. They duplicated the same gesture that Pierre Leclerc had used, only he had smacked gloves against his palm before challenging his rival for Evie's affection with a slap across the cheek.

Shouts from inside the house caused the two policemen to hurry inside. Not rushing because he didn't want to draw attention, Mac walked to his horse, mounted, and rode away slowly. When he reached the corner, he put his heels to the animal's flanks and galloped off.

He had a hell of a lot to do before the entire city was looking for him, and first was finding Evangeline Holdstock.

CHAPTER 4

There were too many convents in New Orleans. Even if he found the right one, he couldn't just waltz in and ask to see Evangeline Holdstock. The very idea of a convent was to protect those inside, to sequester them from the outside world. Mac tried to remember hearing either of Evie's folks mention one in particular.

He finally gave up. He hadn't known Evie long enough to have those kinds of discussions, the rambling, lazy afternoon, mind floating free and memories drifting by kind of talks. Their passion had flared, and they hadn't been willing to bank those fires. His most memorable times with her weren't spent talking of their past.

"Where would he send you, my dearest?" Mac muttered to himself. He noticed the stares he got from people passing by along Canal Street and bit his lip. Talking to himself was a sure way to draw unwanted attention. Considering the patrols along the main streets, usually two or three policemen walking together, he knew any such mistake would land him in jail.

After breaking one cop's hand and shooting another's horse, they would likely string him up from the nearest lamppost.

He rode slowly away from the main streets and down alleys where he could find peace and quiet and think. Who had killed Holdstock? The man wasn't pleasant to anyone, and Mac wondered if he had abused his daughter at some time in the past. He certainly ignored his wife and made her the butt of cruel jokes when they were together.

Micah Holdstock was a banker and over the years must have recruited an army of people willing to slit his throat. How many had he foreclosed on? What businesses had he ruined, whose homes had he taken away? From hints he had dropped, his business extended to things less than legal. Perhaps not illegal but certainly frowned upon by polite society.

Mac knew finding a killer in any of those circles was beyond him. Not only did he travel in the wrong level of society, the police hunted him.

He jerked upright in the saddle when two coppers stopped in the mouth of the alley where he had paused to think. One nudged the other, and they started toward him. Wheeling his horse around, he rode out the far end of the alley, then galloped off. As much as the solitude helped him think, he had to remain in crowds where he became just another face. As long as he didn't stand out, he was safer. For the moment.

"The knife. My knife." He reached behind him and pressed his coat down over the sheathed knife that had killed Holdstock. Keeping it hidden was smart, but how had it gotten to the scene of the murder? "Someone took it from Evie's bedroom. Her pa. He must have taken it."

It made no sense for Holdstock to have furnished the weapon that murdered him. Mac shuddered, remembering the gruesome scene. Holdstock had not killed himself. Someone had taken the knife from him and used it to frame Dewey Mackenzie.

"To frame a rival for her hand," he said. Cold fury built within him. "Pierre Leclerc. You've got some questions to answer, you fancy-pants son of a bitch." He touched the knife again, vowing to use this very weapon to extract the answers if he had to.

Mac remembered hearing that the elder Leclerc ran a shipping company, a big one. He headed down the street toward the docks. The nose-wrinkling smell of dead fish and hot machinery grew as he neared the Mississippi River.

Stern-wheelers and side-wheelers jockeyed for their turn at the docks to unload cargo from farther north and to load cotton, jute, sugar, and other agricultural products from Louisiana. Pitching in the middle of the river were several sailing ships fresh from trips around the Cape and the West Coast and up the Atlantic seaboard and Boston. If Leclerc profited from even a small portion of such incredible commerce, he had to be rich.

If he was owner of the biggest shipping company, he had immense wealth and ought to be easy to find.

For the first time in a couple days, Mac's luck held. He silently thanked Dame Fortune and dismounted in front of a four-story building at the foot of Tchoupitoulas Street near Jackson. Judging by the wagons going in and out of the attached warehouse and the ant-like stream of men hauling cargo from the dockside, this had to be the center of a vast shipping empire. Even without the name Leclerc International emblazoned across the front of the building, Mac figured that out on his own.

He watched the ebb and flow of men and cargo for some time, wondering how he was going to find out where Evie was. Even if Pierre Leclerc had framed him, the man might not know where her father had sent her.

He worried over the problem until almost noon, then perked up when he saw the younger Leclerc come from the side door. The man impatiently looked at his pocket watch every few minutes until his buggy was brought around. He pushed away the attendant, got into the buggy, and drove himself away from dockside.

This couldn't have worked out any better for Mac. Eventually there'd be a place where he could waylay Leclerc. With the Smith & Wesson resting on his hip, he could make the statue of Andy Jackson in Jackson Square talk. Added to that, his desperation to find Evie would give him the wildness necessary to frighten Leclerc. He doubted the man was all that brave without the two burly bodyguards.

As he trailed the buggy, he frowned as a new thought came to him. Those had been Holdstock's bodyguards. Or were they? Did they get paid by Leclerc? Holdstock might have had spies in his midst and never known it. One of them easily could have picked up the fallen knife and used it to kill Micah Holdstock.

The shipping company owner's son crossed Canal and went into the Vieux Carré. Mac's heart beat faster in anticipation of Leclerc leading him directly to Evie. There were several convents in the old French Quarter, all hidden behind high walls and iron gates. He would never have found Evie if she had been sequestered in one of them, but Leclerc could lead him right to her. A quick touch of his hand against his gun reassured him he had the firepower necessary to free her so they could get the hell out of New Orleans.

He frowned when he saw Leclerc step down from the buggy in front of a brothel. If Holdstock hadn't already been dead, Mac would have killed Evie's father for putting her into a whorehouse to keep them apart. He tethered his horse and walked past the door, which opened into an inner courtyard, Spanish style. A quick look around, and then he ducked inside. Many of the rooms had windows that opened into the courtyard.

He worried that finding Leclerc would be impossible without causing too much of a ruckus when he heard the man's arrogant tone coming from a window not ten feet away. Mac hesitated to stare into the room but chanced a quick look.

The woman in the room wasn't Evie. From her exotic, sultry look she was Creole. He sank down near the window so he could spy on Leclerc and the woman.

"Marie, you are so lovely. I want to kiss you all over."

Mac blushed when the sounds indicated that Leclerc was doing that very thing. He heard a bed squeaking.

In his mind's eye, he pictured the two wrestling passionately. He decided this was the perfect time to draw his gun, get the drop on Leclerc, and force him to talk. He had to know where Evie was. And if he didn't, there might be a dead man in a whore's bed.

"Wait, stop, Pierre. No more."

"What? You can't excite me so and then deny me. You can't deny me this. Or this. Or—"

Mac heard a grunt as Marie pushed the man in her bed away.

"What is it?" Leclerc demanded. "Have I made you angry?"

"Of course you have. You think to marry that little slip of a girl. She is nothing. She can give you nothing I can't, but you are marrying her!"

"I don't love her. You, my darling Marie, of all people, know this. Haven't I cared for you better than all your other lovers?"

"Yes, but—"

"Then don't doubt me when I say I marry her for the money she will inherit. She has no male relatives, and her mother is feebleminded and easily talked into anything I want. As my wife, Evangeline will have no choice but to do as I command."

"What will you command her to do? This? Or this?"

Leclerc laughed. Just outside the window, Mac rolled his eyes and gritted his teeth.

"She would die of fright if she tried such wonderful things, my lovely Marie."

"But her father . . ."

"The old man is not a problem. He died this morning." Leclerc laughed so hard that Mac slid his gun from its holster and looped his thumb over the hammer to cock it. Leclerc had not confessed to the murder, but he might as well have.

"So, you are richer? How is this possible?"

"My own father is frail and will not live to the end of the year. When he dies, I will own the shipping company *and* a big bank. Together, shipping and finance, I will be the most important man in New Orleans."

"And the richest," Marie said in a husky voice.

"That, too."

"But you marry her and not me. Will you forget me, Pierre?"

"Never, my darling. I love you. Her, I will only nod toward as we occasionally pass. We will go to all the proper social events as befitting someone of our standing, but it will be your bed where I always return."

"You could take me." Marie giggled. "What would all those prissy women say if you brought your mistress to a fancy ball?"

"Don't joke." Leclerc's voice turned cold. "I will put you in a convent if you try to make such a thing come true."

"Like you did her? You couldn't be that cruel to me, Pierre. You would miss out on me doing this and this." Leclerc groaned in response to whatever Marie was doing. "The Ursuline nuns are known for their sharp tongues, not their clever ones."

Leclerc began to moan louder. Mac stood, back to the wall, hand clutching his revolver. It would take only an instant to kill the man who had thought to ruin his life, but a better fate would be to snatch away his ticket to achieving wealth, power, and social standing in the city. Without Evie at his side, without her father's commercial empire, Leclerc would have his ambitions crushed.

Mac decided that was a crueler fate than being murdered in his mistress's bed.

He slipped his gun back into its holster and left the courtyard. The Ursuline Convent was on Chartres Street, not that far distant in the French Quarter. It would be the work of a few minutes to whisk Evie away and clear out of town, leaving behind all the trouble Leclerc had caused for him.

He found the convent and circled the entire block, trying to locate a way into the high-walled compound. Once he climbed that wall and got inside, getting out would be difficult if Evie tried to bring all her clothing with her. He remembered thinking that a steamer trunk and some smaller bags were missing from her bedroom. Even wanting to please her, he could never scale those walls with such a load.

Around what he considered the back of the convent, he saw a wagon delivering supplies. A heavy gate swung open, and the boxes were dropped just inside the gate before a nun closed it again. From the sound of the locking bar, it was securely fastened against even a battering ram.

"So much to keep the women in," he said softly. It certainly kept him out. On foot, he circled the block again, this time getting an idea.

He tethered his horse near the back gate, then went to the north side. Across the narrow street stood a two-story building with a decent balcony running along the street. Ignoring anyone seeing and commenting on his strange behavior, he climbed a drainpipe, swung over to the balcony, and found that he could see into the convent courtyard—almost. The wall was tall enough to block most of his view, and he saw that the nuns were serious about keeping people out—or in.

The top of the wall had been encrusted with glass shards that would cut him to ribbons if he tried to climb over. But he intended to do something different. Prowling up and down the balcony, he found a heavy rug. Determining the spot closest to the wall, he stepped over the wrought-iron railing, precariously balancing with the rug held in front of him. He gathered his strength and jumped for all he was worth.

If the street had not been so narrow, he never could have attempted such an insane thing. He sailed through the air and landed heavily on the top of the wall.

The rug between him and the crushed glass, he grunted, kicked hard, and flopped over into the courtyard. He landed in a flower bed and stayed in a crouch. Everyone inside the compound had to be deaf not to hear his entry.

Then he grinned. Hymns filtered through the courtyard from the direction of the chapel. The nuns were in the middle of their daily prayers.

He was still alive and free, so his had certainly been answered—so far.

Not knowing how long he had, he slipped inside and began hunting for the section of apartments for visitors. Panic began to set in by the time he reached the second floor of the main building. Then he heaved a sigh of relief. Sitting in a chair at the far end of the hall was the most beautiful sight in all the world.

"Evie!"

His outcry startled her. She looked up from the book she was reading and half stood. Frozen there for a moment, she finally came fully to her feet and turned to face him. By now he had run the length of the hall. He swept her up in his arms, whirled her around, and kissed her.

"What's wrong?" he asked as she pulled her lips away from his. "Aren't you happy to see me?"

"Mac, I—" She pushed away from him, looking flustered. "I never thought I'd see you again."

"It takes more than your pa and Pierre Leclerc to stop me."

Her face turned to stone.

"Evie, please. What's wrong?"

"They put me in this convent until the wedding."

"It'll be our wedding, not yours to that . . . scoundrel."

"Pierre? You mean him?"

"He's got a mistress in the French Quarter. You're not even married yet and he's cheating on you. I swear I'll never do a thing like that, Evie. Ever. I love you." He tugged on her hand, but she resisted. "Come on. We have to get out of here, out of New Orleans."

"I can't, Mac. Not now."

"You haven't taken vows for the order, and your father's not going to boss you around." She might be angry with him later, but he wasn't going to tell her that her father was dead until they were safely away. "You're all grown up. You know your own mind. Say you don't want to stay here."

"No, I don't. I—"

"Then let's go. The nuns are in vespers now. We can get out before they know you're gone. I have a horse. We can ride until sundown, then camp and we'll be away from the city and—"

"Mac, you—" She heaved a sigh, pulled free of his embrace, and sat heavily in the chair. "Everything is so confused."

"We can straighten it out together, Evie. Please, we have to go. We *have* to."

She stared at him emotionlessly for what seemed an eternity.

"I need to do a few things before we go, Mac. That's my room. Wait in there while I tend to them. It . . . it won't take too long. Not more than an hour."

"An hour!"

"Less, then. I can hurry. Go wait for me."

"All right. I trust you. While you're gone, I can pack for you." His mind raced. "If I can get the trunk to the ground floor, I can load it onto a cart. There must be one by the back gate."

"My things," she said in a dull voice. "I never thought about them. Yes, do pack them. Keep busy, and the time will pass more quickly." She stood and let him kiss her.

"The time you're gone will be an eternity. Are you sure I can't help you?"

"This is something I must do on my own." She shooed him toward the room.

He saw that it was more of a narrow cell, with a hard bed and a crucifix mounted on the wall over the head. A window, more like a slit in the wall, let in faint afternoon light. Her trunk and two carpetbags were stacked at the foot of the bed. A small writing desk and stool were the only other pieces of furniture in the room.

"Stay here, Mac. I beg you." She closed the door.

He heard her quick, light steps in the hall as she hurried off. Moving restlessly, he thought to pack the trunk and bags, then realized they had never been unpacked. There wasn't a wardrobe in the room to hang her clothing. He began pacing, now and then wanting to open the door to peer into the hallway to see if she had returned from her mysterious mission. To do so was dangerous if anyone else in this section of the convent was out and about.

Not knowing how long the devotional would run, he began to worry that they would be caught by the nuns. He had no desire to threaten any of them, but he would if that's what it took for him and Evie to get away.

He sat on the bed, then stood and paced. Not able to hold down his nervous energy, he finally opened the door a crack. He couldn't see much of the corridor, so he opened it a little farther. A smile spread across his face.

"Evie!"

She came down the hallway. He stepped out to meet her and suddenly felt as if he had been tossed off a cliff.

To her right strode Pierre Leclerc. And to her left a policeman kept pace.

"There he is! That's him! That's the man who killed my papa!" Evangeline Holdstock pointed an accusing finger, but all Mac saw was the pitiless look on Pierre Leclerc's face.

He had won, and Dewey Mackenzie had lost everything.

CHAPTER 5

"Evie, no!" Mac cried. He shook his head in denial of the accusation and disbelief that she would betray him.

"There he is," she insisted. "That's the man who killed my father."

"She's right, Officer. Arrest him." Pierre Leclerc reached into a coat pocket and drew out a small-caliber pistol. He cocked it and aimed down the hallway at Mac. "Stop, you filthy killer. Stop or I'll shoot."

Mac took everything in with a stunning flash of insight. Leclerc had brought along the policeman to witness a murder. Without doubt, Leclerc had killed Micah Holdstock, and now he intended to kill the only man standing in his way to marrying Evie and controlling a huge fortune.

Mac reached for his pistol but did not draw. If he started flinging lead, he might hit Evie. He wasn't that good a marksman. He fancied himself quick on the draw, but he had never been flush enough to buy the ammunition to learn to be a good shot.

"Do as he says. You're under arrest." The police officer rushed forward and blocked Leclerc's aim. For a horrifying instant, Mac worried Leclerc might shoot the man in the back.

Then they both realized how complicated that would make things. Evie would know Leclerc had tried to blame anyone else—and Leclerc would certainly think to pin that murder on his rival, too. Such a lie would turn Evie against him. Leclerc might succeed without her family's fortune, but the entire scheme had been to gain control of Holdstock's bank and all its assets.

Mac reacted rather than thought through his next action. He shouted to Evie, "Don't marry him. Leclerc murdered your pa!" Using that to sow confusion, he lowered his head and ran as hard as he could for the window behind the chair where Evie had been reading. Arms crossed in front of his face, he crashed through the glass and plunged downward.

Somehow, he turned in the air and got his feet under him. He hit with knees bent and rolled. In the twilight, he lost himself among the flower beds. Flat on his back, he looked up and saw the policeman in the second-story window trying to locate him. The officer might have been armed, but Leclerc definitely was. He shouldered the copper aside and started shooting.

The bullets kicked up tiny fountains of dirt all around. Staying still stretched Mac's nerves almost to the breaking point, but he saw that as long as he lay quietly, he remained hidden.

But from the sounds in the courtyard at the far end of the garden, the gunshots had brought other police running. Again he took the daring route to escape. He waited for two officers to pass him before standing.

"That way. I saw him run that way." He pointed toward the wall. "He's trying to climb the wall!"

When they reacted, he sprinted in the other direction, toward the back gate. Leclerc either didn't see him or had come up empty. No bullets whipped around him. He reached the gate where he had seen supplies being unloaded earlier in the day. The locking bar was heavy and resisted him pushing it aside.

"Come on, come on," he grated as he put his shoulder to the bar. "Nuns move it. I can do as good, even if God's not on my side right now." Heaving with all his strength, he finally slid the bar back far enough to let him slip into the street.

He heard his horse neighing loudly. In the gathering darkness, he couldn't see the horse at all until he almost bumped into it. That worked in his favor. If he couldn't find a horse he knew was tethered here, the coppers would miss it, too. He vaulted into the saddle and turned the horse back into the heart of the French Quarter.

Only then did an officer spot him and open fire. The whistle of bullets past his head spurred him to greater speed. His horse strained as it galloped away from the convent. As he bent low, hearing the police whistles summoning more officers, he experienced the full impact of what had happened.

Evie had turned him in. She had gone to Leclerc,

and he had brought the police. She was going to marry the man who had killed her pa and had no idea how evil he was.

"Why did she stop trusting me? That son of a bitch can't be that persuasive." At least Mac hoped that was so. Maybe he had mesmerized her. He had seen a snake sway back and forth and seemingly paralyze a bird. How Leclerc did that to a woman who had once loved him baffled Mac.

He slowed and looked around to get his bearings. Whatever there had been in New Orleans for him had evaporated like dew in the morning sun. He had no doubt that, if caught, he would hang for murdering Micah Holdstock. No amount of proof would suffice to sway a judge and jury. Leclerc had money to buy them all. After the previous night's bender, Mac didn't have two nickels to rub together. Paying a decent attorney to defend him was out of the question. Anyway, Leclerc would buy off any attorney to rig the trial.

He couldn't go to Evie or her mother for help, for money, for anything. The few people he knew in New Orleans hardly counted as friends. He worked with them or for them. They would abandon him in an instant rather than get mixed up in a murder case.

All his plans had exploded in the span of a single day, and all because he wanted to marry the sweetest, loveliest woman in all the world.

The one who had betrayed him the first chance she got.

"Out of town," he said to himself. "That's the only chance I've got. Get the hell out of New Orleans and away from the law."

As much as it rankled, there wasn't anything he could do to bring Holdstock's killer to justice. Pierre Leclerc would get away with murder. Worse, he would marry Evie and take over her pa's financial empire. Every card fell to Leclerc. It didn't matter what Mac played when Leclerc held a royal flush.

He started north out of town along Canal Street, only to slow and finally stop. Ahead, on streets leading over to the Garden District, were a half dozen policemen. They walked out into the street and eyed everyone moving along toward them. Mac knew it was possible they were after another criminal. He might ride past without being stopped.

"My luck's so bad that won't happen. They're after me. They want to arrest *me*," he said to his horse. The animal turned its head around and peered accusingly at him with a great brown eye. He patted the horse's neck and turned to head the other way along Canal Street, toward the Mississippi River.

If his luck improved, he would follow the banks of the winding river away from town and be free of the police by morning.

His luck didn't hold. He reached the docks and immediately saw groups of police moving quickly to check every pile of cargo and interrogate the dock workers. Whether they hunted for him or were on some other mission didn't matter. He dared not risk boldness now if it landed him in the jailhouse.

He turned to follow the shoreline and immediately saw this way was blocked, too. Reversing course, heading back downriver, toward where Andy Jackson had established his headquarters during the War of 1812, proved equally frustrating.

"Do they have the entire police force after me?" He bit back a curse when a couple of dockworkers turned and stared at him. He had been alone too much of his life and had gotten into the habit of talking to himself. He pretended he spoke to his horse, though he knew it could never understand.

Tipping his hat in the direction of the men, he called out, "I heard tell there's work to be had here, but my directions got confused. Where's the hiring office?" He made a vague gesture in the direction of Leclerc's huge building.

"You ain't the right color, mistah," said the nearest dock-walloper. "From your looks, it don't matter, though. You ain't got the muscle to do a day's work."

Another chimed in, "You wouldn't last an hour haulin' them bales."

Mac shrugged, touched the brim of his hat again, smiled, and rode on, alert for the police making the canvass of the area. Turning back into town and going up Canal Street wasn't possible. An army of blue-coated cops worked their way down to the riverfront. He was caught between the river and a tide of lawmen.

He touched his six-shooter and wondered what it would take to shoot his way out. He discarded that idea.

"A last resort," he told himself. "I've got no call to get myself killed. I'd rather fight it out with Leclerc."

Whether someone overheard the shipping magnate's name or finally identified him hardly mattered. The hue and cry went up. Coppers turned in his direction, and more than one pointed at him, accusing him of being . . . Dewey Mackenzie.

He raked his heels along his horse's flanks and rocketed away, heading for what looked like an open area just north of Leclerc's headquarters. As he passed the building, a dozen policemen poured out. All were armed with rifles and used them. A thunderous roar of gunshots filled the air.

Head down, staying low on the far side of his horse, Mac tried to escape. More than one bullet slammed into his horse's body. The valiant animal stumbled but tried to keep running.

Mac barely kicked free of the stirrups before the horse collapsed. He hit the ground and rolled, momentarily stunned. On his belly, he saw the lawmen running in his direction, firing as they came. His choices narrowed to dragging out his hog leg and shooting at the police or running like a scalded dog. Facing so many armed men didn't look to have a good outcome for him.

He rolled over and over, getting soaked in mud and filth. That saved him. He camouflaged himself so he blended into the shadows of an alley.

"He went this way," came a shout.

"No, no, he's over here!"

Mac touched his gun, wanting to silence the man who was actually on his trail, but if he took the shot, he would announce where he had gone. Besides, even with the terrible danger he was in, he didn't want to kill an innocent man.

Crouched behind a pile of debris washed up on the shore, he waited to see who would prevail. Those thinking he had gone directly to the riverbank won the argument, leaving the solitary cop to stare almost directly at him. Mac barely breathed, not daring to make a move.

But he jumped a foot when something moved beside him. He yanked out the Smith & Wesson and almost fired on a rat bigger than any alley cat he had ever seen. The rat stared at him with fierce red eyes, sizing him up for supper, then walked boldly out from the garbage heap.

The cop saw the rat, drew a bead on it, and fired. His bullet caused the rat to jump into the air and flop over, landing with its life extinguished by a crack shot. The cop came over, kicked the rat, and then called, "Wait for me. Don't leave me behind." He hurried after the others.

Mac relaxed, dropping his revolver back into his holster. Saved by a rat!

He realized his respite was brief, though. When they didn't find him down on the docks, they'd come back in this direction. He stared at the lifeless body of his horse and heaved a sigh of resignation. That was about all he owned in the world, that horse. It had served him well, bringing him all the way south from Missouri.

He stared at the gear and especially the saddlebags still secured to the horse. What few belongings he had were in those pouches. He had dressed in his best clothes to propose to Evie and had never changed when he went on his binge and finally showed up at the Dueling Oaks.

A change of clothes into something more suited to dodging the law rested in the saddlebags. Besides, he wore a coat of mud, and every step he took squished with water that had seeped into his boots.

He had always been careful about his appearance and hygiene, having been raised by a family that had avoided the worst of the diseases ravaging Missouri after the war. His ma insisted they had kept free of scarlet fever and cholera because he washed behind his ears, and his pa had always nodded when she was giving that particular sermon. Mac had never been convinced, but the plagues took lives all around the Mackenzie homestead and left them intact.

He decided being clean felt good, too. Idly scratching an itch, he found some of the tiny mites infesting the Mississippi mud and crushed them. The only way to get rid of them entirely was a hot bath. That wasn't in the cards, but maybe getting his possessions back was.

Advancing slowly in a crouch, he reached the side of his fallen horse. He laid a hand on the horse's neck for the last time. The body had cooled already. A quick try to free the saddle convinced him that wouldn't be possible, trapped under the dead weight as it was.

Anyway, lugging a saddle around while the police hunted him like a mad dog would only lead to ending up like the horse. He turned his attention to the saddlebags. Half were trapped under the horse's body, but the free one had an extra box of cartridges for his S&W and his work shirt, riding coat, and denim jeans. He pulled them out. Everything else he had to leave.

"He's gotta be over here," a policeman said from not far away. "Ain't no way he got past us to the river."

Mac cat-footed through the shadows by the Leclerc building as the police returned from their futile search along the riverbank. He tensed when one discovered he had taken clothing from the saddlebags.

"He's around here somewhere. He rifled through the saddlebags."

"That could have been anybody," another officer said. "The dock's full of thieves. You know that, Ralls. Damn me if you ain't the dumbest copper in New Orleans."

The insult provoked a scuffle between the two lawmen. As others worked to break it up, Mac stood and walked slowly past them, heading in the direction they had already searched. The route was veiled in pitch-blackness. The only way he knew he approached the river came in the way his boots sucked free with every step he took in the mud and the increasing lap-lap-lap of water against the hulls of ships tied to the docks.

When he realized the water rose above his ankles, he turned toward the nearest riverboat. Work crews finished loading mountains of crates and bales on the deck. From the way the ship rode low in the water, he knew it carried a full cargo. He inched his way closer and stared up at the texas deck. The dark kept him from seeing if anyone prowled along. He couldn't even be sure if this was a passenger boat, although almost all the steamboats carried passengers. Some were set up for fancy trips with high-class passengers. Others crowded them on shoulder to shoulder.

He stood a better chance of escaping if this one—the *St. Louis Maiden* was emblazoned on the prow—carried hundreds of passengers. He would never be noticed. If the boat catered to passengers willing to pay premium ticket prices, he'd stand out like a sore thumb.

Sloshing under the dock, he took a quick look around and didn't see any police. He stripped off his filthy clothing and donned the barely cleaner everyday clothing he had taken from his saddlebags, taking special care to move the box of .44 cartridges from the now-discarded dress coat to one of the pockets in his riding coat. Although he had no intention of shooting it out with the New Orleans police, he wanted to be ready.

"There might be a shot at Pierre Leclerc," he said to himself. The soft waves breaking against the pilings muffled his words.

He looked up as heavy boots tramped along the dock just over his head. Turning, he followed them to the end of the landing where the stern-wheeler started chuffing and snorting huge puffs of black smoke from its twin stacks. The *St. Louis Maiden* was preparing to leave, on its way somewhere else.

That destination was fine with Mac. He slipped around and clambered up the rough piling and saw the crew throwing off mooring ropes. The pilot used the steam whistle almost constantly to warn that the riverboat was entering the current in the mighty Mississippi and for all others to give him clear berth.

Without hurrying, Mac walked to the end of the dock. The dockhands had already moved on to other jobs while the crew aboard the boat worked to coil the hawsers that had held it securely to the dock. He judged the distance and realized he was seconds too late to jump aboard. Cursing under his breath, he turned to find the end of the pier blocked by four policemen.

One of them spotted him and warned the others. They ran straight for him.

He took three quick steps toward the charging coppers, spun, and ran as hard as he could. When he reached the end of the pier, he kicked with all his strength. As if walking on air, he kept his legs pumping. The shouts of the police were drowned out by the riverboat's whistle. Then he crashed down to the deck and fell flat on his face.

Bullets whizzed above him the instant before the stern-wheeler felt the rush of the river current and swung about, taking him out of the line of fire.

Mac lifted himself on his hands and saw the police waving their fists in the air and berating each other for letting their quarry escape. One of them shouted toward the boat, no doubt ordering it to come back. Whoever was up in the wheelhouse either ignored the command or never heard it. The boat continued its swing and applied full power, kicking up froth in its wake and pushing upriver. Mac sat and stared at the dark shoreline, laughing. The sound had a hysterical edge to it.

Somehow, against all odds, he had escaped New Orleans, Pierre Leclerc, a bogus murder charge—and Evangeline Holdstock.

CHAPTER 6

"**I** saw someone, I tell you, Captain. He jumped aboard just as we were pulling away from the dock."

"I swear, if you've been drinking again, Thornton, I'll toss you overboard."

Heavy footsteps came in Mac's direction as he heard the voices. He looked around for a place to hide and pressed against a pile of crates taller than his head. A heavy tarpaulin kept water off the crates, giving him an idea. He tugged up a corner, squirmed underneath, then climbed to the top of the pile. Anyone looking down from an upper deck would see a huge lump atop the tower of crates, but he wanted to avoid the captain and whoever had spotted him when he'd boarded so suddenly back at the dock.

Pressed into the top of the crate, he couldn't see but heard everything as the footsteps approached.

"Sloppy work, Thornton. You left the edge of the tarp unsecured."

Mac stifled a grunt as the tarp over his back pulled

taut. He imagined the deckhand securing the end down below.

"It's them new hands, Captain," Thornton said. "They don't have experience, and you don't pay 'em enough to tend to details."

"Lose these crates to the river and I'll keelhaul the lot of you."

"What's that?"

The captain snorted in disgust.

"You whippersnappers never been to sea like real sailors. I rounded the Cape six times and ported across Panama twice taking the damned fool Forty-niners. Saw two men keelhauled in that time. Ropes fastened to their scrawny middles and then pulled under the ship. While we were underway. One survived and never gave any lip to an officer again. The other must have banged his head on the first trip under the keel. He drowned."

"A riverboat's mighty broad of beam. Ain't no man what could hold his breath long enough to be pulled from port to starboard."

"That's my point, Thornton. Get on the hands and have them check the way all the crates are lashed down. I've got to see if the pilot's drunk yet."

"The last one was snockered before we got to Natchez."

"The cargo, Thornton. Get to it!"

"Yes, sir."

Mac heard footsteps swallowed up by the steady thrashing of the stern wheel turning against the river current. He understood enough of how a riverboat ran to know that the captain's duty in port was buying, selling, and handling the cargo. Once the boat was on the river, the pilot assumed responsibility for steering and avoiding the ever-changing sandbars and debris, and navigating the river's course as it meandered from week to week, leaving the captain free to socialize with the passengers.

He stretched out, thinking to catch a few winks before deciding what to do. He wasn't likely to offer much in the way of trading work for passage. Better to rest now and deal with his problem refreshed.

Head resting on his crossed arms, Mac tried to get comfortable, but the constant swaying kept him off balance. He finally got into the boat's rhythm, only to be awakened by gunfire. Jerking up, he strained his neck as he pressed against the tarp. He had forgotten he was under the canvas cover.

He sank back, drew his knife, and cut a long slit so he could look out. The riverboat slipped sideways a little in the water, then the pilot applied full power to the engines. The night filled with glowing cinders, giving him a surreal look at the riverbank. A dozen men lined up along the shore fired rifles into the air. The foot-long tongues of flame from the muzzles caused him to panic. The police had signaled the pilot to turn him over to them.

They waited for him on shore!

He tore a larger hole, preparing to fight to the death. He was glad he had retrieved the box of cartridges from his saddlebags before jumping aboard this boat. Then he heard a loud shout from the prow, where a man held a long, knotted rope high over his head. With a heavy weight on the end, the crewman took depth readings.

"Mark two fathoms!" His cry was relayed to the pilothouse. "We're nearing Twelve Mile Point shallows. One fathom!"

The boat lurched as the flat bottom scraped over the moving sandbar. Mac twisted around and saw the men on shore still firing their rifles into the air. It began to make sense to him. Those weren't police out to arrest him. They signaled the pilot where the last oxbow above New Orleans started, where the shallows were, so the *St. Louis Maiden* wouldn't run aground. A signal fire or a lighthouse would have worked better, but with less fanfare.

The boat continued to slew around, and the engines almost stopped. The riverboat continued to swing about, caught in the current. Then the entire vessel shuddered as if it were a dying beast. The paddle wheel gained speed as power was applied. The huge pistons turned faster and faster, and then the boat exploded forward like a racehorse out of the starting gate. The grating of sand and silt across the bottom of the hull changed to the hiss and pop of cinders racing skyward and the thrashing of the wheel against the river.

Mac settled back down, pulled shut the slit he had cut in the tarp, and again drifted off to sleep, now lulled by the steady throb of the engines and the constant swishing of the stern wheel not a dozen feet aft of him.

He came awake instantly when the tarp was yanked off him, letting in bright sunlight. Rubbing his eyes got the sleep out of them. Then he was sorry he'd bothered.

He saw all too clearly the captain and two deck-hands standing below him.

"Get the hell down off your throne, your majesty." The captain started to order his crew to pull Mac down, but there was hardly any reason to argue.

"On my way down, sir." Mac stood and looked around. The boat wasn't too far from shore, still driving hard against the strong Mississippi current. He tried to guess how long he had slept and how far the riverboat had traveled. They bucked a strong current, and with such a heavy cargo, he doubted the riverboat had gone more than thirty miles. But that was good enough to take him away from New Orleans and all the sorrow there.

"I'm going to throw you into irons. I won't have stowaways, not on my boat."

"Are you planning on keelhauling me?" Mac stared down at the officer and his men.

"If I find a hawser long enough, damned right! And I'll do it with you in shackles."

"We turn him over to the marshal at the next port?" one of the men asked.

"What else, Thornton?"

"I could work for my passage," Mac suggested.

The deckhands laughed. The captain turned livid.

"Like hell. Let one of you landlubbers do that, they'll be lined up for a mile to take advantage of my charity. Get him. Drag him down, and don't be gentle about it." The captain shoved the mate, Thornton, forward.

Mac's hand went to his gun when he saw Thornton had a gaffing hook and used it to climb the mountain

of crates like a monkey up a banana tree. He jumped
to avoid a nasty cut with the hook.

"There's no call to do that," he said. Mac gripped
the revolver's butt but didn't draw. The vicious expression on Thornton's face warned him he ought to
pull the gun and try to avoid serious injury.

Thornton swung again with the hook, this time
catching the edge of Mac's pants leg and ripping off
a piece.

"That's the ticket, Thornton," the captain bellowed.
"Skewer him!"

If it had been one of the crew making that demand, Mac would have tried to talk his way out of it.
When the boat's captain ordered his men to impale
him, Mac knew it was time to leave.

He backed away, then sprinted the few feet along
the top of the crates and leaped to land on another
stack. He didn't try to catch his balance but rather
used his momentum to gather speed. He leaped to
another stack and then sailed into space. Even in the
air he realized he hadn't jumped far enough away
from the side of the boat.

He hit the water and immediately felt the undertow back toward the spinning paddle wheel. Sucked
downward, he fought to keep his breath and not be
battered against the hull. He got his feet up and
kicked powerfully against the side of the ship. He swam
a few feet before being spun around and sucked back
into the deadly paddle wheel. All he could do was
grab one of the paddles and hang on for dear life as
it lifted him.

The paddle wheel lurched to a stop as it caught

for a second on a sandbar. Mac took advantage of the change to kick away from it and drop into the river again. The boat slid over the bar and sailed on, leaving him behind. On the side deck, the captain shouted, and then even those loud curses disappeared in the thrash-thrash of the stern wheel.

Mac had landed on the sandbar. He came up on his knees and began to sink. Realizing this was almost as dangerous as quicksand, he flopped back flat and let himself float over the sandbar. Dog-paddling toward shore, he was glad to see he was coming out on the western shore rather than the east.

He got to his feet and walked a dozen paces from the river, then shook all over like a wet dog. Water flew in all directions. He sucked in a deep breath of fresh air, pressed out more water from his clothes and, relatively drier than when he had been dunked in the river, looked around for his flat-crowned black hat.

He found it about fifty yards away, where it had floated ashore, and wrung water out of it, noting that the dunking had washed away some of the muck that had gotten on the hat during his adventures in the back alleys of New Orleans. He settled the still-wet hat on his head and started walking.

Where he headed hardly mattered, but he thought going west suited him better than going in the opposite direction.

"I do declare, if I never take another step, it'll be a day too soon." Mac sat on a log, worked his boots off, and rubbed his sore feet. "That's got to be ten thousand miles I've walked since I tried to drown myself in the Mississippi."

He moaned softly, wiggled his toes, then pulled his boots back on. Getting soaked in the river had caused his boots to shrink. After a week of walking, he was finally getting them back into their proper size, but that did nothing to ease his aching muscles and blistered feet. With a sigh, he heaved himself to his feet and started walking again.

He had lived off the occasional trapped rabbit and more than his share of squirrel since escaping the New Orleans police. Living off the land wasn't too hard, but it took time. He felt the need to be . . . somewhere. Where that might be was a mystery, but the more miles he put between himself and the beautiful but traitorous Evangeline Holdstock the better he liked it.

He had barely gone a quarter mile along the westbound road when he heard a sound that was pure music to his ears. Coming up from behind, a wagon rattled, creaked, and clanked along. He waited impatiently for the driver to notice him and pull up.

"What's your trouble, sonny?" The old man sitting on the wagon's seat and handling the reins had gray muttonchops and peered at him through eyeglasses thick enough to come from the bottoms of medicine bottles.

"My horse up and died under me," Mac said. That wasn't a lie, but the truth was a bit more complicated, what with the cause being a lawman's bullet.

"You leave your gear on the horse?"

Mac took off his hat, wiped sweat from his forehead, and instead of answering the question finally said, "I don't even know where I am. Is this Louisiana?"

"Your horse died in Louisiana? Then you have been hoofin' it for a spell. This here's Texas."

"Wherever you're headed, I'd appreciate a ride. I can help you unload once you get there." The back of the wagon was full of wooden crates. "It looks as if you have quite a chore ahead if you have to do it all yourself."

"I don't mind a little work. Glad to hear you don't, either." The old man squinted. "That six-shooter on your hip? You know how to use it?"

"I don't shoot men with it, if that's what you're asking. It takes me a couple shots, sometimes more, to bring down a rabbit. By then there's not much left for the stew pot."

"So you're not a gunslick?"

Mac laughed and shook his head.

"I'm just a poor, lost soul looking for a decent job. And by that I don't mean shooting anything—or anyone."

"Climb on up. I'm headin' for Waco to deliver equipment shipped all the way from Boston. I picked it up from a dock along the Mississippi and contracted to freight it into the heart of Texas, more's the pity."

"Why's that?" Mac settled down on the hard bench seat beside the man. His nose wrinkled. The old man hadn't bathed in quite a while. He knew he wasn't a fragrant rose himself, but he tried to bathe whenever he came to a stream. Without soap, the best he could do was soak off the dirt and stink.

"I'm gettin' too old for this kind of work. Truth is, I'm gonna settle down when I get to Waco." He snapped the reins and got the mule team pulling. From the way the wagon moaned under the load, it might take a miracle to get as far as the Texas town.

"What's available in Waco in the way of jobs?"

"Well, sir, you got the rangy, stringy look of a wrangler. There's always more'n one outfit getting ready for a trail drive this time of year."

"Trail drive? Where do they head?"

"North, to Abilene, Dodge City, some of them newer towns that spring up like toadstools after a spring rain. Ellsworth, maybe. A few of the bigger ranches hire upward of fifty men for the drive. Even the smaller spreads use twenty or thirty men. You any good with horses?"

Mac could ride. Other than that, he knew next to nothing about taking care of horses, breeding them, training them, or even picking healthy ones for purchase.

"Can't say that I am, but I'm a quick learner."

"Them drives need wranglers for their remuda. Some have a couple hundred horses for their cowpunchers."

"You're skirting around saying I could get a job actually working as a cowboy."

"Sonny, you need skill and determination and maybe bein' kicked in the head once or twice to take on that job. Mostly, you need experience that you don't have."

"Even the best must have started out as a greenhorn."

"That's true, but times are real hard, and takin' on

a cowboy who don't already know his craft is a stretch for the ranchers."

"I haven't heard. Why's it so hard for the ranchers right now?"

The old man laughed, snapped the reins, and got a dirty look from his lead mule.

"The damned railroads, that's why. It used to be hard getting a cow back east. When it was, cattle fetched big prices. Now the railroads can take entire herds to Chicago and even farther east. That drives down the price for every head delivered. There's always somethin' of a race to get to the railhead first to get the best price. Show up too late with your herd and, well, let's say you not only ate everyone's dust on the trail but you're eatin' something even less tasty tryin' to sell into a market already glutted. You *comprende*?"

"I reckon so," Mac said. "But if there's an outfit looking for a hard worker willing to learn, then I've got me a job, and we'll be the first to reach the rail yards or know the reason."

"That's what I like about young'uns," the driver said. "You got spunk, you got determination, and you got shit for brains. But I wish you well."

Mac barely heard. He was content to ride along to Waco and already anticipated getting a job with one of the big cattle outfits.

CHAPTER 7

Dewey Mackenzie was spun this way and that by the incredible rush and bustle in Waco. He had been dazed by the crush and the number of people in New Orleans. That town was bigger than Waco, but even with the deepwater ships and riverboats coming and going, it couldn't hold a candle to Waco.

For all that, he couldn't find a decent job. Every rancher he approached had already filled his crew for the cattle drive to Abilene or other towns along the railroad up north. Mac was weeks too late getting in line for even the most menial employment on one of the drives.

Waco had its share of jobs, but the best he could do was to swap mucking stables and tending horses at a livery stable in exchange for a place to sleep and one meal a day. Without even a few dollars, he couldn't hope to buy a new saddle or another horse. But he took the job anyway, because there was nothing else.

After a solid week of hunting for something better, he felt trapped. He was getting by and nothing more.

He was perched on a bale of hay thinking about that when the livery owner came up behind him and poked him in the ribs.

"You settin' down on the job already? Ain't been but a day or two since I hired you."

Mac stood up quickly and turned around. He said, "Sorry, Mr. Benbow. I appreciate the chance to work, I really do, but I need money. Just having a roof over my head's good, and the meal goes a long ways toward keeping my backbone from rubbing up against my belly, but there's no way I can get ahead."

"All the outfits are full, I reckon." Benbow rubbed his stubbled chin. "You got to town too late."

"I've found that out. Without a horse, I can't even ride out to any of the ranches to see if the ones forming up their drives outside Waco need help."

"Can't speak to that," Benbow said. He scratched himself. "Now, I will need help here after all them cowboys are gone. Might be I can pay you a salary."

Mac perked up. "Really?"

"Won't be much. Maybe fifty cents a week. You know how slow business is."

Mac's spirits sank again. Two dollars a month, even if he saved every penny, wouldn't buy him even a swaybacked nag after a year's hard work.

"Better to go rob a bank," he said, dispirited.

Benbow frowned. "I'll fire you straight out if I hear any more of that talk. Nobody works for me that's an outlaw."

"I won't be one," Mac said hastily. "Fact is, I tried to sell my six-gun over at the gunsmith shop. All he'd give me for it was two dollars."

"You'd need ten times that for even a broke-down

horse," Benbow said. "The times are rough. There's a panic back east that's causing all kinds of ripples out here. Banks closing, businesses going bankrupt, or so I've heard. I don't put much store by those newspapers that reach Waco a month after getting printed. Better to stay up with the local paper. Yes, sir, the *Waco Examiner* is all I need to keep informed."

He wandered away, talking to himself. Mac understood that. Sometimes when a man is alone too much, talking to himself was the only way to keep from going crazy. He had certainly talked out his dilemma with himself more times than he cared to remember during the past few weeks.

He got to work mucking out the stalls. Then he tried prying a pebble from under a horseshoe on one of the animals stabled there. Benbow wouldn't show him how to actually shoe a horse or even hammer back a loose shoe. All he was good for was cleaning the stalls, feeding the horses, and leading them around for a bit of exercise out in the corral behind the stable. Resigned, he applied himself to the chores until it was time to close the stable for the night.

"You go get yourself a meal over at Sadie's," Benbow said. "I told her to fix up something special tonight."

"Special?"

"Might be her fried chicken. Nobody fixes a hen better 'n her. You tell her I said that."

"Thanks, Mr. Benbow, but I can't go into a restaurant smelling like this." Mac sniffed deeply and almost gagged on his own stink.

"Here's a nickel. Go get yourself a bath over at the barbershop. It's next to the hoosegow."

"Thanks." Mac looked at the solitary nickel in the palm of his grimy hand and wondered how far it would go.

He quickly found out. One bath, no hot water— and the water had been used a couple times before him. But he got a brush and soap, and the barber promised some sweet stinkum for his hair. He pulled shut the curtain around the galvanized tub and stripped down to his long johns. Mac worked to wash his shirt and trousers, then hung them up from hooks on the back wall.

Taking the bar of soap and brush, he pulled down the top of his long johns and stepped into the tub. The cold, dirty water was like a miracle elixir for him. Settling into it, he started scrubbing his back and lathered up so much it looked as if he had replaced the water with suds. He started to sing, then heard someone come into the barbershop.

"Howdy, mister," the barber greeted the newcomer, sounding as jovial as he would with any potential customer. "You lookin' to get that mop of hair trimmed up?"

"Ain't what I'm lookin' for. You seen this owl-hoot?"

Mac scowled. The curtain blocked his view of the man who'd come into the barbershop, but the voice sounded familiar. Using the long-handled scrub brush, he moved the curtain aside just a little. He jerked up and almost came out of the tub, sloshing water everywhere.

"You ain't gettin' more water. What's in the tub's all you get," the barber called. "Now who's this you're huntin' for?"

Mac sank back and held the curtain open the barest amount. Through the slit, he saw a man he had never expected to see again in all his born days. The scarred face with the nose mashed over to one side, the cauliflower ears, the hands that looked like sledgehammers . . . this was Pierre Leclerc's henchman, the one Mac mistakenly had thought worked for Micah Holdstock as his bodyguard.

"This is his likeness. You see him?" The mountain of a man held out a wanted poster. Mac couldn't see the picture on it because the barber held it in both hands and peered myopically at it.

"Can't say I have, but this time of year there's hundreds of new faces passin' through town. What's he done?"

"Murder."

"You a lawman? You don't show a badge that I can see."

"You might call me a bounty hunter. I work for the man who lost his father-in-law. His wife is real distraught"—the plug-ugly worked hard to get the word out, as if he had rehearsed it—"and wants justice done since the law ain't interested after he hightailed it out of New Orleans."

Mac sank deeper into the tub and let the curtain slip shut. His heart hammered so hard, he thought he would create a miniature storm in the water and send a tidal wave out into the barbershop.

"There a reward?"

"A hundred dollars. Says so right there."

Mac heard the poster rustle as Leclerc's henchman pointed it out.

"So it does. Well, now, I ain't seen him. You show this to the marshal? He's a real law and order gent."

"He told me to get lost because he's got his hands full with all these cowboys in town."

The barber gave a mumbled answer. A few seconds later, the outer door slammed shut, and the barber called, "You 'bout done back there? I got a business to run, and you said you don't want your hair cut."

Mac shook his wet hair. It had grown to almost shoulder length. He had considered cutting it himself, but now he decided not to. He needed to grow a beard and mustache, too, to make himself look different from the wanted poster.

"Be out in two shakes of a lamb's tail."

"Shake a tail, all right, but it'd better be yours and not no lamb's."

Mac dropped the brush and soap, stood and looked for a towel. Finding none, he dried himself off the best he could, then put on his still-damp clothes. With some trepidation, he pulled back the curtain and stepped out, sure he would find the barber training a six-shooter on him. To his relief, the man sat in his barber chair and read the newspaper. On the bench where prospective customers waited he saw the wanted poster.

Trying not to be too obvious, he snatched up the poster, folded it, and stuffed it into his coat pocket. This was one less chance for his past to catch up with him. He stepped out into the chilly evening air. Or was he shivering because of the close escape?

"My sweet stinkum," he said, half turning to go back into the barbershop. His hair turned cool in the late breeze and begged for some toilet water. Violet, jasmine, a touch of the Three Flowers pomade his pa always got for special occasions when he went to the barber . . .

With a sigh, Mac turned away from the shop. As much as the perfumed goo would please him, at least until he mucked the next stall, he didn't dare take the risk of the nearsighted barber matching his face with the wanted poster.

He walked along Waco's side streets, wondering how far he could get without a horse. Stealing one would bring down the wrath of the law on his head. The newly formed Texas Rangers reportedly never let a criminal escape alive. They'd either gun down a horse thief or see him strung up.

Mac touched his neck and decided a rope around it for thievery wasn't in the cards for him. It was bad enough that he had been framed for murder back in New Orleans and that Leclerc had sent out bounty hunters to track him down.

His belly began to grumble from lack of food. He turned toward Sadie's, the restaurant Benbow had mentioned. He went in the front, but a short, generously built woman with arms crossed over her chest shook her head. Her dark expression warned him from making a scene.

"Benbow said I could get a meal here," Mac explained.

"Yeah, he told me you'd be around." She sniffed. Mac wished he had dared return for the toilet water. He had scrubbed off the dirt and most of the stable smell, but that extra touch would have gotten him a seat in the restaurant. "Into the back." She jerked her thumb over her shoulder, swirled around, her skirts flaring, and stalked off.

Mac followed meekly. He was pleased to see so many people in the restaurant, all chowing down and obviously enjoying it. Even if he got the scraps, he wasn't going to starve. That the leftovers from their plates might actually taste good was a bonus he hadn't dared hope for until now.

"Sit. Eat."

"Do I get a choice?" He pulled up a chair at a table set off to one side of the small kitchen. The cook worked with admirable speed to get out orders.

"Yeah, you get a choice. Eat what's set in front of you or don't." With that Sadie poked the cook, mumbled something to him, and returned to the dining room.

The cook dropped a plate in front of him, heaped with fried potatoes, grits, and a ham steak big enough to have come from a hog the size of a riverboat. He got himself a glass of water and sat down to begin.

"Here. Biscuits. You gotta have biscuits." The cook set a plate with four golden-brown biscuits on the table beside Mac's plate.

He mumbled thanks around a mouthful of food. He kept eating until he was sure he was going to pop, then kept going. The last meal he'd eaten that was anywhere near as bountiful, not to mention tasty, had been at the restaurant where he'd worked in New Orleans. He wiped up the last of the grease from the ham with the final biscuit, then sat back and rested his hands on his bulging belly.

"Those were about the best biscuits I ever ate," he said. "How do you do it?"

"Here, I'll show you." The cook motioned him over. "Need more. You do what I say."

Before he knew it, Mac was wearing an apron and was up to his elbows in flour and dough. He was sliding them into the oven when Sadie came in with a man who limped slightly. He was weather-beaten and had eyes that darted this way and that constantly, as if he was watching for trouble. Mac couldn't help himself. He moved to see if the man wore a star on his vest.

He heaved a sigh when he saw that wasn't the case. In spite of the low-slung iron on the man's hip and his alert behavior, anticipating trouble, this wasn't a lawman.

"Him." Sadie pointed at Mac. "Not the other one. The other one's a helper."

"I've eaten here often enough to know who you got fixing your grub, Sadie."

"What's this about?" Mac couldn't help himself. The wanted poster weighted a ton in his pocket. He had to know if he ought to slip the leather keeper off the hammer of his S&W and get ready to shoot it out.

"This here's Lem Carson. You talk real polite to him." She shot the cook a hard look, swirled about, and returned to the dining room, which was still filled with customers.

"You fix these?" Carson popped a biscuit into his mouth and chewed. He closed his eyes, and Mac thought the man was going to die, but if he did, he'd be going to the Promised Land happy. The smile crossing his face showed that he appreciated the biscuits as much as Mac had.

"He did," Mac admitted as he poked a thumb at the cook. "He just showed me how he does it."

"A cowboy will ride through hell if there's a decent biscuit at the final roundup." Carson took another biscuit and rubbed his fingers over it. "Nice texture, good taste." He stopped playing with it and munched on it. "I've got a job open for a chuckwagon cook. You interested?"

Mac turned to the cook, who paid no attention.

"You," Carson said. "I'm asking *you*. I know José won't leave Sadie. If you can make biscuits this good—half this good!—I can offer you a job."

"Chuckwagon cook?" Mac felt as if the room whirled around him. That wasn't a job he had ever considered. "You got a job as wrangler to offer? I can do that. I ride and—"

"We got a full company already," Carson said, shaking his head. "I'm trail boss for the Rolling J ranch, the one outside of town owned by Sidney Jefferson. You hear of it?"

"I'm new to town, but I'm willing to sign on. Maybe you got a job as night herd? I can sing passably, leastways that's what the pastor back home always said, but he was a charitable man."

Carson shook his head.

"Wrangler?" Mac said again. "I don't mind doing the menial work." Seeing no response, Mac hurried on, "I'm working in a stable right now. Benbow's, over by—"

"I know the place. And I know Benbow." Calculation came into the trail boss's eyes. "He doesn't pay you more'n a meal a day and a place to sleep. The

Rolling J isn't the richest ranch in Texas, but Mr. Jefferson's not a pauper, either. He hires top hands."

"I can see to your remuda and—"

"*Cook.* We need a cook something fierce since we're hitting the trail tomorrow morning. That means the cook's got to feed the outfit, hit the trail, and set up with lunch before noonday."

"Then get along ahead of the herd for the evening meal," Mac said. "I've never cooked."

"He can do it. He's got the eye," José said, never looking up from a steak he fried on the stove.

"That's a plenty good enough recommendation for me. You'll be paid a dollar a day on the trail."

"I don't have a horse or gear."

Carson looked disgusted.

"What's a cook need any of that for? You drive the wagon, you tend the team, you fix the meals for thirty-seven men three times a day."

Mac was staggered by the work required. He was no cook, even if he had watched how meals were prepared in New Orleans and José had given him the secret to flaky biscuits.

"The one thing that'll send me hunting another cook is if you hit the bottle," Carson warned. "Do you drink?"

"You mean whiskey? I've been known to take a nip, but mostly I'm content with a dipper of water to quench my thirst." Mac spoke the truth and saw immediately this was the best possible answer. It went a ways toward explaining why Lem Carson was so anxious to hire a new cook. The old one must be on a real bender.

"You'll have charge of a couple bottles of whiskey in the larder, but it's not for drinking. Nobody drinks it. Nobody. It's medicinal, and you get to dispense it. The men'll come up with the damnedest ailments you ever did hear to swindle you out of a shot. You don't give that who-hit-John to them, no matter what. The whiskey is for those in real need of having their senses dulled, after getting a leg broke or being kicked in the head by a horse. I don't tolerate drunk cowboys. If I did, Mr. Jefferson would fire me in a second. He's a God-fearing teetotaler."

Mac pressed his hand against his coat pocket. The rustle of the wanted poster helped convince him what he had to do. Without prospects in Waco, working for bare survival and not a penny more at the livery stable, he might as well have drowned in the Mississippi. He had to leave town in a hurry.

"You've got yourself a cook, Mr. Carson." He thrust out his hand.

"Call me Lem. Everyone else does. If I seem friendly, that way you'll take it better when I chew you out." Carson shook his hand, sealing the deal.

"Good. He hired you. Now get out of my kitchen. I got work to do." José made shooing motions, took the biscuits from the oven, and turned back to his frying steak, sizzling and popping in the skillet.

Mac left with Carson, wondering if he had made the worst mistake of his life . . . until he saw Leclerc's bully boy across the street passing out the posters.

CHAPTER 8

"You say we're heading out at dawn?" Mac looked at his pocket watch. After all it had been through, he was surprised it still worked.

Carson peered over his shoulder, then produced his own watch and held it out.

"You're three hours and a few minutes off. There's no time for you to get it to a watchmaker for repair."

"But at dawn, we're off?" Mac shifted to stand a little behind the trail boss so Leclerc's henchman wouldn't spot him. How had the bruiser ever found him? Or was he only hitting the likeliest spots? Why Waco? Was Leclerc willing to send an army of men throughout the state to find him?

"We go to the Rolling J, get you settled in today, make sure you have all the supplies you'll need, then we head out on the Shawnee Trail tomorrow."

"Not in a few hours?" Mac watched the man across the street go into a saloon.

"You surely are eager to hit the trail. I wish all the boys were. Some of them are downright lazy oafs. I've been thinking of taking along a blacksnake whip just for them instead of the shorter ones for use on the cattle."

"You whip the cows?"

"Longhorns are ugly, nasty critters, but the cowboys use the whips to keep them moving, not beat them. You are a greenhorn, aren't you? Come on. It's time to get out to the ranch."

"I don't have a horse. How long a walk is it?"

"I've got a buggy. We can ride in style."

"I need to tell Benbow I'm not going to show up for work."

Carson chuckled.

"That old miser'll have a devil of a time finding anyone to work for what he offers, but I appreciate it that you'll tell him, in spite of the way he's used you so hard these past few days."

"He did stand me for a bath and dinner at Sadie's. Where's the buggy?"

"I'll bring it on around. By the time I get there, you'll have given Benbow notice. Glad to have you working for the Rolling J." Carson slapped him on the back, then limped off into the dark.

Mac wasted no time getting to the stables and finding his employer—his former employer. He took a quick look at the horses in the stalls. A stallion he had not seen earlier shifted from one side to the other, as nervous as if it faced a rattler.

"That the horse of a big bruiser?" Mac asked. "A man with a mashed nose and ears that look like worms got to them?"

"It is," Benbow said, "and you've come to tell me you ain't gonna take care of it."

"Or any of the others." Mac saw that his former boss had already heard through the grapevine how Carson had recruited him. He was glad now he had come personally to tell Benbow. "I'd appreciate it if you wouldn't mention me to that horse's owner."

"He looked to be a hard case. You in trouble with him?"

"He's one reason I'm broke," Mac explained. "He doesn't believe I don't have two nickels to rub together and is more than willing to take it out of my hide. The last time our paths crossed, he tried to kill me."

"He had the look of a man used to doing that for no reason other than he enjoyed seeing blood spill." Benbow nodded sagely. "You done right by me, Mac. I won't mention you to him."

"No matter what? No matter what he says or does?"

"Sid Jefferson's a good customer. If I peached on a Rolling J employee, he might take it into his head to use another stable."

"Thanks, and there's Lem now with my ride out to the ranch."

"You don't go poisoning any of them cowboys, you hear?"

Mac grinned, hoping Benbow kept his word and that the Rolling J herd got on the trail fast. Once headed north, along the Shawnee Trail Carson had mentioned, the sooner he could lose any pursuit. He went out and swung up into the buggy. His weight caused that side to sag. He realized then how light the trail boss was.

"It's an hour out to the ranch," Lem Carson said. And it was, almost exactly to the minute.

* * *

Mac slept better than he had in a month. The bunkhouse was warm, and the bed had a real mattress. Better yet, he didn't have to sleep with one eye open, worrying about who was catching up with him. Let Leclerc send his men throughout the country. On the Rolling J, surrounded by four dozen cowboys, Dewey Mackenzie was safe as could be.

He came awake with a start when a hand shook his shoulder.

"It'll be dawn in an hour. You got to get outfitted and ready for the trail."

Mac blinked his tired eyes and saw Lem Carson standing over him. Beside Carson, a short man with a Colt slung on his hip peered down at him with eyes that cut through any pretense and sliced away at his soul. The fierce look faded a mite when he smiled. The man had a gold front tooth to go along with weathered features, jug-handle ears, and a tuft of silvery beard on his squarish chin.

"This here's Patrick Flagg. He'll make sure you find where everything's hid and get you a team for the chuckwagon. I got to roust the others. Don't make me come back to get him out of the bunk." With that Carson vanished.

Mac wondered who the last warning was aimed at, him or Flagg. He swung his legs around and let his feet touch the cold wood planking. A shiver passed through him; then he pulled on his socks and boots. As he did so, Flagg pulled Mac's pistol from its holster and studied it. After a moment, the man held it up.

"Smith & Wesson Model 3," he said in a slow, raspy voice. "This ain't a Russian model, is it?"

"Nope, pure American. What some folks are calling a Schofield, though I never heard my pa call it that."

"He give it to you?" Flagg broke the gun open, checked the cartridges, spun the cylinder, looked down the barrel, gave the weapon a thorough going over. "This has been through rough times lately. You need to oil it."

"It *has* been a long trail, and you're right. Only I don't have any gun oil."

"Rattler does. Ask him. He's as close to a gunsmith as we got on the Rolling J."

"Rattler? You call him that because he looks like a prairie rattler?"

"He was bit by a diamondback. Terrible case of poisoning. Worst I ever did see. It took the rattler four days to die."

Mac looked for any hint of a smile. Flagg gave nothing away. He secured the S&W in the holster and passed it over.

"You won't be needing that. The rest of the boys all carry rifles. Some of them have sidearms." He patted his own.

"Walker Colt. A sturdy gun," Mac said.

"Ain't never failed me yet. And it's had plenty of chances to. Let's get to the chuckwagon so you can see what more in the way of supplies you'll need."

They walked in silence to the barn. Mac held down his urge to fill the silence with idle chatter. He had realized quickly that Flagg wasn't the kind to appreciate jawing without reason. They stopped when

Mac caught sight of the wagon, a huge affair with a tall back.

"Yours, all yours 'til we get to Abilene. Figure out if you need anything more in the way of supplies while I cut out a team for you."

"Horses? Mules?"

"Which do you reckon you handle better?" Flagg stepped back and gave him a long, appraising stare. "Horses. The mules would eat you alive." He headed off to a corral, climbed the fence, and dropped inside, scattering horses as he worked his way among them.

Mac began keeping a mental inventory of supplies, then quickly realized he couldn't remember everything. He opened small drawers in a cabinet built into the wagon and finally found a piece of paper and a pencil. He drew his knife, stared for a second at the blood still caked on it from Micah Holdstock's murder, then used it to sharpen the pencil. He licked the pencil tip and started his list of what he had. He was sitting cross-legged in the back of the wagon, staring at the list, when Flagg returned.

"You got it all figured out?"

"I need more flour. A barrel or two more. And salt."

"That'll unbalance the wagon, no matter where you hang them."

"I want another couple barrels for water. How likely are we to hit a stretch where there's no water for cooking?"

"Plenty likely. Some of the streams run clear and cool. Others you wouldn't take a piss in for fear you'd catch something." Flagg nodded. "Lem said for me to fire you if you looked to be lost in the wilderness." He turned and started off.

Mac scrambled out and went after him. "Wait, wait! Are you saying you're firing me?"

"Get back on the wagon. We're going into town to fetch your supplies."

"But—" Mac fell silent. He understood. If he had shown that he had no idea what he was doing, he would have been walking back to Waco. As lost as he felt, he had made the right guesses as to what the outfit required on the trail. That made him puff out his chest a little and walk with a strut. He might just make a success of this job yet.

He climbed onto the driver's box and started the team pulling for Waco. Flagg swung up onto a saddled horse and rode alongside.

As they neared town, Mac began to worry that he would be spotted. The last thing he wanted now, when he was so close to getting out of these parts, was to have a shootout with Leclerc's henchman or even the law. As they reached the outskirts of Waco, he pulled his hat down low over his eyes and looked around furtively.

"You thinkin' on stealing something, Mac?"

He jerked around. He hadn't been aware that Flagg was watching him so closely.

"No, just, just the sun in my eyes."

Flagg pointed and said, "There's the store. No need to go on through town. Since it's close to noon, folks will be eating."

"So there won't be many people stirring," Mac finished for him.

"That's a good thing." Flagg didn't explain what he meant by that. He stepped down from the saddle and swung the reins around a hitching post in a practiced move that left the horse secured in a double half hitch. Two quick steps took him into the store. Flagg didn't get in any hurry about talking, but his movements were efficient.

Mac was hardly slower to follow after he secured his reins around the hand brake. He walked into the store to find Flagg dickering with the shopkeeper over a box of cartridges for his Walker Colt. Mac considered a box of .44s for his revolver, then realized he didn't have any money. A dollar a day was a princely sum to earn for him, but he hadn't worked for the Rolling J even one day yet.

"You need bullets for that Schofield, Mac?" Flagg asked.

"I can't afford 'em."

"Get what you need. Put it on Mr. Jefferson's tab. He's got to see us outfitted all proper-like." Flagg watched him carefully, then added, "It's not cheating him. You might need that hog leg along the way, and it's no good without bullets. Although it might make a decent hammer."

"You're right, I suppose," Mac said with a shrug. A smile tugged at the corners of his mouth. "It's not like I'm buying a fancy dress or a lady's button-up shoes."

Mac finally got a smile out of Flagg—a faint one. As he went down his list of what he needed to complete the inventory for the chuckwagon, Flagg wandered about the store, stopping at a pine board just inside the door.

"You need any spices, youngster?" the clerk asked. "Out on the trail, if food gets bad, you can hide the taste if you add enough of this and that. What strikes your fancy?" He pointed to a rack of spices with names that confused Mac. He chewed his lip, admitted he didn't have any idea about most of them, then threw himself on the mercy of the shopkeeper.

"What all do you recommend? Remember, this is going on Mr. Jefferson's account."

Both Flagg and the clerk understood what he meant. Because of his employer, he wasn't going to be gypped. The pile of small bottles grew, the clerk explaining what each was. Some Mac rejected, others he doubled.

"That looks like all you'll need. The Rolling J outfit's going to eat high on the hog," the shopkeeper said, laughing. "Or should I say they'll appreciate the finest beef in all of Texas?"

A new voice came from the doorway. "Now, Seth, you know that's not true. The H Bar H is the finest in these parts, so that makes our cows the finest in all the state." The speaker stood with hands on his hips, looking like he owned the world.

"Howdy, Compass. You fixin' to hit the trail soon, too?" The shopkeeper shook hands with the new customer.

"Any day now, if the Rolling J boys don't clean you out of whatever we need." He turned to Flagg and shook hands. "Good seeing you again, Patrick. Who's your new hand?"

"This here's Mac Mackenzie, our new cook."

"Compass Jack Bennett," the man said, almost crushing Mac's hand in his own. "Wait, don't ask. Everyone does. They call me Compass because I can't get lost. No matter where I am or how they try to confuse me, I know exactly where I'm going."

"A handy skill," Mac said, not sure if he believed the man.

"He's the trail boss for the H Bar H herd."

Compass Jack looked hard at Mac, then said, "You worried about replacing Abel Jones?"

Mac had never heard the name before and didn't answer.

"There warn't nothing able about Abel," Flagg said. "Lem's done good finding a replacement. And if he hasn't, tarring and feathering Mac will be easy enough."

"I'll see you as you drive into Abilene," the H Bar H trail boss said.

"You got that backward, Compass. We'll watch *you* driving your herd of scrawny cows in because we'll have sold ours and will be celebrating."

"And this is the man everyone says is never optimistic. I just never thought you were hallucinating, Flagg." Compass Jack slapped Flagg on the shoulder and began listing all he needed for his drive.

Flagg inclined his head toward the door.

"We got barrels to load," he told Mac. "And that hundred pounds of fancy spices you can't even pronounce."

Mac held up the box containing the spices he had bought. Flagg exaggerated by about ninety-eight pounds. If a pinch was all he needed to give flavor to his meals, the Rolling J cowboys would appreciate the grub on this trip more than they had under Abel Jones.

Before he could ask Flagg about the former cook, he stopped and stared. The pine board beside the door leading into the street had a dozen wanted posters tacked to it. He almost panicked when he saw a couple of them had been torn down. Was his one of them? He swallowed hard, then went outside to help Flagg with the heavy barrels. The quicker he got away from Waco, the better.

Mac was beside himself. He had pots and pans galore, some filled, others waiting to be filled with food he had prepared for the entire crew. They had lined up with their tin plates and spoons, wanting dinner. Mac felt overwhelmed until he got to the point where he reckoned he would either give the entire ranch a bellyache and they would fire him or he would serve a meal they tolerated.

As he slopped the food onto their outstretched plates, he wasn't sure which he had cooked. The few tastes he had done while he worked had been bland. He hesitated to use the spices bought in town, keeping them in reserve as a last-gasp effort once they were out on the trail. He looked up as Lem Carson thrust out his place.

"Fill 'er up," he said.

"Double portion for you," Mac said. As he spooned out his concoctions, he asked, "Where's Mr. Jefferson? I expected him to be here with the men since we're heading out in the morning."

The drive hadn't gotten away from the ranch today after all, preparations having taken longer than expected. Because of that, Mac had been able to use the kitchen in the ranch house to prepare this evening's meal.

"Boss is feeling poorly." The way Carson spoke put off any other questions. Then the next man in line pushed to get his turn at the food.

Mac worked diligently until no one else stood in front of him. He stared. More than forty men had staked out places around the house to sit and eat. They shoveled the food directly from the plate into their mouths, few of them slowing down. When Patrick Flagg came over, Mac had to ask, "Do you want seconds, or are you here to warn me to get a running start?"

"Food's not bad," Flagg allowed as he put his plate and spoon in the big pan where the dirty dishes were collected. "The one you got to please is Carson. He's a picky eater."

"Is that why he fired Abel Jones?"

"Abel got himself run off the Rolling J because he showed up drunk once too often. That and . . . well, that other thing with the goat."

Before Mac asked what more there was, Flagg turned and walked away.

Lem Carson sauntered over. "Aren't you eating?"

"How was it? The food?" Mac tried not to sound too anxious as he asked the question.

"I've had better."

Mac's heart felt like it was about to explode. He waited for the trail boss to fire him.

"I've had worse, too." Carson slapped him on the shoulder. "Be ready to roll an hour before dawn. Me and you, we ride point. I scout the trail, you follow and get set up for supper." With that he walked on, calling to others in the outfit.

The trail boss hadn't fired him after the first meal, Mac thought. That was good. Breakfast would be cold in the morning because he and Carson would be on the trail, finding a place to stop at midday to feed the trail hands before moving on ahead of the herd to repeat the meal for evening chow.

He scraped what was left out of a pot and sampled it.

"Not bad," he said. "Not bad at all, if I do say so myself." He set to work eating what remained and then got to cleaning the pots and pans. He wanted everything ready to go for when they hit the trail.

CHAPTER 9

Mac couldn't believe they'd been on the trail for a solid week and no one had complained about his cooking. As Carson had claimed back in Waco, give them decent biscuits and they'd stick with him through thick and thin. Every time he wanted to change how he fixed the biscuits, just a little to experiment, he remembered how José in Sadie's kitchen had done it and how the biscuits had come out golden brown and perfect. Some of his experiments with the rest of the food weren't too successful, but giving the drovers their bread kept him in their good graces.

He had a barrel of yeasty dough he used to prepare the daily bread. Keeping it through the entire six weeks of the drive had worried him, but Carson assured him this was done all the time. His only worry had to be running out of the dough and having to start a new batch. Lacking the yeast, that would mean buying more from a town along the trail.

"Shawnee Trail," he said. He had tried to follow their tracks on a map he'd found in the chuckwagon. The trail snaked up from way south to Waco. He ignored that part. What lay ahead interested him the most. He'd asked why they weren't following the Chisholm Trail, but Carson hadn't given a definitive answer.

Truth was, he hadn't given any answer at all.

"I pick the route. You follow me and feed the men. Then you follow me some more," Carson had said in a tone that brooked no argument.

Mac had quickly decided he wasn't going to question anything after he saw how hard the men worked. They used eight- or twenty-foot whips, cracking them above the steers' heads to keep them together and moving. He had tried to crack one of the shorter whips and almost yanked his arm out of its socket.

Night herd was the least desirable chore, so the men rotated the duty. Three days as drovers, three as wranglers, three as night guards. The wranglers provided him with helpers, those who weren't tending the huge remuda of horses or taking care of the gear. He was four days into the drive before he found Rattler and had him take apart and oil his S&W.

"Good pistol," Rattler had said. The man was gaunt to the point of starvation, but Mac never saw anyone eat more chow than Rattler when they lined up for meals. He had deep, sunken eyes and hands so tiny they might have been a woman's. But the strength in them belied any femininity. Rattler, like most of the cowboys, walked bowlegged from so many years in the saddle and still stood an inch taller than Mac.

"It was my pa's. He left it to me when he died."

Mac forced the memory away. His family had been loving, and both his ma and pa worked hard to raise him right, but he was on his own now with them six feet under in a cemetery in southern Missouri.

"You any good with it? As a marksman?"

"Can't say that I am." Mac hesitated to mention the time he had spent in front of a mirror, practicing his quick draw. He had fancied himself a gunman for a while, then realized he had no money to buy ammunition and actually learn to hit anything, even if he was lightning fast clearing leather.

"You should get Flagg to give you some lessons. Never saw a man who shot straighter than him."

"Aren't you better?"

"Naw, all I do is tinker. You need something fixed, ask me. But I get the fantods thinking about facin' down someone intent on killin' me. This here hand would shake like a wet dog, yes, sir." Rattler held out his hand. It was as steady as a rock.

Rattler wandered away, leaving Mac with his freshly oiled revolver. Somehow, the gun fit better in his hand, and he felt more competent. That was crazy, he knew, but it was the truth. He took off the gun belt and stowed it away in his chuckwagon. There was always something to do, and he got to starting the hundreds of smaller chores that needed to be attended to before getting down to fixing another meal for the entire crew.

As he worked, he heard loud voices, then the rush of men not tending the herd as they circled around.

"String him up!" That cry built until most of the Rolling J cowboys were shouting it as they waved their fists in the air.

"Settle down. Let me through. Get back." Lem Carson pushed his way through.

Curious, Mac went to the ring of men, shouldered his way forward, and saw three men in the middle. Carson stood between two other men, a hand on each hombre's chest to push them apart. Mac recognized Deke Northrup, a hothead who had been in a couple of fights since they'd left Waco. From all he could tell, Northrup wasn't good enough at his job for Carson to put up with such behavior, but he had a following with some of the others that made Mac scratch his head.

"He tried to steal one of our longhorns." Northrup shoved Carson's hand off his chest, balled his fist, and started to punch the other cowboy.

"You got some explaining to do, son," Carson said sharply. "What were you doing sniffing around the Rolling J herd when you got stock of your own to tend to?"

"I got turned around riding night herd," the second cowboy said. He was young, and a little on the scrawny side. "I thought I saw a couple stragglers from the H Bar H herd mixed in with yours. I was wrong."

"Wrong?" Northrup sneered. "You're not wrong, you're lying. You're a rustler looking to steal our cattle!"

This time, when he pushed forward, he got past Carson and took a swing at the H Bar H cowboy. The punch missed by scant inches but provoked a response.

The H Bar H wrangler lurched forward and grabbed Northrup. The two grappled, nothing much happening, until Carson grabbed them both and again separated them.

"You head on back to your herd," Carson ordered. "Tell Compass Jack to keep better track of his own cows."

"Ain't the trail boss's fault I got lost. And I wasn't tryin' to rustle your no-account animals. Why would I want to? Anybody figuring to eat a steak carved from one of them would choke on the gristle!"

"Enough of that. Get out of here." Carson shoved the cowboy away. With ill grace, he left, the ring of Rolling J hands parting for him.

Deke Northrup stood there for a second, his face dark with anger, then suddenly he clawed his revolver out of its holster, evidently intent on shooting the H Bar H cowboy in the back anyway.

"Look out!" Mac cried without thinking.

Carson moved again, this time putting his own life in jeopardy. He stepped around swiftly, blocking the shot with his own body. Mac caught his breath when it looked as if Northrup would shoot anyway, not caring if he gunned down his own trail boss.

"You up to pulling the trigger, Deke?" Carson spoke in a low voice, but every word cut Mac's senses like a knife. "Put the smoke wagon away."

Northrup gritted his teeth. His hand trembled the slightest amount, but he finally relaxed and slipped the gun back into his holster.

"Don't cross me, Carson. Don't ever do it again."

"I can say the same thing about you, Northrup. Don't forget who's in charge here and who's only a cowboy riding herd."

Northrup grumbled and turned away, stomping

off. Carson watched for a moment, then called, "The show's over. Get on back to work, all of you. Do it now!"

Mac had never seen the trail boss this angry. He looked fierce enough to chew nails and spit tacks. As the cowboys drifted away, Carson stormed off. With a deep sigh of relief that no one had died, Mac returned to his chuckwagon and the work ahead of him.

As he prepared yet another meal of steaks and potatoes for the men, he tried to figure how much longer the potato supply would last. Eating on the first part of the drive proved to be high cuisine. He worried about the vegetables rotting in another week. Then he would have to find more by rooting around the countryside or going into nearby towns to buy more. Which worked best depended on how much money Carson would give him. Being such a tenderfoot forced him to depend on advice from others, and that made him look like he wasn't doing his job.

Above all else, Mac wanted to do his job well. Despite his early misgivings, he found he liked working as a cook. Without him, there wouldn't be a trail drive or men willing to ride endless hours to move the herd north. So far, he hadn't gotten any complaints about what he fixed. And José's way of baking biscuits still kept the men smiling.

"You want to learn to use that gun you lug around?"

Mac jumped at the voice behind him. He had been lost in planning for the next meal.

"Howdy, Flagg," he said as he turned around. "You must have been talking with Rattler."

"Have."

"What will it take? To learn how to use the gun, I mean."

"You got a couple boxes of ammunition. I remember you agonizing over buying them back in Waco."

"Mr. Jefferson paid for them, true. I haven't had any call to fire even one round, so it seems to me that I kinda did him out of the money."

"Learn to hit what you aim at," Flagg said. "If it comes in handy later on, he'll have gotten a bargain. You have a minute or two?"

Mac saw that he did. The chores were endless, and they would wait for him. What he had on the fire cooking wouldn't require anything more than occasional stirring on his part.

"I can spare the time."

"We'll start easy so all you'll need is a loaded gun. Six rounds." Flagg looked around the chuckwagon and picked up an empty tin can. He tossed it a few inches into the air, caught it, and then walked some distance from the cooking fires.

Mac strapped on his gun belt and made sure the Smith & Wesson slid easily in the holster as he trailed Flagg outside the camp. For a second, he thought Flagg was going to toss the can high in the air and expect him to hit it on the fly. He had seen a traveling sideshow with a lady marksman able to do that very thing for hours on end, but it was beyond him and would only waste ammunition. Flagg made it easy on him, balancing the can on a stump.

"Don't jerk on the trigger," Flagg said. He motioned for Mac to shoot the can and then backed off.

"Should I draw and—"

"You'll blow a hole in your leg doing that. Be gentle. Take the gun from the holster. Point it at the target. Cock. Pull back real gentle on the trigger."

Mac felt a little put off by not practicing his quick draw, but he wanted to learn, and Flagg was the teacher. He drew, held the pistol at his side, then raised it slowly, cocked, and fired. When the can didn't jump off the stump, drilled smack dab in the middle, he frowned and tried again. Once more he missed.

"Sun's in my eyes."

Flagg lifted his Colt and fired. The can flew into the air, reflecting sunlight as it spun. He never said a word when he retrieved the can and put it back in place.

"Try again. You got four more tries to hit it, or at least scare it a little."

Mac held his temper down. Flagg insulted him. He held the six-gun level, aimed, and fired. The can teetered but did not fall over.

"Closer. The air whistled past it. You're turning your wrist before you fire." Flagg came over to him, grabbed his arm, and held his hand straight. "That way."

Mac squeezed off another shot. The can flew sideways.

"Still turning your wrist. Might try practicing with a splint to hold yourself in line. That's enough for now."

"I've got one more shot," Mac protested.

"Save it for next time. We got to chow down and—" Flagg turned, lifting his head like a wolf sniffing the night breeze.

Mac smelled nothing, but he felt the vibration coming up through the ground.

"Is that an earthquake? I remember one back in Missouri."

"Stampede!" Flagg yelled. "We'll need every hand to turn it. Get on a horse and get your ass out there!"

Mac started to reply but found himself staring at thin air. Flagg had hightailed it faster than Mac had ever seen him move. He wasted no time, running after the cowboy for all he was worth.

Mac got back to the chuckwagon in time to see Flagg galloping away. It took him a few minutes to saddle a horse from his team. The mare didn't take kindly to this change in job, going from harness to saddle. Mac fought the animal at every stage.

Then he realized the horse didn't mind the saddle. It was frightened of the stampede. The ground now shook so hard the pots and pans hanging from hooks along the sides of the chuckwagon rattled.

"Come on," he told the horse when he finally got mounted. "We got work to do."

Mac galloped after Flagg, not sure what to do but certain he would understand once he reached the herd.

He slowed the closer he came to the herd. The prairie had been covered with the longhorns as they walked along all peaceable-like. Now they kicked up a cloud of choking dust that obscured everything but the danger of being in their way as they mindlessly ran themselves into the ground.

To his amazement, he saw the cowboys trying to get in front of the herd, using their whips to snap above the heads of the cattle in the lead, trying to turn their direction.

It didn't matter which way they moved the herd, as long as they forced them to turn. This caused the ones at the back and far edge to run extra distance. Tiring out the leaders was the goal, and the cowboys, with their whips, made it sound like a war had started. Then Mac realized he heard gunfire over the herd's pounding hooves. Those without whips fired into the air to force the cattle away from their headlong plunge across the rolling land.

Almost as quickly as it started, the stampede petered out, and within minutes, the two thousand head were milling about, looking for clumps of buffalo and grama grass to eat. He heard more than one cowboy cursing the stupid beasts. He had to agree. It almost made him afraid to eat one of the longhorns for fear he might swallow some of the stupid.

He did what he could to get stragglers back into the main herd. That few minutes of effort convinced him the life of a cowboy wasn't easy. A great deal of skill went into riding and herding.

"You done good, Mac." Rattler drew alongside, took off his hat, and used his bandana to wipe away sweat from his forehead. "Then again, if you hadn't helped turn them damn fool critters, they'd have stomped your chuckwagon into the ground. That was the way they were headed."

"I never noticed." Mac looked around and saw the cowboy was right. "What started them running?"

"Who knows? They take it into their heads to run, they do. It only takes one to get spooked and the rest follow. Why, one time I—"

"Wait. There's a commotion over there." Mac pointed to where a dozen of the cowboys had formed a circle. They were all looking at something on the ground.

Rattler settled his hat onto his head and began swearing a blue streak. He wouldn't tell Mac why but galloped toward the tight knot of drovers. Mac followed as fast as his horse would take him. His heart sank when he saw a man lying on his back, staring up at the sky.

Lem Carson would never see another cloud or star again. He was stone dead.

Flagg and Northrup knelt beside the fallen trail boss. They stood and faced off. Mac thought they were going to throw down on each other from the way they stood. He hit the ground and ran forward, ready to do what he could.

"It was that son of a bitch from the H Bar H," Northrup said. "It had to be. No other reason for the herd to stampede."

"Cows don't need a reason," Flagg said. "Did you see him?"

"The H Bar H hand? Hell no, but I didn't have to. He was trying to steal our cows before. When I caught him, he decided to take some revenge." Northrup looked down at Carson's body. "He was a damned fool to let the rustler get away scot-free like he did. We can take care of that, though, can't we, men?"

An angry cry went up. Several turned their horses in the direction of the H Bar H herd, maybe five miles distant.

Suddenly, silence fell when a shot rang out. Mac

jumped. Flagg had pulled his gun and fired into the air to get their attention.

"Lem's dead. Don't go starting a range war for no good reason. He wouldn't like it."

"He got killed in the stampede started by that H Bar H hand. We can't let that go unpunished. Why, it's nigh on murder!" Northrup started to mount, but Mac's voice froze him in his tracks.

"It may have been murder," Mac said. "Carson's got what looks to be a bullet hole in his head. He was tromped on by the longhorns, sure, but he might have been shot out of the saddle before they ran over him."

He knelt and rolled Lem Carson onto his face, then pointed to the tiny hole in the back of the trail boss's skull. Blood and bone hid the wound until he pushed back enough hair to show it.

"The bullet went in here but never came out the front."

"That means it was fired from a long ways off," Northrup said. "It must be them H Bar H punchers. They set up a sniper to shoot Carson and—"

"Might have been shot close by with a small-caliber gun," Flagg said. "What's the caliber of that piece hanging on your hip, Northrup? I seem to remember you carrying a .24."

"It coulda been an accident," another cowboy chimed in. "I was firing my six-shooter after I lost my whip in the stampede, and I can't account for any of the rounds. I think they all went into the air, but I couldn't swear to it. None of us can. Lem might have got unlucky where his head was at when a bullet came down."

"He might have been hit by any of us," Mac said, seeing the logic in what was said. He had no love for Deke Northrup or the way the man acted, but even if the bullet in Carson's head matched that from Northrup's gun, that proved nothing. Flinging lead all around in the middle of a stampede meant some of it went where nobody intended. Northrup might have shot the trail boss, and it might have been accidental.

What bothered Mac was the possibility that it hadn't been an accident. Carson had humiliated Northrup when he had backed him down earlier over letting the H Bar H cowboy return to his herd.

"Some of you, get a grave dug and plant Carson in it," Northrup ordered. "We've got to bed down the herd for the night and—"

"Who made you trail boss, Northrup?" Flagg stepped over Carson's body and stopped a couple feet from the cowboy.

"Nobody made you trail boss, either, Flagg."

"I've been with the Rolling J for three years. You just signed on."

"So working for Jefferson longer means you're in charge? Hell no, it don't. I know more about cattle than you can ever learn."

Some of the cowboys snickered at that. Mac felt the tension rising.

"We can send a rider back to the Rolling J and ask Mr. Jefferson who he wants to ramrod the herd on to Abilene. Or you can back down and let me take the job."

Flagg never lifted his voice, but the cold edge to it

chilled Mac. He felt death building in the air, death beyond that which had already visited Lem Carson.

"Let's vote who takes the herd to Abilene. All who want me, raise your hands." Northrup looked around, glaring.

Mac counted fast.

"And those of us what want Patrick Flagg, get those filthy paws into the air," ordered Rattler. His was the first hand to lift. One by one and then faster and faster, the outfit voted.

"It's not even close," Mac said. "Ten for Deke Northrup. Thirty-five for Patrick Flagg."

"Two men short." Rattler looked down at Carson, then amended, "One short. Who didn't vote?"

"I didn't vote for myself. There was no call to," Flagg said. "This isn't something to be put to a vote. Now get the herd bedded down. All of you." He turned to Mac. "Except you. You get evening grub ready." The cowboys mounted and headed away.

"I'll see to burying him," Mac said, seeing as to how none of the cowboys had lingered to help with the chore. "Any particular place?"

Flagg looked around, then pointed to a small hill.

Mac nodded and said, "He'll have a good view from there."

"Take him over. I'll get a shovel and help dig."

"I'll ask Rattler to make up a marker," Mac said. "He's handy with small things."

He heaved the trail boss's body up over his saddle, letting him dangle over on either side. He stared at Carson for a moment, then called to the new trail boss.

"Flagg, did you notice that—"

"That Lem wasn't killed by any bullet falling from the sky? Yeah, I did. That hole shows he was shot from behind, maybe even from a little lower with the gun pointing up." Flagg looked toward the group surrounding Deke Northrup. They talked and weren't working on the herd.

Mac felt the tension, even at this distance. Without another word, he led his horse toward the hill, where they buried Lem Carson and had a short service for him just before everyone ate a quiet evening meal.

Chapter 10

"Looks good. Set up your wagon here," Flagg said as he reined in. He spoke without looking at Mac, who had gotten used to the man's ways after a week of him working as trail boss. Flagg never said much, but when he did, he meant it.

"Why quit so early?" Mac asked from the chuck-wagon seat. "We've got another hour or two of daylight."

"There's a river to ford. We'll tackle it the first thing in the morning. We start now, darkness will drop before we got half the herd across."

Mac understood that. Having to deal with the longhorns in the dark was foolish at best and deadly at worst. Even with many of the eight-foot-spanning horns polled, they were deadly if they took it into their feeble brains to swing about just as a rider came past. More than one rider had had his horse gored to death. And so far, one rider had been laid up with a horn through his leg. This had been Mac's only call to do any doctoring, which fell under his job description along with damned near everything else that wasn't riding and herding.

"Should I whip up something special to get the men ready for the morning?"

"Save it for breakfast. Steak and whatever you got left."

"No eggs," Mac said, knowing what Flagg meant. The man liked nothing more than eggs for breakfast, but putting in ten or even fifteen miles a day left no time to ask after freshly laid eggs at the farms they passed. The few dozen eggs he had bought in Waco had lasted for only a couple days of travel.

Some of the food had gone a bit stale, and Mac was happy he had bought the spices. Toss enough pepper into any dish and the bad taste and smell went away. He tried not to serve too many meals like that, but there had been a stretch of more than four days when he'd had no other choice. The going had been hard, and there had been no chance to replenish his larder with fresh food.

"Before you start, let's get in some practice with that hog leg of yours," Flagg suggested when he had swung down from the saddle.

This surprised Mac, and he said so.

"It ain't that I expect trouble from Northrup and his boys," Flagg went on, "but you ought to be able to hit the broad side of a barn even if you're not locked inside. You got any empty airtights to plink at?"

"A couple."

"Set up six. Over yonder."

Flagg secured his horse to the chuckwagon's back wheel. He stretched and walked around to get the kinks out from long hours spent in the saddle, scouting the trail for the herd. By the time he was ready, Mac had his S&W unlimbered and the cans set up.

"You got six shots. You take out all six of them cans. No need to hurry, but think about moving along right sprightly, as if your life depended on throwing lead that way."

Mac took a breath, squared his stance, lifted the Model 3, and cocked the hammer. He squeezed off a shot, cocked, repeated, and worked his way down the line, hitting all six cans and feeling good about his improvement.

Flagg snorted and said, "You only scared that last can. You're still canting your wrist, turning it a mite. Keep it upright. You won't miss as much."

With that, Flagg tugged on the reins, pulled them loose from the wagon wheel, and mounted. He looked down at Mac.

"You get that iron reloaded and serve a meal fit for a king. The boys have put in some hard days since Carson was killed."

Flagg rode away to scout the river where they'd have to ford in the morning. A low line of scrubby trees twisting across the flat, open landscape marked the stream's course.

Mac worked steadily until the herd caught up and the cowboys started bedding the cattle down for the night. The last hour of daylight made it more difficult to get them settled. Mac wasn't one to brag, but his meal matched the best he had done. After the crew had shoveled down the grub, he cleaned up and was ready to turn in himself when he heard rustling in the trees along the river.

"What's that?" He nudged Rattler and tapped his ear, urging him to listen.

Rattler frowned, then said, "Sounds like it might be a turkey. You got it in mind to shoot one of them?"

"Or more, if it comes to that. The Rolling J has some mighty fine beef, but it gets tiresome eating steak every day of the week."

"For this many men, you'd have to kill a flock."

"Want to come with me and see what we can scare up?" He saw the answer on Rattler's face.

"Can't make it. I got the first two hours of night herd. You got any requests for me to sing?"

"Not that off-key rendition of 'The Whorehouse Bells Were Ringing,' " Mac said. "I never heard anyone sing it worse."

Rattler grinned and lifted his cracked voice in song.

> *"The whorehouse bells were ringing,*
> *And the pimp stood in the door.*
> *He'd had a hard on all day long*
> *To screw some dirty whore."*

"That's the one you *don't* sing," Mac said as he grimaced. "You don't do a bad rendition of 'Lorena' or 'In the Days of Forty-Nine.' Stick with those."

"You just don't want me stretchin' my vocal chords and tryin' anything different," Rattler said in mock complaint. "Maybe that particular song brings back memories for you that ain't too happy?"

"It's mighty dark out in the woods. You might sing something to keep the cows agitated. I can find my way back to camp by following their lowing when they complain about your scratchy voice."

"You can't fool me. You want to get away from all them fellers snorin' their fool heads off."

Mac couldn't deny that. Already half the men were pulling blankets over their shoulders and curling up for a night's sleep. A few sat around the fire swapping tall tales and outright lies for the sheer pleasure of it. One or two of them managed fine stories that kept the others entertained, but mostly they talked about their lives and ladies they'd left behind. A few opined about the ladies they would find in Abilene, but only the most inventive didn't repeat themselves by this time in the drive.

Rattler rode off for his turn at night herd. He had one more night, and then he moved to morning patrol, getting the herd moving at first light. The cowboys all rotated through the day, working the point, sides, and back of the herd, eating dust, then got to watch the cattle for two hour shifts at night. Rattler wouldn't be back on night duty until they were almost in Abilene at the railhead.

Mac found a burlap sack and strapped on his gun belt. He had no intention of trying to shoot a turkey in the dark. He was pleased enough with his improvement as a marksman, but to hit a bird on a pitch-black night would require more luck than skill. Hiking steadily toward the sounds of turkeys gobbling and thrashing about in the underbrush, he slowed and finally stopped to get his bearings.

It occurred to him that wild hogs might find these trees along the river particularly fine for a home. He touched the S&W at his side, sure that the large-caliber bullet could bring down all but the biggest hog—if he saw it in time to draw and accurately fire.

"No hogs, just turkeys," he said softly as more gobbling came from straight ahead in the woods. He took careful steps, trying not to make much noise. In the dark, he might as well have led the entire Union Army in full assault. Twigs broke and leaves crunched under his boots no matter how cautious he tried to be.

The gobbling stopped. He kept walking and found the underbrush where turkeys might be inclined to make nests. Dropping to hands and knees, he began hunting. Luck favored him that night. He found a nest with half a dozen turkey eggs in it almost right away. Carefully, he put them into his sack and continued hunting. After a futile half hour, he gave up.

"Wore out all my luck in the first couple minutes," he muttered. As if mocking him, turkeys gobbled somewhere not too far away. He slid his gun from its holster and considered taking a wild shot to scare the birds, maybe flush them out into the open.

Good sense made him pouch the iron. A shot would bring Flagg and half the camp running to see what was wrong, not to mention the always-present chance that it could spook the cattle and start a stampede.

Backing out of the trees, he looked around in the darkness until he located the spot where he had parked the chuckwagon. The fires scattered around the campsite had burned lower until they were barely visible. When Mac got back to camp, he added firewood to some of them to help ward off the night's chill.

When he was finished with that, he placed the

turkey eggs in a basket and wrapped them with cloth to keep them from breaking. Whatever he did with them for breakfast in the morning had to be something special. There wasn't any need to rush the decision, though. With that to feed his dreams, he curled up under the wagon and went to sleep in minutes.

"Get on across with the wagon first," Flagg told him. "Then we'll get the herd moving."

Mac looked at the rapidly flowing river with some trepidation. His heart slugged heavily in his chest. He had forded rivers before—but they were creeks in comparison to this stream.

"There's no place to ford? We have to swim?"

"Afraid so, Mac. Get going. You're holding up the herd." Flagg waved to Rattler and two others now taking point for the herd, getting them ready for the crossing.

Keeping that many longhorns swimming in the same direction and not letting the current carry them away was going to take most of the morning. Mac felt guilty for being so slow to get the chuckwagon moving. The current sent logs as thick as his body sailing along in the middle of the river. If he got hit with one of them, it would be like a battering ram smashing in the side of the wagon. He would go right to the bottom—

He stopped thinking of ways he could die and lose the chuckwagon. Snapping the reins, wishing he had a whip to get the horses pulling faster, he entered the river. Keeping the wagon upright proved to be a chore, but one he was equal to. He found himself shifting his weight back and forth on the seat, trying to maintain the vehicle's balance even though that probably had little real effect on it.

The horses disliked swimming as much as he did and kept heading for the far bank. The current in the middle of the river proved too strong to plow right on straight through. He angled the team downstream a little, keeping them working until the lead horse found purchase and leaned into the harness. The next found solid ground and then the rest.

In a few moments, Mac was safely on the shore, heaving a sigh of relief. He brought the horses to a halt, tied the reins to the brake lever, and dropped to the ground. He had stopped on a slant so water would drain from inside the wagon. A quick check showed he had wrapped everything properly to be kept safe from the water. Almost everything was dry or at least could be dried out in a hurry.

Best of all, his turkey eggs had survived the crossing. He had dreamed about them the night before but hadn't come up with a decent way to prepare them.

He turned to the river and waved to Flagg. The signal wasn't necessary. The trail boss already had the first few hundred cattle in the water and was leading them across.

Mac waited for Flagg to reach the shore and come over to him.

"What do you want me to do?" he asked. "Wait for you to scout?"

"I have to be sure the herd's across. You go ahead and do the scouting. We'll follow your trail."

"What if I don't find a good trail?"

"You've ridden alongside Carson and then me the whole time we've been gone. You know what to look for and how to set up camp when you find it. We'll be caught up by noonday. Have a good feed ready for us. The men'll need it after the work we're putting in getting them damned cows on this side of the river."

Mac puffed with pride that Flagg thought highly enough of him to scout the trail. He watched as the cowboys rode alongside the few dozen cows they brought across each time. Only a handful of cowboys remained on this side to keep the herd together while the rest of the hands returned to bring more across. It was a tedious, dangerous crossing.

He made one last check of the chuckwagon and the team, then started northward looking for good grazing, easy passage, and a place to park to prepare lunch. Moving faster than the herd today, he found a decent spot and began the midday meal, making a special batch of biscuits since that pleased the outfit more than anything else he cooked.

As he moved the big kettles off the fire to wait for the Rolling J cowboys, he heard the sound that he had lived with for weeks now. The herd came slowly over a low hill and into a shallow valley he thought perfect for grazing. Alongside were a couple dozen of the cowboys.

He waved and got Rattler's attention.

"You surely do have it easy, Mac," Rattler called. "All you got to do is ride along, whump up a meal, and then ride on. We got to keep those filthy long-horns moving together."

"Everyone's got problems," Mac said, knowing Rattler wanted to blow off steam after a hard morning. "Where's Flagg?"

"About a hundred head got separated as we were crossin'. They washed on downriver. Him and a half dozen of the others left us to come on ahead while they retrieved them varmints."

"A hundred head's worth a pile of money," Mac said. "Thirty, forty dollars a head?"

"Might be that, might be less. Surely that, though, if we get to Abilene ahead of the other herds. It's a matter of racin' 'em now to get top dollar. Hey, are those biscuits I smell bakin' in that Dutch oven?"

"They are, and you can wait your turn like everybody else. Might be, I hold off feeding you until Flagg and the others get back."

"Do that and you'll have a mutiny on your hands," Rattler warned.

"There's a stream yonder. You've got time to bathe. You smell like a wet dog."

"I got plenty of bathin' done this morning, thank you 'most to death, but Flagg told me to ramrod the outfit until he gets back. Save me some of them biscuits now, you hear?"

Rattler let out an exuberant whoop and rode away, leaving Mac to complete his preparations.

He worked steadily and got the meal lined up, mentally going over when he started what and how long it took to cook. The beefsteaks were the quickest since most of the men preferred their meat so bloody that it mooed when a knife cut into it. He put a kettle of water on over a fire to boil so he could toss in some greens he had gathered. The men didn't like weeds boiled until they turned to mush, as too many of them claimed, but he had yet to see one of them that didn't lick the last bit off their plates. Variety helped keep up morale as well as preventing them from getting sick from any number of diseases. Mac took some pride in the fact that he hadn't given any of the outfit food poisoning yet.

"Where you keep it?"

The sudden question made him turn around. "What's that?" he asked. Mac tried to keep the disgust from his voice as he saw who had ridden up to the chuckwagon.

Thumbs Fontaine was thick with Deke Northrup. While it could hardly be said he was Northrup's second in command, that probably wasn't too far off the mark.

"You got a couple bottles of whiskey," Fontaine said as he crossed both hands on his saddle horn and leaned forward. "Me and the boys want to celebrate gettin' across the river. That was one nasty chore, and we want to whoop it up."

"The whiskey's only for medicinal use," Mac said. "You know that. And you know Mr. Jefferson doesn't like any of his hands boozing it up out on the trail."

Fontaine spat to the side and then said, "That was Carson's idea, not the owner's. Hell, why do you think they call it the Rolling J? Jefferson rolled on out of a poker game so drunk he could hardly stand. He held four jacks."

"Never heard that story. I always thought it had something to do with his name being Jefferson. Now get on out of here. Food's not gonna be ready for another hour."

"That'll give me and the boys time to finish off

one of those bottles." Fontaine dismounted, went to the chuckwagon, and started pawing through crates, hunting for the liquor.

"You don't listen. Your ears as broken as your thumbs?" Mac grabbed Fontaine's right wrist and twisted. One of the malformed thumbs should have pointed up at the sky. Instead it stuck out at a crazy angle. The thumb on his left hand was just as misshapen.

Fontaine jerked away, his face fiery red with anger.

"Don't you ever say nuthin' 'bout my thumbs."

"Why not? That's why they call you Thumbs, isn't it? Or maybe you spend all your time with a thumb stuck up your butt. I don't see you doing much work."

Mac expected the punch and dodged it. What he didn't expect was someone coming up from behind and grabbing his elbows to keep him from returning the blow. He struggled, but he was too firmly held, his chest and belly vulnerable.

"You got a big mouth. You got a big belly, too." Fontaine unleashed a short, hard jab straight to the midriff.

Mac was ready for it and tensed his stomach. The blow still doubled him over. The man holding him pulled him upright. The next time Fontaine hit him took the wind out of him. He sagged to the ground and rocked under the impact of kicks from both sides. He drew up his arms to protect his head as he curled into a ball. Try as he might, he couldn't get his breath back. The pain in his chest got worse, and then one of the booted feet caught him in the head, stunning him. A few more kicks landed before the words came from a long ways off.

"I found the bottle. Let's get this to Deke so we can empty it 'fore the rest get back."

"What about him?" Another kick thudded into the small of his back. Mac hardly felt it.

"What about him? If anybody asks what happened to the booze, we'll say we saw him guzzlin' it. Ain't that what happened, cook?" Another kick dug in the pit of Mac's stomach. He started dry heaving as the world spun around him.

He knew the two cowboys had walked away, not because he saw or heard them but because the punishment stopped. Mac lay there for an eternity before Rattler came trotting up. The lanky cowboy swung down quickly and hurried over to help him sit up.

"What in blazes happened to you, Mac?"

"Fell," Mac grated out. "Got clumsy and didn't watch what was going on around me."

"Like hell!" Rattler started to repeat the question, but one look at Mac silenced him.

"Like hell," Mac agreed. He let Rattler help him to his feet, but that was all. He could do his job himself.

And he wouldn't be caught without his gun next time.

CHAPTER 11

It hurt to move. Every time Mac sucked in a breath, pain boiled up inside him and the top of his head threatened to blow off like a riverboat venting steam from its boiler. He rested his hand on the butt of his S&W, then carefully pulled the gun up a few inches before letting it drop back into the holster.

"I can do it," he said softly to himself. He imagined himself facing down Fontaine. "I need to get him to tell me who held me. Then, then—"

Mac's hand flew for the gun. He drew smoothly, cocked, and almost fired, holding off on the trigger at the last instant. The ease and speed of his movements startled him. What made his gut clench even tighter was the notion that he would have fired if Fontaine had been in front of him.

Can I kill him? I'll have to. Can I?

A surprising calm settled over him. He strode off to find Fontaine. Not only could he pull the trigger, he would. Nobody sucker punched him and then beat him up. Nobody.

Boisterous singing came from the men passing around the whiskey. As Mac came closer, he saw Fontaine tipping back the bottle, only to have it snatched from his hand before he drained it.

"Don't hog it, Thumbs!" said the man who had taken it. "I got as much right to it as you."

"About time we enjoyed something on this drive. I'm fed up with—" Another man began, then broke off what he was going to say. He nudged Fontaine and got his attention. "Lookee there, Thumbs. We got company. You don't want to be unneighborly now, do you? Did you save enough of that crappy firewater to share?"

Fontaine turned, saw Mac standing there, and laughed.

"Ain't necessary to share with him. He's a teetotaler. He won't swill this fine booze like a real man. He had plenty of chances to do that, and he never so much as tried one little nip."

"You and your friend shouldn't have stolen that bottle," Mac said. He watched carefully. The man standing beside Fontaine stiffened when Mac mentioned a friend. He knew now which of the men following Northrup had helped with the beating.

"The way I see it, whatever you got in that chuckwagon is for all of us," Fontaine snapped. "I wanted it, and you wasn't inclined to dish it out, even a shot at a time."

"I'm here to remedy that. I'll take you two on, one shot at a time." Mac squared his stance.

"Oh, lookee there. The little boy thinks he's—"

Mac drew and fired in one smooth motion. The bottle and what little whiskey remained in it exploded in Thumbs's hand. A quick move cocked the S&W again. The roar of the .44 was deafening and caused a sudden silence to fall around the camp.

"You little son of a bitch." Thumb Fontaine clawed for the gun on his hip. He jerked to one side when a man came up behind him, grabbed his wrist, and shoved him away.

"You settle down. I'll handle this." Deke Northrup stepped around Fontaine and hooked his thumbs in his gun belt. Sneering at Mac, he went on, "So you think you got a spine? You think you're some kind of gunman? Let's see if you can stand up to me, boy."

Mac knew Northrup intended to rile him so he'd do something stupid. A wrong move now meant he died. Mac promised himself he wasn't the one going to be fitted out for a marble top hat.

"Step away so I don't get excited and shoot the rest of them," he said.

"Oh, listen to him," Northrup jeered. "He thinks he's faster 'n me. Hell, boy, I'll let you keep that six-shooter trained on me, and I'll still outdraw you and put a bullet in your worthless carcass."

Mac was young. He wasn't stupid. He went into a crouch and fanned off two quick rounds. The man with Fontaine, the one he believed had held him so Thumbs could beat him up, caught both bullets in the leg, just under his holster. A split second later and he would have hauled out his smoke wagon while Northrup was distracting Mac.

Mac swiveled back to cover Northrup.

"You done having these owlhoots do your dirty work for you, Northrup?"

"I don't know what you're talkin' about, boy."

"So they did it on their own. That's good to know. I'll have to reload after I take care of you."

His vision narrowed to a dark tunnel with Deke Northrup at the far end. He never saw the man come up from the side and shove him hard. Mac stumbled and went to his knees. Strong hands grabbed his gun hand and yanked his S&W away.

He looked up into Patrick Flagg's weathered face, but Flagg wasn't looking at him. Flagg faced Northrup.

"You try to go for that pistol, Northrup, and I swear I won't even bury you. I'll let the buzzards eat your worthless flesh."

Northrup still glared, but a wary look had come into his eyes.

"That's mighty big talk, Flagg. Why don't you let your pup here fight his own battles?"

"This is about us, Northrup. Ever since Lem died, you've been hankering for a fight."

"You're not the one to head this drive, Flagg. You're old and washed up."

"Then the two of us ought to make one good cowboy," Mac said as he got to his feet. "You think he's too old and I'm too young. You got the pair of us to fight." He saw Flagg's reaction out of the corner of his eye. Flagg wasn't pleased one little bit. Mac didn't care. What Flagg said about Northrup was true. The two of them had been spoiling for a fight ever since

Carson's death. But Mac had his own quarrel with Fontaine and the man beside him.

Try as he might, Mac couldn't remember that one's name. It didn't matter. He had enough fire-power left to take both of them out if Flagg handled Northrup.

"For two cents, I'd leave you dead on the ground, Flagg. You're a no-good, no-account, cowardly snake." Northrup moved his shoulders, as if shrugging out of a coat.

Flagg didn't stir. Not a betraying twitch, not a muscle, except to say, "If that's the way you want it, Northrup. One of us is going to the Promised Land, and it's not going to be me."

The two stared at each other. Northrup broke first.

"You got it wrong, Flagg. I want the job as trail boss because I can do better, but—"

"Clear out, Northrup. You'll be twenty miles from the herd by sundown, or I swear, you'll never see the sun come up in the morning."

"If I go, I take my men with me."

"Do whatever you have to, but I'm trail boss, and you're only a hired hand."

"The Rolling J owes me and my boys for the time we put in. Nine of them, me, a month on the trail, I make that, uh, three hundred dollars."

"See Mr. Jefferson back at the ranch. He'll give you your salaries."

"You can't steal that money from us, Flagg. We earned it."

"If you ride out, you've all forfeited it. You signed on to stay with the herd all the way to Abilene. Now, what's it going to be? We got cattle to move, and I'm getting all tired out jawing like this."

For the first time, Flagg moved more than a little, sweeping his duster back and exposing the butt of his Colt. His intentions were plain.

Northrup stared back at him for a second, jaw clenched so hard it looked like his teeth might snap. Then he said, "We're not wanted here, boys. Get your gear. We're clearing out."

Mac took a step forward, wanting to call Northrup and Fontaine cowards, but Flagg slapped him across the chest with his left hand. He hit a bruise left by Fontaine's boot and sent a stabbing pain into Mac's chest that shut him up before he could say anything. He kept silent, backing up Flagg, as Deke Northrup and his men gathered their tack and walked toward the remuda, grumbling as they went.

"They'll likely steal some horses along with taking their own mounts," Mac said.

"Won't. I made sure of that."

"You've got someone guarding the remuda?"

"Rattler's there."

Northrup and his crew rode off a few minutes later. Flagg watched them until they were out of sight. Once they were, he turned sharply to Mac.

"That was the stupidest damned thing I ever heard of. You'd be dead right now if I hadn't pulled your fat from the fire."

Mac said, "They stole supplies."

"The whiskey." Flagg nodded. "I can smell it a mile off."

"They beat on me to get it. I wouldn't give it to them."

Flagg sighed and gave a slight shake of his head. "Mac, you're not a bad cook, but you're about the stupidest, greenest tenderfoot I ever laid eyes on. Northrup wanted to kill you. He sent Fontaine and Ferguson to get you riled up."

"Why? That doesn't make any sense."

Flagg shook his head and walked back toward the chuckwagon.

"He don't give one good damn about you," he said over his shoulder. "Northrup wanted me. He wanted to get me mad and have the rest of the outfit back him if it looked like I wasn't fit."

"We stood together," Mac said.

"Yeah, we did. And now we have to each do the work of two men since Northrup took his boys with him. You wanted a job as a cowboy. You might be riding night herd for a shift. And I have to ride point during the day. That means you get to drive the chuckwagon *and* scout our trail."

"I'm sorry I didn't plug Fontaine."

"You'll be even sorrier Northrup didn't plug *you.* The work on this drive just got a hell of a lot harder. Now, is there anything left to eat? I rounded up a hundred-ten head of cattle and brought 'em in. Those longhorned bastards are grazing, and since it don't look like I've got any more sense than one of them, I should be, too."

"I can always scare something up for you," Mac said. "I've even got a bottle of whiskey left if—"

"No! Lem said no drinking on the trail. But I will settle for a couple of those biscuits of yours."

Mac grinned.

"And stow that six-shooter of yours," Flagg added. "There's no need for a cook to wear a gun."

With that, Patrick Flagg walked away, leaving Mac unsure how to feel. He had stood up to Northrup and his men, but without Flagg's backing, he'd likely be in a grave about now. Thinking over all that had happened, he returned to the chuckwagon to prepare the biscuits Flagg yearned for.

"I swear, I thought my luck had changed," Rattler said as he and Mac plodded along on horseback with the vast herd to their left. "Instead, I got you as my partner."

"Flagg said—" Mac clamped his mouth shut when Rattler made a dismissive gesture.

"We all got to do double duty, I know that. And there's not a minute what goes by that I don't curse Northrup and the men with him."

"Especially Fontaine," Mac said, almost under his breath. He spoke loud enough for Rattler to hear. The glum look on his face told the story. Rattler shared his feelings on the matter. It was good to see those troublemakers gone, but it was hard on every one of the Rolling J cowboys remaining who now had to do the work of two men.

"All you got to do is ride at the side of the herd and keep them knucklehead cows from wanderin' off, thinking to find a little better graze. And," Rattler said, heaving a deep sigh, "we're gettin' into Indian Territory. That means they'll try to steal as many head as possible, then dicker with Flagg to pay 'em even more cows for safe passage."

"I heard him talking to the men working the horses." Mac nodded. He understood all this and didn't envy Flagg one little bit. "He's afraid we'll lose more of our mounts."

"Never decided if the twenty head we lost two nights back just ran off or if they were stolen," Rattler said. "We lost track of 'em, so it don't matter. What counts most is keepin' the herd headed toward Abilene."

"I saw dust to the west of us when I was scouting this morning. Another herd's running alongside."

"That's all right out here on the prairie, but when we get closer to the railhead, it might be a problem. The ones what get to the railroad first get the best prices for their cattle. Now you drop back some, 'bout halfway from here to the drag."

"I'll need to ride ahead in a couple of hours to fix the noonday meal." Mac had scouted the route as he drove the chuckwagon ahead, parked it when he located a suitable spot, and then ridden back to help with the herd. He was riding four times as far as the men and expected to do not only some of their work, but that of the trail-boss scouting, and then take care of his own chores as cook.

He ought to have been angry about that. Somehow, though, it made him feel good, wanted, important for the first time in his life. His euphoria died down as he realized he had felt this way once before, when Evangeline Holdstock had caught his eye. Having her as his lady had made him feel as if he were successful at last. It didn't matter that her pa hadn't wanted him anywhere near his daughter. She had enjoyed his company and would have married him if it hadn't been for . . .

He jerked around, seeing something moving at the edge of his vision. The cattle ambled along slowly, but they kept up the pace that got them decent miles to the north. He rode a few hundred yards straight away from the herd and looked around at the woods where he thought he had seen something. A black streak. Movement. He wasn't sure what it was.

Maybe a wolf, but more likely an Indian stalking the herd and waiting for the chance to cut out a few head for his own use.

Mac prowled around for a few minutes but failed to find whatever it was that had spooked him. Wanting to keep hunting but realizing the cattle were going to drift away from the herd without his constant supervision, he rode slowly back. Even occasional glances over his shoulder didn't catch whatever he had seen by surprise. By the time he was shouting, waving his hat, and sometimes using a loop of lariat to whack the balky cattle back in line, he forgot about it.

Checking his pocket watch and then looking up at the sun for corroboration told him it was about eleven o'clock. He made one last attempt to bunch up the cattle close to the main herd, then rode faster to find Rattler.

"Time for me to get back to the chuckwagon," he called.

"Don't burn the damned biscuits this time. You turned them into charcoal lumps last night."

"That didn't stop you from eating six of them."

"I needed the roughage. Your damned cooking's got me all stoppered up tighter'n a banker's wallet."

"I got a bottle of camphorated tincturate of opium."

Rattler looked aghast. "You tryin' to kill me? That's a paregoric and would stopper me up even tighter."

"I'm just offering you the chance to show your true colors," Mac said with a grin. "Build up enough pressure and you'd purty near explode."

"If I get to that point, I'll make sure to find you."

Mac rode off at a gallop, Rattler still going on about what it would be like once the dam broke. He doubted if any of the men actually suffered from his cooking, but he decided to hunt for more greens to throw into the pot. A diet of nothing but beefsteak and taters got boring after a couple weeks, no matter how good the steaks were. He was running low on the potatoes and needed onions for some flavor. The whole ride back to where he'd parked the chuckwagon, he pondered on how to fix the same food in different ways.

As he rode up to the wagon, he slowed. Something felt wrong to him. He rode in a wide circle. His team had been put into a rope corral and nervously pawed at the ground, as if something had frightened them.

Mac touched his right hip and found only denim. Very few of the cowboys rode with their six-shooters, and Flagg had ordered him to leave his in the chuckwagon. Carrying an extra three pounds of iron all day wore a man down, especially one not used to carrying a gun. The rifle snugged in a saddle scabbard would do if he needed a weapon.

Mac slid the rifle out and worked the lever to cock it before getting off his horse and walking up to the wagon. All he heard were expected sounds—and the horses neighing some distance away. The breeze died down, and the prairie turned downright quiet. He dropped to his knees and looked under the chuck-wagon in case anybody was hiding on the far side.

Nothing. In spite of the loneliness of the camp, he made a complete circuit, on guard the whole way.

"I'm scaring myself for no good reason." He lowered the hammer on the rifle and stashed it back into its sheath. Humming as he worked, he got the saddle off, put the horse in with the others, then turned to the chore of fixing a big meal for a passel of hungry cowboys.

He took the lid off a barrel of flour and scooped out some into a pot. He started to get a second scoop, then stopped. While he hadn't worked long as a trail cook, he had developed certain instincts. Using his finger, he poked at the flour in the barrel and moved it around. The sun turned crystals in the flour into diamonds. He licked his finger and scooped up some of the sparkly bits.

"Salt." He spat it out. "Somebody's dumped salt into the flour."

He started pawing through the barrel and saw someone had done a damned good job of mixing in salt to ruin the flour.

Maybe he hadn't been mistaken earlier about seeing someone sneaking around and heading into the woods. They could have reached camp long before him and ruined the flour. He started checking the rest of the larder for signs that there were troubles worse than salt in flour.

CHAPTER 12

"What are you doing?" Flagg stared at the almost empty barrel as Mac shook a burlap sack filled with flour. White dust fluttered down a little at a time.

"Somebody's trying to keep us from delivering the herd," Mac said, then explained what had happened.

"You never got a clear sight of whoever was in the woods?"

"I don't even know if what I saw wasn't a wolf or coyote. It could have been a man riding a horse. I only caught a glimpse. If he rode real hard he'd get back to camp enough ahead of me so he could do this."

"Is that working?" Flagg stood on tiptoe and looked into the almost empty barrel.

"Not too good," Mac admitted. "I keep trying to think of other ways to separate out the salt from the flour, but this seemed to be the best. The flour's a lot finer than the salt, but the burlap's too coarse. It lets both through."

"This is a waste of time." Flagg rubbed his stubbled chin, pushed his hat back to scratch his head and finally said, "We're not more than five miles from a settlement. Get on in and buy more flour."

"I can use most of this since I bake by adding salt. Only I can't control how much salt's in it, and everything might taste salty."

"Northrup." Flagg's voice was flat and angry.

"I suspect him, too," Mac said with a shrug, "but we can't prove it."

"Doesn't matter," said Flagg. "Who's going to arrest him for what he'd only deny? No marshal worth his salt would look at this as anything other than a prank."

"You made a joke," Mac said, amazed. "Not a particularly *good* one . . ."

"Didn't know I did. Get the food fixed for the men, then cut out a couple heifers and get into town. Sell them for what you can and buy more supplies."

"It'll be faster if I take a couple of horses as pack animals rather than driving the chuckwagon."

Flagg nodded and went off. Mac didn't miss how the trail boss kept touching the butt of his Colt, then moving his hand away. Mac figured he was thinking the same thing. If Northrup ever happened to come into range, he was likely to get himself shot. Putting salt in the flour was hardly enough reason for murder, but Mac would lie like a trooper to get Flagg off with the law if he did put lead in Northrup.

That idea bothered him. He was honest, and lies didn't come easy to his lips. Telling lies had gotten him into trouble more times than he cared to remember, but he spoke his mind. Remembering the

truth was easier than building a house of lies and trying to keep them all straight. He hadn't earned any
special place in Micah Holdstock's esteem for that
trait, either, since he was one of the few who didn't
suck up to the man just because he was rich.

The meal went well. Mac had several wranglers
help him clean up and then pick out three horses to
use as pack animals. Figuring which cattle to cut out
was a chore beyond his skills.

Rattler chose three heifers for him, then drove
them over to the camp.

"You think you can handle 'em all right, Mac? You
do all right with horses, but cows got a mind of their
own. Unfortunately, it ain't much of a mind, but they
scare easy."

"I'll do what I can. If I'm not back to fix dinner,
send out a rescue party."

"I'll ask Flagg if I ought to drive the chuckwagon
ahead. I've never been much of a scout, but the
land's pretty flat hereabouts."

"I hadn't thought of that. I'll have to find where
you make camp rather than just come back here."

"Straight on north, five miles," Rattler said. "If you
hurry, you might be able to get back by sundown."

Mac checked his watch and shook his head. He
wasn't sure how he could be that quick, but spending
the night in some town whose name nobody knew
didn't appeal to him, especially when there was another meal to fix.

"I'll hurry. That might run all the meat off the
heifers' bones, but I'll make do."

The first mile along the trail into town proved the
hardest. By the time the second mile had vanished

under his horse's hooves, he had the knack of herd-ing the cattle. As Rattler had suggested, he had no trouble with the horses and reached the town after less than an hour on the trail.

Not knowing where to go, he rode directly to a general store he spotted almost immediately and called to the proprietor. A smallish man with a big bushy mustache came out, his hand hidden under his apron.

"What can I do for you, mister?" he asked with a wary frown.

"I need to sell these fine cows and spend all the money on supplies from your store. Where can I get top dollar?" Mac saw the sudden change in the man's expression. He had worded it exactly right. If he didn't get top dollar for the heifers, the storekeeper came out on the short end of the stick.

"The town's butcher. A little ways down the street. Let me talk to him and see what he can do." The man squinted and sized up the cattle. "You with a herd?"

"The Rolling J ranch's herd out of Waco."

"Them ain't diseased cows, now, are they? Texas fever?"

"Splenic fever? No, sir, they are healthy. Not a one in the herd's shown any sign of splenic fever." He em-phasized the proper name to keep the man from at-taching blame to every cow from Texas. Calling it Texas fever was a trick ranchers in Kansas and Ne-braska used to make Texas cattle less attractive to buyers. Somehow the name had come to be used this far south into Indian Territory.

"Good. Good." The store proprietor moved his

hand from under his apron. As Mac had thought, he clutched a six-gun against the wild Texas cowboy who had blown into his town unexpectedly.

The notion that he was someone to defend the town's honor against appealed to him in an odd way. That meant he was more of a cowboy than a drifter. He belonged with the trail crew, no matter that he was only the cook.

He herded the cattle down the street, following the storekeeper to a butcher shop. Twenty minutes of dickering got him a hundred and fifty dollars. The butcher started to hand it to him, but Mac shook his head and pointed to the storekeeper.

"I said I was going to spend the money on supplies. Give it to him. He'll let me know when I've chosen that much in flour, potatoes, and whatever else he might have in stock."

"I've got some carrots. You have much interest in onions and peaches?"

During the next hour, Mac and the storekeeper haggled over the prices as the supplies piled up on the store's counter, but eventually he had three horses laden with enough foodstuffs to keep the outfit well fed until they reached Abilene.

"Anything else you need, son?" The proprietor stood on the boardwalk, looking pleased as punch. He had earned a good day's income off the Rolling J and sounded expansive.

Mac thought about it for a second, then said, "Actually, there is something more."

"Terbacky? Chaw or for smokin'? Give me a minute or two and I can get you a bottle or two of firewater."

Mac shook his head to those offers. "That penny candy on your counter. The peppermints. I reckon the men would enjoy having some candy."

"Wait a second." The man went into the store and returned with a large brown-paper-wrapped parcel. "That ought to be enough to take care of everyone's sweet tooth."

"Much obliged."

"Anytime you're passing by, come on in, and I'll see that you're fixed up with whatever you need."

Mac led his small caravan of packhorses out of town and was a mile away before he realized with a laugh that he hadn't even heard what the place was called.

He settled down and reached a fork in the road, the one leading back in the direction he had come from the noonday camp. The other angled off to the northwest. Where Rattler had driven the chuckwagon was something he had to find out, but taking the new road sent him in the proper direction and shortened the time it would take him to get down to using some of the flour and potatoes for the evening meal.

He had ridden almost an hour and started thinking he ought to look for either the herd or wagon tracks when he heard hooves pounding behind him. Mac turned in the saddle.

He went cold at the sight of three masked men galloping after him. He reached to pull out his rifle, but he was too late. A lariat spun through the air, settled over his head and around his shoulders. He yelped as he was pulled from the saddle and hit the ground hard. Arms pinned at his side, all he could do was bounce along, dragged by the outlaw who had roped him as surely as any dogie waiting to be branded.

"Got the packhorses?" one of the men called.

Mac craned around to see who answered. He thrashed furiously when he recognized the thief. The mask concealed his face, but nothing hid Thumbs Fontaine's hands as he reached for the reins of the pack animals.

"String the little peckerwood up," Fontaine said. "He deserves it."

"By his neck?"

"That'd be fine with me, but it ain't what the boss said. We want to send a message."

Kicking and struggling, Mac was hoisted into the air over the limb of a big oak tree. He swung around at the end of the rope, caught in the wind as much as by his own attempt to get free. Each of the outlaws rode past, close enough for their horses to bang into him as they let out exuberant whoops. The impacts sent him back and forth like the pendulum on a regulator clock. The rope cut cruelly into his upper arms. When his hands started going numb, he stopped fighting and started thinking.

He could die from being strung up like this, no matter what Fontaine had said. As he worked his right hand to the middle of his back while he still had some feeling in it, his fingers brushed over the hilt of the knife sheathed there. Carefully, he drew it and pinked himself a couple times but got the blade under the rope. Now the swinging helped move the rope across the keen edge.

Mac dropped suddenly when the rope finally parted.

He landed on his face in the dirt. When he struggled to his feet, the outlaws were long gone with his supplies. Staring at the knife, he slowly returned it to the sheath.

"It saved me just like it killed Holdstock," he muttered. Cursing as he walked, he headed out to get back to the herd, not sure what kind of reception he would get from Flagg and the others.

"You're for certain sure it was Fontaine?" Flagg looked like a thunderstorm ready to pour down all over the countryside.

"His thumbs gave him away. I recognized the voices of the others, too. They left with Northrup. I swear, I didn't see them in town, but they must have seen me and decided to rob me."

"The loss of the supplies isn't as bad as losing more horses."

"But the cows!"

"We've got most of the herd left. Three don't matter. We haven't had the big losses to weather or rivers like we've had some years."

"I got fifty a head for them."

"You done good, but we're not likely to return to the town and get that kind of money again," Flagg said.

"The butcher's got three heifers hanging in his store he needs to sell," Mac said, realizing what Flagg meant. He had flooded the market with top-quality beef. If they waited around a week or two, they might get that much per head again.

However, he knew Flagg wasn't about to stop for anything now.

"I can feed the men with what we've got in the chuckwagon," Mac went on. "It won't be as fancy as before, but they won't starve."

"Yeah, right," Flagg said, hardly listening. "There's no marshal who'd track down road agents for such a small theft. If Northrup had robbed a bank or stagecoach, they'd have a posse out in nothing flat. But a drover getting robbed of flour and horses?" He shook his head. "I've got a big score to settle with him."

"*We've* got a score to settle," Mac corrected. "This is three times they've done me dirty."

Among the men who had assembled curiously at Mac's return on foot, Rattler said, "Yeah, Flagg. Mac's right. We all have a stake in this. Northrup's stealin' from all of us." The lanky cowboy raised his voice. "I say we bed down the herd and track those sons of bitches down and do what's right. They strung up Mac here. I say we string them up, only with the ropes around their dirty necks!"

A cheer went up from the rest of the crew. More than one suggested even more drastic measures that would make an Apache blanch in fear.

"Hold on! Quiet!" Flagg bellowed loud enough to cause the cattle to begin lowing. "Settle down. Nobody's going after Northrup and his band of vipers."

"But, Flagg, we got to. They stole our food. They tried to hang Mac! They can't do that to our cook!"

Mac felt a little pride at how much support he had among the crew, then he turned somber, realizing he had caused this. If he hadn't let himself get robbed, there wouldn't be talk of a posse and lynching North-rup and his men.

"We're not vigilantes," Flagg said with his usual dour solemnity. "We're cowboys. We're wranglers working for Mr. Jefferson. Our job's not to see North-rup kicking his last dance at the end of a rope. We are hired to deliver Rolling J cattle to Abilene. And that's what we're going to do, not go chasing off around Indian Territory."

Another voice came from the crowd. "We can't let them get away with this." Whoever spoke got a murmur of agreement.

"I was the one they robbed," Mac said, "and I don't like it. Not one little bit, but Flagg's right. After we deliver the herd, then we can think about taking on Northrup."

He listened as the argument bounced around the assembled cowboys and slowly died out. The initial blood fever had passed.

"But what about eatin'?" Rattler asked with a stricken look. "We're gonna starve 'fore we get to Abilene."

"I won't let that happen. I know a few tricks I haven't shown you yet. You won't go hungry. You've got my promise."

Mac had no idea what he was going to do to keep that promise, but he'd think of something.

After a moment, Rattler shrugged and said, "Hell, you ain't pizened us yet."

"Yet," another cowboy said. "He ain't pizened us *yet*. This'll give him a chance!"

Laughter passed through the outfit, then the men

began drifting away, some for night herd and others to bed down. Mac heaved a sigh.

Flagg caught his eye, winked, and then went off to be sure everyone knew their increased duties. That one look made Mac puff up with pride. He wasn't a complete waste. He even hummed to himself as he cleaned up and finally spread his bedroll under the chuckwagon and went to sleep. Dawn came early for him . . . dawn, breakfast, and scouting ahead for the trail for the herd.

CHAPTER 13

Every muscle in Mac's body ached. That was becoming an all too common occurrence.

He stretched, regretted it, and rolled onto his side, thinking to grab just a few minutes more sleep. The sounds around camp roused him. He was the axle around which the entire trail drive turned now. Without food, the cowboys couldn't work. And not only did he have to feed them, he had to show them the trail for the herd to follow.

Pushing himself up, he arched his back like a cat and felt better when the spine cracked. He rubbed his arms where the rope had been when Fontaine and his henchmen hung him up like a side of beef.

He fed the men, packed the chuckwagon, and waved to Flagg as he left to scout the trail. Not for the first time, he wished the trail boss rode alongside, giving him hints about how to actually blaze the trail.

Twenty minutes into his day after breaking camp, he made a disturbing discovery.

Another herd had already come this way.

"This is the Shawnee Trail," he told himself. "Of course other herds will follow the same route to take advantage of cattle having come this way before."

He snapped the reins and turned his team into a route running alongside the cut-up grass. More than once, he found where the herd ahead of the Rolling J had watered from streams.

The grass might be well cropped, but there was still plenty for another herd. This was the promise of the Shawnee Trail rather than heading out across Indian Territory on a new road.

He tried to decide if they were actually out of Texas yet or if they had more miles to go. That didn't matter, other than measuring how long they had left on the trail. But with the work done for him today by the earlier herd, he pressed on, found where they had set up their camp, did a quick calculation and decided the Rolling J herd could make another few miles before dark. This might be a fifteen-mile day.

A hilltop presented a good spot for him to survey the land. He took out a crumpled piece of paper and used the stub of a pencil to sketch out the way two streams meandered around and where the best feed would be. The Rolling J didn't have to graze the herd on already overgrazed land. Slowly turning in a full circle, he completed his crude map, then stared toward the west. Curls of white smoke rose from a wooded area. People were camped there, and from the amount of smoke reaching for the sky, it was a large number.

Mac caught his breath when he spotted four riders heading toward the trees. Shielding his eyes with his hand and squinting, he got a better look. His heart jumped a little when he realized the riders were Indians.

From what he knew of the tribes, these were Comanche. After a few minutes, they entered the woods. No gunfire or other commotion resulted. They had rejoined a larger group. From what he knew of the Lords of the Plains, he reckoned more than fifty Indians were camped not four miles from where the drive had to travel.

He turned and looked farther east, wondering if they could skirt the Indian encampment by going miles and miles in that direction. The rolling hills there would slow their progress. Worse, getting through those hills required more scouting than simply standing on a hilltop and sketching out a map. He had found the best trail. With another herd maybe a day or two ahead of them, they risked not showing up in Abilene in time to get decent prices for their stock. They couldn't afford to delay.

Leaving the chuckwagon parked at the foot of the hill down by a creek worried him, but he had to get back to tell Flagg what he'd found. Making the decision, he unhitched a horse and jumped aboard. Riding bareback would have scared him only a few weeks ago. Since then, he had ridden horses in every possible way. He bent low and tapped his heels against the horse's flanks to get the most speed possible from it. It had taken him hours to locate the best spot to pitch camp, but it took less than an hour to find the leading longhorns in the herd.

"Where's Flagg?" he called to Rattler, who was riding point. "I got something real important to tell him."

"He's on the other side of the herd. What's the problem?"

"Stop the cows. Don't go any farther until Flagg tells you." Before Rattler could question him further, Mac spotted Flagg and rode his tired horse as fast as he could for the trail boss. He skidded to a halt beside Flagg. Words poured out of his mouth as he breathlessly tried to let the older man know what he'd found.

"Slow down. Take a breath. Then tell me what's got you so fired up." Flagg rested his hands on the horn and leaned forward in the saddle, looking calm enough to give Mac strength. If anybody would know what to do, it was Flagg.

He spilled the whole story in one long rush, then gasped for breath.

"Fifty?" Flagg looked and sounded skeptical. "That's a powerful lot of Comanche this far north. They don't tangle much with the Five Civilized Tribes."

"But," Mac said, "are we even in Indian Territory yet? I tried to figure it out and couldn't."

"We are. Not by much, but we are. That stream we forded a couple of days ago was the Red River, and that's the border. You say another herd passed that way a day or two earlier?" Flagg stroked his stubbled chin. "That's likely the H Bar H herd. Compass Jack knows this country like the back of his hand. If anybody's beat us this far, it'll be him."

"But the Indians! What do we do about them?"

"It might be a hunting party. Could be a war party, but you would have heard about it if it was."

"Me? How?" Then Mac settled down and thought. "In the town. They would be all abuzz if the Comanche had a war party raiding the countryside."

Flagg nodded once, lost in thought. He spat, then took the reins in hand and got his horse walking.

"We keep on going. They might not be Comanche. Could be Creek or Fox or Seminole, this part of the country. Maybe Sac. We don't know."

"But what if they *are* hostiles?"

"All the more reason to keep going and for you to get back to the chuckwagon. If we lose what supplies are left, we'll have to give up on the drive. Ain't heard of it happening too often, but some outfits have lost their chuckwagon and just quit right there on the spot"

"I won't let that happen. That's *my* chuckwagon!"

"Glad you feel that way, Mac. Now ride on back and get supper fixed. We'll be along with the herd before you know it, if the trail's already blazed for us."

"It is."

"And tell Rattler to disregard whatever you told him."

"How'd you know—never mind." Mac touched the brim of his hat in acknowledgment of the trail boss knowing him that well.

He turned his horse's face back in the direction he had just come. By the time he got to the chuckwagon, he knew that stretch of trail better than any other. Every inch of the way he had been alert for Indians, waiting to be ambushed by Northrup's men, or just hunting for spots to graze the herd. He didn't see any hostiles along the way and was grateful for that.

The noonday meal was less elaborate than he usually fixed, but from the way the cowboys gobbled it up, he hadn't lost anything in how he prepared it. As Mac finished cleaning, Flagg rode up and dropped from his horse to stand nearby.

"You up for an adventure?" the trail boss asked.

"That's all I've been having." Mac rubbed his arms where the ropes had cut into him. "What do you have in mind?"

"You and me are going to take a ride. Who do you trust to drive the wagon?"

"Any of the men who have been teamsters in the past, I suppose."

"Rattler drove a freight wagon for a spell down in San Antonio before he signed on with Mr. Jefferson," Flagg said. "Let him drive on, if the road's as clear-marked as you say."

"Where will I be?"

"Since you know where it is, riding with me to scout that Indian camp."

Mac's eyebrows rose in surprise. "In broad daylight?"

"That's what makes it an adventure. I need to know why they're here and what tribe they are. Comanche are bad news. A local tribe is another matter."

"What if we're not back before nightfall? Who'll feed the men?"

"Better hope we get back by then, or they'll set to feedin' themselves."

"Now you're scaring me." Mac had to laugh in spite of what he was about to do.

Flagg found Rattler and gave him his new orders, then he and Mac rode out. They angled west for a few miles, to a spot Mac calculated to be due south of the Indian camp. Tension thickened inside Mac as they headed toward it in silence.

Flagg motioned for him to dismount when the woods began to thicken. The undergrowth made riding more difficult unless they followed game trails.

"We'll go on foot," Flagg said quietly. "Walk soft. If it's a war party, they'll have sentries watching."

Mac walked on pins and needles, trying to step where Flagg did since the trail boss moved silently. He was concentrating so much on what Flagg did that he ran into him when the trail boss stopped suddenly.

"Down."

Mac sank to the ground and wiggled ahead until he peered around a thick sweet gum tree. He caught his breath at the sight of the Indian camp. Counting softly, he got to thirty men. There might be a few more scattered around, but he was confident that was most of them.

"Not as many as I thought," he whispered.

"Still plenty," Flagg said, equally quietly. He put his finger to his lips to shush Mac.

For an hour, they watched those in the camp go about their business. Mac looked for a squaw or child but saw only braves. He didn't know enough about ornaments or the way they wore paint on their cheeks and decorated their horses to know which tribe he was spying on. About mid-afternoon a band of five braves rode in, whooping and hollering. They passed within a dozen yards of where Flagg and Mac hid in the thick brush.

He got a good look at some of the horses herded by the Indians and caught his breath. Surprise made him rise up slightly.

"That's a Rolling J brand! They stole our horses!"

Flagg pulled him back down and clamped a hand over his mouth. Simmering with anger, Mac watched as the Indians strutted around, pounding their chests and obviously boasting about how they had stolen the horses. Ten head was hardly going to stop the trail drive, but it made it all the more important to be sure the horses were rotated properly to keep from tiring them out. More horses increased their options. Fewer made it more difficult, just as the loss of the food had.

"So, what are we going to do about those thieves?"

"Not much we can do," Flagg said. "Let's go back and find the herd. The quicker we get out of this country, the better."

"Are they Comanche?"

Flagg nodded.

"Are they on the warpath?"

"Raiding." Flagg tugged at Mac's arm to get him heading back to where they'd tethered their horses.

Mac was glad he was with Flagg. The man never lost track of where he was. With Comanche raiders nearby, hunting for an hour to find the spot where they'd left their mounts would have been worrisome.

When they reached the horses, Mac waited for Flagg to mount, but the trail boss didn't.

"What's wrong?" Mac asked, still quietly even though they had put some distance between themselves and the Indian camp.

"Listen. More horses coming. Lots of them."

"If a second raiding party stole more of our horses, the entire drive might be in jeopardy," Mac said.

Flagg leaned his head to one side as he listened, then said softly, "That's a bigger herd. Maybe twenty horses."

"We have to steal back our horses."

Mac wouldn't have thought it was possible to surprise Flagg, but the older man stared at him, mouth gaping.

"What the hell are you saying, Mac?" Flagg asked when he found his voice.

"You said it yourself. The drive won't be possible with forty head of horses gone. Let's steal them back."

"From a bunch of Comanches? That's worse than poking a wasp nest with a stick. It's more like sticking your thumb in a grizzly bear's eye."

"I've done worse."

Flagg looked at him for a moment and then laughed. He slapped Mac on the back and said, "I just bet you have. What do we do? Just ride in and take our horses back?"

"Why not? You distract them, and I'll get the horses."

"So you want them shooting at me while you sneak around?" Flagg scowled. "Reckon that makes some sense. I can outride you, and getting shot at doesn't bother me like it once did."

Mac wondered what Flagg meant by that, but with the sun dipping down, this was the time to act.

"Circle around and make a ruckus. I'll be ready to go for their remuda."

"Remember, Mac, horses are money to them. You're robbing the bank, in a manner of speaking. No man likes to have his bank account stolen."

"And no man likes to have his horse stolen." Mac patted his horse's neck, then swung into the saddle. His rifle pressed into his knee, but there wasn't any call to draw it. What he had to do was best accomplished by being sneaky, not noisy. The last thing he wanted to do was draw attention to himself. He started to offer his rifle to Flagg, but the trail boss had already ridden off, meandering through the trees and hunting for the trail used by the Comanche to reach their camp with the stolen horses.

Mac waited, then made his way directly to the camp, waiting when he reached the edge of a clearing. In the twilight, he made out a few campfires here and there, getting the layout of where the Indians were. He sucked in his breath when he heard more horses approaching, only these came from the north.

As he wondered about those hoofbeats, he heard a single gunshot. Then came a thunder of hooves and more gunfire. This awakened the camp. Indians sprang up in places where he hadn't even thought anyone was. They raced to their horses and mounted quickly, riding out, whooping and hollering. Two more gunshots rang through the evening, more distant. He hoped that meant Flagg was hightailing it away.

With his breath seemingly frozen in his throat and his heart hammering in his chest, Mac rode directly to the rope corral the Comanche used for their stolen horses. He gathered bridles and tugged at a few. The ones with Rolling J brands followed him immediately. The others, the ones most recently put into the corral, hung back. On impulse, he rode alongside one of those animals and looked at the brand.

"I'll be damned," he said softly. "That's an H Bar H brand. Their herd can't be much ahead of ours."

He had his hands full with the small herd of Rolling J horses, but a sudden wild impulse struck him. With his lariat out and used liberally on the rumps of all the horses, he got them moving from the corral, both Rolling J and H Bar H branded horses. If he was going to retrieve his own mounts, he might as well do the same for Compass Jack Bennett and his stolen horses.

Mac moved the horses away from camp. Just as he began to think he was going to get away scot-free, an Indian let out a bloodcurdling shriek somewhere close by. Mac jerked in the saddle and looked around to find the brave.

Then he knew exactly where the enemy was. The Comanche pounded up on foot and launched himself like a Fourth of July rocket straight for Mac. The Indian's strong arms circled his horse's neck, twisted, and brought both horse and rider to the ground. Mac kicked his feet free from the stirrups and flung himself aside so the horse wouldn't land on him. His feet hit the ground. He stumbled, almost fell, then caught his balance and swung around. His hand went to his hip, but he had left the Smith & Wesson back at the chuckwagon.

Then he felt those strong arms that had bull-dogged his horse do the same to him. He was twisted around and slammed down hard. Somehow, he ducked his head, and the Indian lost his grip. Spinning, he faced his foe. The Indian reached for the knife sheathed at his waist. Mac duplicated the other man's attack. He dived, arms circling a sinewy neck. He jerked around and sent the man stumbling. The Comanche's knife slipped out of his hand.

They faced off a few feet apart, the knife on the ground between them. Mac started to grab the knife. So did the Comanche. They collided, exchanged blows, and bounced apart, the knife still in the dirt.

"Those are our horses," Mac panted. "You're a thief." He wondered if the brave understood English. There wasn't any recognition on his face. Mac hadn't intended to do anything but distract him from circling, feinting, trying to grab the knife without being knocked down.

Without really thinking about what he was doing, Mac let instinct guide him. The Indian dived, scooped up the knife, and stumbled to get back to his feet. Mac snared the wrist holding the knife as he reached behind his own back and found the knife he carried there. It slid easily from its sheath.

Just as easily, it went into the Indian's chest, angled up, and punctured his heart. The Comanche was dead before he hit the ground.

Panting, Mac stared at the knife he had pulled free from the other man's body. It had taken more than one life now. First blood had been in the hand of someone else as it was drawn across Micah Holdstock's throat.

"You showed it what to do, Leclerc," Mac said bitterly. "I know you did."

He plunged the knife into the ground to clean off

the blood, used the sharp blade to cut off a beaded strip woven into the Comanche's hair, and then sheathed his knife.

He looked around and saw that the horses hadn't mindlessly stampeded. Instead, they milled around, his horse emerging as their leader. Running hard, he overtook the animal, grabbed the saddle horn, and pulled himself up. It took some work, but he got the herd of close to fifty horses heading in the direction where he hoped the Rolling J herd had bedded down for the night. He was going to have one hell of a story to tell.

He hoped that Flagg was there to listen to it and then tell his own tale of daring.

CHAPTER 14

Mac hadn't ridden a mile when he knew he was in more trouble than he could handle. The faint gunfire as Patrick Flagg decoyed the Comanche away had long since faded in the distance. He worried that the trail boss had been caught or, worse, killed.

He knew how loco this plan was, and how many things could have gone wrong with it. Having Flagg lead an entire pack of warriors away was the most dangerous part of it. If anyone could have done it, Flagg was the man. but dying for a herd of horses was flat out wrong.

"Whoa, get back to going east." Mac called to the horses, as if they understood or would obey if they did. He checked the stars to be sure he still followed the route he had taken originally and saw that the horses had veered away to the north.

For whatever reason, the horses had taken it into their heads to go in the wrong direction. Riding around, Mac cut off the leading horse and forced it toward the east. The animal carried an H Bar H brand. He wondered if one of the Rolling J horses would be better at the front of the herd. Twice he tried to get one of his outfit's horses to lead, and twice he failed.

How the horses chose their leader wasn't something he wanted to dwell on. He got antsy when he realized every failure to keep them running gave the Comanches a chance to come after him.

They would kill Flagg, discover they'd been robbed, and come after the thief with blood in their eyes. That was what he knew would happen if he didn't get the horses back to the Rolling J crew. Only with the twenty or so riders left to fight the Indians could he hope to make this daring theft work.

The horses angled back northward, away from the route Mac wanted. Galloping to the front of the herd again, he used his lariat to whip the horses from their chosen route and more toward where he guessed the Rolling J would bed down for the night. Then, above the thudding hooves and whinnying horses, he heard something that struck fear into his heart. More hoofbeats, a lot of them, coming up fast behind him. Mingled with the sound came shouts from angry throats. Indian throats.

Mac had no idea how much time he had before they overtook him, but they had found the trail easy enough. Even he could have done that in spite of the darkness. So many horses tore up the ground as they raced along. Mac vowed they wouldn't get all the horses, especially the one he rode. If he had to abandon the others, so be it. Better to have a story of failure than to lose his scalp.

"Damn it, why won't you keep going in the direction I want?" He swatted at the lead horse, only to be ignored. The horse had a mind of its own. "What? You smell your barn stall? Is that it?" He started to lasso the horse and forcefully drag it toward the east.

As the pursuing hoofbeats welled up, he gave up the attempt and leaned back to pull his rifle from its saddle scabbard. The Indians had caught up with him. He swung around, lifted the rifle, and squeezed off a round. In the dark he fired blind. He heard the commotion the bullet caused but saw nothing to show he had even come close to any of the braves. Another round didn't produce any better results. Then the leading Indian galloped toward him, a war lance leveled and aimed at his chest.

Forcing himself to remain calm, Mac got off a third shot. The Comanche tumbled over the head of his horse and somersaulted along the ground to land flat on his back, staring up at the stars. Mac started to congratulate himself on a good shot when he realized the horse had stepped into a prairie dog hole. The Indian would have gone down, shot or no shot from a tenderfoot's rifle.

He pulled the trigger again, aiming into the middle of the black mass surging toward him. The hammer fell on a dud. He levered it out and a bullet whined past his head. Confused, he stared at the rifle, got a new round in, and heard two more bullets sail past him. A quick pull got another bullet out of his rifle barrel, but it joined a dozen others, all coming from behind him.

Mac let out an excited whoop and called, "This

way, boys! I got the horses the Indians stole. Give 'em hell!" He fired until his rifle came up empty.

By then the Comanche tide had broken, turned back, and retreated. They had no stomach for fighting what had to be the entire Rolling J outfit.

"You did it," Mac went on excitedly as riders clustered around him. "You boys surely did pull my fat from the fire."

Mac grinned at the rider beside him, but that grin turned into a puzzled stare. Mac's mouth opened, then closed. When he got his senses back, he asked, "Who're you?"

He looked at the half dozen others and didn't recognize a solitary one of them, either.

"Who are you?" He asked again as he worked to get his rifle reloaded, but the man beside him reached over and plucked it from his grip.

"Ain't no need for you to fire that no more."

"Who are you?" Mac asked for the third time.

"We're the owners of these here horses. Thank you kindly for fetching them back for us."

"Wait, you can't take those horses, too. Those are Rolling J horses."

"Not anymore. They belong to us for all the trouble we went through."

"Come back here!" Mac reached for his knife, only to realize a blade against almost a dozen armed cowboys was a one-way ticket to the boneyard. He caught sight of the brand on the rump of one rider's mount as the man trotted past, keeping the horses bunched in a tight knot.

H Bar H.

"I was going to give back your horses!" Mac shouted after them. "You can't keep the Rolling J's!"

His words faded in the night, ignored. In a few minutes, he sat alone in the darkness. The pounding hooves had disappeared to the north. Mac took off his hat and smacked it against his leg in frustration.

"That pretty well explains why those horses weren't inclined to go the way I wanted. They knew where their home was—with the rest of the H Bar H remuda."

He considered heading back to the Comanche camp to find Flagg, then realized all he would accomplish by doing that was to get himself killed. Once more finding the nighttime stars to guide him, he headed east for a couple miles, picked up the trail of the Rolling J herd, and turned northward. By midnight he rode into the camp.

"That you, Mac? Damn me if I didn't think you was dead." The sentry snorted as he shook his head. "Truth is, I lost a dollar bettin' that you were."

"I'm glad you lost that bet. Who's been acting as trail boss? I need to talk to him."

"What's wrong with Flagg? He rode in a couple hours ago."

"Where? Where is he?" Mac trotted into camp and found the trail boss quickly enough. Flagg, Rattler, and a half dozen others sat around a low fire, drinking coffee.

"Mac!" Rattler greeted him. "'Bout time you showed your face. Pull up a rock. Have some coffee that don't take a layer of skin off your tongue." Rattler held up his tin cup. "I fixed it myself."

Quickly, Mac swung down from the saddle. "Flagg, you're not dead. When the Comanche came after me, I thought—"

"I'm better than any bunch of redskins." Flagg coughed and looked sheepish. "Truth is, I fell off my horse and lay in a ditch while they rode past. When they found out they weren't chasing anything except an empty saddle, they came back hunting for me. By then I was ready. I jumped one of them, took his horse, and came right on back. But what about you?"

Mac rushed to get his story out and ended, "So the H Bar H riders took all the horses, even ours. And I was going to return their horses!"

"At least they ran off the Indians," Flagg said. "Dealing with Compass Jack is easier than arguing with a Comanche raider . . . although not by much."

"Let's get over to the H Bar H herd and get those horses back right now!"

"Settle down. We both need a night's sleep, and you have to fix breakfast for the boys tomorrow morning. Then we'll ride along and see what kind of a deal we can make." Flagg spat. "I'm afeared Compass Jack is going to ask for a few head of cattle to give us back our own horses. That's still cheaper than leaving our scalps with the Indians." He took off his hat, ran his hand over his mostly bald head, then laughed. "Them Indians would have been mighty disappointed lifting this scalp. There's not as much of it as there was once upon a time."

Mac was all fired up and sure he could never get to sleep, but once he unsaddled the horse he'd been riding, he supposed there was nothing else to do but turn in. As he passed Flagg on the way to his own bedroll, the trail boss slapped him on the back and said, "Glad you got back all safe and sound."

"Thanks," Mac said, touched by the gesture.

"Yeah. Rattler's coffee is worse than yours."

Mac felt as if he had ridden into the Comanche camp and was surrounded by warriors wanting nothing more than to count coup on him before killing him. He stood close to Flagg, who kept his distance from Compass Jack Bennett. The two trail bosses had started with a staring contest. When that proved unwinnable on either side, they resorted to threats. Neither was moved. Mac felt they had sanded down the rough to the actual matter now, but lead might fly at any instant.

"You got horses with the Rolling J on their hindquarters, Compass Jack," Flagg said. "You know why they got those brands? Those are Mr. Jefferson's horses."

"They were all mixed up in a herd of ours," Bennett replied. "That means they were out running free, and we claimed them cayuses."

"After Mac here stole them back from the Indians, who'd taken horses from both of us. We don't want much. Just our horses back. We'll let you keep the ones of yours that were stole by the Indians, even though it was a Rolling J man who got them back."

"Now ain't that mighty fine of you, letting me keep my own horses? If my men hadn't come along when they did, you wouldn't have this fellow beside you. He'd be dead and buzzard bait by now."

"Looks like we're even."

"How can that be?"

"He got your horses back from the Indians, you saved his life."

"We're keeping them. Those horses are property of H Bar H now."

Mac caught his breath. That was about as plain as Bennett could put it.

"You want me to offer a few head of longhorns in exchange for the horses, don't you? I won't do it." Flagg sounded adamant.

"There ain't much else I'd trade ten horses for, not out here." Compass Jack sounded as set in his ways.

Mac felt a rush of inspiration. Sometimes boldness was called for. He said, "There might be something you'd hanker after that I'll bet you haven't had since leaving Waco."

Compass Jack frowned at him, as if seeing him for the first time. "Now what might that be?"

"We'll trade you a custard pie for the horses." Mac's heart felt like it was about to explode in his chest. He had no business getting involved in Flagg's dickering, but he read both men pretty good. Neither was going to budge.

"You will?"

Mac had to laugh. Both men asked the same question at the same time.

"I will. If I get you a custard pie before evening chuck, you'll give us back our horses."

Compass Jack didn't hesitate. "Son, you've got yourself a deal," he exclaimed as he grabbed Mac's hand and pumped it like he was drawing water from the center of the earth. "Now you go fetch that pie."

He nodded to Flagg with a smirk, turned, and began yelling orders to his men to get the H Bar H herd moving. Flagg took Mac by the arm and steered him away.

"What was that about? You can't deliver no damned custard pie. We lost our horses. Worse, when I ransom them, Compass Jack will charge me a couple longhorns per head now."

"We need the horses, right?" Mac's mind raced. "I can deliver that custard pie. Let's get back to the outfit."

The ride back passed in utter silence, Flagg glaring at Mac and saying not one word. For his part, Mac went over the times he had watched his ma fixing pies. When they returned to where the chuckwagon was parked, he hit the ground, tossed his reins to the nearest cowboy, and never paid any more attention to what happened to the horse. He had work to do.

Getting out the fixings, he worried about the flour laced with salt. If he put plenty of spice in, that wouldn't be noticed. He had cinnamon enough to hide any salty taste in the crust.

"I need milk," Mac called to Rattler. "Get on out to the herd and find a couple cows to milk. There's got to be some with their udders still full."

"Might have to nose out a calf, Mac. You wouldn't want that, would you?" Rattler laughed, and the men crowded behind him did, too.

"Damned right I do. Get to milking."

"Where are you getting eggs?" Flagg motioned for a couple of cowboys to get out to the herd with a bucket for the milk. "You think of that?"

"I've had a half dozen turkey eggs bouncing along for a few days that I didn't know what to do with. Frying them wouldn't do any good since I could only serve a few of the men. This benefits everybody."

The questions flew fast and furious. Mac ignored them and only spoke to impress men into his service. When they realized he was handing them more work, they began drifting away. That suited Mac just fine. By the time the milk came, he had whipped up the turkey eggs and started the crust.

Milk, eggs, spices, he had the custard filling ready to pour into the crust after it had baked a few minutes. He sampled it. The taste was odd because of the salt, but he poured in the custard and returned everything to the Dutch oven before he leaned back to rest.

"You got a full meal to prepare. Get to it." Flagg took special pleasure in driving him.

Mac felt good about his pie. Food was served and consumed, with more than a few of the cowboys asking to sample just a little of the pie. One even came up with a complicated idea of slicing out a piece, then scooting the rest of the custard around to cover the spot where the sample had been removed. Mac chased them away, using his wooden cooking spoon to rap knuckles and push joking men back.

"All ready, once it cools down a mite," Mac told his trail boss. "I'll need a few hands to go with me to make sure those horses don't get away from me again."

"I'm going. I got to see Compass Jack's face when you give him that pie." Flagg whistled, got three men saddled and ready.

Mac found a crate and carefully placed the pie inside. Using burlap bags, he made a cushion, then gingerly settled down in the saddle with the crate in front of him. Riding as if he carried a crate filled with nitroglycerin rather than a pie, he headed north to where the H Bar H herd had bedded down for the night.

Compass Jack sauntered out to greet him. The trail boss looked up and grinned.

"Come to tell me you promised something you can't deliver?"

Mac lifted the lid on the box and said nothing. The trail boss's nose twitched as the aroma wafted out. He took a step closer and licked his lips.

"What's that in the box?"

"What's it smell like?" Mac asked.

"A fresh-baked pie. You have one in there? You baked a custard pie?" Compass Jack reached up, but Mac held onto the box.

"We have some horses to cut out of your corral. Then I'll pass it over."

"Let me look at it. Let me sniff." He did exactly that as Flagg and the other Rolling J cowboys went to the H Bar H remuda to retrieve their mounts.

"Here you go," Mac said, handing the crate over. "I have to ask one thing, though. How are you going to divvy it up among your men?"

"That bunch of scoundrels?" Compass Jack laughed. "I'm taking a piece. I ought to eat it all for myself." He looked sly. "But I won't. A couple of my boys got shot up fighting the Indians. They get first dibs on a piece. After that, well, we'll see."

"Not much will be left," Mac predicted.

"Won't bet against that." Compass Jack took another sniff, then looked at Mac when he was sure Flagg could hear. "You want a job cooking? I can bury my cook where his body'll never be found."

"The maggots will betray the burial plot," Flagg said.

Compass Jack shook his head.

"Won't happen. He's already put every last one of them slimy little worms into his biscuits."

"Mac has a job. Don't you, Mac?"

Mac heard the joshing tone and knew things had been patched up between Compass Jack and Flagg.

"I'd have to watch my back. Every single man in the Rolling J outfit would come to kidnap me back. Sorry, Mr. Bennett, I'll stay where I am."

Flagg got the small herd of Rolling J horses moving, leading the way back to their camp. As Mac stepped up, Compass Jack reached out to take his arm.

"Just so you know, he's aiming to steal your herd."

"Who's that?" Mac frowned.

"Deke Northrup. Him and his gang wanted jobs with the H Bar H, but I chased them off. While he was here, I overheard him saying he had big plans for the Rolling J cattle. Watch your back. He's a mean one."

"Thanks," Mac said, stepping up into the saddle.

Compass Jack had already called for his cook to bring his sharpest knife and cut the thinnest pieces possible. Mac smiled. It wasn't possible to make a small pie stretch out for more than forty men, but every one of them would at least get a taste. As he galloped after Flagg, his exhilaration at doing good faded, and Compass Jack's words began to gnaw away at him.

"Damn you, Northrup." He put his heels to his horse to catch up with Flagg and tell him what he had learned.

CHAPTER 15

Mac drew alongside Flagg and said, "It might just be that we've got a problem."

"Nope, no problems, thanks to you," Flagg said. "Was that pie any good? Surely did smell good."

"The flour I used for the crust had salt in it, but you could hardly taste it by the time I added enough spices. But that's not the problem."

"Problem is you can't make one of them for us. You had to give the pie to Compass Jack Bennett, damn his eyes." Flagg laughed. "That old cayuse owes me for this. Stealing Rolling J horses is one thing, but taking a pie ransom the way he did is something else. When we get to Abilene, I—"

"Flagg! Listen up. You had ridden away already when Compass Jack told me what he'd overheard. Deke Northrup is planning on rustling the herd. The Rolling J herd!"

Flagg cocked an eyebrow. "Do tell. I wondered where he went when he and them mangy dogs of his left us in the lurch the way they did."

"Northrup's shown he won't stop at anything to make trouble for us. Fontaine and the other two owlhoots could have killed me if I hadn't cut myself free." Mac instinctively reached and touched the knife sheathed at the small of his back. That knife had saved him, all right, just as it had taken Micah Holdstock's life.

"He'd find himself in worse shape than we are. We're shorthanded, but we got more riders than him. Almost twice as many. How's he expecting to drive that many cows to Abilene? Those knuckle-headed longhorns would be scattered from here all the way to the Canadian border in a day. He'd need every last one of his gang to ride night herd. Nope, Mac, you worry too much."

"Compass Jack thought fit to warn me."

"Because he knew I'd say to him what I just said to you. Ain't gonna happen, no way, no how. You get yourself a good night's sleep. You have to be up early to feed everyone and then get to scouting our trail."

"I looked around the H Bar H camp," Mac said. "Following them all the way into Abilene might make scouting easier, but our cows are going to get mighty hungry. There wasn't hardly enough grass for Compass Jack's herd. If we come along a day later, ours will starve."

"Good for you, keeping your eyes open and not getting all caught up in the horse–pie swap. I saw that, too. That means your job just got a bit harder. The Shawnee Trail stretches out across the countryside for miles and miles. Find a spot we can use that hasn't been cropped like a bunch of damned sheep have passed through."

Mac watched the trail boss herd the horses into the corral they had built for the night. He tried to lift his arms and stretch. His muscles refused to give him that much effort. He ached all over and barely kept his eyelids from drooping. Flagg had told him to get some shut-eye. That was about the best advice he remembered getting. He put his horse into the corral, trooped to the chuckwagon, and spread his bedroll underneath.

He went to sleep with visions of pies, apple and cherry and pumpkin and mince, all tormenting him. He wanted to make them all and lacked the ingredients for any of them.

The next thing he knew, it was time to fix breakfast. Even then, he regretted not fixing up a mountain of eggs for the men. They had to do with beefsteak and whatever else he could dredge up from the larder.

And biscuits. He might not have pie for the herders, but he had biscuits.

"Which way are you heading, Mac?" Rattler asked when the meal was over.

Mac finished closing the drop-down table on the chuckwagon and looked back at Rattler.

"I can't follow the H Bar H herd, so I'm going to head more to the east. There must be a river in that direction from the way the land slopes. Find it and there'll be grass aplenty for the cattle."

"Don't you go gettin' lost. You're gettin' out of ridin' with the herd so you can cook for us. You're 'bout the best hire Lem Carson made." The old cowboy spat, then added, "'Cept me, of course. And

Flagg. And then there's that consarned Billy Duke. And . . ."

Rattler walked off, listing every cowboy in the out-fit.

Mac had to laugh. The way they all worked, humor was necessary for lubricating the troubles between them, but he wondered about Billy. Others besides Rattler had said he had a wild streak that barely stayed under control.

Mac pushed that thought from his mind. Scouting the new route mattered more than any single cowboy out there singing to the cattle. Wagon rattling along, he cut away at an angle to the trail left by the H Bar H herd and an hour later saw that he had guessed right about a river. It flowed between rolling hills and disappeared in the direction of the Mississippi, though that was mighty far off. Getting the team turned, he followed the riverbank, hunting for a spot to ford.

Not another mile along the river, he saw debris floating that showed a town lay upriver. From the amount of junk, it wasn't too far off. Thoughts of swapping another few cows for more supplies filled his imagination. Unless Compass Jack or another herd had come by recently, those settlers would need fresh beef as much as the ones in the other town. Top dollar per head was his goal.

He found a decent place to make camp and began work on the noon meal. Before long, he looked up and saw two riders watching him. After he beckoned them over, the pair trotted closer. Badges gleamed on their chests, but he had no trouble figuring which was the marshal and which was the deputy. The deputy looked to be about ten years old, although he had to be older than that. The marshal pushed back his hat so a shock of gray hair poked out.

"Howdy," the marshal called. "Are you setting up a permanent camp here?"

"No, sir, I'm waiting for the rest of the Rolling J herd to catch up with me. As quick as I feed the crew, we'll push on."

"Push on," the marshal repeated. "Do tell."

"There's a town not far from here, unless I miss my guess. Are you in need of fresh meat? If you are, we can do some trading. Prime beef for supplies."

"Supplies."

Mac grew a little irritated. All the lawman did was repeat what he said and didn't give out the information he needed. Any worry that the marshal might have recognized him passed quickly. The man had a far-off look in his eye, and the boy with him wanted to be somewhere else. Anywhere else, from the way he fidgeted. He reminded Mac of the children at Thanksgiving dinner being put at the small table in the kitchen while the adults sat around the dining room table. The deputy acted like he wanted to be with the adults but found that they didn't have half the fun the kids did.

"What's the name of the town?" Mac decided to try a different tactic to get the marshal talking more freely. Who didn't want to brag on the town where they lived?

"I call it Hell, but the residents prefer Lewiston."

"Lewiston sounds more accommodating."

"Does it now?" The marshal reached for the gun on his hip and looked off into the distance to the southwest. Mac turned his head to check and saw Flagg riding toward them, his horse moving at a steady lope.

When Flagg rode up, he reined in and asked, "And who might this be?"

Mac introduced them the best he could, saying, "Lawmen from a settlement nearby. I didn't catch your name, Marshal. Or your deputy's."

The marshal relaxed and took his hand away from his gun as Flagg dismounted and went to stand beside Mac.

"Name's Wilkinson, and this is my boy, David."

"Pleased to make your acquaintance," Flagg said, but his tone indicated he was as wary as Mac had become of the lawman.

"Good thing to talk to the trail boss since you're the one what has to pay up for passage."

"How's that?" Flagg stepped away from Mac.

This caused Mac to catch his breath. Flagg acted as if lead was about to fly. Mac bent into the chuckwagon and opened the drawer where he kept his S&W. Leaving it there but close at hand, he turned back to the conversation playing out between the men.

"Well, Mr. Flagg, as town marshal, I got to levy a passage tax of a dollar a head on your cows. You have to go right on by Lewiston, you do, and that causes all kinds of disruption in our business."

"That's two thousand dollars!" Mac blurted out the number before he could control himself.

"That many head, eh? Well, now, Mr. Flagg, you either turn your herd around and go back the way you come or pay the passage tax. In gold, if you got it. If you're thinkin' on payin' in scrip, well now, there's a convenience tax added on. I'd have to take three thousand dollars in greenbacks."

"I can understand that," Flagg said. "Most banks issuing paper money are bankrupt."

"Glad you understand. Now pay up or get out of here. This is town property where your cook's set up. I wouldn't want to deliver a fine for not obeying a peace officer."

"You want two thousand dollars for the herd to go *past* your town. And you want rent for my cook fixing a meal beside a river that looks like it's free for anyone to use." Flagg rested his hand on the butt of his Colt. "That sounds like highway robbery to me."

"You accusin' a lawman of bein' a crook? That's a crime, too, in Lewiston."

"If I had to guess, everything is a crime in Lewiston." Flagg turned toward Mac and said, "There's nothing we can do but pay the passage tax."

"You got that kind of money?" Marshal Wilkinson's eyebrows arched in surprise. "How much more you carryin'?"

"I suppose you want to know so you can invent new taxes and take that, too!"

Mac's outburst caused the deputy to drag out his black powder Remington. It was almost as big as he was, but it didn't waver or quake in his steady grip.

"That's not too friendly."

"That's a crime in Lewiston, isn't it? Have your boy put down his gun. We can talk this out." Flagg glared at Mac, and he didn't blame the trail boss. He had let his emotions get out of control at how unfair this was. The marshal was as much a robber as Thumbs

Fontaine and his partners when they'd hog-tied him and strung him up so they could steal the Rolling J supplies.

"No need for a parley," the marshal said. "The law's clear. Pay up or go back."

"If we don't do either?" Flagg squarely faced the lawman.

Mac tensed. This was the question that had to get answered.

"Won't come as a surprise to you if I confiscate the herd, will it? See? It's cheaper to pay the tax what's owed the city of Lewiston."

"It isn't possible to offer a few head of cattle to you to forget the whole matter, is it?"

Mac blinked at the marshal's speed. He had his gun out, cocked and pointed at Flagg so fast there wasn't hardly a blur.

"Now that's a crime, Mr. Trail Boss. You tried to bribe a peace officer. You get yourself across that horse, and let's get on into town. We got a right fine lockup and a cell waitin' just for you."

"What's the fine?" Mac ignored Flagg's attempt to silence him. "How much will it take to get him out and free? We need him to handle the herd. There's nothing but greenhorns working the cattle otherwise."

"Is that a fact? Five hundred dollars. That'll get him his freedom. Then we'll talk about the two-thousand-dollar passage tax." Wilkinson motioned with his pistol for Flagg to mount.

His boy rode over, plucked Flagg's Colt from his holster, and tucked it into his own belt.

"Can you rustle up the money, Cook?" Wilkinson

sneered, forcing Mac to decide between answering with a word or his own six-shooter. He chose the one Flagg would approve of.

"Can."

"Better get him out of jail before the judge comes through. Then it'll be prison for certain." He waved his pistol around, pointed with it upstream, waited for Flagg to start, and said, "You watch our back trail, David. Don't let nobody but this one come on into town. I don't want any trouble. The townsfolk don't cotton much to whoopin' and hollerin' by rowdy cowpokes."

His horse reared, pawed the air, then galloped off, leaving Mac with emotions mixing anger and fear. There wasn't any doubt Flagg would pay dearly if the fine wasn't paid. As far as Mac knew, the only cash money Mr. Jefferson had given them was around three hundred dollars. It might be in Flagg's bedroll, but that still came out a couple hundred shy of the ransom demanded.

And there was no question about it. This was a road agent, only he wore a badge.

"I say we all ride into town and shoot it up." Rattler waved his fists in the air. More than one of the cowboys joined in the call for action.

"He's got a point, Mac. We can't let Flagg stay in the hoosegow." Billy Duke didn't shake his fist. He drew his gun and fired it into the air.

Mac saw the shot coming, and he still flinched at the loud roar.

"That's just going to make matters worse," he said. "We have to figure this out."

"I reckon I'm 'bout the most senior hand left in the outfit," Rattler said. "That makes me actin' trail boss. Billy here's got a good idea. We don't have near enough money to pay any fine to spring Flagg. What else can we do?"

"If I read the marshal right, he wants us doing that very thing—riding into Lewiston and trying to shoot up the town. He's looking for an excuse to seize the entire herd."

"A lot of them mayors and marshals demand money to drive past them, but they only ask for a few head of cattle. That's part of the business, and in the past Carson forked over the beeves without so much as a cold, hard stare." Rattler grabbed Billy's hand and pulled it down and whispered to him. Billy holstered the six-shooter but looked put out rather than repentant.

"I want to do what Billy's suggesting," Mac said. "I really do. But if it makes matters worse, if it loses Mr. Jefferson his entire herd, nobody comes out ahead other than that crooked marshal and his boy."

"That's what we do. We kidnap his kid and hold him for ransom. We swap him for Flagg, and we go on." Billy Duke looked proud of himself for thinking up the harebrained scheme.

Mac chose his words carefully, not wanting to split the outfit. They had to work together or they'd all be out of a job—or worse. Marshal Wilkinson looked like the kind who would lock them all up or leave their bodies for the buzzards. With the town situated along the Shawnee Trail the way it was, the lawman had worked this swindle before. The people in Lewiston might go along with it because he shared, or maybe he kept them cowed by threatening them. Without knowing, Mac saw no quick solution to their problem.

"Three hundred's all there was in Flagg's bedroll?" he asked.

"Mac, there wasn't even that," Rattler said. "I'm not too good at countin', but I'd say there was only two hundred. There's no tellin' if Carson left him the whole amount or if he spent some along the way. Hell, for all I know, one or the other of them lost it in a poker game."

"We haven't hit any towns where they'd have gambled," Mac said, distracted. "We don't have the money"—he looked around the circle of faces and saw they couldn't scrape together another fifty dollars among the lot of them—"so we have to do something else."

"You said he wanted the entire herd, so offering a few head to him's not goin' to work." Rattler started to wind up for a speech rallying them to shoot up the town. Mac beat him to it.

"I can get Flagg out. And not pay the ransom for moving the herd." He saw how skeptical Rattler was and how disappointed Billy was. He hurried on. "I'll need what money Flagg had."

"That's not enough to pay Flagg's fine!" Rattler sounded disappointed that Mac hadn't been paying attention.

A slow smile came to Mac's lips.

"It's not, but it'll be plenty for what I have in mind.

Here's what we have to do. All of us." He held out his arms and pulled Rattler and Billy Duke closer as if hatching the greatest conspiracy since Lincoln's assassination. As he talked, they warmed to his cock-eyed scheme.

They agreed to it because they didn't have any other choice.

Chapter 16

Mac felt every eye on him as he rode into town. The nightlife in Lewiston stirred and moved toward one of three saloons but took a pause to study him like he was some exotic bug buzzing about. He kept his eyes straight ahead as he passed the third of the saloons, Gus's Watering Hole. It was the least crowded and closest to the jail. He wondered if there was a connection between those two facts.

He dismounted and went to the jailhouse. His hand shook as he reached for the latch. He stepped back, took a deep breath, and remembered all he had survived. Comanches and Northrup's killers and working double—triple!—duty with the drive. Before that he had escaped New Orleans by the skin of his teeth. He had avoided a double danger there. Going on trial for Micah Holdstock's murder would have been the worst, but he wondered if, after seeing how Evangeline had taken so quickly to Pierre Leclerc, he had dodged trouble by not marrying her, too.

"I can do this," he said softly. When he reached for

the latch this time, his hand was rock steady. He opened the door and stepped inside to face a scatter-gun aimed in his direction.

"You've got quite a way of greeting strangers, Marshal," Mac said calmly. "Real hospitable."

"You ain't wearin' a gun. Turn around. Lift that duster."

"All I've got on me is my knife."

"You just drop it here on my desk." Marshal Wilkinson rocked back in his chair and balanced the shotgun on the desk edge as Mac divested himself of his only weapon. "That's real good. Now, you got the money?"

"I do. I want to be sure Mr. Flagg is still among the living."

"Ain't no reason why he shouldn't be."

"I'm all right, Mac. You got the money?" Flagg's words came from the back of the jail, set off by a wall and closed door.

"Now, you two stop that palaverin'. This is a legal matter, not a social one. Fork over the money. On the desk."

"I had to be sure you were an honorable thief."

"You want to end up in the cell next to that owl-hoot?" Wilkinson rocked forward and lifted the shotgun to menace him. Mac never batted an eye. He had come this far—too far to back out.

"I want to buy you a drink, Marshal. Your choice of saloon. I see there's three of them. Which do you prefer?"

Wilkinson frowned. The shotgun never moved an inch off dead center of Mac's chest.

"You thinkin' on takin' me to a saloon whilst the

others come and spring him?" He canted his head back in the direction of the cells. "That's not happenin'. I'm too smart for that."

"How did you know I was at the door and not someone else? Really, Marshal Wilkinson, you have everyone in town on the lookout for you. If anybody snuck in, you'd know it right away. I wanted to be sociable, but if you don't want a drink . . ."

Mac let the invitation die off. From the two empty bottles in the office corner he guessed Wilkinson didn't go long without dipping his beak in a shot glass filled to the brim with whiskey.

"My scouts all say you rode in alone. Ain't nobody else out on the road leading into town."

"See?" Mac tried to look innocent. He must have succeeded because the marshal lowered the shotgun. Now if he fired, he would only blow off Mac's balls.

"Ain't comin' out of my fine. The fine for your trail boss, that is."

"Agreed. I don't want us to part on bad terms, and, well, you've seen how he is." Mac glanced toward the rear of the jailhouse. A locked wooden door between the office and the cells prevented him from seeing Flagg. "He can be downright cantankerous."

"He's got a mouth on him, that's for sure."

"Wet your whistle, Marshal. I'm buying. Is Gus's Watering Hole next door good enough?"

"I have to get my deputy in to watch the office." He bellowed like a bull, sucked in more air, then repeated the call.

Mac smiled, nodded and waited. He was not surprised to see the youngster who had been with Wilkinson earlier come in from a small room at the side of the office, rubbing sleep from his eyes. Running this town was a family enterprise.

"Yeah, Pa. What is it?"

"You keep the office whilst I'm out. Lock the door after me. If anybody tries to break in, you shoot the varmint in the cell. You hear?"

"Like I done before?"

The boy's question turned Mac cold inside. He knew they had run this swindle before, but hearing such a young man admit he had murdered a prisoner on his pa's orders chilled him. The wrong ones were out of the cell.

"Like you done before, David. You're a good boy. I won't be long. Me and this son of a bitch got some business to tend to."

"At the saloon?"

Wilkinson tried to backhand his boy. David was too quick for him.

"You don't sass me. Now set yourself down and point this shotgun at the door. Anybody you don't know comes through, you blow them to Kingdom Come."

The boy settled into the chair, looking as arrogant as his pa.

Mac looked over his shoulder uneasily at the boy, worrying he might take it into his head to start shooting. He didn't have any love for his pa, that was obvious, and Mac doubted he liked much of anyone else. He breathed a sigh of relief as he stepped out into the chilly night.

"There's the best place in town. I'm the only customer at times."

"That seems odd, doesn't it? If it's so good, why are you the only one there?" As soon as the words left his mouth, Mac knew he was on thin ice. The marshal didn't understand why people in town would avoid him. Or maybe he did. No man wielded the power he seemed to without enjoying it and thinking on how to gather even more.

"Nice place, ain't it?" Wilkinson pushed through the swinging doors and went to the bar. He slapped his hand down a couple times and ordered, "Your best, Gus. Give me your best whiskey, and don't be slow about it. I got a successful business deal to celebrate."

"Coming right up, Marshal." A ruddy-faced man in an apron behind the bar poured a generous drink into a tumbler, then asked Mac, "What's your pleasure?"

Mac knew better than to answer that truthfully. He looked at the marshal, then his whiskey.

"That looks mighty good. I've been on the trail so long it'll take more than one to cut through the dust."

A moment later, he hoisted his glass and saluted the marshal.

"To . . . business."

The marshal gulped his drink down in a single swallow, banged the glass in a demand for more. Gus obliged. Mac shook his head. He was still working on the first one.

"I need some money for the drinks," the barkeep said.

"Right here, sir, right here." Mac pulled a roll of greenbacks from his vest pocket and dropped them on the bar. "Keep the liquor flowing. I want to seal the deal with Marshal Wilkinson good and proper."

"Well that you should." The marshal got another three fingers of whiskey poured into his glass. He showed no sign of slowing his drinking. "I'm gonna be four thousand dollars richer, Gus. This gent's agreed to pay for passage for his herd." Wilkinson frowned. "You got to bail out that trail boss of yours, first, don't you?"

"I'll drink to that, Marshal. If he wasn't such a good friend, I'd let him rot in your jail, but we need him on the job. Can't have anybody slacking off, can we?"

"Nope, no, sir, you can't."

"It's too bad your boy is such a lazy one."

"What? He ain't!"

Mac motioned for the bartender to give the marshal another drink. Wilkinson downed it and got another drink, his face fiery red now.

"How's he better than you, then?" Mac kept goading the marshal, finding the soft spots to poke hardest at. All he wanted was to keep the man drinking. Even a professional drinker like Wilkinson had a limit. Having a new antagonist in town spurred him on, but it still took a bottle and a half of the whiskey before he started to wobble on his feet.

Mac moved slowly from foot to foot. The trade liquor he had imbibed took its toll on him, too, but the marshal had outpaced him three drinks for every one he swilled. Still, Mac had never been much of a drinker. He watched the marshal's eyes try to track his back and forth movement. When the bloodshot eyes actually crossed, he knew he had succeeded in this part of his plan.

He started to scoop up the money remaining on the bar, but Gus was quicker.

"I know what you're doin'. This is mine."

"You'll have to come up with one hell of a story."

"I can think up the woolliest stories you ever did hear. Nobody in town much likes him or that snotty-nosed brat of his."

Mac nodded, got his arm around the lawman, and steered him for the door.

"Don't you pass out on me, you hear? We've got to get you back to the jailhouse so you can let my partner out."

"Why? You ain't paid his fine. You ain't paid nothin'."

"It's in your office. On your desk. Don't you remember?"

"Oh, yeah, sure, I remember." Wilkinson managed to stumble along under his own power. Mac trailed him.

"David, it's me, your pa. I'm comin' on in, so don't you shoot."

"Aw, come on in, then." The boy sounded as if he had been awakened.

Mac considered this even better. As the marshal opened the door into his office, Mac slid Wilkinson's gun from its holster. The lawman never noticed.

"Where is it? I don't see the money." He fell forward, braced with both hands flat on the desktop.

"David took it," Mac said.

"What?" the youngster exclaimed. "I didn't take no money!"

Wilkinson lunged for his son, knocking the shotgun to one side. Mac stepped around and pointed the marshal's gun at the boy.

"Get the keys to the cells."

"You stole my money." Wilkinson fell heavily across the desk and flopped onto the floor. "Gimme it."

Mac waited for Patrick Flagg to come from the cells in the back of the office. He took in the situation in a flash.

"What the hell are you doing?"

"Get him into the cell, maybe one alongside his boy. The two of them might not get along together." Mac pursed his lips, then said, "No, put them together. The town might enjoy a trial of one of them killing the other with his bare hands."

Flagg grinned wolfishly, dragged the protesting marshal into the back. He came back, grabbed the boy's arm, and hauled him into the cell block as well. Keys clicked and cell doors slammed.

"You've got something in mind. What is it?" Flagg asked when he came back into the office.

"We need a trail boss something fierce right now," Mac said. "Moving a herd at night isn't something any of the others have any experience doing."

"How many miles do we have to go, do you think?" Flagg rummaged about in a drawer, found his gun belt and six-shooter. He strapped them on as he left the office.

Mac started after him, then stopped. A stack of wanted posters showed no sign of having been examined. He hastily flipped through them, then stared at his own likeness peering back at him. Pierre Leclerc had convinced the New Orleans authorities to put up a hundred-dollar reward on his head for the murder of Micah Holdstock. He crumpled the poster and stuffed it into his pocket before following Flagg outside.

"Where's your horse?"

"At the town livery, if Wilkinson didn't sell it to someone." Flagg climbed up behind Mac as they rode to the stable. Less than five minutes later, Flagg rode out and asked, "Where do we head?"

Mac had gotten his bearings. He remembered what Flagg had claimed about Compass Jack Bennett and how the man never got lost. That ability would have served him in good stead now, especially since the herd was already on the move.

"That way," he said, pointing north out of town. He followed the pointer stars in the Big Dipper up to the North Star and refined his route.

Once outside Lewiston, Mac tried to make a guess where the Rolling J longhorns might be by now. They had been on the trail almost two hours. He tried to get his bearings using the stars, but heavy clouds hid the sky and the constellations he depended on for nighttime guidance.

"You know the Rolling J will never be allowed to come this way again?" Flagg's tone was neutral.

"There was no other way I saw to get you out of the hoosegow and save the herd."

"There's one other thing I regret," Flagg said.

"What's that?" Mac felt on edge, waiting to hear.

"I missed one of your meals with those biscuits."

Flagg laughed, surprising Mac. He hadn't heard the trail boss in such high spirits in quite a while. It was time to bring him down to earth.

"You're missing more than the biscuits. I used most all the money you had in the bankroll for buying supplies."

Flagg sniffed.

"At least you enjoyed a drink or two with the money. I've never seen a man quite as drunk as that marshal. How'd you know it would work, getting him so snockered?"

"I didn't." Mac touched the marshal's gun still tucked into his waistband. He drew it and sent it spinning into the night. It landed in a puddle, causing a small splash. "I smelled whiskey on him when we first met. That was all I had to go by."

"You're going to have my job one of these days, Mac."

"What? And deprive you of your biscuits? Nobody in the outfit can cook half as good as me."

"Give Rattler your recipe and who cares what else he cooks, as long as he delivers on those heavenly hunks of cooked dough."

They joshed one another as they rode. Then they settled down. Mac had to ask, "How long do you think we've got before the marshal gets a posse on our trail?"

"He'll have to sober up first, but you're right about him. No man with that sort of power lets anyone make a fool out of him. If it had been just him locked in the cell, we might be all right, but he lost face in front of his son. Wilkinson has to make good on catching us."

"Do you hear cattle up ahead?" Mac tilted his head and strained to hear the smallest sounds in the night. On this open prairie stretching northward, the loud sigh of the wind drowned out most normal sounds.

"I do. That way." Flagg looked up. "We're catching a bit of luck."

A drop of moisture suddenly brushed Mac's cheek.

He knew he wasn't crying, so he said, "Driving the cattle in a rainstorm's good luck? How do you figure?"

"Think on it, Mac. Wilkinson tries to find our trail, but the rain's washed away all trace we were even here. That's the good luck."

Heavy drops of rain began to thump against the brim of Mac's hat. He peered into the murk and thought he made out silhouettes of longhorns moving away from him. What the trail boss said might be true. A posse wouldn't want to brave a late-summer thunderstorm just to appease their marshal, but the weather posed its own problems.

By the time they caught up with the back of the herd, it was raining to beat the band. Distant thunder made the cattle uneasy. Mac hoped they wouldn't stampede.

"I need to find who's driving the chuckwagon. The hands will want breakfast whenever we take a break."

"Go on, Mac." Flagg hesitated, then called out to him. "Hey, Mac!"

"Yeah?" Mac was thinking about how to keep driving when the ground got muddy and the chuckwagon slipped and slid around. "What is it?"

"Thanks." With that Flagg trotted off.

Behind him, in soaked clothes and with water dripping in an almost constant stream from the brim of his hat, Mac grinned.

He knew they weren't safe yet, not from the angry marshal and not from the chance of a stampede because of the storm, but for the moment he felt good. Damned good.

CHAPTER 17

"I'll never be dry again," Rattler grumbled from the seat of the chuckwagon. He pulled his yellow oilcloth slicker around him and kept his head down against the driving rain.

"When you get to Hell, it'll be hot enough to dry you off," Mac said as he swayed back and forth on the seat beside Rattler, who was still handling the reins. He had to agree with the cowboy about the weather. Since he had sprung Flagg from the Lewiston jail and caught up with the herd moving into the storm, it had not stopped raining.

A few times it looked like it was going to let up. It lied. After a pause, the rain pelted them even harder than before. Glancing up and swiping water from his eyes, Mac doubted he could see fifty feet. The only good thing about the rain was that it would wipe out their trail and maybe keep Marshal Wilkinson from following them. Other than that, Mac couldn't find anything good to say for the incessant rain. It had been so bad, he didn't know if it was still night or had turned to morning yet.

From the way his belly grumbled, he had to bet on morning. He fished out his pocket watch and held it up to get a better look at it.

"What time is it?" Rattler shouted over the drone of the rain hammering against their hat brims before running in tiny rivers down their slickers.

"Nine. Don't know if that's night or morning."

"Got to be morning. When do you think Flagg is going to let us take a break? I'm ready to eat."

"Me, too," Mac admitted, though he would need at least an hour of preparation before he fed the hands. Building fires and cooking anything in this downpour was going to be yet another obstacle to overcome.

"No lightning in this storm. We're lucky that way," Rattler went on.

"Some luck. We might be driving the herd in a giant circle and will end up back in town." If that happened, Mac vowed to shoot it out with the law, even the younger Wilkinson. That one looked to be a real menace sooner rather than later. He had heard stories of gunmen who were barely into their teens. The boy fit the bill exactly and already had the arrogance of a killer.

"Mac! Mac!"

"That's Flagg," Rattler said. He slowed the team as the sheets of rain fell endlessly around them.

A shape loomed up out of the murk and turned into a man on horseback. "I couldn't find you," Flagg said as he drew rein beside the wagon. "No sense trying to fix food. You got enough to serve cold?"

"I do. Won't be much, though."

"Better than nothing. I'm calling a halt to the drive for a while. The men are falling out of the saddle, and the cattle are getting cranky."

"Nobody wants a cranky longhorn," Mac agreed. His humor was the only thing dry this morning.

"Go on and dish up the food, then take a break. You've been awake as long as anybody."

"You, too," Mac said.

"I got some sleep in a nice warm cell, though the cot had bedbugs." Flagg scratched to make his point. He grinned, his gold tooth shining in the dark. The smile faded. He wheeled around and galloped off to take care of yet another problem with the herd.

With his usual thoroughness, Mac fixed what he could, cleaning out most of the dried fruits and jerked beef from the larder. The airtights he saved for later. If the rain didn't let up, he'd have to serve the peaches and tomatoes for the evening meal.

As the men came riding in and gratefully took whatever he dished out to them, the rain began to let up. By the time Flagg rode into camp, the rain had stopped, and the clouds were parting enough to show occasional patches of blue sky.

Flagg dismounted and said, "I hate to do this, Mac, but can you ride out to the far side of the herd and see if you can find Billy Duke? Nobody's seen him for more than an hour. Last anybody talked to him, he was fixing to chase after twenty head that had broken away from the herd."

"If I find him, do you want me to help him drive the cattle back?"

Flagg nodded, picked up a plate with a scant assortment of dried food on it and began chewing on a tough piece of jerky.

Mac cleaned up the best he could, then chose another horse to ride since the one he had pushed so hard during the night shied from him as he approached. It hardly seemed fair that the horses got treated better than the men who rode them. Being cook was hard enough, but having trail scout and now cowboy added to his jobs left him so exhausted he walked around in a daze most of the time. Flagg berated cowboys who slept in the saddle, especially during night herd, but Mac wanted to find out how they did it. There wasn't likely going to be any other time for him to catch a few winks.

When he found Billy Duke and they got the errant cows back to the herd, he would have to drive the wagon, do some scouting, and fix the noonday meal. With the ground the way it was, he likely wouldn't be able to make more than a mile or two of progress. The chuckwagon's wheels might even bog down in the mud until it was impossible to move.

"When it happens, I'll worry about it," he told himself. He tipped his head down and let the rain drip off the brim. The horse lulled him into a half sleep that almost betrayed him. Only a loud shout woke him.

"What? What? Billy?" Mac looked around, rubbing his eyes to get the sleep out of them. He saw the cowboy ahead of him, herding a dozen head of cattle.

"Hey, Mac. I got 'em back. All of 'em."

Mac rode around and came up on the far side of the small herd to keep them together. The larger the

number, the easier it was keeping most of them together. When the longhorns formed tiny bunches
like this, they moseyed off, ignoring the others. Mac
had never figured out how the cattle decided on a
leader, but they did. Sometimes it was the biggest
bull, but other times there seemed no rhyme or reason to which critter they followed.

"How many were there?"

"All these. A dozen. They wandered off in the middle of the storm. It took me forever finding them.
They'd gone due west and were down in a hollow."

"Good work, Billy." Mac used the end of his lariat
to move two stragglers along. As he did so, he saw
something out of the ordinary. He rode closer, bent,
and wiped mud off the rump of the nearest heifer.
"This isn't one of ours."

"Of course it is, Mac. What are you saying?"

"I don't know brands, but this looks like 23. It's
not the Rolling J."

"A cow's a cow. Don't go gettin' all prairie lawyer
on me."

"The brand means it belongs to another herd. Did
you see other riders?"

From the glare Billy Duke gave him, he knew the
answer.

"You take the 23 branded cows back. I'll see to getting ours into the herd. Flagg's got them moving—"

"No."

Mac turned on the cowboy. Billy Duke was a year
or two younger, but his experience with cattle out-
stripped anything Mac claimed. In the pecking order
of Rolling J riders, Mac had never figured where he
stood. Flagg listened to him and sometimes even fol-

lowed his ideas. But he wasn't a cowpuncher. The others, ones like Rattler, joshed with him as they did others riding herd. But he was a substitute because of Northrup taking his men and hightailing it. The only thing he knew for certain was that he had been hired as the cook.

Cooks didn't give orders. Cooks took them.

"If you don't want to do it that way, you get the Rolling J cows back. Tell Flagg how hard you worked finding them, and take credit. I don't care. I'll see that these are returned to wherever they belong."

"That might be a dozen miles off. There's no telling when those cows got cut off from their main herd. We've lost a couple dozen since we started. This will go a ways toward making up for them."

"It's not rustling, not exactly. But it's wrong to keep them, Billy. I'll drive them back to wherever the 23 herd is bedded down."

"Damn it, Mac, you're taking food out of our mouths if you do that. Every cow sold in Abilene adds to the pile of money to be split amongst us cowboys."

Nothing had been said to him about that. He had been hired as cook, and likely Lem Carson only gave bonuses to the cowboys. Even if it was true that the total profit for the herd was divvied up, it was wrong. And a couple cattle wouldn't amount to much more than a dollar or two when split twenty ways.

"Are you that hard up, Billy? I'll give you some of my pay, if you are. I'm getting a dollar a day."

"I'm getting more, but that's not the point, Mac. We're busting our butts out here and deserve every penny paid us."

Mac saw that arguing wasn't getting him anywhere.

It was a crime to steal another man's cattle. Accidentally cutting a few into your herd after the storm they'd endured was one thing, doing it on purpose was another.

"Get them back to Flagg." He swung his rope in short, swift arcs that whacked the rumps of the 23-branded cattle.

"Mac." Billy's voice had turned velvet and soft. That was warning enough, even if staring down the barrel of his gun wasn't.

"You'd shoot me over the cattle?"

"I would. I like you, Mac, I do, but I went through hell getting those cattle. You're not giving them away."

"Giving them back," he corrected. Billy Duke looked serious about squeezing the trigger. He had no idea what drove the man to want to commit murder on someone he had known and been friends with for a month or more, but the intent was there. Mac read it in his eyes.

"We'll drive them all back and let Flagg decide. But I am telling him. Whatever he decides, I'll abide by. Will you do the same?" Mac thought he was secure in that. He knew Flagg pretty well. The man was honest and did the right thing. He wouldn't keep cattle he knew were stolen from another herd.

At least, Mac didn't think he would. Billy's actions had surprised him. It was possible Flagg's would, too.

After a tense moment, Billy shrugged and slid his gun back into leather. Working together, they moved the tiny herd back. Mac tried to memorize the markings on the cattle. Once they mingled with the far larger Rolling J herd, it would be difficult, if not impossible, to single them out. This could be done in Abilene when the cattle were run down a chute and examined one by one. Spread all over the prairie was another matter.

When he saw Flagg, Mac waved his hat and beckoned him over.

"I got work to do. No time for jawing, Mac."

He quickly explained the situation, not mentioning how Billy Duke had gone out of his way to steal the 23's cattle.

"So they were just grazing with ours?" Flagg's disgusted tone showed the depth of his concern about the errant cattle. "We need to find this herd—I don't know where the 23 calls home—and get word to the trail boss that we have their cows."

"Three cattle, boss," Billy Duke said. "There's only *three*. Why not square it with them in Abilene, if they even notice?"

"That's why." Flagg looked past them to a trio of riders coming fast toward them.

"Rustlers!" Billy Duke clawed at the gun on his hip, but Mac almost fell from the saddle as he lunged and grabbed the man's arm. He kept the lead from flying by doing that.

All three of the approaching riders had rifles resting across the saddle in front of them. Seeing Billy's move caused them to bring their weapons around.

"Howdy!" Flagg called, raised his hand in greeting and trotted out to meet the men.

"You stay here," Mac ordered. Billy Duke growled like a cougar but took his hand off his six-shooter. "I'll be right back."

"There's no call to give the cows back."

Mac tried to ignore the comment. He joined Flagg, who already was parleying with the man obviously in charge. The rider was older, had a touch of iron gray hair in his sideburns, even if he wasn't more than forty years old. His gaze was as piercing as Flagg's, but there wasn't a hint of smile on his lips. Flagg tried to jolly the trio, but they weren't having any of it.

"You stole our cattle. We want them back."

"You belong to the 23 brand?"

"The 23's down near San Antonio. Damned right, it's our brand. Those are my cows you stole."

"They got separated from your herd during the storm," Mac said. "We rounded up some of our strays, and yours were with them. I only noticed when we got back. I'm real sorry this happened."

The trail boss looked Mac over, then turned back to Flagg without saying anything. The set to his body spoke louder than words.

"Why don't you boys go fetch your cows?" Flagg said. "There's not been any harm. You get 'em, and we can all get on to herding up to Abilene."

"We ought to get a lawman out here. You tried rustling our cattle." The 23 trail boss glowered.

"Do whatever you like," Flagg said. "We're moving on as soon as we get a meal in our bellies. The storm set us back a day or two, and we'd like to make up the time."

"Try that and it'll be a range war. I promise that."

"No need to be unreasonable. Mac here's admitted it was a mistake. Doesn't seem like one that ought to garner anything more than a 'thank you.'"

"You need to pay for stealing those cows."

"Well, sir, you have a one-track mind. It's on those tracks, and it's heading for a solid wall. I don't have to do this, but if it smooths your ruffled feathers, why don't you take a couple of our cows as payment for your aggravation?"

The trail boss exchanged looks with the two cowboys with him. He nodded brusquely to them and pointed to the Rolling J herd. They trotted off.

"Makes life easier," Flagg said agreeably enough. Then his tone hardened. "This ends the matter."

He wheeled about and galloped away. Mac started to apologize again but saw there wasn't any chance he would get an acknowledgment. He trailed behind Flagg and overtook him halfway back to the Rolling J campsite.

"Flagg, hold up. We need to talk a minute."

"What is it? Billy Duke just caused us to lose a couple cattle."

"The 23 trail boss didn't deserve it. If anything, he owed us for saving his cows," Mac said. "But you're right about Billy. He wanted to keep those longhorns and did what he could to lose them among our herd."

"I'll keep an eye on him. He's got an itchy trigger finger. That's not good in a cowboy who's supposed to be watching over the herd."

"He's a hothead, but he's not wrong. Not entirely."

Flagg shook his head and rode away without giving his opinion.

As Mac got the chuckwagon ready to roll, Billy Duke rode into camp and hit the ground on the run. He grabbed Mac by the arm and spun him around.

"What's got you so fired up?" Mac held his irritation down. He had work to do.

"They took the cows." Billy was almost out of breath and looked to be on the verge of tears. "They took the cows."

"Flagg told them they could get their own back and take a couple of ours for their trouble."

"They took more 'n a couple. They took a couple *dozen*. Those owlhoots rode away with twenty-five head, and most of them were ours!"

Mac had no words. He just stared at the hot-headed cowboy, wondering if he was exaggerating— or if the 23 trail boss had outright stolen Rolling J cattle.

CHAPTER 18

"**D**id you tell Flagg?" Mac asked. "He's got to know. This is serious."

He chewed his lip, thinking about his part in the rustling. Too many problems piled up for him to bear all the responsibility, but somehow he was always in the middle of trouble every time it broke out. He felt a tad guilty that he hadn't convinced Billy Duke not to steal the cattle in the first place.

Only he wasn't in charge. Mac tried to figure out why he took such responsibility on himself when he wasn't anything more than the cook, though that job had changed day by day until he might as well have been the trail boss, too. Cook and scout and wrangler—and the one who had sprung the actual trail boss from jail and sent the herd racing on in the storm when the rustling had occurred. He filled all those jobs and maybe some he hadn't even bothered to consider.

None of this was his doing, but he felt responsible anyway.

"If I tell him, he'll fire me for sure, Mac," Billy said. "There's no way I can afford to lose this job and forfeit all my pay. I need the money somethin' fierce."

Mac studied the young cowboy. This wasn't the first time he had heard a note of panic from Billy when it came to money. That was the heart of this entire mess.

"Why? We all need the money. Working the Rolling J herd is the way we earn it, but you make it sound like a matter of life and death. You've got three squares, a horse whenever you want, and you pull down a decent salary for the work you do."

Billy shuffled his feet and looked around, dropped his gaze, and nodded. He spoke in a mumble too low and garbled to be understood. Mac said nothing, knowing the cowboy would spit it out if he had a mind to.

"Most of the cowboys don't have a family. I do, and that's only part of my woes. The crops failed, and my ma got real sick and died. Pa's not been the same since."

"That's a shame, but your pa can't expect you to support him the rest of his life."

"There's Jenny and little Tom, too. My wife and son, and they ain't got nobody else. Tom's only three. They all live together in a one-room cabin outside of Waco. There's not a whole lot I can do to keep from losing the farm, but the money from my wrangling can save them. She tries to hide it, but Jenny's got the consumption, and Tommy's on the sickly side. I never saw a young'un who was so pale and thin."

"You left them for a trail drive to Abilene?" Mac wondered what he would have done in those circumstances. "There wasn't a job around Waco? Mr. Jefferson has a few men working what's left of the herd on the Rolling J. Without someone keeping those cows healthy, there won't be a spring birthing or a drive next year."

"I asked. He said it was the trail or nothing. Nobody else would give me a job, and I was desperate. Please, Mac, don't tell Flagg."

"How likely is he to notice the missing cattle? What with the storm and all, he might never notice they're missing."

"Maybe not, but I need the bonus money those cows would fetch in Abilene. It's not much, but a few dollars means the world to me. I ain't spent one thin dime since I signed on. It all went to Jenny." He fumbled in his pocket and pulled out a soaked letter. He thrust it at Mac. "See? She writes me. Ain't been nowhere lately to pick up mail. No address even if I went into town, but this letter reached me just before the herd left Waco."

A quick glance at the water-stained ink showed it to be almost illegible. But Mac did make out the last two lines: *Love, Jenny, Tommy and Pa.*

"What are you suggesting?" Mac asked a question and didn't really want the answer. He cursed his foolishness when Billy said, "I'm gonna steal 'em back. I'll find our cows in the 23 herd and drive them all back. I promise, Mac, I won't touch a one of them others. Let the 23 keep theirs. All I intend to do is recover what's by law ours."

"The 23 trail boss never should have taken advantage of Flagg the way he did. I heard him say to take a couple cows as payment for all the trouble. Flagg never said to take a couple dozen."

"You cover for me, Mac. Please. I'm beggin' you."

If Flagg knew what Billy Duke intended, he would go up like a Fourth of July skyrocket. Whether he would bother confronting the 23 trail boss about the theft was something else. They were in a race to get to Abilene after so many delays. He knew the H Bar H herd was least two days ahead, maybe more. Compass Jack Bennett would get to the railroad ahead of them and claim the best price per head. That reduced the value of the Rolling J herd a mite. This new theft by the 23 cut it down even more. Not only would they receive less for each head of cattle, there'd be fewer to sell.

"You can't hope to get to the 23 herd, find the cattle, and drive ours back all by yourself before morning. Flagg would see you were gone and ask questions nobody'd want to answer."

"Do what you have to, Mac. I'm going." Billy sounded so desperate Mac grabbed his arm and spun him around.

"One man can't do all that. Two stand a better chance." Seeing Billy's confused look, he shook the young cowboy and said, "Us, damn it. You and me. We'll both go. But if you can't find ours straight away, we turn around and ride on back. Money or no money in Abilene, you can't risk your neck. Where'd your wife and boy be then?"

"And Pa," Billy said in a choked voice. Tears welled

in his eyes. He thrust out his hand and shook Mac's hand, hard. "You're the best friend a man could ever hope for, Mac."

"Don't get us killed. That's all I want."

They mounted and rode into the night. Mac's thoughts drifted as he rode, his mind slipping and sliding around from exhaustion as if it were on an icy pond. He jerked awake when Billy whispered, "There, Mac, there's the 23 herd."

He tried to make out the shapes of the cattle in the light of a waxing crescent moon. Scant illumination showed a small herd of close to a hundred head.

"What are the chances our cows are in there?"

"The only way to find out is to look. Come on."

"You look, I'll keep watch." He touched the S&W he had strapped on before leaving. It was dangerous going armed at night, but he had the feeling in his gut that any trouble would be life or death. If he had to shoot it out with the 23 cowboys, he wanted something to shoot with.

Billy Duke walked his horse among the cattle. Mac nodded in approval. If the young cowboy had tried forcing his way into their midst, he would have stirred the sleeping cattle. The horns these cattle sported could gore a man to death if they made a quick turn. Worse, his horse would go down first, leaving him on foot amid frightened, angry longhorns swinging their heads this way and that. It might take a man a day to die from what a single horn could do to his body.

Mac rode the perimeter, trying to make out the brands. In the pale moonlight, he caught sight of only a few. All the stylized 23, the middle stroke in the 3 being the bottom of the number 2. He saw the larger herd some distance away and heard the cowboys singing to them. He had to grin. Those cowboys didn't sing any better than those riding for the Rolling J. And these cattle didn't much care, either, about the quality. Only the soothing sound that wasn't a wolf sneaking up on them mattered.

"Get on back to the main herd," a man's voice ordered abruptly from behind him. "You know the boss wanted these to stay away from the others until he checked them for the fever."

Mac half turned in the saddle before he realized it was one of the 23 hands who gave the order.

The rider practically yelped in surprise. "Hey, you're one of them cowboys from the other herd. What're you doing here? Rustler! We got a rustler!"

"Now, wait, I—"

Mac ducked low when the cowboy unlimbered a pistol and fired. A foot-long orange and yellow flame spurted in his direction, and the slug whined just over his head. Not intending to do so, he sent his horse lunging directly into the cowboy's. They collided amid a tangle of flailing hooves, shouts, and gunfire.

Mac grabbed the other man and dragged him from the saddle. They hit the ground hard, but he had a split second to prepare. He landed on top of the cowboy. This advantage proved fleeting. The man kept shooting wildly. None of the bullets came close to Mac, but he had to dodge the end of the barrel or he would have caught an ounce of lead in the chest.

Moving fast, he caught the drover's wrist and forced

it back and around until he dropped the gun. Then Mac worked to pin the man. That proved harder than getting him to drop the gun, but at least the danger from getting a bullet in the gut was past.

"We're not doing anything," Mac grunted as he fought.

"Rustler!"

"You're the one who stole our cattle." Mac rolled over and found himself pummeled by wildly flying fists. He got his forearms up and took the blows there.

He feinted to the right, then used a left jab to the man's midriff to double him over. Grabbing him by the shoulders, Mac held him in place as he brought his knee up under his chin. That ended the fight. As the cowboy collapsed, Mac staggered back and gasped for breath. Then he heard more gunfire.

Knocking out one cowboy did nothing to stop a half dozen others charging in his direction. He saw less of the riders than he did the muzzle flash as each fired at him. Mac stared, thinking he could tell the difference between the six-shooters and the rifles. Then shock passed, and he knew he had to hightail it or he'd end up in an unmarked grave—if he was lucky enough to be buried.

He looked around frantically. His horse hadn't run far. Whether it was too tired or wanted to remain near someone it considered a friend didn't matter. He whistled, got the horse's attention, then approached it. With a single vault, he landed in the saddle. Lead whipped through the night all around. He bent down so the horse's neck protected him as he dug his heels into the animal's flanks to get some speed. The urging wasn't necessary. The gunshots spooked the horse and sent it racing across the prairie.

Worse, the gunfire spooked the small herd. They shifted around, thinking it over, and one finally panicked. The rest followed. The herd headed back for the Rolling J stock.

"Billy! Billy!" Mac's cries were drowned out by the thundering hooves that shook the ground and filled the air with kicked-up dirt and grass.

He lost sight of the cowboys who had fired on him. He thought he heard distant warnings and more gunshots. Mostly, Mac heard nothing but the stampeding cattle and the thudding of his own horse as it galloped after the herd.

It looked for all the world like he had started the cattle running in order to steal them. Reaching the far side of the herd, he kept his horse galloping, in spite of the danger. He remembered the horse that had stepped in a gopher hole. In the silvery half-light, only shadows danced along the ground. The unsure footing caused the horse to panic even more. It pounded ahead to the front of the herd.

Mac looked around wildly for Billy but didn't see him. Drawing his gun, he fired it in the air and yelled until he was hoarse. He had to turn the herd. For whatever reason, cattle would stampede straight ahead until their hearts exploded, but turn them and the urge to run died down. A few minutes after that, a frightened cow would be ready to graze again—or even go to sleep. When his gun came up empty, Mac worried that he had failed. Then another rider raced past him.

"Billy!"

"Get back to the herd! This ain't gonna end good for anybody."

Billy Duke cut in front of the lead longhorn and used a whip on its head. The distraction from fear to anger caused the steer to turn. That slowed the stampede. Then Billy forced the small herd at almost a right angle to the original path. The cattle slowed and stopped.

"You did it, Billy. You got them to—"

Mac fell silent when he saw what Billy had noticed already. This small bunch of cattle was easy to turn. The gunfire and the approaching stampede had passed itself along to the much larger Rolling J herd. Like a giant, lazy wave along the Mississippi, the cattle stirred. Mac saw the rise in front ripple across the cattle as more of them came awake to the danger.

The ground had shaken before with only a hundred head of cattle stampeding. As the entire Rolling J herd began to run, it felt like an earthquake.

Mac had hoped never to see such an awesome, frightening sight as two thousand cattle charging madly across the prairie.

But that was what he saw now.

CHAPTER 19

Moonlight gleamed off a churning sea of horns as the stampede built up speed. Mac started toward the herd, but common sense held him back. To ride in front of that moving wall of gristle and bone meant certain death. He kept his head down and cut off at an angle.

Only then did he remember why the herd had begun its slow, unstoppable run. He looked around for the 23 riders, but they were nowhere to be seen. If their herd caught the scent of fear from the Rolling J stock, they had as much trouble on their hands as Flagg's outfit.

Mac sat straighter and tried to make sense out of the shadowy, unstable mass of cattle. They cried as if they were being killed. And some were. A stumble and fall meant being trampled to death. More than a few slowpokes became victims. Their carcasses were left behind as the mindless tide surged away.

"Billy!" Mac shouted until his voice began to croak. Hunting for the other cowboy brought him only a sinking feeling as he saw how thoroughly the ground had been chopped up by thousands of hooves. The moonlight hindered more than it helped. Casting shadows made anything more than a slow walk difficult, if not downright dangerous.

He rode in a zigzag pattern in the wake of the stampede, hunting for Billy Duke. When he didn't find him, Mac snapped the reins and brought his horse to a canter. He wanted to gallop in the other direction, but the stampede required someone to head it off. He had seen how a few gunshots and some whooping and hollering had turned the smaller herd when it stampeded. But getting in front of the two thousand head herd was suicidal.

In spite of that knowledge, Mac picked up the pace. He reached the rear of the herd more quickly than he thought he would. The cattle had already turned, curling around, but they weren't slowing down. With his head down, he got the most speed from his horse that he could. Pulling even with the side of the herd, he took lariat in hand and began whacking the cattle to force them toward the center. This forced the longhorns running behind to slow and try to follow the one in front. This broke up the flow of the stampede, just a little.

Heartened by his success, Mac kept up his work. Soon enough, entire segments of the herd had collided with slower-moving cattle, and the stampede stalled and finally became nothing more than the brutes milling about. Mac kept riding because he had only stopped a few hundred, and thousands more still ran wildly into the night.

He saw others from the Rolling J doing much the

same as he had done, but their efforts were less successful because they tried to turn greater numbers.
Joining the efforts of a cowboy he recognized as
being from San Antonio but for whom he had never
done more than serve a meal, Mac got a few of the
frightened cattle to stop. But his arm felt ready to fall
off. He touched the gun at his side and remembered
he had already exhausted it on the earlier stampede
when he was with Billy Duke.

"What do we do?" he shouted to the other cowboy,
but the pounding hooves drowned out his question.

Everything happened with lightning swiftness. His
companion's horse stumbled and fell, sending its rider
flying. Mac saw his work with the herd wasn't slowing
the run. Turning his tired horse, he came around. The
cowboy wasn't hurt, but his horse had broken a leg.

"Gotta do this. Hate it 'cuz he was a good horse."
The cowboy put a single bullet through the horse's
head.

"Here," Mac said, dropping to the ground. He
handed over his reins. "You know what you're doing.
I don't."

"Ain't gonna do much until the leaders wear
themselves out. But all I can do is try." The cowboy
took the reins and stepped up. "You watch yourself.
You bake real good biscuits."

With that he disappeared into the night. Mac wasn't
sure if it was a compliment or not, but he took it as
one. He had his place in the outfit. It just wasn't in
the saddle trying to herd cattle. Plodding along, he
tromped through the field torn up by the stampede.
More than one cow lowed in pain, legs broken just
like the cowboy's horse. Mac stopped by one pain-

wracked animal. He drew his S&W, broke it open, and ejected the spent brass. Fumbling around in his pockets, he found six cartridges, closed the gun, and took a deep breath. His first shot failed to kill the cow. With a better grip on his emotions, his second round put the animal out of its misery.

Mac ran out of bullets before he got back to the chuckwagon.

He sat for a few minutes, dead in body and soul. Then he searched for more ammunition, reloaded, tucked a handful of cartridges into his coat pocket, and saddled another horse. The distant noise had died down. He wasn't sure what that meant, but he had to find out. He rode into the dawn and saw dozens of fallen longhorns. One had dug its horn into the ground and been carried up and around by the rush of the cattle behind, breaking its neck. By the time Mac reached the small knot of wranglers, he had become deadened to any feeling for the animals.

Then he found reason to let his shock expand and totally encompass him.

Flagg stood beside two bodies stretched on the ground. Both were covered by slickers. Mac dismounted and walked forward slowly. Boots sticking out from under one of the raincoats looked familiar.

"Billy Duke?" His voice, already hoarse from shouting, came out in a barely discernible croak.

"Afraid so. And the other's Huey Matthis."

Mac didn't know Matthis beyond serving him meals three times a day. The men tended to become tightknit, small circles of friends hardly known outside their own personal circle. But first and foremost, they had been riders for the Rolling J ranch.

"What happened with the herd?" Mac saw dozens of cattle milling around, hunting for tufts of blue grama to graze on but disturbed by the coppery smell of blood that descended on the land like an evil fog.

"They ran into a river and turned. That was all it took for two men to break the stampede." Flagg's eyes darted to the bodies on the ground. "They saved a half dozen others. This is a damned shame."

"About the stampede," Mac began. He was responsible for Billy's and Huey's deaths. He had gone with Billy Duke on a fool's errand. If they hadn't gotten caught by the 23's night herders, gunfire wouldn't have spooked first one herd and then the other.

"We don't talk about it. Not ever," Flagg said. "I'm not superstitious, but putting some things into words makes them happen again. We can't afford that. First off we bury them."

"Here?"

"Where they fell is as good as any other."

"I'll help," Mac said, feeling even guiltier. "Flagg, I have to tell you something."

"No." Flagg fixed him with his ice-cold stare. "You won't say a damned word."

"But—"

Flagg took a quick step and bumped his chest against the cook's. He glared at Mac. His nostrils flared like a bull pawing the ground and getting ready to charge.

"No." He shoved Mac away, causing him to stumble. "Everyone's going to have twice the work as before. These two are dead and a half dozen others are so banged up they can hardly ride."

"They can ride in the chuckwagon."

"No, Mac, they *will* ride in the chuckwagon. You're going to tend to them 'til they're healed enough to get back to the herd."

Mac looked down at the slicker-covered shape that had been Billy Duke. A faint morning breeze caused the slicker to flap just a mite, as if the body beneath was trying to come back to life. Mac felt sick and looked away.

"He had family in Waco. His wages ought to be sent to them. A wife, boy, and a pa who's in a bad way."

"When we get to Abilene, you take care of it."

That was additional punishment for the calamity he had caused, Mac supposed.

"No good deed goes unpunished," he murmured. He wasn't sure if Flagg overheard. The trail boss turned away and barked orders to get the cattle bedded down in one herd instead of stragglers spread over half of Indian Territory.

Mac began digging and took longer than expected when he hit a layer of red clay almost as hard as rock. He scraped and chopped and finally dug down below it. Both men would rest easy here, safe from being dug up by hungry animals. He had heard a man had to be buried six feet under because coyotes could smell a decaying body if buried any less deeply. Mac knew nothing about that. Billy and Huey would be under clay that even the most determined animal would have trouble clawing through.

He fashioned crosses for them and used his knife to scratch crude names into the wood. As he drove the crosses into the ground, he heard men all around him. Tears in his eyes, he saw everyone in the company, including Patrick Flagg, had come back.

"Go on, Mac. Say a few words."

"I'm not a preacher. Fact is, I never spent much time in church, so I don't know what to say."

"Do it," Flagg ordered with a lash in his words.

Mac drew in a deep breath, then said, "Dear Lord, accept these two good men. Their lives were full of trouble and pain, but they died doing honest work. They saved others who rode alongside. Bless them." Mac wondered if this was enough, then decided it had to be. Looking down from Heaven, seeing everything, God knew what had happened and would accept Billy Duke and Huey Matthis for what they had tried to do before dying.

He hoped Billy's rustling wouldn't count too much against him. Mac swallowed hard. When his time came, he hoped it wouldn't count against him, either.

Returning to the chuckwagon, he fixed breakfast for the men. It was quiet, somber, and none of the joshing went on that he had come to expect. For that he was glad.

As he cleaned up, Flagg came to him, looking worried.

"We got a problem, Mac. That river stopped the stampede good and proper, but it also put us miles off the Shawnee Trail. I don't know where to ford the river here, and if we did, we'd have to cross back if we got ourselves caught in an oxbow. Every river we ford costs us a few more cattle."

"What do you intend to do?"

"I'm riding with the herd along the river. I want you to cut across country and find out if we can stay on the west side of the river. We've lost so much time, we'd need to make up a week or more to get to Abilene before some of the other herds."

"The H Bar H?"

"Compass Jack's got us beat, no matter what. I don't begrudge him that because he's a good man. The others beating us to the railroad makes my hackles rise."

"You want me to drive the wagon?"

"Let Rattler do it. He got his leg all bunged up. Him and the others who got injured last night have to ride in the wagon anyway. You take a horse and do the scouting."

"Flagg, I want to tell you something about what—"

"Quit lollygagging and ride. I said we have a week to make up, and I mean it. Go, go!"

Flagg shooed him away like he was only an annoying fly. Mac found a horse in the remuda, saddled it, and reflected on how he had his choice of tack now. They had gone through so many men that less than half their original company remained. If they lost any more men, finishing the drive might not be possible.

He set out to scout the trail Flagg wanted. Not crossing the river would save them a day or more. He knew how the trail boss worried they would find a bend in the river and have to cross twice. With the wind in his face and warm sun on his back, he set out to find the best route possible. The Shawnee Trail had proven a good course for them, but he had no idea how to find the already blazed trail again, except by pure luck. As he rode, he worried about coming across the 23 herd.

Flagg had to know about his part in causing the stampede. Billy had paid with his life. Flagg's punishment had been even crueler. Mac wanted to confess. Instead, he had to let the guilt fester inside. All he could do was try to learn from it and make things right again by doing the best job possible.

With the crew being so shorthanded, he wondered if he would ever sleep again this side of Abilene. Cooking, scouting, riding night herd, he had more than any two men would handle. It would only get worse the longer they were on the trail. He yawned, stretched, and tried to get comfortable in the saddle. Finally deciding the more he ached, the easier it would be to stay awake, he bounced and bobbed and let the horse's gait jolt him constantly. After a couple miles, he settled down and found a more comfortable seat.

Punishing himself served no purpose and only made it more likely he would make a mistake. Riding atop a hill, he rubbed his eyes clear of sleep and carefully studied the lay of the land. It was good country, with rich earth and clumps of trees scattered around to provide wood for the buildings he spotted. A decent-sized farmhouse sat on a level patch of ground not a mile off. Behind it rose a red-painted barn.

Mac found himself grinning in memory. His pa's farm had looked like this. He imagined the sound of chickens in a coop and maybe pigs oinking as they rolled around in their pen, waiting to be slopped. Huge swathes had been cut through forests to make way for farmland. Driving the herd through a nester's farm would bring out the guns and recriminations, but it was late enough in the year that some of the crops had been harvested. Those fields might benefit from a herd tramping through, breaking up the earth as good as any disc harrow and turning under weeds to serve as fertilizer for next spring's crops.

He rode down the slope toward the farm. Barren fields stretched as far as he could see. Perfect for a herd to tromp through, all he needed was the farmer's permission.

So intent on gauging distances and directions, he didn't hear them come up on him.

"I swear, mister, I will shoot you out of the saddle if you move a muscle."

He moved more than a muscle. He was so startled he jumped a foot and caused his horse to shy. Mac turned and saw a farmer with a rifle clutched in his hand and two strapping young boys alongside.

"Just go on an' plug him, Pa," one of the youngsters urged. "It'll save us a passel of trouble if he don't go get the rest of his gang."

"Whoa, wait, don't go doing what your boy says." Mac raised his hands. "These are your sons?"

"Are," the farmer said. He dressed in bib overalls, heavy boots, a denim shirt, and a straw hat so tattered along the brim it did little to protect his face from the sun.

"I've got a business proposition for you."

"Ain't gonna bring your filthy cows through my property." He lifted the rifle and sighted along its barrel. From Mac's vantage, it looked as if he peered down a bore the size of a shotgun.

"Easy now. Your crops are in. We'd be willing to swap a prime heifer or two for passage."

"Nope." The nester tucked the rifle into his shoulder as if he anticipated a heavy recoil when he fired.

"You people done ruined more'n one of our fields with your cattle," one boy said. "We been told all about how you destroy everything in your way, and he wouldn't lie to us." He glanced at his father for encouragement. As far as Mac saw, the farmer said and did nothing, but the boy took heart in that. "You're next thing to criminals for what you do to good farmland. You deserve eternal damnation."

"Those fields haven't been touched," Mac said. "I used to work on my family's farm up in Missouri, and I can appreciate your concern. I—"

"Git."

The farmer motioned with his rifle for Mac to ride on.

"You don't want to shoot me. I'm not armed, except for my rifle, and it's sheathed. We can discuss this and come to—"

The farmer pulled the trigger.

CHAPTER 20

The bullet passed within an inch of Mac's nose. He jerked away so abruptly that he fell off his horse. He landed hard, then had to curl up in a ball to keep the horse from stepping on him as it nervously pawed the ground. Rolling got him away from the hooves. He came to his feet, sorry now that he hadn't worn his Smith & Wesson.

Then he realized the farmer had no qualms about plugging him. If he'd slung his gun belt around his waist, the nester had reason to kill him outright. With both his boys as witnesses, the murder would be overlooked by the local law.

Mac held his hands up to make sure the farmer saw he wasn't going for a hideout gun.

"I'm not armed. You can't murder me in cold blood."

"Not cold."

"Do you cut down anyone who rides up to your spread?"

"Farm. Only cowboys call it a spread."

Mac saw the determination in the man's face. He believed he was protecting his farm against destruction, and no amount of talk would convince him otherwise.

"I'll go. Let me mount and ride on out." He started to lower his arms, but the set to the farmer's body made him freeze. He kept his hands over his head as he went to his horse, found the reins, and pulled himself up into the saddle.

Even mounted, he held his hands up where they were in plain sight.

"I don't take kindly to being shot at like that."

"Kill him, Pa," one of the boys said. "It'll save trouble later. It will!"

Mac saw that the boy's attitude was come by honestly. The farmer considered the merits of doing as his son suggested.

"No need for any more shooting," Mac said quickly. "I'm leaving."

"Don't come back." The farmer pointed with the rifle, then pulled it back into line with Mac's chest.

Hands still up, using his knees to guide the horse, he turned and started the animal walking away. More than anything in the world, he wanted to gallop. He felt the gun centered on his spine. Another bullet would shatter his backbone, killing him if he was lucky and leaving him paralyzed if he wasn't.

Still, lighting a shuck like that would show how frightened he was of the farmer and his two sons. It never paid to show weakness. But when he topped a rise some distance away and out of sight of the farmer, Mac brought the horse to a gallop to get as far away as possible from the homicidal sodbusters.

As he rode back in the direction of the herd, Mac

took care to memorize every detail of the country-side. This was the route they needed to get back on schedule, but the farmer stood in their way. Going around him and his property was possible, but Mac worried that would only add to the delay.

Flagg saw him before he located the trail boss. Trotting up, Flagg looked grim.

"I hope you've got good news, Mac. I crossed the river, and sure as shooting, we'd be going into the middle of a damned oxbow, like I feared. If we don't find a quick trail on this side of the river, we'll be an-other week behind getting to Abilene. Give me some good news. You find a good way to the west?"

Mac explained his problem with the farmer. He took his hat off and examined it for new holes. The bullet had missed both him and his hat, but that was the only good luck he'd had.

"I've come across men like that farmer," Flagg said as he eased his back in the saddle. "There's no rea-soning with them."

"If we had some money left, he might be con-vinced by the flash of greenbacks." Even as the words left his lips, Mac regretted reminding the trail boss how he had used the drive's money to pay for liquor to get Marshal Wilkinson drunker than a lord. It had been necessary to spring Flagg from the jailhouse. That incident brought back unpleasant memories for both of them.

"He's got at least two boys. Probably a wife. Maybe other family in the house. Younger boys, girls. That's quite a brood to feed. A cow would give them fresh meat for a week. Two cows, with one's meat jerked and salted, would last them through the winter." Flagg looked at the clear blue sky. "This part of the country gets mighty fierce Blue Northers blowing through come January. Snow two feet deep makes a body rely on stored food. We can be the difference between starving and living to plant in the spring."

"Maybe you can make the case to him. I was warned off." Mac remembered the whine of the bullet past his face. "And watch out for his boys. They're young but bloodthirsty."

"I crossed a well-traveled road a mile back that away," Flagg said, pointing. "It has to lead to a town. You go on in and ask around for other ways to move the herd through. That one farmer might have a bug up his ass for no good reason. Others liking the taste of prime beef can be persuaded."

"How many cattle can I offer?"

"Use your own good judgment, Mac. Right now, I'd give half the herd to get the rest through, but that's a mite extreme and my aggravation speaking." Flagg rode away, leaving Mac to stew. He had a new job. Not only was he cook and scout and wrangler, now he was a negotiator.

Kicking at his horse's flanks, he got onto the road Flagg had found and turned toward town. A twenty-minute ride took him to the edge of the settlement. He looked around before slowly riding down the middle of the main street. Nobody turned away from him. They all showed the usual curiosity about a stranger, but nothing hostile. Not one of them scowled at him or spat like the farmer. The nester had taken one look and opposed him and the herd going across his land.

Mac tied his horse to a ring in front of the general

store and went inside. He heaved a sigh when he saw all the supplies he couldn't afford.

"Howdy, mister," the proprietor greeted him. "What can I do for you?"

"Not a whole lot unless you're willing to swap a cow or two for supplies. I'm with a herd that's been on the trail for close to six weeks, and we're running low on a lot of things, like vegetables." Mac took a deep sniff of a box holding onions and garlic bulbs. Those would go a long way toward giving flavor to whatever he fixed for the cowboys.

"Don't swap like that. Wish I could."

"Could? Is there something keeping you from dealing with a trail drive?"

The man had close-set eyes and a long, pointed nose. The mustache on his lip twitched like a mouse's whiskers. He looked around as if someone might trap him. Two women at the back of the store measured cloth from a big bolt. The clerk looked back and shook his head.

"Can't do business like that. Can't."

The women stared coldly at Mac. He politely touched the brim of his hat and flashed a smile. The younger woman's lips crinkled up in the beginning of a return smile, only to be quickly quashed by the older woman. Turning back to the clerk, he asked in a low voice, "Who's the woman wearing the gold cross?"

"That's the pastor's wife. And her daughter Ruth."

"It didn't take her long to come to a conclusion about my character, did it?"

The clerk started to laugh, then sobered and nodded brusquely.

"They got their reasons. Now if you want to buy something, it's cash on the barrelhead. No trading."

"Much obliged." Mac turned to leave, only to find the door blocked by a man with big girth and a star pinned on his vest. He nodded politely and said, "Marshal," then waited for the lawman to move so he could leave.

The marshal didn't budge.

"You come on with me," the lawman rumbled. "We got to talk."

A thousand things flashed through Mac's head. Not the least of which was the chance that this star packer had seen the wanted poster like the one he'd snatched off the marshal's desk in Lewiston and taken from the barber in Waco. But the man stood with his thumbs hooked behind his gun belt. He made no move for the heavy iron dangling at his hip. If he intended to arrest a man wanted for murder in New Orleans, he likely would have brought a scatter-gun with him. At the very least, his revolver would be pulled and aimed, not resting easy in its holster.

"I always enjoy a friendly chat."

"That's what it'll be." The marshal stepped back and let Mac out.

As he exited the store, the hairs on the back of his neck rose, waiting for the marshal to draw that six-shooter and buffalo him. Or worse. Getting shot in the back made an arrest a lot easier. But the marshal huffed and puffed as he caught up.

"Over there's my office."

"That's convenient. Right next to the saloon."

"I didn't pick it. With the saloon that close, I have to break up more than my share of fights that would otherwise take care of themselves. Yes, sir, I've seen two men whaling away at each other like mortal enemies. After a few punches and maybe a bloody nose or swollen eye, they use each other to stand up, then go back in to drink. They've gotten to be best of friends."

"But now you throw them in the calaboose?"

"Something like that. We got men who hate each other's guts now when they ought to be drinking buddies. Why, two men who came to town as partners now cross the street if they see the other. Mark my words, one of these days, one's gonna shoot the other, probably from ambush and in the back." The marshal shook his head sadly. "That'll be a pity. Both of them are good men."

"A man like you should be able to talk them out of their feud. Why don't you move the jail away from the saloon? There must be other places that would serve as well."

"Out of sight, out of mind." He heaved his belly up and down, using both hands. With that he went into the jailhouse, strode around to his chair and sank down. The wood creaked as it took his bulk.

Mac looked around. There wasn't a chair for him to sit. He moved closer to a sheaf of wanted posters nailed to the wall. He didn't see himself peering back from the top one, so he figured it was safe to stand there.

"We want you folks to just keep on going," the marshal said. "This is a peaceable town, 'cept when drovers come through. Then things get out of hand."

"We have to move on pretty quick, Marshal," Mac said, "but if we cross the river, it'll add a week or more to our travel. That farmer out west of town took a shot at me."

"That must be George. Him and his boys are pretty . . . religious."

"I ran into the preacher's wife and daughter over at the general store. That was an experience."

"I'm sure it was. Let me guess. The girl took to you right away, and Mrs. Hunnicut didn't." The marshal grinned at Mac's expression. "If it was the other way around, you'd be out of town by now, driving your herd like a son of a bitch."

Mac frowned. "Are you saying it's the preacher's wife who's against us driving the herd across farmland?"

"You didn't hear that from me—no, sir. I'll lie like a trouper if you say I did, too. I have to live in this town, and the pastor's got an iron grip on folks and their opinions."

"And his wife has an iron grip on him."

"You are one smart gent."

"Why is she so opposed to trail drives? Or is it the men? I promise we won't come into town, not a one of us. There won't be fights or saloons shot up. Nothing of the sort."

"You'd be surprised how many trail bosses make that claim." The lawman cleared his throat. "And I'm always surprised how many keep that promise. But one of them didn't when Mrs. Hunnicut was a youngster. Promises were made and broken. The drive went right through one of her pa's fields with winter wheat just sprouting. Ruined it. The family came close to going bankrupt."

"And?"

The marshal bounced his paunch, then stood.

"You're way too smart to be a cowboy. You ought to get a job where you can use that brain of yours. I never heard, and she don't tell anyone, but I suspect something else went on."

"Forcibly?"

"Never had that feel to her words. More like she fell for one of the cowboys, and he used her for his own pleasure before moving on with the herd."

"She can't blame every cowboy for what one did!"

"It's not logical, but if you've ever been in love, you know logical's not got a whole lot to do with it." The marshal eyed him closely. "I see a glimmering there. You *do* know. Now, clear on out of town, or I'll have to run you out on a rail. You're smart enough to know why."

"Where's the pastor's church?"

"Now, son, you're showing me a stream of black, tarry stupid. Getting Pastor Hunnicut to talk his wife into letting you do squat is not going to happen. Ever. Not this side of the Pearly Gates."

"I don't want to drive the herd up there," Mac said, eyes rolling toward the heavens, "but I have an idea that might appeal to both the preacher and his wife."

"More power to you. Just don't make me arrest you." The marshal shooed him out of the office and followed into the street. "And it's not a cell you'll be seeing the inside of if you try wooing Ruth Hunnicut as a way to her ma. It'll be the inside of a coffin."

"Don't worry, Marshal."

"I won't worry. I never do. I just keep the peace

and make sure Mrs. Hunnicut doesn't disapprove of whatever I do."

Mac watched the rotund marshal waddle away and started to fetch his horse back at the general store. He hesitated. A quick look at the stack of wanted posters would tell him if Leclerc had spread the word about the murder at the Dueling Oaks this far north. He twisted this way and that, then decided not to look. The marshal wasn't the kind who ignored details, not if it kept things quiet in town. A notorious murderer would have him hauling out his six-gun as fast as he could. While he might not be all that fast reaching around his beer gut, a dozen deputies might rove the town keeping the peace, too, for all Mac knew.

He mounted his horse and rode slowly through the town. Townsfolk weren't hostile at all, and this marshal certainly didn't have an attitude like Marshal Wilkinson. Everything rational could be talked about. At least he hoped so. He halted when he saw the church steeple rising behind a store on the main street. Cutting down an alley, he found the road running to the church. It was well kept, whitewashed, and had two men cutting weeds down in the front. To one side stretched a cemetery divided off into sections.

As he rode past, he saw that both the Elks and the Masons had maintained plots for their members. The rest of the cemetery showed some disrepair, but not enough to cause mention. As he rode to the side of the church, his half-baked idea turned into a solid conviction.

Before he could enter the front, the preacher came

out, clutching a Bible to his chest as if it would protect him from any bullets Mac sent his way. He was a medium-sized man with a mostly bald head and watery blue eyes behind a pair of spectacles.

"Good afternoon, Reverend." Mac took his hat off and held it with both hands, waiting for acknowledgment.

"My wife saw you in Mr. Dunlap's store," the preacher said without returning the greeting.

"If that's the general store, I reckon she did, sir. She was measuring some mighty pretty cloth, for a dress, unless I miss my guess." Mac held back his opinion that it would be a dress for their daughter because that would just derail whatever goodwill he had going so far.

"She's handy with needle and thread."

"I'm sure she is, sir." Mac said nothing more. The preacher got a bit nervous. When he started to speak, Mac cut him off. "I've talked with your marshal. A fine lawman, isn't he?"

"Yes, he is. I—"

"He agreed that a town social is exactly what everyone needs before the weather gets real cold."

"Social? What're you talking about?"

"On behalf of the Rolling J ranch and Mr. Jefferson, the owner, we'd like to host a church social." He pointed to the area freshly cleared of weeds. "That's a fine place for me to do the cooking."

The sky pilot frowned, obviously baffled, and said, "What are you going on about?"

"Why, I'm sorry if I didn't make it clear. I'm the Rolling J cook, and my boss would appreciate the chance to show his appreciation for everyone in town by doing a Texas-style barbeque right here. You can do a little preaching, the folks can socialize. Why, I suspect this might draw in people you haven't seen in a while, maybe not since Easter."

"There are, indeed, those who only make it to church at Easter and Christmas."

"Well, they'll want to sample prime beef done up special just for them. If you want to make it a pot-luck, you can get the ladies involved and let them show off their cooking and baking skills."

"That's a good idea. Something Mrs. Hunnicut has been talking about."

"We have to move on soon," Mac said. "The next couple days would be fine for us. I'm sure we can get everything arranged by then. How many cows should I fix? One? Two? There'd have to be a donation to the church, of course. A couple more cows?"

"A donation?"

"I can dig a roasting pit over there, away from where it would cause any trouble and be easy to fill in afterward. You'll never know it was there."

Mac and the preacher walked about the yard, making arrangements until Mrs. Hunnicut came out of the church with her daughter trailing behind. It took a bit more convincing, but with both the preacher and his daughter working on the woman, she finally relented. From there, Mac felt as if he were racing downhill, the wind at his back.

All he had to do now was convince Patrick Flagg that hosting a church social was the way to get the herd moving again.

CHAPTER 21

"You're such a good cook," Ruth Hunnicut said, peering into the pot Mac stirred slowly. "Are you going to keep cooking like this after you're married?" The honey-haired young beauty looked at him with wide brown eyes. Her earnest expression made him a tad uneasy.

"Only if I had a houseful of children to feed."

"How many children would you like?"

"I cook for twenty or so cowboys. At least that many."

"Twenty?" She looked perplexed. "That's a powerful lot of kids running around. What job would you do to keep them? And a wife?"

"Why, I'd have to be out on a trail drive most all the year."

"Oh, you," Ruth said, playfully slapping at the hand clutching the wood spoon. "You're pulling my leg. I know it."

"You want to take over stirring the beans while I

tend to the brisket? It looks like we're getting another ten or fifteen people coming to the social."

"I'd be honored . . . Mac." Her hand lingered just a moment on his as she took the spoon.

He didn't quite run to take care of starting a new batch of barbeque, but it came close. Flirting with the pastor's daughter was playing with fire. She had her cap set for him, and he wanted no part of it. She was pretty enough and certainly of marrying age— and that's what spooked him. Pickings for a husband in this town might be slim. Her pa might not chase off would-be suitors, but he didn't doubt her ma did. Mrs. Hunnicut bustled about like a queen bee, talking to the women and berating them for not getting their husbands and brothers to church more often. Her husband's approach was gentler.

Mac saw himself caught in this town, tied to Ruth's apron strings, and browbeaten by her mother. It was a terrifying picture.

As he worked on the beef, Flagg came over. The trail boss watched for a spell, then said, "I've got to hand it to you, Mac. This is one fine shindig."

"No dancing. Mrs. Hunnicut doesn't believe in it."

"But I've watched the preacher. He's enjoying himself. You think he'll talk to them about letting the herd cross their farmland?"

He glanced in the direction of the farmer and his two sons. A woman, undoubtedly the farmer's wife, talked a blue streak with Mrs. Hunnicut.

"I promised the preacher a couple more cows after we're finished. That ought to convince him to have words with Slausen, his name is. For the good of the congregation."

"Slausen?" Flagg shook his head. "His boys stick close to him, like they'd get lost if they strayed too far."

"They want to see him shoot me between the eyes. They're a nasty bunch."

"And that filly's not so nasty. I saw how she was making cow eyes at you."

"I'd sooner juggle sticks of dynamite." Mac began ladling out the sauce and pouring it over his cooking beef.

"Good. It shows you haven't lost your senses."

"I want to get back on the trail. Cooking for all these people is fine, but I'd rather it was just the riders."

"I don't know, Mac. Cooking for that little girl's likely to get you into her bed. I heard what she was saying."

Mac aimed a spoonful of sauce at Flagg, who dodged it. He made the rounds of several ladies and the potluck they had brought, praising them on such fine vittles. For his part, he wasn't lying. Tasting anyone else's cooking proved a real treat, and some of the women were mighty fine cooks. It was too bad the outfit remained with the cattle and had been ordered by Flagg to keep the longhorns ready for movement.

Or maybe it wasn't too bad, Mac reflected. Being on the trail for so long, away from both liquor and women, he didn't trust them all to be on their best behavior, even at a church social. No liquor being served might make the men all the more insistent about forcing themselves on the women. That was a sure road to losing all the goodwill he had created with the pastor and, hopefully, his wife.

He had to grin. Ruth Hunnicut certainly had good-will to spare for him. He turned back to his work and tried to forget about Ruth.

Slausen came over, his two sons trailing behind him like bad odors.

"Give me some of that," the farmer said with his usual dour expression.

"My pleasure." Mac served him, then the boys. He wanted to press the matter of driving the herd across his fields but held back. The man had the look of someone spoiling for a fight. Better to let the preacher approach him and do the convincing. The preacher and his wife had more influence than anyone else would, at least, though the man had the look of someone so pigheaded that nothing would change his mind.

The Slausen family moved off in a tight knot, working on barbecue, beans, and a bit of peach cobbler one woman had brought. Mac's scheme of making this a potluck took away the need for Flagg to figure out how to pay for any food that wasn't on the hoof. He was talking to an elderly couple when he caught sight of a man riding up and looking around. Something about his attitude put Mac on alert.

"Do either of you know the newcomer?" He pointed at the rider with his spoon.

The man turned, adjusted his spectacles, and then made a sour face.

"That good-for-nothing has no place here. That's Lucas Langdon. His pa used to be a rich man but lost it all in the war. Everyone thought Lucas had gone off and joined the army, but chances are good he was off hiding somewhere. He comes into town to make trouble every month or two."

Mac didn't ask which army. That didn't matter. Lucas Langdon dismounted and swaggered over to a table, sampling things with his dirty fingers as he went from one end to the other. The congregation parted in front of him, not wanting to tangle. Mac stepped out, wooden cooking spoon in his hand. He was all too aware that he had left his S&W in his saddlebags, and his horse was corralled out back of the church.

He blocked Langdon's path and said, "Why don't you grab yourself a plate?"

With a sneer, the man said, "Now why would I want to do that? I can get what I want just fine." Langdon reached out and plucked an ear of corn off a platter, took a bite, and tossed it over his shoulder.

Mac stepped up, poking the bowl of the spoon into the man's solar plexus. He got a grunt of pain from him.

"Now that was perfectly fine corn you threw away. Pick it up before the ants get it."

"Who the hell are you, little man?" Langdon pushed Mac back. His hand drifted down to the big iron swinging on his hip. The move looked practiced and intended to cow anybody facing him.

Mac wasn't inclined to be intimidated.

He whacked Langdon's knuckles with his spoon. The gunman yelped and took his right hand away to suck on his bruised knuckles.

"You shouldn't have done that," Langdon said ominously.

"Behave yourself or leave. The saloon's still open. I think they're serving pigs' knuckles for lunch. That'd suit you better than food for people."

Langdon reared back to punch Mac, but the cook didn't retreat. He stepped up and drove the spoon into the man's gut again. This pushed him off balance, so he staggered and failed to deliver the blow. Mac never gave him a chance to recover. He kept walking and poking with his spoon. When the chance presented itself, he whacked Langdon on the side of the head with the spoon, causing him to drop to one knee. Mac towered over him now.

"It's about time you left. Now."

Mac felt someone at his elbow, taking hold of it. He glanced back and saw Ruth Hunnicut. Her eyes glowed—and it was in adoration for him. Everything he did from cooking to facing down a bully made him even bigger in her eyes.

"Don't even think on it." The cold words came from Mac's right.

Flagg had pushed back his coat so he could grab for his Colt. Lucas Langdon was getting his balance back, although still on his knees, so he could draw and gun down Mac.

"That's all right, Mr. Flagg. This gentleman was just leaving. He was just leaving without causing any more trouble." Mac lifted the spoon and held it as if he wanted to lay it alongside Langdon's head again.

"We ain't done, you and me," Langdon blustered. "When you don't have a gunslick protecting you, it'll be just you and me." Langdon got to his feet and backed away.

Every inch of the way, Mac thought he would slap leather. A step to the side interposed his body to protect Ruth Hunnicut if lead should fly. It didn't. Langdon backed down, turned, and almost ran to his horse.

"Oh, Mac, you're about the bravest man I ever did see." Ruth clung to his arm and pressed her cheek against his shoulder. If the situation had been different, he would have liked that. As it was, the commotion had caused everyone to notice, and that included the preacher and his wife.

"Are you all right, dear?" Mrs. Hunnicut came over and pried her daughter's hand loose from Mac's arm. "You must have been so frightened by that bully."

"Oh, no, Ma, not with Mac here to protect me. Not only does he cook, he's a hero!"

"That's not what happened," Mac said hastily. "I mean, I can cook, but it was Flagg who ran off Langdon."

"The ruffian." Mrs. Hunnicut swung her daughter around and marched her away. Ruth looked back at Mac and smiled. He wasn't sure who her mother meant when she spoke of a "ruffian."

"Mr. Flagg, you should take off that sidearm. It is not appropriate for this gathering." The preacher looked pained having to say that. It made clear who his wife thought was the barbarian at the party.

"That's all right. I've got to be getting back to the herd. The sooner we move out, the better."

"I . . . I'll speak with Mr. Mackenzie about that

later." The preacher looked around to see if his wife was out of earshot. She was, but he thought better of delivering the permission Flagg needed to send the herd tromping across Slausen's field.

"We're getting more folks in to serve all the time, sir," Mac said to distract the preacher. "Now might be a good time to let everyone know of the Lord's bounty."

Setting the man on the path he understood proved a good thing. Mac kept cooking and serving until the preacher got onto a stepladder and began his sermon. Mac found himself caught up in the flow of the man's words and even let some of the important ideas creep in. It had been a long time since he'd been in church.

He turned somber as he recalled that the last time had been for his parents' funeral. And the next time he had expected was for his wedding with Evangeline Holdstock.

Reverend Hunnicut got fired up, and when he got a second wind, he gave every indication of taking the rest of the afternoon to say his piece. Mac cleaned up and put his kettles aside, making sure to stash away some of the best food remaining on the tables so the Rolling J hands could have a feast of their own when he got back.

As he heaved a pot around to put it in the back of a wagon he had borrowed to move his gear, he heard a shrill scream that died abruptly, as if smothered by a gag. He ran around the side of the church and saw Ruth Hunnicut struggling against Lucas Langdon's overpowering strength. He had tied his bandana over her mouth to prevent her outcries and held both her wrists in one big hand.

"Let her go!" Mac charged toward them, then dug in his heels and stopped dead in his tracks.

Langdon had his revolver out and pointed directly at him. The smirk on the gunman's lips made anger boil up inside Mac. Bullet or no bullet, he was going to wipe that look off Langdon's face. Seeing the change in his attacker's demeanor, Langdon shifted the gun to Ruth's temple.

"Come any closer and I'll splatter her brains all over the back of her daddy's church. No amount of whitewash will ever get the stains off."

"Let her go. This is between you and me."

"I hated you the second I laid eyes on you, you little son of a bitch," Langdon said. "That's true enough, but I've had my eye on this one for a long time. Her and me, we're riding out of here and gonna enjoy ourselves. At least I am until she wears out."

He cocked the gun when Mac started forward again. Ruth struggled in his grip, then let out a tiny "oh!" He smacked the gun barrel alongside her head, knocking her out. With a heave, he lifted her belly down over his saddle. Never moving the pistol from her head, he mounted. Mac knew what was going to happen then.

He was already diving for cover as Langdon rode out, spraying lead all over the place. As the swift rata-plan of hoofbeats faded, Mac came up dirty but unscathed.

Several members of the crowd that had attended the social rushed around the church, drawn by the shots. Mac called to them, "That was Lucas Langdon! He kidnapped Ruth!"

The preacher stopped short with a look of horror on his face. That lasted only for a second. Then a fierce expression that belied his normally mild appearance came over him. He turned and exclaimed, "I'll get my horse!"

Mac stopped him. "I'll take care of it."

"The marshal, he—"

"Really?" Mac had nothing against the marshal, but he hardly looked up to the task of facing down a gunman like Langdon.

"He . . . he's in town. It would take him forever to get after them. By then—"

"I'll take care of it," Mac repeated. He didn't wait for the reverend to contradict him. He ran to his horse, opened the saddlebags, and strapped on his gun belt. The heavy weight at his hip didn't slow him at all as he vaulted into the saddle and galloped after Langdon and his hostage.

For the first time, he appreciated the time he had spent scouting for the herd. His sharp eyes picked up details as he rode along that he might have missed with less experience hunting for a trail. Here and there he saw a hoofprint, but the crushed grass and broken limbs made the trail easy to follow. Langdon had only a few minutes' head start on him, but the man galloped full speed while Mac had to track more slowly. It still proved easy enough because Langdon arrogantly thought no one would come after him.

Mac had to admit that no one at the church social was likely to, not after Patrick Flagg had left to tend to the Rolling J herd. They were all churchgoing men, and not one of them had worn a gun. Life in this town had been too easy, and outlaws like Lang-

don ran out of control against a marshal who barely
fit through a normal-sized doorway.

A small shed off to the side of the road drew Mac's
attention. He reined in and sat watching the shed,
not sure what made him do so. Then he heard a
horse nickering. Rather than keep on what looked
like the trail, he rode around the shed and recognized Langdon's horse tied to a sapling. He had run
the man to ground.

From inside the cabin came tiny sounds that turned
him cold inside.

"Langdon! Get your ass out here right now!"

Mac knew better than to believe the man would
do any such thing. He rode closer to the ramshackle
shed and jumped onto the roof. One boot went
through the old, rotten wood. The other failed to
find purchase. Flopping down, he slid a few inches,
caught himself, and looked over the edge.

Langdon fired a few shots through the roof, tearing holes inches away from where Mac lay.

"Ruth!" he shouted. "Are you hurt?"

"Mac? Is that you, Mac?" She sounded terrified, as
well she might. "He . . . he's tied my hands. He—"

The woman's words cut off abruptly. Mac imagined the owlhoot clamping his hand over her mouth.
He counted to three and then almost laughed out
loud. Langdon let out a howl of pain. She had bitten
him.

Since jumping onto the roof hadn't really worked,
he swung off and dropped to the ground. One step
forward let him kick the door in. It slammed back
and pulled off its hinges. Ruth knelt on the floor

with her hands bound behind her back. She looked up at Langdon, who clutched his left hand. Blood dripped between the fingers on his right hand.

"You can't even handle a woman," Mac told the kidnapper. "I'm nothing but a drover, but I'm going to put you in your grave."

Langdon wiped his bloody hand on his shirt, then reached for his pistol. Ruth surged up and slammed into him, knocking him against the far wall. Again the old wood gave way. Langdon toppled through it.

"Out, get out. Run!" Mac grabbed her and shoved her behind him in the direction of the road.

He kicked away more of the rotted wood wall and stepped out. Lucas Langdon scrambled to his feet and squared off, his hand hovering over his gun.

"Come on, let's see what you're made of," he jeered. "I've killed more men than you got fingers and toes." He turned slightly to reduce the distance he had to move to get his gun out and pointed in Mac's direction with his left hand, a move intended to distract his opponent.

"I doubt that. But maybe you believe it because you're too dumb to have ever learned how to count."

The world moved in slow motion for Mac. Fingers curled around the butt of his Model 3, closed. He drew and used his left hand to fan off a round. Another and another. Somewhere he realized that Langdon hadn't even cleared leather as the third round drove through his chest.

As slow as the world had become, it just as suddenly sped up. Mac saw Langdon straighten. His limp fingers released his hold on the gun. As if coming to attention, Langdon's knees stiffened. He toppled backward like a tree cut in the forest and crashed to the ground, dead before he hit.

Mac had not only outdrawn him, he had outshot a gunman. All three of his rounds had found deadly targets in the man's chest. He heard a gasp and looked up to see Ruth Hunnicut staring at him. Her brown eyes were wide, and her mouth gaped.

"You killed him," she finally got out. "You killed him and saved me!"

"Reckon so," was all Mac could say.

CHAPTER 22

Mac rode slowly, uncomfortable with Ruth Hunnicut's arms around his waist. Her hands kept moving down too low. Finally, she settled for gripping his gun belt and resting her cheek against his back.

"Nobody's ever had anything so terrible happen to them in town," she said.

"I'm sorry you were the victim," he said.

"I . . . I like it that you saved me." She clung to him a little tighter, making him even more uneasy. Such behavior, especially involving the preacher's daughter, would get him strung up amid the cheers and jeers of the congregation. Her ma would be the one putting the noose around his neck.

"Anyone would have done it." The words sounded hollow to him. No one he had seen in this town was likely to ride to her rescue the way he had. The marshal might be good for dealing with drunks, but facing down a desperado like Lucas Langdon stretched far beyond his capabilities as a lawman.

"But it was *you*, Mac. You did it."

He saw the church steeple and slowed a little more. He should have enjoyed the ride back with a pretty girl clinging so intimately to him, but dealing with her pa, and especially her ma, occupied his thoughts almost completely now.

"And you can cook." Ruth laughed at this and turned to kiss his shoulder. "You're so different from every other man in this town."

"There's your pa. Climb on down."

"Let's ride up like this. I want—"

He shifted his weight and caught her off balance. She yelped as she tumbled off. Hanging onto his waist kept her from falling, but it took her a moment to get her feet under her. By then, he had maneuvered his horse a few feet away. If the preacher saw how she was clinging to him, he didn't show it.

"Ruth! Thank the Lord, you're safe!" He grabbed her and hugged her so hard he threatened to crush her. She fought free and held him at arm's length.

"You should thank Mac instead. He saved me. And he shot that terrible man. He killed him before he . . . before . . ."

"She's safe, sir," Mac called. "The marshal ought to know what happened and fetch in Langdon's body and his horse."

Pastor Hunnicut didn't look at Mac. Instead he gave his daughter a thorough looking-over to be sure Mac wasn't lying.

"He didn't touch you?"

"Mac rescued me before that!"

"I meant him." The reverend looked hard at Mac.

"No! He was a perfect gentleman. He kept Langdon from doing anything."

"Thank you, young man."

"Do come on in and have a drink of water. You must be thirsty after so much . . . excitement." Ruth's come-on was obvious, even to her pa. Especially to him.

"You need to get back to your herd." The reverend spoke in a flat tone.

"It'll be mighty good if we can find the right trail." Mac knew he shouldn't say such a thing, but he wanted to get on with the cattle drive as soon as possible. "If we don't move on right now, we'll have to stay around town for a spell."

Ruth squealed with glee at the prospect of the herd lingering in the vicinity. This decided her pa.

"I need to counsel Mr. Slausen and his family." He took Ruth by the arm and swung her about, almost frog-marching her to their small house set behind the church. She looked over her shoulder, not understanding what was going on.

Mac smiled and waved, then kicked at his horse to get it galloping away. As he rode around the church to where the social had been held, he saw that the owner of the borrowed wagon had already pulled out with all his kettles and pans. He got to the road and reached the herd in less than a half hour. Flagg already had the cowboys spread out around the herd, at point, at the sides, and many more than usual behind the herd to keep them moving.

Flagg rode alongside him and asked, "Where the hell have you been, Mac? That fella from town brought out your pots and pans so Rattler could put them back in the chuckwagon, but he didn't know where you were."

"There was some excitement after you left."

Flagg's forehead creased in a frown. "More trouble?" His tone sharpened even more. "Something to do with that Ruth filly?"

"Yeah, but not what you think. The important thing is that the reverend is going to talk to that farmer who's in our way."

"Talk? That's all?"

"Get the herd moving," Mac suggested. "The reverend has a new reason to be on the side of us clearing out."

Flagg looked at him curiously, then yelled out his orders. Bullwhips cracked above the longhorns' heads. The cattle lowed and began to stir. Then the entire mass surged with movement.

"Where's the chuckwagon?"

"Rattler's already on the trail." Flagg laughed. "He surely did have a high opinion of how good you are at convincing people. He even bet a few of the suckers in the outfit that you'd get us moving through that farmer's field."

"I hope he made a fortune." Mac hesitated, then asked, "How much did you make?"

"I don't bet on things like that," Flagg said. As he rode to the head of the herd, he called back, "Twenty dollars!"

As the drive passed within view of the church an hour later, Mac thought he saw Ruth standing in the field where they had held the social, but he didn't slow down to pay his respects. That would only make matters worse for all of them. She was a young girl and would find a beau one day that her ma and pa approved of.

And if she didn't, she should leave town and find a bigger city with more prospects. She certainly deserved better than a cook for a trail drive.

As Mac thought that, he felt a touch of pride. He knew what he was, and he liked it. Back in New Orleans he had had no idea what to do to earn his daily bread. It hadn't mattered, as long as Evangeline Holdstock was by his side.

But now he fit into a group that was tighter than a family. The cowboys relied on each other and risked their lives for each other and knew who their best friends in the world were.

Ruth Hunnicut would have been a good choice to take him away from a life of being a drifter, but as long as he was with the Rolling J outfit, he knew he had a job and wasn't randomly wandering. They had a destination, a daily job and purpose. Delivering the herd fed thousands of people back East and kept even more in business down around Waco. What he did was important.

He caught up with Rattler just a bit to the east of the Slausen farm.

"Good to see you decided to join us," the lanky cowboy greeted him. "I'm getting sick and tired of driving this here buggy. I need a sturdy pony under me."

"Keeps your knees from knocking, you bowlegged son of a gun. Get out of my wagon!"

"Why not? I done et everything in it worth eating. And there was damned little."

"That's because you can't even boil coffee."

Mac traded his horse for the driver's box on the chuckwagon. He settled down, reins in hand, and felt at home.

"Is it true you made a killing betting I'd convince the farmer to let the herd cross his land?"

"Why else would I bother keepin' your wagon in such good shape? Good to have you back, Mac. And the gossip was right? You did get his permission to cross?"

"Let's not dally. I'll lead the way, and you see that Flagg doesn't let any strays get loose. That farmer's got an itchy trigger finger."

Mac had to wonder what else of Slausen's anatomy itched. He obviously did whatever Mrs. Hunnicut told him. Such thoughts were not too charitable, but Slausen hadn't missed with his shot by more than a couple inches. Mac doubted the man was that good a shot. It might have surprised the farmer that he missed at all, not that he almost hit his target.

"Up ahead. That's the farm." Mac pointed. Rattler let out a whoop and galloped away to let Flagg know it was all clear.

Mac hoped that it was. As he drove the wagon past the front gate and into the furrows left after the final harvest, he saw Slausen and his two boys out in front of their house. The preacher was talking to them, alternately pointing and praying. Then Mac lost sight of them when the chuckwagon hit the furrows and began bouncing him all around.

Keeping the team pulling across the field took all his skill. From the clatter in the rear, he doubted Rattler had secured all the pots and pans properly. If the kettles and other implements used for the social had been piled in somewhere, he'd be satisfied. A touch of nostalgia warmed him. He remembered some of the socials he and his family had gone to in Missouri. Neither his ma nor his pa had been overly religious, but they attended when they could and had insisted that he be baptized.

Would the pastor who had done the baptism condemn him for the life he'd lived so far? Probably. But Mac didn't feel like he had done anything wrong. Shooting Langdon had been more than an act of self-defense. He had rescued a kidnapped girl and saved her from being violated. Whatever a court decided in the matter of Langdon, if he had gone to trial, wouldn't have been enough. Hanging was too good for a man like that.

"If that's blasphemy, so be it," Mac said. He snapped the reins, got the team to pull the chuckwagon over one last furrow, and wide-open space stretched before him. With as much speed as possible, he raced across the prairie. There was a lot of time to make up.

The drive's luck ran out on the fourth day after crossing the Slausen farm. The herd had cut up the ground, making it easier for the farmer come springtime planting, but Mac doubted if the man had thought about that at the time. His ears had burned from the preacher's exhortations that this was the proper thing to do, the neighborly thing. Mac would have bet a brand-new hat that Reverend Hunnicut had never mentioned getting a certain chuckwagon cook out of the county.

Not too surprisingly, Mac didn't miss Ruth one bit.

He did miss Billy Duke and Huey Matthis and others who had died along the route. Their absence came back to haunt him every day, not only because he felt a pang of guilt over his part in those deaths but also because they had pulled their own weight in the outfit. Doing the cooking, scouting, and occasional night herd was wearing him down to a nubbin.

And now he brought the chuckwagon to a halt because a dozen grim-faced men armed with rifles blocked the road. He sat and stared at them for a minute. They stared back. No one spoke until Mac decided it was up to him.

"Is there a reason you fellas are blocking the road? You don't have the look of road agents since you aren't wearing masks."

A wiry man came over, his step quick and nervous so that he almost crow-hopped like a horse in a snake pit. He looked up with sharp eyes and an expression that brooked no argument.

"You're scouting for a Texas herder, ain't you?"

"I am. The Rolling J herd is three or four hours behind me. Now if you'll kindly step out of the road, I'd like to find an open area to set up so I can feed the men before they bed down the herd for the night."

"Turn 'em around."

"What's that? You want the men to go back?"

"Don't bring that damned herd through here. Go back to where you come from."

Mac looked at the posse. Fighting it out with so many men amounted to foolishness. Even if he'd had his S&W strapped on, six was the most he could hit. Twice that many would return fire with rifles, even if each of his rounds found a target.

"There's more of us in town. Lots more, and we're all determined to keep your poxy herd away from our livestock."

"The Kansas border's not too far north, is it? What if we keep on driving through the night and got into Kansas?"

"Your cows are sick. We don't want them even passing by us." The man swung his rifle around and aimed it at Mac.

Quickly, he held up both hands, palms outward.

"Whoa, hold on now. Don't go shooting the cook. And our Rolling J longhorns aren't sick. Every last one of them is healthy enough to have made it all the way from Waco."

"So you're sayin' the sick ones died along the trail? That means they infected the ones still on their legs. Turn around. Leave."

"I'm not the one you need to talk to. Our trail boss can assure you the cattle are healthy. All of them. He's an expert."

"The only way he'd get to be an expert is if he saw enough cases of Texas fever."

"You folks stay right here. I'll be back with Mr. Flagg before you know it."

"Don't bother!" The man shook his rifle in the air like a Comanche getting ready to attack.

They watched Mac like a hawk as he turned his chuckwagon around and headed back down the road. He found Flagg after only a short time since the trail boss rode at the front of the herd.

Mac explained the trouble. "I tried to convince them we don't have any sick cows, but they wouldn't listen. And there was a powerful lot of them to keep me from making them listen."

"They might have reason to block a herd. If another infected herd's already passed by, they have every right to think trailing herds will be carrying splenic fever, too."

"I told them you'd palaver with them. You've dealt with fearful men like them before."

"Hell, I've dealt with worse than that. I keep you and the rest of the outfit from shooting each other every single day."

"I'd never shoot any of them."

"No, you'd poison them." Flagg pursued his lips. "You get on a horse and come back with me. They'll recognize you and maybe not kill me outright."

"Should I wear my gun?"

"Won't hurt."

Flagg impatiently waited for Mac to find his gun belt and get it settled around his waist. Swapping horses with the first rider who came by was as good a solution as possible, though Mac didn't like an inexperienced cowboy driving his chuckwagon.

"It'll be all right," Flagg assured him. "What can Caleb do to it you haven't already done?"

"Break an axle. Hit a rock and throw a wheel. Let the team spook and run away. Or—"

"Shut up, Mac."

He shut up.

They rode in silence until they reached the blockade where Mac had encountered the posse. The man he had spoken to before walked out in front. Mac looked around and counted noses. They had called in reinforcements. More than a dozen new rifles had been added to the blockade, and each man looked fiercer than his neighbor. For the first time, Mac feared for not only his life but for that of Patrick Flagg as well.

"I'm the trail boss," Flagg announced himself as he and Mac reined to a halt. "My cook tells me you've got the wrong idea about our herd."

"Not wrong," the spokesman declared with emphatic confidence. "Infected. Texas fever. You keep them cattle away from ours. We don't want to start shooting to protect ourselves, but we will if we have to."

"No need to get riled up. My herd's clean. We haven't had a single case of splenic fever—"

"Texas fever," the man corrected.

"*Sickness* since we started out from Waco," Flagg said. "On the trail, I haven't heard of any other outfit with diseased cattle, either. Let us pass through, and we'll be gone before you know it."

"One cow falls over, it'll infect all ours!" The man's harsh rhetoric agitated the others. They began cocking their rifles.

Flagg shrugged his shoulders. The men might not have noticed, but Mac saw how this moved the trail boss's gun hand closer to the butt of his Colt. He shifted in the saddle so he could throw down on the posse, too, but he knew that if lead started flying, he and Flagg would end up ventilated. The best they could hope for was to take a few of the locals with them.

"Inspect our herd," Flagg suggested. "Get a vet out here and have him look over every cow. He'll see that there's no sickness to be found."

"I suppose you got a vet with you what'll state that?" The man spat. "That's no solution."

"The solution," cried another toward the back of the assembled townspeople, "is for them to turn around and go home. Let their damned, diseased cows die somewhere else."

"I see you folks have a strong opinion on the subject. Do you have a vet in town, too?"

The man stared at Flagg, not understanding. Flagg went on, "You bring your own vet out and check our longhorns. He'll find they're clean."

"Why would we go and do a thing like that?" The man was suspicious, but Mac saw cracks forming in his resolve.

"Because I'll donate five heifers to your town for the biggest shindig you ever did throw."

"Our vet?"

"Your vet," Flagg said, nodding. "Get him out and examine the herd. The sooner he does, the quicker we'll be on our way."

Mac inwardly groaned. He was bone tired. If the vet came out later, the men would have to move the herd through the night. That meant no dinner for them. And it meant he had to press on and scout the trail in the dark. If he found traces of earlier herds coming through, that would solve the problem. The West Shawnee Trail wandered all over this area, splitting up into splinter routes that converged back in Kansas for the final drive into Abilene.

But here? He had some fancy trailsmanship ahead of him. After the vet gave his approval.

"Doc Wilson don't work for free."

"We'll pay his fee—if he finds even one cow that's infected."

"If he don't?"

"You'll pony up his due. The offer of five cows stands. You can sell one of them and pay him without having to dip into the town treasury."

The posse leader looked from man to man, then pointed. The indicated vigilante hopped onto his horse and raced off toward town.

"He won't be an hour."

"That'll give me time to get my herd settled down."

"Not here! Keep 'em away!" The cry went up through the posse.

"We'll just bed them down where we are, then," Flagg said. "We're a ways out of town, so you don't have anything to worry over." He muttered under his breath. Mac hoped none of the vigilantes heard what he called them and their town.

When no bullets came flying their way, he relaxed. They would lose a day on the trail, but he could fix a proper dinner for the men while they waited for the vet to arrive. After a night to rest, the herd could be moving again with the dawn.

Time lost wasn't good, but this worked out the best all around for Mac. He might even get a decent night's sleep if he didn't get tapped to ride night herd for a couple hours.

They settled down to wait for the vet to reach them so they could escort him to the cattle.

CHAPTER 23

"Infected." The word came flat and hard out of the veterinarian's thin-lipped mouth.

Mac and Flagg exchanged surprised looks, then the trail boss exploded.

"What the hell do you mean, infected? There's not a trace of disease in any of the cattle!"

Dr. Wilson closed his bag and stood, moving away from the longhorn he had examined. He locked eyes with the trail boss and never flinched when he repeated his verdict.

"Infected with Texas fever. I'd recommend the entire herd be killed. Douse them all with kerosene and light it."

"There's damned near two thousand longhorns in this herd. You can't be serious!"

"I know my job. These cows are sick. Look at this one. About ready to fall down and die." Wilson shoved hard against the longhorn. The steer swung its long horns around, trying to gore the man for such an indignity. The ungainly horns caused it to stumble when it missed sinking the tip of its left horn into the vet's belly.

"It can outrun a racehorse. You're nothing but a fraud. They paid you to lie about the condition of my herd!"

Dr. Wilson signaled. The two vigilantes who had accompanied him from town came over, hands on their rifles. They stayed at a distance.

"What's it going to be, Doc?"

"Kill the lot of them. Texas fever."

Mac turned, went into a crouch, and had his Model 3 out and cocked, aimed at the nearest townsman.

"You shoot that steer and you'll be buried with it."

"Mac, calm down." Flagg sucked in a deep breath but didn't take his own advice. He turned red in the face from anger.

"They're crooked, Flagg. They want to steal our herd, and this is their way of doing it. The doc here knows the cattle are fine."

"They're sick, every last one of them. Look at their eyes. You can see the whites all around. That's a sure-fire sign they're sick. And listen to them. They're bleating like damned sheep. That's not normal. They're all infected."

"Where'd you get your training? There's nothing wrong with them being frightened or lowing the way they are. They're frightened, not sick." Flagg rested his hand on his gun. "How much did they pay you to lie?"

"The mayor told me you'd pay up since the cows are yours, and they're all sick."

"In a pig's eye I'll pay you one red cent, you crooked son of a bitch!"

Flagg reached out and grabbed the vet by the lapels of his threadbare coat and shook him so hard the man's teeth clacked together.

Mac took his eyes off the men who'd ridden from town with the veterinarian. This almost cost him his life.

The first rifle bullet tore through his hat brim. He swung around and fired. His usual deadly aim was off because the longhorn swung its head back at that moment and banged one of its polled horns into his back. Stumbling forward, he went to his knees.

This saved his life when the second rifleman opened fire. The round went over his head, but his hat picked up another hole, this one through the crown. Mac flopped forward and rested his elbows on the ground so he could steady his aim. The Smith & Wesson roared again.

This time he caught one man in the thigh. The vigilante yelped, dropped his rifle, and grabbed for the wound. Blood oozed through his fingers. Since there wasn't any spurting, Mac knew he hadn't hit the main artery.

"Drop your rifle," he ordered the other man. "Do it or your partner will get another round. This one will be through his head!"

"Don't listen to him, Guy," the wounded man grated. "He only wants to kill us both so we can't tell anyone about the sick cows."

For two cents, Mac would have plugged them both. Flagg stopped him.

"You men, get back to town. Take this quack with

you." Flagg kicked Dr. Wilson in the butt and sent him stumbling toward the other two. "Leave your rifles. I don't want you shooting at any of my men as you make dust."

"We'll be back," Wilson said. "We'll destroy the whole damned herd."

"You'll never see it if you're dead, you lying weasel." Flagg kicked again at the seat of Wilson's britches. He missed this time, but the veterinarian jumped as if he had connected.

"I'm bleeding to death, Doc. Help me," pleaded the man shot high in the leg.

"Back in town. I'll see to you back in town." Dr. Wilson stepped up onto his horse and galloped away.

The wounded man moaned. His partner stared at the blood as if he had never seen anything like this before. He turned dull eyes up at Mac and said, "You shot him. You shot him!"

Revolver back in its holster, Mac went to the man and roughly knocked him to the ground. He whipped out his knife and cut away the bloody fabric. The wound was only a crease. He pressed the tip of the knife into the wounded man's throat to keep him still, took off his bandana and tied it around the thigh just above the bloody groove. He tightened it more than necessary just to see the man wince.

"Get him to a real doctor. Not that quack. I wouldn't let Wilson opine on whether the sun's shining. He'd as likely get it wrong as he would see the light."

The two hobbled away. The wounded man's partner helped him into the saddle, and they both lit out like their horses' tails were on fire. Mac watched them vanish into the twilight.

"Stupid sons of bitches," he grumbled.

"Maybe not so stupid if they keep us from getting through to Kansas. We can't go back to Fort Gibson and find another branch of the Shawnee Trail. That would put us two weeks behind schedule."

"We're running low on most supplies, too. We have enough for another two weeks, maybe ten days," Mac said. "Then I don't know what we'll do."

"Eat nothing but cow meat." Flagg kicked at a dirt clod, then stomped on it in anger. "I should have known they'd try this."

"They're ransoming the herd?"

"Maybe, I don't know. It might just be that they're sincere. If that's the case, no amount of bribery will get us past their town without swinging far out of the way."

"Do you think it's possible to ever convince them the cattle are healthy?" Mac chewed on his lower lip as he thought.

"What are you thinking?"

"There must be another town around here. There's always a string of towns near the borders of states. What if I find another vet and have him check the herd? If he's honest, he'll know there's nothing wrong."

"Then you take him into town and have him convince the vigilantes to let us pass by?" Flagg shook his head. "That sounds chancy to me. What if he's a goddamned liar, too?"

"We might have to shoot our way past if that happens. But a second opinion has a better chance of swaying the townspeople and keeping anybody else from getting shot."

"The man you winged'll bring the marshal back

with the rest of that posse. We're liable to be in for a fight no matter what anyone says, even another animal doctor."

"I can stay and fight." Mac touched his gun. It wasn't the way he wanted to deal with their problem, but if it came to that, he would. Letting the townspeople destroy the herd would not only ruin the Rolling J ranch, it would deprive all the cowboys who had driven the cattle this far of their pay.

"One gun, more or less, won't matter. You stand a chance of convincing them not to kill all our longhorns."

"A slim one," Mac said. He mounted and headed toward the town, taking a fork in the road to avoid riding into that rattlesnakes' den.

Almost reaching Kansas was a lucky break for the drovers. Towns popped up on either side of a boundary. Some preferred to live in Indian Territory where the land was cheap, and dealing with the tribes could be easier than trying to convince bureaucrats in some far-off capital of their needs. But across the line in Kansas was the United States again. Laws were different and understandable, at least to Mac. He kept his head bowed as he rode into the chilly wind.

He crossed into the state and saw he had guessed right about a town being close by. With increasing hope that his ride would be worthwhile, he trotted into town and looked around. Finding the vet proved easier than expected. The man had hung his shingle beside the town's livery stable.

Mac went into the tiny office and was almost overpowered by the pungent odors. His nose wrinkled, and his eyes started to water. A smallish man with a big mustache sat at a table with open bottles of the smelly chemicals and beakers holding his mixtures, many of them corked.

"Sorry about the smell. I'm whipping up a batch of medicine for a sick horse out on the Gorman spread." He pushed away from the table, adjusted his eyeglasses, and saw Mac more clearly. "That likely means nothing to you since I've never seen you in town before. What can I do for you?"

Mac explained the Rolling J's dilemma.

The vet took off his glasses and nervously polished them, put them on, then tried once more to clean the lenses as he thought about all he had heard. Finally sucking in a deep breath, he said, "Convincing them's not likely to be possible. I've argued with Doc Wilson endlessly 'bout what symptoms to look for in an infected cow."

"He mostly makes up symptoms, as far as I could tell," Mac said.

"You didn't hear it from me, but you're right. I swear, he got his degree from an ad in one of them dime novels. Send in a few dollars, get a degree by mail. I suppose they're lucky he wanted to kill animals and not people with his bogus degree."

"You'll look at the cattle?"

"You're not asking me to find that they're free of Texas—of splenic fever?"

"No, sir, I'm not. You look, you decide. It's my belief and that of the trail boss, too, that the cattle are free of any disease."

"What might be your position that you're sure of that diagnosis?"

Mac hesitated, then said boldly, "I'm the cook."

The vet's eyes widened, then he laughed.

"You're an honest man, aren't you? And who better to know the condition of the herd than someone who slaughters a cow every day or two and has to prepare it?"

"Nobody," Mac said. He looked around and saw the nameplate on the vet's desk. "You're Dr. Pointer?"

"Alan Pointer." The vet stood and thrust out his hand. Mac hesitated. "Go on, the chemicals won't kill you. They might even fix what ails you."

Mac shook hands and had to ask, "What do you think ails me?"

Dr. Pointer gave him a once-over before saying, "Nothing physical. You have the look of a youngster carrying the weight of the world on your shoulders." He picked up his bag, tossed a few items from the table into it, snapped it shut, and asked, "How far's the herd?"

"An hour's ride. Maybe more if you're driving a buggy."

"Then I'll ride. The sooner I look at your cows, the sooner I can get back to whipping up a new batch of medicine."

The ride back to the herd took less time with Dr. Pointer pushing the pace. Mac's horse struggled to keep up, being tired out from being ridden so long before.

"That's the varmints, eh?" Pointer drew rein, cocked his head to one side, and listened hard.

"What is it? What do you hear?"

"A contented herd and a cowboy with the most God-awful voice I ever did hear singing 'Lorena' to keep them quiet."

"That's probably Rattler," Mac said. "He doesn't know too many songs. Be glad you're missing his rendition of 'Dixie.' "

"That would require me to shoot the herd—to save them from such torture," Pointer said. He looked up as Flagg and two others rode up.

Mac introduced them.

"You go check anywhere in the herd you like, Doc. If you want my men to ride with you, they will. Otherwise, get started." Flagg glanced at Mac, then back to Dr. Pointer.

"The way you boys approached this makes me think there's no trouble at all. If there was, you'd want me to look at only a couple of your longhorns."

"Any of them." Flagg hesitated, then asked, "Did Mac arrange for a fee?"

"We avoided that. If you're like most drovers, you're short on money about now. Is that so? I thought so," Dr. Pointer said. "You pay me in cash money if the cattle are sick. I'll take three of my choice if they're not."

"Agreed."

"Well, now, Mr. Flagg, this inclines me to think even more that you've got nothing to hide. Let me get started. I'll need one of your hands to hold a lantern. Otherwise, I can make my own way through the herd." He looked at Mac. "When I'm through, you fix me a cup of coffee and something to eat."

"I will," Mac said. "They tell me I make the best biscuits they've ever tasted."

Pointer snorted.

"I'll be the judge of that. And your herd." With that he rode among the half-asleep cattle.

"You impressed him. Good," said Flagg. "He sounds like a man who values honesty."

"I'd better get those biscuits started, then, so he can see I wasn't lying."

"Throw out the coffee Rattler made. We don't want to poison the man before he delivers his report." Flagg wheeled about and began a circuit around the entire bedded-down herd.

Mac found the chuckwagon and sampled the coffee. He spit it out, tossed what he had put in a cup after it, then poured the pot onto the ground. If it poisoned the soil, so be it. By the time he had a new pot boiling and had settled in to cook, Dr. Pointer rode up, Flagg beside him.

"You better have a good cup waiting for me," the vet said. "That was mighty thirsty work." He let the words hang for an instant to see if Mac got the hint. He did. Not even looking to Flagg for approval, he poured a shot of the medicinal whiskey into the coffee before handing it to the vet.

"That hits the spot. And I've cut out my heifers. They look to be good eating."

"All clear?" Mac let out a breath he hadn't realized he was holding. There hadn't been any doubt in his mind what a competent veterinarian would find, but the strain still wore on him. "No sign of disease?"

"Not a trace. I suppose you want me to talk to those yahoos in town so you can move the herd in the morning."

"We do, Doc. You mind going on in tonight?" Flagg motioned to Rattler and another cowboy to get back to the herd.

"Not at all. You boys keep my cows with your herd. When you get across the state line, you can deliver 'em to me. I'm a better vet than I am a drover." He smacked his lips as he finished the whiskey-laced coffee, wiped a drop from his mustache, and tossed the cup back to Mac.

"You go on, Mac. I need to be sure there's no more trouble with the herd." Flagg shook hands with Dr. Pointer, mounted, and rode off into the night.

"Good man, Flagg. He's a competent trail boss."

"I agree, Doc," Mac said, getting a new horse from his team to ride. Best to let the one he had ridden earlier rest.

"You pick up on what he says and make it your own."

"How's that?"

"You're learning from him. You can do worse. You looking to be trail boss one day yourself?"

"I enjoy cooking for the outfit too much," Mac said.

"You do whip up a fine batch of biscuits. They could use some butter or honey, though. Or gravy. Gracious, I'm making myself hungry just talking about food."

Mac settled astride his mount and followed the doctor away from camp toward town. He hoped the vigilantes wouldn't shoot them out of hand as they approached.

"Being a chuckwagon cook's not an ambition too many share, but if you like the job, more power to you. Me, there's nothing I like more than curing a sick animal. Or like tonight, finding there's nothing I need to do because they're all healthy." Pointer grumbled some about the fools in town jumping at their own shadows.

Mac kept an eye peeled for the roadblock. The men had moved back into town for the night. He and Dr. Pointer rode down the main street. A few men stirred, but the town was quiet. Where he would present the reputable vet to give his clean bill of health answered itself as he rode past the marshal's office.

"We don't want you in town," a harsh voice said from the building's porch. "You might be infected. Or your horse."

"Sorry to disappoint you," Mac said to the man he had argued with out on the road. Like a magnet drawing iron filings, others came to stand by their leader. Enough carried rifles that Mac got uneasy watching the crowd form.

"I'm Alan Pointer, vet over—"

"We know who you are. Doc Wilson warned us about you and your quackery."

"See here, I know my job. I am not a quack, unlike Wilson. He—"

"Doctor, please," Mac whispered urgently. "Don't rile them."

"Rile them! They're fools if they believe one word that charlatan says. The herd outside town is healthy, not a trace of Texas fever or anything else infectious."

"Liar! What'd they pay you to say that?" Dr. Wilson came up, shaking his fist in the air. "You'd have us all die!"

"You need to read your medical books, Wilson. There's—"

Dr. Pointer let out a yelp as a man grabbed him and dragged him from the saddle.

Mac went for his gun but never finished his draw before a rock hit him on the side of the head and brought him crashing to the ground. As he tried to scramble to his feet, men grabbed his arms and held him immobile.

"Tar and feather the liar!" Wilson did what looked like a war dance, stomping about in a circle and waving his arms over his head. Mac wondered if any of the crowd would notice how crazy the vet appeared.

His unasked question was answered immediately. Two men came running up with a rail. Another opened a bag of feathers and sent them fluttering into the air. Another ran away shouting that he was going to get a pot of pitch. Even then Mac doubted they were sincere until two men started a fire in the middle of the street.

They were going to tar and feather Dr. Pointer. The vet struggled in the grip of two men while others crowded close. Mac took in the situation in a flash. If he didn't act now, Pointer and probably he, too, would be dabbed with burning tar and then doused in feathers before being tied onto a hitching post and bounced out of town.

He sagged, as if passing out. Both men holding him bent to follow him down. With a surge, he stood and threw his arms backward. Caught off balance, they sat heavily. Spinning around, Mac directed his fist at the back of the head of the crowd's leader. The man stumbled and fell into the pair holding Dr. Pointer. Stepping over them, Mac swung his fists with strength aided by fury. He punched two more and got the vet free.

"Horse. Ride!" He shoved Dr. Pointer in the direction of his nervous horse.

The veterinarian didn't have to be told twice. He took a giant leap, flopped belly down over the saddle, then spun around and properly got into the saddle. To his credit, he looked back to see if he could help his rescuer.

"Go, now, ride! Go!"

Mac flailed about, his fists bony cudgels that caused the crowd to retreat. He refused to give up the fight, even as his strength began to fade. Trying to make his way to his own horse became impossible when Wilson and another man blocked him. He ducked and weaved, then landed a good jab to the vet's belly. A fist sunk wrist-deep caused Wilson to double over, gasping for air.

Mac felt a moment's pleasure, then despair crushed down on him as hands pulled at his arms and yanked him spread eagle. The men who had gone after the pitch pot raced back to join the fray. Mac found himself held so he couldn't move a muscle.

"Let me go! You heard Dr. Pointer. The Rolling J cattle are clean!"

"Lies, I tell you, all lies!" Wilson frothed at the mouth. Clutching his belly and half bent over, he started his peculiar war dance again. "String him up! He's trying to murder us all with his sick cattle."

Too many in the crowd believed him. Mac was yanked hither and yon, then dragged toward a scrub oak tree at the edge of town. From nowhere, someone produced a rope with a hangman's knot tied in it.

"You have to give me a trial! This is murder."

"He's right. We have to give him a trial. I'm judge. What say you, gentlemen of the jury?"

"Guilty!" The resounding cry echoed through the night.

Mac watched the rope sail high over a limb and swing ominously. They tied his hands together and boosted him onto his horse.

"Hang him, hang him high!" The chant tore at his soul. Rough hemp abraded his forehead as they tried to slip the noose over his head.

CHAPTER 24

Mac jerked his head around to keep the noose from falling down around his neck. As he fought, he twisted his wrists to free himself from the sloppy job they had done tying his hands. He was able to pull his left hand free, but he couldn't reach around to his right side and draw his gun.

Blood roared in his ears, but he heard someone in the crowd shouting a warning that he still had his gun. Writhing around failed to keep his head free. The noose dropped around his neck. He grabbed with both hands, getting his fingers between the rope and his throat as the horse bolted. Mac swung free, hanging on for dear life. He kicked and tried to work around to reach the hangman's knot and loosen it so he could shuck off the rope.

Hands grabbed at his feet. He kicked hard and connected with a nose. Blood spurted. He kept swinging, fighting, and then he heard a distant thunder unlike anything he had ever heard.

Only he *had* heard this sound before—the night Billy Duke had died. The pounding of a cattle stampede was unlike anything else in the world. Jeers around him changed to screams of fear. The hands on his boots disappeared. He swung around and pulled hard, taking the strain off his neck. Although he still wasn't able get his head free, he had the chance to reach behind him with one hand and find the handle of the knife sheathed at the small of his back. He drew it and slashed repeatedly at the rope above his head.

The strands of rope parted, and Mac crashed to the ground, only to face a new danger. Running hell-bent for leather toward him were a hundred long-horns. With a desperate spin, he got behind the broad trunk of the oak where they had tried to hang him. He barely reached safety. Horns flashed through the air inches away from him. Panting with fear, he pressed his back against the tree.

For a moment, he thought he was imagining the voice calling his name. Then he looked around and saw Flagg leading a riderless horse and shouting at him.

The words blurred under the roar of hundreds of hooves slamming into the ground, but Mac understood. Putting away his knife, he took two running steps and vaulted into the saddle as Flagg rode by. This wasn't the horse he had ridden into town on. That didn't matter. It was going to be the horse that took him out of town.

"Got here just in time!" Flagg shouted.

"I hope you brought the whole damned herd and that it smashes this town to splinters."

"Only a couple hundred. Rattler's moving the rest along the road outside town."

"Damn."

Flagg laughed, bent low over his horse's neck, and lit out after the small herd that had scattered the vigilantes so willing to stretch Mac's neck. Mac joined the trail boss and worked his way around to the far side. With the cattle between them, they did their best to steer back toward the main road. They merged their cattle with the main herd and kept moving, though at a slower pace now.

"Can we get across the state line tonight?"

"We're gonna try, Mac, you can bet that we're gonna try." Flagg fell back to bring up the rear of the herd and keep stragglers from getting captured by anyone from the town.

Mac rode around and did what he could. The times he had ridden herd stood him in good stead. He knew how to bring back those wanting to take off on their own. As he swatted at the lumbering beasts, the lariat he held reminded him of the noose that had been draped around his neck. The cattle returned to the main herd and moved along at a decent clip.

Far behind the herd he heard gunfire. Flagg tangling with a few brave souls coming from the town, Mac thought. He started to join the trail boss in his defense of their trailing cattle, then decided his current mood would only cause someone's death. They had tried to murder him. He wanted justice. Plugging a few of the men would do nothing to ease his anger, even if it might keep other drovers farther behind the Rolling J herd from suffering a similar fate.

Realizing his need to vent his anger would only result in death, he galloped forward to put more distance between himself and the settlement. The thought that one bullet through Dr. Wilson's worthless skull could save lives later kept haunting him. Then Rattler began slowing the herd to a steady walk. Mac caught up with his friend.

"Glad to see you decided to do some work tonight, Mac." Rattler grinned ear to ear.

"Where's the chuckwagon? You didn't try to make more coffee on your own, did you? You'll poison everyone, including yourself."

"I don't know who's drivin', but the wagon's in the lead. Caleb might have taken over the chore." Rattler drew rein and turned half around in the saddle. "You hear that?"

"Gunfire," Mac said. "I reckon Flagg is having it out with those crazy bastards from the town."

"That might be, but there's a powerful lot of shooting. Listen."

Mac's fury from before rekindled. Flagg's six-gun would have run out of bullets after the first volley. The reports kept coming. He counted fifteen in the span of a few seconds. It sounded as if a major battle had erupted behind them.

"I'll see what's going on. You're right. All that can't be Flagg."

"And it ain't stoppin'. If they got him, why'd they keep on shootin'? The last time I heard that much gunfire was at the Battle of Palmito Ranch when we whupped the Yankees good and proper."

The words faded as Mac raced back to support

Flagg. He passed the rear of the herd, then realized more cattle lay in front of him. He skirted them so they could catch up with what he had thought were the stragglers in the herd. He spotted Flagg up ahead.

"What's wrong?" Mac came to a halt beside the trail boss. Flagg reloaded his Colt and didn't look over. "Won't they ever give up?"

"There's another herd moving through, almost overtaking ours. The damned vigilantes opened fire on them and killed a handful. That set off a fight between them and the cowboys in the other crew."

"Another bunch of cattle?" Mac craned around. The animals he had passed were nowhere to be seen. They had either stampeded off the road or had joined the tail end of the Rolling J herd. "What should we do?"

"If anyone points a gun at you, shoot him. We can keep the vigilantes bottled up long enough for Rattler to drive the herd into Kansas."

"What about the other drovers?"

"If they shoot at you, return fire. But I don't think that'll be a problem with the jackasses from that settlement shooting into their herd."

Mac waited, his S&W clutched in his hand. More than once he had to wipe sweat off his brow, in spite of the gathering cold. He glanced up at the sky and estimated that it was well past midnight. It might even be dawn in a couple hours. He had trouble telling because of the clouds moving in to obscure the sky and turn the land into an inky nightmare of indistinct shapes.

"The other herd's veered away from the road and

heading due north. Let's make tracks." Flagg holstered his iron. Mac did the same and galloped alongside.

"Who are they? The other herd?"

Flagg shook his head.

"You don't know?"

"I don't care. They came along when we needed a diversion. They did us a favor, so I wish them luck and hope they didn't get too shot up, but I saw a couple dozen head of cattle brought down."

"They must have known the town was crazy if they tried moving during the night."

"They're in the same pickle we are, being late along the trail. Maybe they wanted to make up for lost time." Flagg shook his head. "Or, as you say, they knew the trouble waiting for them along the road past that damned town."

"What was that town's name?" Mac slowed as Flagg did to give their horses a chance to catch their breath. "I never heard."

"Piss Pot. Shithole. I know what I call it, and don't care what their name is."

That suited Mac just fine.

"Polecat Creek," said Flagg as they crossed a stream several days later. "We're getting closer to Abilene."

"Then there's nothing much to worry about now, right?" Mac started whistling a jaunty tune as he rocked along on the chuckwagon seat, but he stopped when he saw how Flagg suddenly looked irritated. "What's wrong?"

He gazed ahead across the Kansas prairie, with its patches of colorful sunflowers. Goldenrod spewed pollen into the air, making both man and beast sneeze, but the large green balls of Osage oranges were downright lovely. Traveling over this mostly treeless land had its drawbacks, but Mac had stocked up as much as possible on firewood and stacked it in the chuckwagon. The vast herds of buffalo had left dried chips behind. Those burned with smoky heat, but they would do to fix meals when the firewood ran out.

Flagg grunted. "Indians. Osage. The Comanche still raid this far north. And every time it looks like we're getting easy passage, something goes wrong."

"Do you think we'll have trouble crossing any of the rivers?"

Flagg shook his head.

"The Chikaskia River might give us some trouble, but this late in the year that's not likely. Before we get to the Arkansas, we'll camp at Skeleton Creek."

"That sounds ominous. Is it?"

"Skeletons as far as the eye can see." Before Flagg could describe it in greater detail, Rattler came galloping up, waving his hat above his head to attract attention. "Now what's he want?"

"Boss, we got a band of Osage wanting a few cattle for passage. They claim this is their land. What should we do?"

"I'll handle it. If we had any tobacco, that'd satisfy them more than a few head of our cattle." Flagg looked expectantly at Mac.

"Sorry, no tobacco. The men might have some

among them, but I didn't stock much, and what I did was lost back in Indian Territory."

"I thought as much. Keep scouting, Mac. We'll catch up. It won't take long to get those Indians paid off."

Mac watched Flagg and Rattler ride away, then turned on the seat to watch where he was going. He shielded his eyes to get a better view of the prairie. Almost any direction was flat and clear enough to give decent passage. Using the sun, he got his bearings. The West Shawnee Trail curled up almost due north to Abilene. He felt good about reaching this point, and from the flat prairie he got a good view of any trouble ahead.

The faint breeze blowing across the land brought with it heavy clouds from the northwest. He aimed straight north and let the horses set the pace. More often than not, they spotted prairie dog holes that could break a horse's leg when Mac didn't. Only when they were rushed did such disasters occur.

Rocking gently from side to side as the wagon found ruts left by prior travelers, Mac felt drowsy and almost dropped off to sleep once or twice. He forced himself to stay awake by leaning over the wagon edge now and then. Less than two miles from where Flagg had left him, he saw how the ground had been cut up by the passage of another herd. On impulse, he secured the reins and jumped down to study the dirt rims of a few hoofprints.

He had gotten good at estimating when another horse or longhorn had passed. The sides of each print were only slightly crumbled from wind. There hadn't been any rain to erase the tracks. From prior experience and listening to what some of the better trackers among the cowboys claimed, he knew that another herd had passed this way less than a day ahead. The flat land reduced visibility to about three miles.

Not for the first time, he wished there were hills as there had been in Indian Territory to climb. Good visibility then had been twice what it was in the flatlands. He didn't worry about watering the cattle. This close to Abilene, there was a sense that reaching the railroad had become a race. At least that was the impression he got from Flagg.

Another five miles brought him to a meandering creek without more than a few saplings for shade. That bothered him less than the lack of firewood. The earlier trail drive had used whatever wood there had been. He parked the chuckwagon, hobbled the horses, and let them graze on the buffalo grass and drink from the stream while he took a burlap sack and hunted for buffalo chips.

An hour of hunting built a pile almost three feet high. He had cooked a few times over dried dung and had a feel now for how long each chip would last. The evening meal, along with breakfast, was easily taken care of. The cowboys could add to the pile if they wanted to keep a fire burning all night. As chilly as it got on occasion, many of them would be happy to range out farther than he had on foot and fetch back a dozen or so chips for their own nighttime fires.

He started a fire, began working on dinner, and had it ready when he sighted the leading steers. They scented water and came faster now. Flagg and the rest of the outfit made no effort to slow them. They were saddle weary and wanted food and rest as much as the longhorns wanted water.

"You got food for us, Mac? Damnation, but you are what they call efficient." Rattler dropped to the ground, rubbed his aching rump, and led his horse to a rope corral Mac had built between three saplings. If the horses thought about it, they could break free. Being near the water, they weren't likely to go far.

Inside of an hour, Mac had fed the entire crew. One by one, they turned in their plates and spoons. Rattler was the only one to complain about the meal.

"Damned biscuits taste like buffalo droppin's." That said, he found a mount, saddled, and went out for a two-hour patrol around the perimeter of the herd. Mac cringed when he heard the man begin singing to the cattle.

"We made good distance today. This part of the trip lets us get fifteen miles or better. You think you can make it that far before stopping to fix supper, Mac?" Flagg picked his teeth with a thick-bladed knife.

"As easy going as it was today, there shouldn't be any trouble getting at least that far tomorrow before I stop."

"There'll be trouble. I feel it in my bones."

"Indians?"

"You mean the Osage? Not them. They were happy to get anything I was willing to hand over. I gave them ten head. That'll keep their village fed for a month or longer. They might even have enough to tide them over when it gets cold."

"It does do that," Mac said, remembering the Missouri winters. Those here in Kansas couldn't possibly be milder.

"That's right, you're from these parts and not New Orleans." Flagg sheathed his knife.

Mac tensed. He didn't remember telling Carson or Flagg where he had been before he came to Waco. With Leclerc's men dogging his footsteps, he wasn't going to let it slip he had ever been near New Orleans. A quick pat of his coat pocket made a crinkly sound. The wanted posters he had taken in Waco and Lewiston still rested there. If he had any sense, he would use them to start a fire, but something made him keep the incriminating evidence of being a fugitive.

As long as he had them in his pocket, neither Flagg nor anyone else could see them. Making it this far north ought to have let him outrun the long arm of the law.

"I need to go tell Rattler to sing on key," Mac said. "He's getting on my nerves. Who knows what he's doing to the cattle."

"They don't seem to mind. Who knows about a longhorn? They might like his singing." Mac had to laugh at Flagg's reply.

He packed everything and laid out what he would need for breakfast, took his bedroll, and crawled under the chuckwagon to sleep. Being a scout had some advantages. Because he had to range so far ahead and fix the meals, he hadn't been sent out on night herd in a few days. Flagg's anxiety about reaching Abilene had grown, and he wanted the route to be the best Mac could find.

With the land as flat as it was, Mac knew he would have them sailing right on into the railhead in a few days. A week at the outside. With that thought tantalizing him, he slipped off into a light sleep, only to awaken a short time later.

"What a dream," he said, rubbing his eyes. "I'm even dreaming of trains."

He sat up, banged his head against the bottom of the chuckwagon, and rolled out to get to his feet. He cupped his hand behind one ear to listen better.

"A freight train. I did hear a train. We must be closer than I thought."

Then he recognized the sound. More than once growing up he had heard this same noise.

"Tornado!" The yelled warning mingled with that of a half dozen other cowboys. They heard the roar, too, as the twister came toward them.

CHAPTER 25

Mac scrambled to pull on his boots as some of the cowboys ran past him. "What do we do about the herd?"

His question was drowned out by the rising wind. Turning in a full circle, he located the distant tower of clouds. During the day, the formation would have been obvious: the flat bottom, perhaps the color of corroded copper, the funnel dipping down toward the ground until it finally touched. When that happened, all hell broke loose. Winds of impossible ferocity tore away at the very earth. Trees were uprooted and entire houses picked up and turned into splinters.

He had seen one farmhouse picked up, carried three miles, and deposited so gently the windows weren't broken or the door frames knocked out of square. But out here on the wide-open prairie, the only things to be picked up were cattle and horses.

And cowboys.

He made his way to the rope corral. Many of the

horses were gone, either because the men had already saddled and headed out to control the herd or they had simply taken off, running in fear. The three horses left fought him as he dragged and pulled and cajoled them to the front of the chuckwagon. He hitched them up the best he could, leaving the left front spot open. He climbed into the driver's box and sat, reins in hand.

Mac had no idea where to go. Which way would avoid the dancing, bobbing, erratic tornado?

The times in Missouri that a twister had swept past, he had never been allowed to watch. The family always crowded together in the storm cellar, buried next to their house. Now Mac wished his pa had let him watch so he would have some idea what to do.

With the sky totally black with clouds and the air filled with gusts of wind and a whine that rose until it hurt his ears, he realized no amount of study could have prepared him to deal with a tornado. It went where it wanted, and it went randomly. Bouncing this way and that, it reminded him of a dark bare-knuckle fighter avoiding punches and jabs, only there was no opposing fighter and the stormy body filled with lightning flashes.

He snapped the reins and forced the horses to pull as he shouted at them. With only three hauling a load where four worked normally, he made them concentrate on the job rather than their fear. At least, that's what he told himself as he struggled to find a trail across the prairie and avoid thinking of the monstrous windstorm coming for him.

He worked the horses up to a quick walk, straining as they went. Not knowing it, he headed for the herd

and soon found himself surrounded by the frightened longhorns. The steers swung their deadly horns
back and forth. Mac feared losing a horse to one of
the slashing movements and hung back. The herd
moved away, then began to stampede. The slowest
cow proved faster than him with his wagon pulled by
a trio of horses.

Mac was content to follow the running herd. He
hoped all the cowboys had avoided being trapped in
front, yet knew that was the only way the herd could
be stopped. From before, when Billy Duke and Huey
Matthis died under the cattle's cutting hooves, he
knew someone had to race to the front and, using
whip or gun, force the leading longhorns to turn
from their course. Force them across the front of the
herd, making the scared ones behind the leaders
turn or run into the cattle in front.

He wasn't sure who rode that section of the herd.
He said a silent prayer not only for that rider but for
all of them.

Deafened by the spinning storm, he kept his
horses pulling until they were exhausted and stumbling. Even then he kept them moving. It took him a
full minute to realize the roar had gone from the sky
and that he could stop whipping the team.

He pulled to a halt and looked around in the night.
The cloudy tower filled with lightning and death had
disappeared as suddenly as it had appeared. The roar
in his ears died, and he turned the chuckwagon
around to return to where he had parked it earlier.

As he drove, he saw that the herd had calmed, and
the cowboys worked to reform it into a single giant
mass. As he returned, he hunted for stray horses.

Dark shapes moved in the night that might have been escaped horses, but he couldn't be sure. Without even the flashes of lightning, it was worse than driving around in an inkwell.

At least the herd had stopped its stampede.

Hoofbeats sounded in the night. Mac waited until Flagg caught up with him and inquired about the condition of the wagon and team.

"We're all right, but I'll need another horse when I get to scouting in the morning."

"Sorry," Flagg said, "but there might not be enough horses to go around. We'll round up what we can, but they scattered across the plains when the tornado roared past."

"It missed us," Mac said. "Lucky the stampede wasn't worse. Nobody was hurt, were they?"

"Not that I know. I need to—" Flagg cut off his words in mid-sentence as a raindrop fell and spattered on the brim of his hat.

At least, Mac thought it was a raindrop until he saw the white, slushy residue. Then he heard a splat on his own hat. He looked up and cried out in pain. A hailstone landed on his cheek hard enough to open a tiny cut.

"Oh, damn." Flagg raced off again into the night as the hail began falling faster.

By the time Mac returned to where they had pitched camp, stones the size of marbles hammered at him. Lightning crashed through the sky again, giving the world an eerie aspect. He saw the cattle, the riders, everything in his world with that one flash. Then the storm began pounding away in earnest with hailstones of increasing size. Mac unhitched his team and dived under the wagon to watch hail the size of hen's eggs bouncing on the ground.

Then mixed into the thunder from the storm came the sound he had come to fear most. The herd stampeded again.

The ice piled up until it was ankle deep and showed no sign of slowing as it hammered down. Mac hesitated to go out, but he knew the herd was again in danger. The Rolling J outfit had so few cowboys left that he felt guilty staying safely under the chuckwagon even one more minute. After brushing off his clothes, he took his yellow slicker from his gear, donned it, and went out to saddle a horse. The hailstones drove him to his knees in one heavy downfall driven by a gust of wind that threatened to rip off his hat. Only the wide-brimmed hat kept him from being bruised.

Once more in the saddle, he headed out to find the herd. Seeing even a few cattle in the storm counted as a victory for him. Without being told, he rounded up the stragglers and drove them toward the spot where the herd had begun its stampede. From here he located a larger segment of the herd. With the hail hitting him like bullets, he kept his head down and let his hat absorb as much of the punishment as possible.

"Glad you're out here! We can use the help!"

Mac barely heard the voice over the noise of the hail bouncing off his hat brim. He wiped rain from his eyes. Rattler had ridden up, and he never knew it until the cowboy shouted at him.

"What needs doing? I can't make heads or tails of this."

"We got the stampede stopped again. The cattle

are millin' around, but there's another problem." Rattler pointed to the cattle Mac had brought back to the herd.

"I don't understand." He swiped at the rain in his eyes again and then saw what the other cowboy already had. The brands on these cattle didn't match any on the Rolling J longhorns.

"That's a Lazy B brand. You put cows that aren't ours into the herd."

"Where's the Lazy B?"

"I don't know, Mac, but they must be close. Their herd scattered either from the twister or the hail, and we got a few head of theirs."

"And they got some of ours?"

Mac watched Rattler shrug. Who could know in this storm?

"Flagg! Over here. Flagg!" Rattler waved to get the trail boss's attention.

The trail boss rode over and barely glanced at the cattle Mac had added to the herd.

"We got more'n fifty Lazy B cattle mixed in with ours," he said without preamble. "Don't worry about that now. Make sure ours aren't fixing to stampede again."

"How can they have any energy left?" Mac marveled at how easily the cattle spooked and how strong they were. Swinging that eight-foot span of horns had to exhaust a steer, but they always found a reserve of stamina to make life miserable for the drovers.

"Because they are the Devil's creature, that's how." Flagg spat. The hail was still falling, but at a slower rate. As Flagg rode off, his horse's hooves crunched on the ice.

Mac had heard the resignation and exhaustion in Flagg's voice. The man was reaching the end of his trail even before he delivered the Rolling J herd. So much responsibility when he hadn't signed on for it had worn him down to a nub.

He glanced at Rattler, who pointed. Together they rode away from the herd, found tiny knots of cattle trying to escape, and worked to drive the strays back. By the time they had rounded up more than a hundred head, the storm had stopped, and the distant horizon showed dawn's pink fingers creeping around black clouds. The weather was clearing.

"We made it through another night," Rattler said. "I'm gonna sleep all day long."

"Unless Flagg wants to get the herd on the trail to Abilene," Mac said.

"You have to fix us breakfast, too."

"And get the chuckwagon rolling to scout ahead so Flagg can move the cattle." In spite of so much soul-crushing work looming in front of him, Mac felt oddly exhilarated. Once more he had helped save the herd and keep their goal in view.

The nearer cattle mooed, drawing his attention. Two riders he didn't recognize worked their way through the Rolling J herd. He called to Rattler and got his attention.

"They're not cowboys Flagg just hired, that's for certain." Rattler pushed back his slicker and freed his six-shooter.

"They're likely not rustlers, either. They're cutting out the Lazy B stock." Mac put his heels to his horse and trotted to speak with the cowboys. "You fellas finding any Rolling J cows in your herd?"

"Haven't looked," one of the riders replied. "Still rounding up the ones we lost in the storm." The cowboy had lost more than one bar fight in the past. His nose was broken and smeared off to one side. Scars crisscrossed his left cheek but not his right. Although he didn't wear facial hair, he had the bushiest eyebrows Mac had ever seen. It took considerable willpower not to stare as the eyebrows wiggled up and down like woolly worms.

"I herded a dozen or so into our herd at the peak of the storm. Rattler here noticed the Lazy B brand. Where do you hail from?"

"South."

"Where in the south? Texas? The Rolling J is outside Waco."

"Know that." The man's horse cut suddenly, turned, and worked the cattle trying to return to the Rolling J herd.

Mac rode over to keep the Rolling J cattle from joining the Lazy B head going back to their herd.

"Where's your herd bedded down? Since you've cut out yours, we'll need to look for our brand and return them. Unless you want to swap?" Mac watched the bushy-browed man intently. His eyebrows rippled as he scowled and then relaxed.

"Nope."

"What do you mean by that? You intend to keep our cattle? Maybe we should keep yours, just until we cull your herd."

"We got ours. Time to hit the trail."

Before he snapped his reins and got his small herd moving, Mac cut off his retreat.

"Nope," Mac said, duplicating the man's tone.

"What do you mean?" His busy eyebrows rose in an arch, as if he had no idea.

"We need to talk to our trail boss about what he wants us to do. Rattler? Go fetch Flagg."

"We're leaving." The Lazy B rider started to circle around Mac, only to find his way blocked again. This time Mac rested his hand on the butt of his Smith & Wesson.

"It's mighty neighborly of you to want to talk with our trail boss," Mac said.

"Don't want to talk." Now the man reacted. He pushed back his coat and reached for his gun. Before he had the weapon half drawn, Mac pointed his cocked S&W at him.

"We want to talk. I don't want to shoot, but you just said you have a few head of our cattle that you won't return or let us fetch back. That sounds like rustling to me, stealing another rancher's cattle."

"You don't want to start flinging lead around. You'll lose."

"You'll lose first," Mac said.

For a split second, he thought the Lazy B rider was going to throw down on him. That would make killing him self-defense, but Mac saw it as shooting a fish in a barrel since he had his pistol out and aimed. Something in his expression must have changed from doubt about shooting to certainty. The other outfit's cowboy let his six-shooter slip back into its holster without making any other hostile move.

"The law might see this different. You're the one with the drawn gun preventing me from taking what's rightfully mine."

Mac never wavered. He lowered his six-gun only

when he heard Rattler returning with Flagg. The trail boss would know how to handle this.

"My man's told me you're here to collect your cows. Glad to see you recovering them," Flagg said. "Why don't I send my two men with you to bring back any Rolling J cattle in your herd?"

"You'd spook my cattle riding around through the herd. After the tornado and hailstorm and a pack of wolves we shot at a couple nights back, they're likely to stampede again. I'm not inclined to let that happen."

"Your men can return any of our cows, then," Flagg said. "One way or the other, we want our cattle back."

Mac chimed in, trying to lighten the mood.

"They miss their friends." Mac saw that his small joke fell on deaf ears. Neither the Lazy B rider nor Flagg took notice of him. They engaged in a staring contest.

On the one side, Flagg's face looked like a craggy, weathered image cut out of stone. On the other, the Lazy B rider's visage might have been something carved into a tree trunk.

"You owe us," the other cowboy said. "After what you did to us back in Indian Territory, you owe us."

"We didn't do anything. I've never heard of the Lazy B brand before," said Flagg, perplexed.

"Them townspeople were chasing you, screaming about your herd infected with Texas fever. We were passing by when they gave up shooting at you and started in on us."

"Lazy B," muttered Mac. It came back to him now. A few head of cattle with that brand had mingled with the Rolling J's. He had noticed but did nothing about it since he'd almost gotten his neck stretched by the lynch mob. Between the rope burns and wanting Dr. Pointer to get away, he had ignored the cattle.

"That wasn't our fault," Flagg said. "Those people were loco, all of them."

"I'd heard of them. That's why I wanted to sneak by their town, but you riled them up. We figure to have lost fifty head of cattle."

"Did they shoot that many?" Flagg showed his first sign of emotion. The corners of his lips threatened to curl up into a grin.

"Yeah."

"That's another problem to face along the trail. Nobody ever claimed driving a herd to market was easy." Flagg gripped his saddle horn and leaned forward. "That said, how are we going to agree on both of us getting our property back where it belongs?"

The bushy-browed cowboy thought for a moment, then smiled. Mac thought of a wolf looking at a rabbit, wondering how slow it was.

"I'm willing to let any of your boys hunt through our herd for, what is it, Rolling J branded cattle."

"In exchange for?" Flagg had asked the right question.

Mac caught his breath when he heard the request and Flagg's answer.

"This seems right fair to me," the man said. "We let you get back your cattle. You let the Lazy B herd in to the railhead before yours."

Flagg leaned back and said in a voice almost too low to hear, "Like hell."

CHAPTER 26

"I never caught your name," Flagg went on.

"Why do you want to know?" The man thrust out his chin belligerently. The scar pattern on his cheek began to pulse a sickly pink, and his nose twitched like a squirrel sniffing the air.

"It makes it easier to say who I think is one dumb son of a bitch."

Mac worried this would start them shooting at each other. Both men looked to be on the edge of a gunfight, but the Lazy B rider only sneered.

"It's fitting to know who's your better. Name's Weed. Willie Weed, but my friends call me Jimson."

"No reason to know that since you'll never be among friends if you stay in the middle of the Rolling J herd," Flagg said. "Now are you going to let my men hunt through your herd for Rolling J cattle?"

"Are you going to let me take my cattle to market ahead of you?"

"That sounds like we have come to what they call an impasse." Flagg never took his eyes off the Lazy B rider as he called to Rattler, "If our herd stampeded, where'd it go?"

"Might go north, might go northeast toward their herd. I scouted it out. The Lazy B ain't more'n a mile off, boss."

"You wouldn't do that!" Weed protested. "Starting a stampede is crazy. Both our herds would be hurt."

"That doesn't have to be the way this works out, Weed. We each get our proper stock and go on our separate ways."

"I did a quick count," Mac said. "We have more of their cattle than they do of ours. That sounds like a fair trade, each of us going our own trail." He lied through his teeth. He hadn't come to any such reckoning, and Flagg knew it. Weed must, also, but it gave him a way to save face.

"Our cows are better quality. If you have more, you'd be stealing from us." Weed glanced at his partner, who looked confused at the argument over the cattle.

Mac doubted Weed's friend was a mental giant, and if they made Stetsons in the proper shape, he would be wearing a tall, cone-shaped one and be sitting in the corner. If he had ever gone to school, that would be natural for him. Mac doubted he had seen the inside of a classroom, much less had ever worn a much-deserved dunce cap.

Flagg stayed silent. Mac and Rattler did likewise, putting pressure on Weed to offer the solution they wanted. He finally did.

"You three. Nobody else. Come on over to my herd, and you got one hour, no more, to find any cattle wearing your brand."

"Fair enough. You and two more of your men can ride through the Rolling J herd hunting for your cattle. Nobody else."

"I'll send men. I'm not taking my eyes off you three."

"Suit yourself." Flagg signaled to a trio of night riders heading in to sleep and told them what he was going to do. Mac saw them sag in the saddle. They knew they had to extend their shift another hour. Worse, with the cook heading off with the trail boss, their breakfast was going to be delayed.

Weed and his partner galloped back toward the other herd, leaving Flagg, Mac, and Rattler in the dust. Flagg motioned for them to ride on either side so he could talk to them.

"Keep an eye out for our brand and others, too. I get the feeling Jimson Weed up there's something of a rustler. The law would like to know how many different ranches he's herding cattle for legally—and which he's not."

"Gettin' our longhorns back ought to be enough, boss. Weed looks like trouble." Rattler kept moving his slicker back so his gun was easily drawn. He finally shucked off the oiled cloth and rolled it as he rode. This freed his holster.

Mac thought that was a good idea and duplicated the process, only with less skill. He almost dropped his slicker but finally tucked it under a rawhide string on his saddlebags. By the time they reached the Lazy B camp, Flagg was ready for action, too.

"Do you think they'll try to drygulch us?" Mac looked around the camp. The men stirring all looked like hardcases. He'd as soon expect to see their pictures on wanted posters as them herding cattle south of Abilene.

"When you see other brands, don't react," Flagg cautioned. "These men didn't start with a rancher's herd. They stole these cattle, picking off strays from other herds on the drive north."

Mac looked at Flagg. The trail boss ground his teeth together. His hand shook just a mite as he held the reins. The idea of a roving band of rustlers didn't set well with him, not at all.

"Is there any need to go too deep into their herd, boss? If our cattle joined up, they'd be on this side." Rattler didn't flinch as the Lazy B cowboys stared at him like he was going to be a buzzard's dinner.

"Play the cards as they're dealt. We don't want trouble." Flagg rode toward the herd, then stopped. "Watch your backs. Weed didn't send any of his men to fetch the Lazy B cattle in our herd."

Mac rubbed his hand across his coat to dry the perspiration. While there could be any number of reasons, the one that burned brightest in his head was Weed gunning them down, getting more Rolling J riders over and killing them. They'd have numerical superiority over the remaining drovers. Stealing the entire herd would be easy enough if they outnumbered the remaining Rolling J riders by two to one.

"Do you suppose Northrup has anything to do with them?" Mac looked around. "He promised to steal our herd."

"Don't worry none about Deke Northrup. He's

halfway to Canada by now. I know his kind. He talks big, but when push comes to shove, he's nowhere to be found." Flagg shifted around and squinted to get a better look at the cattle. "There's a pair of ours. Rattler, tend to them while Mac and I hunt some more."

Rattler spat out a curse, but he did as he was ordered. In a short time, Mac had located eight more Rolling J cows and had driven them back to where Rattler waited impatiently. Their tiny herd grew in size when Flagg drove back a dozen.

"You see any of those boys ride over to our herd?" Flagg wheeled his horse around as he spoke to Rattler in a low voice.

"Boss, those lazy louts never moved off their butts. There's the same number here as when we rode in."

"I was afraid of that. They'll ambush us, given the chance. Keep your gun ready. You do the same, Mac."

Mac slipped the leather thong off his S&W's hammer. The chance of it bouncing out as he rode increased, but he warily kept one hand near the butt now. If more than one of the Lazy B riders threw down on him, he would drill at least one of them and maybe more. He was glad now that Flagg had insisted on him practicing not only his draw but his marksmanship. Getting clear of the holster first didn't matter if he couldn't hit anything.

Mac imagined the other cowboys as being tin cans and whiskey bottles sitting on a fallen log. One by one, he fanned off rounds in his mind and hit each one squarely.

"Mac! Pay attention. Weed is making his way through the herd. I don't know what he's doing, but it doesn't look right."

Mac forgot his fantasy of gunning down a half dozen of the others and tried to make out what Weed was up to. Turning and cutting, he moved a bunch of cattle away, toward the far western side of the herd as if hiding it.

"He heard you say to check only this side of the cattle for ours," Mac said. "Let's see if I'm right." He snapped the reins and got his horse into a trot, only to find himself swallowed up by milling cattle. Trying to rush through the herd had been the wrong thing to do. The cattle reacted.

Flagg kept his horse at a slow, steady walk. The cattle parted as he came, towering over them. Swinging left and right in the saddle, Flagg guided his horse among the shiny horns faster than Mac would have thought possible. Seeing how well this tactic worked, he slowed his headlong rush and worked over to Flagg's wake. Even following the trail boss this way proved difficult. As quickly as the steers parted for Flagg, they closed back in and blocked Mac. Cursing under his breath, he made as much progress as he could but fell back minute by minute.

He heard Flagg call out to Weed, "That's mighty nice of you to cut out our cattle for us. All these have Rolling J brands."

Weed's reply was muffled. Mac saw Flagg ride closer, then he and Weed grappled and fell from their horses. This caused a reaction in the nearby steers. They moved away to form a small clearing in the center of the herd. They also crowded back toward Mac, further blocking his path while the two men wrestled.

Mac stood in the stirrups but only saw an occa-

sional arm or leg rising and falling. Weed and Flagg
fought, but who was winning remained hidden by
tons of beef. Seething at the slowness of his progress,
he moved toward the small area where Weed finally
swung and decked Flagg. The Lazy B rider got to his
feet and stumbled back. Mac whipped out his revolver
and started to shoot when he saw Weed going for his
gun. The distance was too great for him, but it didn't
matter. A longhorn bumped into Weed and knocked
him to his knees.

This gave Flagg a chance to get to his feet. Mac
worked closer and yelled, "I'll be there in a second.
Hold on!"

He came within a couple yards of the two men.

"You were trying to steal Rolling J cattle," Flagg
said. He had squared off. His hand rested on the
leather holster slung at his side. His fingers tapped
once, twice, then became perfectly still as he bent
forward slightly, ready to draw.

"Your herd is mine." Weed's hand flashed for his
gun.

He was fast. Flagg was faster. He cleared leather
and fired, the round catching Weed high in the right
shoulder and spinning him around. From his vantage mounted and looking down, Mac saw what Flagg
couldn't.

"Shoot him again. He—"

That was as far as Mac got before Weed ripped off
another shot. Flagg stood upright. He raised his gun
for another shot, then sank down as if the bones in
his legs had turned to mush. Mac raised his pistol
and aimed the best he could on a nervous horse buf-
feted around by longhorns. Flagg had taught him to

aim properly. He squeezed the trigger, felt the kick of the Model 3 in his hand. Then the world went berserk around him.

The cattle snorted in fear and stirred. He broke through the final ring of longhorns and dropped to the ground, kneeling beside Flagg. The trail boss looked up. His eyes were clear, but his lips were drawn back in pain.

"Damned son of a bitch shot me in the gut. Mac, don't ever let anybody tell you getting shot doesn't hurt. Hellfire. That's what it feels like."

"Don't move. I'll get you out of here." Mac almost laughed at the irony. Flagg lay wounded on the ground, and the first cow he saw as he looked around carried a Rolling J brand. He got his arms around Flagg's back and heaved him to his feet. For an instant, Flagg stood under his own power. Then his legs quit on him again, almost carrying Mac to the ground. Heaving, Mac got him up and onto his horse.

Only then did he go hunting for Jimson Weed. He pushed past frightened steers and found a patch of sticky mud where a considerable amount of blood had been shed. Gun waving around, he sought the man who had gunned down Flagg. Past a dozen heifers clustered together, he saw Weed's hat bobbing up and down. He took aim and fired.

"No, Mac, don't. Don't." Flagg's weak warning came too late.

He had clean missed Weed, but the report pushed the herd into a full frightened run. Whirling around, he found his path back to his horse and Patrick Flagg blocked by several steers. He scrambled onto the nearest longhorn, found purchase with his boot against a horn, kicked and launched himself through the air. He skipped over a second cow and landed hard, belly down over the rump of his horse. The animal reared, tossing him off.

Mac lay on the ground. All he saw surrounding him were hooves backed by thousands of pounds of fear. He curled up, got his feet under him, and climbed to his feet. His horse reared. Flagg tried to stay in the saddle and control it. As the front hooves landed hard on the ground, Mac threw his arms around its neck and pulled hard, bringing the horse to its knees. This let him mount with Flagg behind him.

The horse got back to its feet, giving Mac a horrifying view all around of a herd building up steam for a full-out stampede.

"That way." Flagg rested his arm on Mac's shoulder to point out a thin spot in the sea of cattle.

The horse understood, even if Mac was slow to see the opportunity for escape. They raced through the increasingly thin herd until they burst out behind the stampede. Mac brought the horse around and stared at the destruction moving away from them. Hooves pounded at the muddy ground so hard it felt like an earthquake. He almost galloped after the herd, thinking only to get in front and turn the lead steers.

Then he felt wetness on his back. Flagg still clung weakly to him, but the blood leaking from his belly wound soaked into Mac's coat, vest and shirt.

"Hang on," he said. "I'll get you back to the chuckwagon and get you fixed up before you know it.

Then we can go after the Rolling J cattle mixed in with the Lazy B stock."

"Ride, stop stam . . ." Flagg's voice trailed off.

Mac worried he had died, but the man straightened himself and shifted his grip so he hung onto Mac's gun belt. Fingers slipped underneath gave a more solid way of staying atop the horse.

Ride fast? Ride slow? Mac worried which was better for the wounded man. He decided getting to the wagon and what supplies he had there mattered more than the jolting gait of the horse as it galloped. By the time he found the chuckwagon parked beside a stream, the sun had poked all the way above the horizon.

"I'll have good light to bandage you up," he told Flagg.

"I'm gonna miss your biscuits. Damn, boy, you do them good."

"You won't miss them. I'll whip up a batch for breakfast. And for tonight, too. You can have those biscuits at both meals. And anytime until we get to Abilene."

"Good. I like that." Flagg started to slide off the saddle. Mac grabbed his arm and lowered him the best he could. It almost sent him falling to the ground, but he kept his balance and also prevented Flagg from taking a tumble.

Arm around the trail boss, he walked to the chuckwagon and heaved. Flagg helped and flopped into the bed, resting on a pile of burlap sacks. He rolled over onto his side and rested his head on a curled arm.

"That's not much of a pillow. Here." Mac slid a sack of beans under the injured man's head. Flagg lay flat on his back, staring up at the clouds moving sluggishly across the sky.

"Might rain again. Hope no twister. Hail. Can't stand more hail."

"Take a sip of this. It's medicinal." Mac helped his patient swallow a little whiskey. When Flagg kept it down, he gave him some more.

"Never wanted to drink on the trail. Bad."

"This is medicine, not booze." As Mac talked, he used his knife to cut away the blood-soaked vest and shirt above Flagg's wound. "I'm no doctor, but it doesn't look too bad."

"Is the bullet still in me? Got a pain in my back."

Mac rolled Flagg onto his side and cut away more vest and shirt. The exit wound was three times the size of the entry.

"You are one lucky galoot. I don't have to go digging around inside you to find the bullet. It went smack-dab through."

"Go back. Find it," Flagg said. He grinned. "Want a souvenir."

"The scars on your tired old body will have to do. By now the cattle have tromped the lead into the ground." He grumbled a bit and said loud enough for Flagg to hear, "I hope they stomped Weed into the ground, too."

"Trampled weeds. All kinds." Flagg tried to laugh but winced in pain.

"More medicine, then this." Mac poured the alcohol onto the wound. Flagg arched his back and cried out. As he came off the sacks, Mac poured more onto the bigger wound in his back. Flagg passed out from the pain.

Mac had some medical supplies. He unwrapped bandages and wound them around Flagg tightly enough to prevent more bleeding. He was trying to make the man comfortable when Rattler rode up.

"By all that's holy, how'd Flagg get shot?" He came over and examined Mac's bandaging and nodded in approval. Rattler picked up the bottle, obviously thirsting for a taste. Looking at Flagg made him put the cork back in. "He needs it more."

"What about the stampede? I don't hear the uproar out there anymore."

"I tell you, Mac, them cows won't have an ounce of fat on 'em when we get to Abilene if they keep tryin' to run off like that. We turned them at the creek, not a mile away."

"What about the Lazy B rider? The one I suspect is their trail boss? Weed's his name."

"Is he the one what shot Flagg?" Rattler gripped his six-shooter.

"He'll pay for gunning him down," Mac said. "I swear it. What about our herds?"

"The two are all mixed up like that salt in the flour. It'll take a day or longer to cut ours out." Rattler hesitated, then asked, "With Flagg down and out like this, who's our trail boss?"

"You, I reckon. You're experienced and—" Mac lost his balance when Flagg reached up and took his arm in a surprisingly strong grip. The man's eyes fluttered open, but he looked squarely at Rattler.

"Mac. Mac's . . . trail boss. I say so." Flagg closed his eyes and passed out. His breathing became shallow and uneven, but he was still breathing.

"I can't," Mac said. "I'm a cook."

"You didn't know nothing about cooking 'fore you signed on. At least now you know all about riding herd and scouting. From his condition, I'd say you're pretty good at doctoring, too."

"I can't do all this. I have to cook. I have to scout. I—"

"Hey, fellows!" shouted Rattler, waving to the cowboys coming in from turning the stampede. "Mac here's the acting trail boss while Flagg is laid up."

"Good," said the nearest rider. "That's real good. Now where's breakfast? A trail boss never lets his men go hungry."

Dewey Mackenzie tried to argue, but no one listened to him.

CHAPTER 27

"He's out of his mind. He's been gut-shot!" Mac threw his hands up in the air, frustrated that the Rolling J cowboys wouldn't listen to him. "He's passed out."

"I heard Flagg as clear as day sayin' that you're trail boss whilst he's recoverin'." Rattler looked around at the other hands, who were eating the breakfast Mac had prepared hastily. "Some of you boys heard him, too, while you were ridin' up. Ain't that so?"

"That is the gospel truth," one cowboy said. Others joined in until Mac knew he faced rebellion if he didn't assume command of the trail drive.

"I'm doing half a dozen jobs already," he said, more to himself than any of the men. "Why not trail boss, too?"

"As long as you don't let Rattler fix the coffee, I'm good with doing what you say, Mac."

This proved to be the general consensus, over Rattler's protests that he was able to boil a decent pot of coffee. The men gathered round and stood silently.

It took Mac a second to realize they were waiting for his orders.

He looked at Flagg but got no help there. The trail boss slept peacefully now. His breathing still sounded like a smithy's bellows, and his face was pale, but that could be blood loss and shock. There wasn't a whole lot more Mac could do for him. But the herd? It had to be tended right away.

"Get back out there and cut out the Lazy B cows. Then I'll go and talk to them about getting our cattle back."

"Why not call it even? We got more of their scrawny runts than they do of our prime beef," Rattler opined. "More in our herd, better in theirs." He scratched his head. "That don't sound right. You say we get ours back, then we do, Mac. Let's go, fellas."

Mac finished cleaning up after their breakfast, poured some water into Flagg's mouth. Flagg choked at first, then got the hang of swallowing while he was still passed out. Mac took that as a good sign the trail boss would make it. He finished packing, made sure Flagg was comfortable on a bedroll and some burlap sacks, then hitched the team and started out, hunting for a trail to follow. The ground was all torn up from the storm and the many stampedes of two entire herds.

He cut across and headed for the spot where the Lazy B cowboys had camped. It was time to settle accounts with them. Before he got halfway, he reached back, retrieved his gun belt, and strapped it on. It felt right dangling at his hip. And this time he wasn't going to hesitate to use the S&W, should it come to that.

He pulled up outside their camp and jumped down. He felt their eyes on him as he walked up boldly and asked, "Where's Weed?"

"What do you want with him?" a man asked in a surly voice.

"He shot my trail boss." He didn't bother adding that Flagg had shot Weed or that he had taken a couple potshots at the man as well. With any luck, someone would tell him that Weed's body had been trampled.

"We don't know where he got off to. We ain't seen him since yesterday, before the last stampede."

Mac heard the lie. He went to the man and stood with his face inches away. A sudden twitch as if he went for his gun made the man jump out of his skin.

"Next time I move, there'll be a six-shooter in my hand. Where's Weed?"

"He . . . he . . . we're tellin' the truth. We ain't seen him. The son of a bitch musta lit out and left us on our own."

"He was your trail boss?"

"As much as anybody."

Mac wondered at that, then considered how many different brands he had seen on the cattle in the Lazy B herd. The initial herd must have been small. Unlike most drives, the Lazy B herd had grown through picking up strays from other ranches and undoubtedly a tad of rustling. He didn't care about stolen cattle. He wanted Rolling J cows back and demanded it of the handful of cowboys gathered.

"You've got until noon to cut out my cows. My crew is working to get anything with a Lazy B brand driven over here."

"Why should we do what you want?" The most arrogant of the cowboys came up, thumbs hooked into his gun belt. Mac sized him up.

"You don't have a trail boss, do you?"

"No, but—"

Lightning speed brought Mac's S&W out. He swung it around and laid the barrel alongside the man's temple. He went down like a tall tree sawed down in the forest. Mac put his boot in the middle of the man's chest to hold him down.

"Then I'll be your trail boss, and I've given you an order. Disobey and . . ." He let them imagine what he would do as he swung his gun around in an arc, covering each man in turn.

"You heard him. Get his cows outta the herd. Come on, come on!"

The Lazy B riders belied their brand as they hurried to get to work. Mac took his foot off the downed man. With his gun still in his hand, Mac glared down at him.

"You going to lie around all day, or are you going to work cutting out those cattle?"

"G-going now, boss." The man rolled onto hands and knees, then shot off like a stepped-on dog.

Mac returned to the wagon, climbed into the driver's box, then glanced at Flagg. The man's eyes were open. A small smile spread until it went ear to ear. He closed his eyes and went back to sleep. Mac took that to mean Flagg had overheard everything and approved of the way he had handled the reluctant cowboys.

About noon, he prepared a meal for his cowboys.

As they ate, he listened to their tallies on Rolling J cattle recovered.

"They took off after they brought us our cows," Rattler said. "It was real odd. They worked, slow as molasses, but they worked. It was almost like they intended to give us back our due but do it real slow."

As the men reported, Mac kept count. He frowned when he added up the numbers.

"We lost more than a hundred head. How's that possible? Did you scout the area for stragglers?"

"Of course we did, Mac." Rattler looked disgusted. "We're not greenhorns. No offense."

"They did a piss-poor job of cutting the cattle," said another cowboy. "And I swear their herd was tiny."

"Tiny." Mac tried to remember seeing the extent of the Lazy B herd. "Rattler, you jump on your horse and run it hard to the north. Come back when you see the Lazy B herd."

He finished serving the meal and began cleaning up when Rattler returned. The man's tanned face was fiery red with anger.

"Boss, they hit the trail with their main herd at dawn or before. They must have made off with those hundred head we couldn't find."

"So they've got almost a half day's start on us. Weed wanted to dicker with Flagg about reaching Abilene first."

"That'd slice off half the money we'd get for every head," protested Rattler. "The earlier we get to the railroad, the more we get."

"We've been snookered," Mac said. "They not only stole some of our cattle, they stole a march on us."

"We can overtake them. If we get goin' now, we can catch up and give 'em what for." Rattler slapped his sidearm to show what he meant.

Mac had had enough gunfighting to last a lifetime. Flagg was in a bad way, and he had to do the job of trail boss and almost everything else. The only bright spot was being able to order the others to ride night herd in his stead. The downside to that was doctoring Flagg. He was hesitant to leave the chuckwagon and his patient for too long.

"Rest the herd for another half day. I'll go scouting. While I'm out finding us a decent trail, I'll be thinking on the matter."

"You can't let them beat us to Abilene. You can't, Mac." Rattler got even redder in the face as his anger rose again.

Mac slapped him on the shoulder and said, "That's not going to happen. I don't know how we'll do it, but we'll be there watching those miserable snakes in the grass coming into the rail yard. You wait and see."

This mollified Rattler, but as Mac drove the chuckwagon out to scout the trail for a five- or six-mile travel day, he wondered how he could deliver on the promise.

He felt as if he had been on the trail all day, though his pocket watch told him it was less than three hours. Mac looked over his shoulder now and then to see how Flagg fared. The trail boss moaned and rolled about, showing he was still alive. That heartened Mac but made the trip seem even longer. Hunting for smoother terrain so he wouldn't bounce Flagg all over the wagon bed required more concentration and took him away from scouting a route for the herd.

Mac was so occupied with Flagg that he rattled up a low rise before he saw the curl of white smoke ahead. He halted and stared down the slight incline to a spot beside a creek where half a dozen Indians camped. Reaching for his gun, he knew he was in big trouble if they decided to come after him. Fighting rather than running was his only way out.

Then he hit on a third way, other than opening fire or turning tail. Neither of those promised to work well since they outnumbered him and, with their ponies rested, could easily overtake him.

Mac stood in the driver's box and waved, then called to them.

"Hello! Can I come down?"

The Indians crowded together and talked. One rose from around their campfire and motioned for Mac to join them.

None of the others went for weapons or even glanced toward bows and arrows stacked nearby. As Mac slowly made his way down the slope, he saw that the Indians had two rifles among them. He had more to fear from the knives at their belts than he did longer-range weapons—so of course he drove right down to them.

He hopped down and waited.

"You are cattleman," the standing Indian said. Mac tried to make out the tribe. They weren't Comanche. The Five Civilized Tribes in Indian Territory were well settled and didn't roam around the plains.

"Osage?" That reaction was one of distaste. "Shawnee?" This produced a more positive reaction. "Pleased to make your acquaintance." He thrust out his hand, then pulled it back when the Indian made no move to shake. "You're right. I'm trail boss for a herd going to Abilene."

"Iron horses there."

"That's the reason we're going." Mac hesitated, then asked, "Do you know the fastest way there if I have to drive the herd?"

"Cattle?"

"Texas longhorns," he confirmed.

This set off a long dialogue among the Indians. After some discussion, their leader nodded.

"We know quick way. Faster than on trail there." He pointed to the west, where the Lazy B herd had to be traveling. Swinging around, he pointed northeast. "There. Faster."

"That's not where Abilene is."

"Faster." The Shawnee dropped to one knee and sketched a map in the dirt.

"Would you scout for us and show the route?"

This produced more discussion. Their leader shook his head.

"Map, no scout. You give us cattle."

That moved the discussion in a different direction. For more than half an hour, Mac dickered with them and settled on giving the Shawnee ten head. In return, they let him make a map of the route. The only paper Mac had turned out to be the wanted poster he had taken from the Lewiston marshal's office. It made him uneasy using the back to draw the map, but he decided it put the poster to a better use.

"Are you sure about the direction?" Mac again felt uneasy that this route took them off at an angle away from Abilene.

"Our trail. You use Shawnee Trail. Know country." The Shawnee leader pounded on his chest with a fist and pointed to the northeast.

"Done. I will bring cattle to thank you for this." He held up the map. All the Indians nodded and whispered to each other. It made him wonder if he had been lied to, but he had to take the chance.

It was time to roll the dice. He climbed onto the chuckwagon and headed back to the herd. Rattler had arrived at the spot they had agreed on at breakfast and impatiently looked around for the chuckwagon—and his noon meal.

Mac creaked to a halt and motioned Rattler over.

"Cut out ten head of cattle."

"Which ones? You dealing them for something we can use?"

"I am. I have a map that'll get us to Abilene ahead of the Lazy B herd." He pulled out the wanted poster and hastily turned it over so Rattler couldn't see the picture. "I got this from some Shawnee Indians. They have the trail named after them, so they should know all the shortcuts."

"I'll have the boys cut out some of them Lazy B branded steers. They're scrawny little things, anyway."

"That's fine." Mac jumped down, checked on Flagg, and then began opening the drawers and getting out his kettles to prepare the noon meal. "You see that the Indians get the cattle. You personally. I don't want to make them mad at us."

"It wasn't a war party or you'd be missin' your scalp. That means a huntin' party. You givin' them that many cows will feed their village all winter long. You sure you want me to cut out that many?"

"Do it. Now get moving or you won't get back before all the food's gone."

He watched Rattler hustle off. Had he done the right thing by getting a map from a band of Indians he had never met before and had no information about? It hadn't occurred to him that the Shawnee were a hunting party rather than on the warpath until Rattler mentioned it. Why should they offer any help to drovers crossing what had been their hunting ground for a long time?

Mac pushed such worries aside as he fixed up a stew for the cowboys, then used Flagg to test how good it was. All the man had to say was a weak, "Needs salt."

Mac decided he was right and poured in a handful of salt.

He hoped he was right about the new trail cutting off time from the final push into Abilene, the railhead, and top dollar for the Rolling J longhorns.

CHAPTER 28

"That's the bend in the river," Mac said, moving the map around so it lined up with the terrain they crossed.

"Mac, we been travelin' a whole day, and we're goin' away from Abilene. I swear, it's back there." Rattler pointed to the northwest.

"I'm not Compass Jack."

"Thank the saints for that," Rattler said. "The H Bar H outfit's a tough one to work for, and they don't have a cook near as good as you."

"I guessed that when he offered me a job." Mac folded the map and put it back into his pocket. More than once, he had almost exposed the back side to Rattler and the others, showing his poorly rendered photograph. None of the Rolling J cowboys would turn him in for the paltry reward, but he wanted to keep them moving toward the railroad without any conflicts of loyalty.

He *hoped* they were going in the right direction. He couldn't think of any reason for the Shawnee Indians to direct him on a wild goose chase, although Rattler and the others probably could give him a long list. He accepted all that, but in this world, you had to believe somebody sometime. Why he chose to believe the Indians wasn't something he could put his finger on.

The hunting party had been delighted to get the cattle. He hadn't seen a hint that they felt guilt over giving him the wrong directions. If anything, there had been pride in giving information others lacked. At least he hoped that was what he read on their faces.

"Go on and ford the river," he ordered Rattler. "It looks rough going for another couple days. Then it ought to be a race into town."

"You get that from the map?" Rattler shook his head sadly. "I think we'd better get used to the idea of takin' the herd all the way to St. Louis. That's the direction we're goin'."

"Get to the herd. I've got to set up camp for the night."

"You get across the river in the wagon without any help?"

"Flagg can help. He's doing better."

"About that, Mac. The map ain't the only thing you're not seein' right. Flagg don't have any color in his face, and his hands shake."

"He took a bullet through the gut. It'll take a spell, maybe a long one, before he's up and kicking again."

"You're seein' things that ain't there." Rattler sighed. "Never mind. I ain't arguing with you 'bout anything. I'll get to point on the herd and start them across the river in a half hour or so." Rattler rode away.

Mac watched him go, then made sure Flagg was resting comfortably. Only then did he climb onto the driver's box and start his team pulling toward the river. He had studied the banks earlier and found a rocky spot that showed where others had crossed in the past few days. He wasn't a good enough tracker to know if the tracks were from shod horses or Indian ponies. Finding a scrubby tree on the far side, he fixed his gaze on that as a goal and got the team pulling.

The horses balked, then found some purchase on the slippery river bottom. As the current caught the chuckwagon, he began slipping downstream. Keeping the tree in sight, he guided the team back, partially against the current. Flagg moaned in the rear of the wagon, but Mac had his hands full with the team. Halfway. Then the horses got better purchase and pulled hard, wanting to be out of the cold, running water. With a final surge, the horses dragged the chuckwagon onto dry land again.

Mac let out a whoop of joy. The map had shown this ford. It had given him the trail up to this point and hadn't been wrong. From this point on, it would be rough for five or ten miles, then easy going.

"Easy going," he said aloud. "We'll get to Abilene before those crooks working for the Lazy B."

He gave the team a once-over, checked Flagg, and began to lay out a trail for the herd. The ground turned rocky and rough, almost overturning the chuckwagon in one stretch. He gritted his teeth and plowed on, too stubborn to admit the Indians had sold him a bill of goods. By the time he was ready to stop, he worried that the wagon wouldn't hold up much longer. More than once, he feared a broken wheel or cracked axle.

He rolled to a level if rocky spot and began fixing the evening meal for the men. It would be some time before the herd arrived because of the rugged terrain. Mac sighed as he fixed the biscuits. He had about run out of dough. No more yeast, the flour was close to being all used up, and there wasn't a lot more left in the larder. If he wanted to give the men the biscuits they enjoyed so, he would have to turn back and find the more traveled part of the West Shawnee Trail into Abilene. That would put them a week to ten days behind the Lazy B and most likely many of the other herds. Selling the cattle would be a disaster, and Mr. Jefferson would barely break even, if Mac's figures were right.

But at least he would have delivered the herd.

"Not bad," he said to himself, "for a first-time, greenhorn trail boss who has no idea what he's doing."

As the biscuits came out of the Dutch oven, he looked up to see Rattler and several others riding up.

"Get the food before the varmints do," he called. More than once, he wished he had a dinner bell to properly summon the men to chow down. That had been the farthest thing from his mind when Lem Carson had recruited him to be cook back in Waco.

Now it would have been fitting, traditional, something he would have enjoyed using.

"Biscuits! It's about time we had something to celebrate," Rattler said. He was first in line and had two biscuits downed before he got to the main course. "I do declare, Mac, I doubted you. No more."

"Why's that?" Mac started to tell the men he had

decided to turn back, but another eight rode up. Better to tell as many as possible once and not let gossip spread. It was his job as trail boss, after all, to keep the men informed.

"They're beddin' down the herd just over the rise." Rattler laughed, the sound building and coming out full-throated. "As if there's anywhere in Kansas that counts as a rise."

The newcomers lined up for chow, and Mac decided the time was right. The men left to tend the herd would be in to eat within an hour.

"I've got an announcement to make," he started.

"No need to get all long-winded," Rattler said. "We already know."

"How do you know?"

"We got eyes. You may be the scout, but we saw it with our own eyes."

"What did you see?" Mac was too confused to think straight.

"The tracks. Two or three of the boys said they recognized this stretch of tracks. They wanted to keep goin', but I thought you had a reason for stoppin' so soon."

"To eat. To feed you and let the cattle graze." He still didn't understand what Rattler was talking about.

"They can graze plenty in the fattening pens. That's what they're for. Good biscuits. Any left?" Rattler went to poke about in the Dutch oven, hunting for the doughy lumps.

Mac pressed close and asked in a low voice, "What the *hell* are you talking about?"

"The herd. We're almost there. Abilene's not more than five miles off. None of us thought this shortcut you took would amount to a hill of beans, and here you landed us in the rail yards, five days sooner than if we'd followed the old trail."

Speechless, Mac stared at Rattler, thinking he was joshing him. Neither he nor any of the others had that sly look of putting one over on him. Their joy was real, as was their bragging about what they'd do when they got paid. Mac left them around the buffalo-chip fire and hiked to the top of the rise. The herd shifted restlessly as most of the cattle ate and others started falling asleep.

In the distance, he heard a steam whistle. Echoes of steel wheels clattering against tracks came a short time later. In the twilight, he saw a tower of black smoke from a stack. Dancing fireflies of embers darted about as the distant train sped westward.

Toward Abilene. He had done it. He had brought the herd to market.

"It's a good thing we're almost there," Rattler said. "I can't stand another breakfast without biscuits."

"I'll drive on in and be sure the yard's ready to take Rolling J cattle," Mac said. He looked anxiously into the rear of the chuckwagon, where Flagg lay unmoving. He had hardly moaned all night long, and he burned up with fever. "I'll get Flagg to a doctor, too. He's in a bad way and getting worse."

"He's a tough old bird. He'll do all right." Rattler said the words without conviction.

"You bring the herd in, and we'll celebrate." Mac wasn't even sure he remembered how to celebrate anything. Life on the trail had been so fraught with danger and disappointment, being free of it seemed impossible.

"See you in Abilene, old son." Rattler touched the brim of his hat in salute, then let out a yell that rolled across the prairie. Others in the outfit took it up. They all knew the end of the drive was nigh.

Mac settled down in the driver's box and started the last few miles into Abilene. The sound and smell of a city devoted to shipping cattle rose quickly. The trains huffed and puffed. Even the horses felt the energy and spirit and began pulling faster. He reached the town sooner than he expected.

He patted his pocket with the map given him by the Shawnee Indians out on the prairie. That had been the best deal ever made, ten cattle for a week saved on the trail.

"You up to doing some dickering, Flagg? They know you and you can get top dollar." He looked back at the trail boss. Flagg was even paler, if that was possible. He thrashed about weakly as fever dreams danced in his head.

Mac saw the road branching one way to the rail yards and the other into town. He never slowed as he took the road into town and began asking everyone he saw along the way where he could find a doctor. Selling the herd was important. A man's life was more important, especially when it was Patrick Flagg's.

He found the doctor's office at the edge of town. Not bothering to see if the doctor was in, he heaved Flagg over his shoulder. The man was as light as a feather. Mac went to the door and kicked at it a couple times to announce his presence.

"Got a patient, Doc. You in? Is anybody inside?"

The door opened. A man hardly a year older than Mac himself stood there. He tried to grow a mustache. The few bristles showed it wasn't too successful. Worse, the man's sandy hair was already receding, giving a curious young-old look to him. He peered at Mac through thick glasses.

"Bring him on in and put him on the table. You're lucky I'm still here. Miz Rodriguez is about due to deliver." He snorted. "Has been for two weeks. I wish she'd get done with it. I've got a bet that it'll be a boy." The doctor peered at Mac. "The Rodriguezes have four daughters already. Poor Paco deserves a son after all he's been through."

"This is my trail boss. He's been shot."

"He was shot some time ago, wasn't he? That's one powerful fever." He stripped away the bandages and frowned as he poked at Flagg's wound. Mac grimaced. He hadn't seen the green growing around the bullet hole before. The doctor called, "Elise, fill the tub with cold water. I've got a fever to bring down fast." He never looked up as he continued probing the wound. "Elise is my missus and acts as my nurse."

He heaved Flagg onto his side and examined the exit wound in his back.

"How long's he been like this?"

"He was shot almost a week ago."

"And you've bounced him around in that wagon ever since. Amazing. This man's constitution is pure steel."

"What can I do to help? I've been tending him since he was shot."

"Well, you can—" The doctor recoiled when Flagg reached up and grabbed Mac's arm in a strong grip.

"Mac, get to the rail yard," Flagg rasped. "You want to deal with Ready Reedy. He'll give you an honest deal. Ready Reedy. He—"

"You settle down now," the doctor said, prying Flagg's hand free. "We'll do what we can for you." He looked at Mac. His expression spoke volumes. There wasn't much to be done for Flagg. But the doctor had said he had a strong constitution.

In that Mac took hope.

"I'll be back to let you know how the deal went," he promised. "Ready Reedy. I won't be long."

"So long, Mac. You're a helluva cook. Scout. Trail boss. Go. Go." Flagg collapsed onto the table, eyes closed. Only the fluttering of hie eyelids showed any life remained.

Mac hesitated, then saw there wasn't any more he could do. He owed it to Mr. Jefferson to get a decent price for the cattle, and since the trail boss wasn't able, he would act as Flagg's assistant. As he left, the doctor and his wife were wrestling a limp Patrick Flagg into a bathtub sloshing over with water to bring down his fever.

All the way to the rail yard, he told himself Flagg would be fine. Get a good deal. Ready Reedy. Get a good deal from the cattle broker and Flagg would snap right back to his old self.

"Ready Reedy," he called to men hanging on the fence of a cattle chute. They prepared a pen full of longhorns to go into a cattle car on a siding.

"Yonder. Kansas Range and Cattle Company."

"Much obliged." He parked the chuckwagon beside the office and took a deep breath. His job was almost over. He opened the door and stared. His mouth dropped open as he heard a familiar voice say, "That's him, Marshal. That's the rustler I told you about. His name's Mackenzie, and he's a dangerous one. You be careful arresting him."

Deke Northrup smirked as the marshal came forward, revolver drawn and ready to fire.

CHAPTER 29

"Hold on, Marshal. I haven't done anything. What's the charge?"

Even as the words left Mac's lips, he knew whatever trumped-up charges Northrup had filed against him amounted to nothing compared with murder down in New Orleans. Without thinking, he pressed his hand against his coat pocket where the wanted posters with his pictures rested.

"What's that?" the lawman snapped. "What do you have in that pocket? Pull it out real slow."

With the marshal's six-shooter trained on him, Mac wasn't in a position to do anything else. He felt anger boiling inside as Northrup looked on with his smug attitude.

"It's a map made by the leader of a Shawnee band I came across. They helped me to get here ahead of some other herds." He carefully drew out the wanted poster. He had folded it several times, with part of his face showing.

The marshal grabbed it from his hand.

"The back side, Marshal. That's where I drew the map."

The marshal carefully smoothed it out and laid it on the table. One corner curled up. Mac vowed to throw down on the lawman if he saw the reward for the man Northrup accused of being a rustler.

"It's a map. I recognize this river. And here's Slow-poke Gulch. You cross that with a herd?"

"I did. Once past it, getting into Abilene was easy."

"This only shows he came with a stolen herd. It doesn't prove anything else," Northrup said. "Look, Marshal, I filed charges against him and Patrick Flagg a week back. You know all the details about how them and their gang stole my herd."

"Liar!" Mac started for Northrup, only to have the marshal's gun jammed into his belly.

"I have witnesses. Fontaine told you the same story."

Without realizing it, Mac ran his fingers over his upper arm where Fontaine and his cronies had strung him up like a side of beef.

"Thumbs Fontaine and two others robbed me. They robbed me after they poured salt into my flour. That got them and Northrup fired."

"So you admit you were with Northrup's herd?" The marshal squinted with one eye.

"He worked for Mr. Jefferson and was only a cow-boy with the Rolling J. He's not the owner."

"He made the claim that he was."

The other man in the room, who had been silent until now, spoke up. "I've been a broker here in Abi-lene for years. The Rolling J owner's a steady cus-tomer of mine and has decent cattle, but I've never seen either of these men before, Marshal."

"Contact Mr. Jefferson. He owns the Rolling J. He'll tell you." Even as Mac spoke, he knew that wouldn't accomplish anything, even if Jefferson replied. Lem Carson had hired him, not the rancher. Jefferson didn't know him from Adam.

"That's a sure way to keep us all in town for a month," Northrup protested. "There's no reliable telegraph to Waco, not after the war." Northrup looked proud of himself for that one. "Besides, this one's a youngster. The real criminal is Flagg. He's the mastermind behind the rustling."

"He's being tended with a bullet in his gut," Mac said, speaking before he realized it might be better to keep quiet. If Northrup thought Flagg was waiting for him, he'd be more skittish and might even spill the truth by accident. Knowing the trail boss was in a bad way only added to the man's arrogance.

"Good riddance. Now, Marshal, are you going to throw this rustler into jail or not?"

"I can't do that on your say-so, Northrup. I know, you got witnesses, but that doesn't mean a thing to me. I need a bill of sale, a letter from this Jefferson fellow. Mr. Reedy knows him, so if I see a letter I'll take that as evidence of who's running this herd for the Rolling J."

"The herd's just now coming in," Reedy said, looking out the door. "I see the brand."

"Get them all logged in and tallied up, Mr. Reedy," Mac said. "Did we beat the Lazy B to the train?"

"Lazy B? I don't know that ranch. I haven't heard of other brokers taking in a herd, either. Only one got here before you."

"We need to get a price so you can send the cattle off to Chicago," Mac said.

"Hold on! He's not the one who can sell the cattle. I am. Arrest this damned rustler, Marshal. I demand it!"

"Cool down, Northrup. I don't remember a dustup like this before. I need to talk to Judge Francis about what to do. Until then, those cows don't go nowhere. They don't leave, either back down the trail or off to Chicago. Understand, Mr. Reedy?"

"Plain as you can make it. From the look of them, they need some time in the fattening pens. The trail's run off a lot of weight."

Mac said, "We've gone through tornados and hailstorms and—"

"Don't mean a thing, Marshal. He stole them. I don't care what he went through bringing my cattle to market." Northrup stood with his chin jutting out. Mac wanted to take a swing. One good shot to the jaw would knock the lying rustler out cold.

He held back, knowing that would get him into trouble and strengthen Northrup's claim to the herd.

"I'll do some asking around. Neither of you gents leave town, hear?"

The marshal started to scoop up the map, but Mac grabbed it. They had a small tug of war over it.

"This is mine, Marshal. It doesn't have any bearing on ownership."

"Reckon not." The lawman released the wanted poster. Mac hastily jammed it into his pocket and out of sight. He vowed to burn it the first chance he had.

Only a strange vanity had made him keep such damning evidence this long.

"You keep those thieves away from my cows after you get them into the fattening pens," Northrup said. He left, making a point of shoving Mac out of his way.

"Keep calm, youngster," advised Ready Reedy. "We'll get this worked out."

"I'm the Rolling J trail boss with Flagg all laid up."

"If you'd ridden in and Northrup wasn't muddying up the waters, I'd take you at your word. You seem honest enough." Reedy sniffed. "More'n the likes of him. But you heard the marshal. The herd's impounded until the judge rules who's allowed to sell it."

Mac added, "And who's allowed to take the money."

He stepped out into the bright Kansas day. The cowboys had gathered around, looking expectant. Telling them the truth would only cause big trouble. Rattler had a hair trigger, and the rest weren't far behind after all the hardships they had endured on the trail. Knowing that Deke Northrup was trying to cheat them out of their pay would cause a ruckus unlike anything Abilene had ever seen before.

"I need to do some more negotiating before the herd's sold."

"When do we get our money, Mac?" Rattler spoke for the rest.

"First, the longhorns need to get some weight put back on. That'll get us better money. You fellows 'bout ran their legs off, the ones you didn't eat." He tried for some joking. He got a smile or two. They wanted their pay. He didn't blame them.

"It won't take long. I promise you," he said.

"How's Flagg doin'?" Rattler asked. Only a few cowboys had remained after being told their pay wasn't forthcoming.

"Not too good. The doctor's looking at him. He had a high fever, but dunking in ice water's supposed to help with that."

"Gettin' shot's just the thing he needed. That's the first bath Flagg'll have had since we left Waco." Rattler laughed at the joke. Mac smiled weakly. The memory of how Flagg had told him to get the herd sold lingered.

He wasn't sure how he would tell the trail boss they might lose ownership of the herd. That it was Deke Northrup attempting to pull off the theft made it even worse. He wished Flagg had listened to him when he said that Northrup was pure poison, but keeping the herd moving back then had been more important than running Northrup and his gang to ground and finishing them off.

The more important matter to attend to now was proving he had authority to sell the herd. Mac had no idea how he would do that. Even if Flagg waltzed in right then, Reedy said he didn't know him. The cattle broker was well known, but that didn't mean he knew all his customers. With most ranchers changing their cowboys from year to year, the only one who would have been known was Lem Carson. And he was dead.

"What are you going to do, Mac? We don't have money for a real bender, and none of the saloons in this town will run a tab for a cowboy."

"Smart businessmen, them," Mac said. He watched

as more cattle were driven up the chute into freight cars. "Those must be from the herd that beat us to town."

"The H Bar H," Rattler said. "I saw the brand."

"Do tell." Mac rubbed his chin. "Maybe I ought to drop in on Compass Jack Bennett and congratulate him for getting here ahead of us."

"Cadge a drink from him. He took quite a shine to you." With that, Rattler wandered off to join the others from the Rolling J.

"He did take a shine to me, didn't he? He offered me a job as cook." Mac walked fast to the corral and climbed up next to a cowboy counting the longhorns as they were loaded onto the freight car.

"I'm looking for Compass Jack. Where's he hanging out right now?"

The cowboy he spoke to jerked his thumb over his shoulder.

"In the railroad office. He's always doing a new deal." The cowboy looked him over. "Do I know you? You look familiar."

"Our paths crossed on the trail. Thanks for the information." Mac hopped down and found the railroad office. He sucked in his breath. If this didn't work, he had no idea how to prove ownership of the herd. He went into the office.

Compass Jack sat with his feet up on a desk, glass of whiskey in hand. Across from him sat a man with a matching glass. Between them on the desk sat a half-full bottle of liquor.

"Can I help you?" asked the man behind the desk. Neither of them dropped his feet to the floor.

"Soon, I hope, if you're the shipping agent. Right now, I need to ask Compass Jack a question."

"Jack, you've gone too far this time. Using my office to do your business? I should charge you."

"You do, Ned," Compass Jack drawled. "Triple the going rate, if what I hear's true."

"Naw, only half that." The railroad agent lifted his glass in salute and downed the whiskey. He poured another shot as he waited to see what was unfolding in his office.

"Do you know me?" Mac asked.

"Now that's an unexpected question. Hell, yes, I know you. You're Flagg's cook. And you can argue with the best of 'em and win. I know. You talked me out of a nice profit."

"Flagg's laid up over at the doctor's office."

"Too bad. So?" Compass Jack put his glass down carefully on the edge of the desk. "There's not a whole lot I can do."

"I'm not asking you to do anything on that score. I need something else from you. I need you to go to Ready Reedy and identify me as being the legitimate trail boss for the Rolling J herd. After Flagg got shot, he appointed me."

"So I can't ask him about that? Is that the problem?"

"The problem is Deke Northrup." Mac carefully laid out the way Northrup had lied and what had to be done so he wouldn't steal the herd—and do it legally.

"You want me to tell Reedy I know you from the trail and that Northrup got fired?"

"He tried to get a job with you. You turned him down."

"That decision makes me out to be a genius." Compass Jack picked up his glass and swirled the amber fluid around, watching the light play off it before downing it in a single gulp. "I won't do it."

"What?"

"I won't tell Reedy any such thing. Or the marshal."

"But—"

"I won't do it unless I get paid." Compass Jack grinned wolfishly.

"How much? How many head of cattle?" Mac fought to hold his anger in check. This was outright thievery. He wondered if Compass Jack was in cahoots with Northrup.

"You don't have enough cattle to pay me." Compass Jack dropped his feet to the floor, put his hands on his knees, and leaned forward. "I'll tell you what I do want."

Dewey Mackenzie stared at the H Bar H trail boss in amazement when he heard the price.

CHAPTER 30

"This better be good. I've got an important meeting." The judge puffed himself up and fingered the gavel lying on the desk in front of him.

"She can wait, Benjamin. This is important." Ready Reedy stood in the middle of the small group gathered before the beefy, ruddy-faced judge.

"You'll address me as Judge Francis, sir. This is an official, if somewhat informal, legal proceeding. And I resent your innuendo."

"No innuendo, Judge," Reedy said. "Ursula will wait for you. But," he went on hurriedly when the judge reached for the gavel, preparing to give it a solid rap on the desk, "we got the parties to the dispute gathered to give evidence."

"Not all the parties. Where's this Northrup fellow?" Judge Francis peered down his nose at a paper in front of him.

"We can take care of that varmint later, Judge," said the marshal. "You ought to hear what Mr. Mackenzie has to say."

"So let me hear it and be quick about it. I know the dispute." The judge shook the paper. "What's your evidence that you're the rightful owner of the herd? Rather, the rightful agent acting for Rolling J ranch owner Sidney Jefferson?"

"Northrup claimed I ran him off and stole the herd. I've got a witness to what happened. Compass Jack Bennett is—"

"I know who he is." The judge cast a baleful glance toward Bennett. "Jack's been a regular in this court for years."

"I always bail my men out, Judge," Compass Jack said. "You have to admit that they've never done more than put a few bullet holes in saloon ceilings."

"One bullet came tearing through the floor right next to the bed where Ursula and me was—" The judge cleared his throat. "This court knows you to be an honest man. What do you have to say?"

"It's like Mac says. Northrup tried to take the Rolling J herd when their original trail boss died. Northrup was run off by Patrick Flagg, who became the new trail boss." He glanced in Mac's direction. "I think he was also run off by Mac, though that's a supposition on my part."

"Sup-po-sition," the judge said, savoring the word. "Where's this Flagg who took over when the prior trail boss was killed?"

"He's laid up with a gunshot wound. I took over and am acting trail boss and agent for Mr. Jefferson, Your Honor."

"It sounds as if your trail drive was particularly dangerous, young man, what with two trail bosses dying or getting shot. So, Jack, you contradict what

Deke Northrup said to both Reedy and the marshal? This young fellow is the rightful agent for the herd? You'd swear to that in an affidavit?"

"I would and have already done so, Your Honor." Compass Jack handed a notarized statement to the marshal, who passed it along to the judge.

"I got to ask. Is this youngster paying you anything?"

"Sir, no money's changed hands. And I'm not accepting any of the cattle in his herd to say any of those things." He pointed to the affidavit.

Mac smiled, just a little, at the way Compass Jack skirted the real question, but he decided this answered the judge's concerns without muddying the water.

"Ready, Jack, Marshal, hear my verdict." The judge harrumphed and continued. "I find that Dewey Mackenzie is the only rightful agent for the Rolling J herd and that this lying sack of buffalo chips, Deke Northrup, is to be arrested on sight for attempted rustling. Now get out of here. I have an appointment to keep." He rapped the gavel smartly and stood.

"Tell Ursula howdy for me, Judge," Compass Jack said with a grin.

"Get out of here, Jack, before I find you in contempt of court."

The H Bar H trail boss shook hands with the judge and let him hurry from the courtroom without another word.

"We've got a deal to complete, Mr. Mackenzie," said Ready Reedy. "The sooner the papers are signed, the sooner those Rolling J beeves can be shipped."

"And the sooner I can pay the men."

"We all have our priorities," Reedy said.

As Compass Jack and Mac started out, the marshal called out to them.

"You really want me to arrest Northrup?"

"He tried to steal the longhorns. Of course I do, Marshal." Mac heard something in the lawman's words that made him curious enough to ask.

"Well, it's like this, son. I got it on good authority that Northrup and his gang lit out when they heard that Compass Jack was going to tell the judge what went on."

"Get a posse. Chase him down." Mac frowned when he realized that wasn't going to happen.

"I need all my deputies patrolling the streets. You and Compass Jack are among the first herds to get to town. When the rush starts, I'll have upward of five hundred drunk, horny cowboys shooting up Abilene. I can wait until the last of the herds gets shipped out, but that'll be another month. Might be less, but likely won't be."

"You're telling me Northrup will have a month's head start?"

"By then he could be in Montana or God knows where else. Even if I took out after him this very minute, I don't know which direction he went."

"Only that he left Abilene," Mac finished.

"That's about it." The marshal looked contrite, but he was the kind of man who could look that way without much effort. Mac doubted he felt the least bit regretful about letting Northrup go.

Mac looked at Compass Jack. The H Bar H trail boss took out his pocket watch and made a point of examining it. He snapped the lid shut and looked for all the world like a dog on a leash wanting to be set loose.

"Thanks for your honesty, Marshal." Mac shook hands. "I've got to pay a debt."

The marshal started to say something, then left abruptly, not wanting to know if Compass Jack and Mac had lied to the judge about a payoff.

The truth was, they had.

"It's been close to an hour, Mac. Come on. You owe me."

"Hold your horses. I'm coming." Mac fell in beside Compass Jack as they hurried to the back of a nearby bakery.

Mac went straight in and exchanged greetings with a man wearing a flour-streaked apron and a floppy chef's hat.

"It's about ready to come out," the baker said. "Smells real good, too."

"He's one fine cook." Compass Jack pulled up a chair at a table. "Now serve me. I only got a tiny taste of that custard pie, but it was about the best I ever had. My men gobbled it up as a reward for their work."

Mac pulled the pie he had fixed from the oven, using a towel to keep from burning his hands. He placed it on the table in front of Compass Jack.

"There it is, Jack. An entire custard pie, just for you."

"Who says you didn't bribe me?" Bennett took a knife and fork, cut through the pastry, and scooped some of the still-liquid filling onto a plate. A quick taste put a look of delight on his face. "I wasn't joking, Mac. You want a job cooking, come to work for the H Bar H. The men will love you."

"It's hard baking a pie out on the trail." Mac had to laugh. "It's hard getting biscuits baked. Enjoy your pie, and thanks for seeing the judge."

"I'd have stood up for you, pie or not. But this makes the drive all the better." He began eating the still-hot pie, blowing on every forkful.

Mac had work to do and left for Ready Reedy's office. Dickering with the man proved harder than he expected. Reedy knew his business and made a good profit driving a hard bargain, but after all Mac had been through, he wasn't going to roll over and play dead. He fought for every dime and even got a day's feedlot fee taken off, adding close to a hundred dollars to Mr. Jefferson's profit.

"You come back next year, Mac. I'll know you then and give you an even better deal."

Mac shook hands and left with Reedy's check in hand, the ink still wet. He headed directly for the bank used by the Rolling J and deposited it. The bank president assured him cash money for salaries could be withdrawn the next day. Mac tucked the deposit slip in his pocket. He touched the wanted poster with the map on the back and vowed to get rid of it and the other one from Waco right away.

He stepped outside into the cool autumn and took a deep breath. With some time to waste, he headed back to the rail yards. The more he learned, the better he would be as a trail boss.

Only he didn't want to be a trail boss. He saw the way Compass Jack Bennett had dug into the freshly baked pie with such gusto. The men in the Rolling J outfit never stopped telling him how good his biscuits were. Figuring out ways to stretch the sparse supplies had been a challenge, but an exciting one. He felt real accomplishment when he served up supper or dinner made from only a paltry few items left in the larder.

Fixing beefsteaks and stew was easy enough. He had a herd to choose from for prime cuts of meat, but giving the men something more than the same fare day after day made him feel good. Cooking wasn't something he had ever expected to like, but he did.

If he came back to Abilene, with the Rolling J or H Bar H or some other outfit, he'd come as a cook.

"Hey, you," came a call from the corral. "You're with the Rolling J, aren't you?"

"I am." Mac went to the corral fence, where the cowboy hung like a scarecrow, counting the cattle as they went into a car. "What's the problem?"

"You ain't got all your herd in one place, that's what. See?" The man pointed.

Mac caught his breath. As sure as the sun rose every morning, a longhorn with the Rolling J brand trotted past on its way to being loaded. Then he saw a different brand and another. Finally, the answer came when a half dozen carrying Lazy B brands followed up the chute.

"Where's the trail boss for the Lazy B?"

"They just got in and rushed their cows through. I heard that Reedy took 'em for a bundle, underpayin' by half or more."

That meant most of the Lazy B herd had been stolen, and they wanted the evidence of rustling moved out as fast as possible.

"Cut out any Rolling J cows. I'll give you one for every five you put into another corral."

"Them's stolen? The ones bein' loaded now?"

"Where's the Lazy B trail boss?"

The cowboy pointed across the yard and asked, "You want me to fetch the marshal?"

"Tell Reedy. That'll be good enough. I can handle this myself."

He slipped the leather keeper off his hammer and checked to be sure the gun slipped out easily. Willie "Jimson" Weed was supposed to be dead, but the shenanigans of letting the Rolling J outfit cut out a few of their own cattle while the main herd moved to Abilene warned him that Weed might be responsible.

Mac wished the stampede had smashed the ugly trail boss to a bloody pulp. Weed had shot Flagg. Taking care of him had been more important than anything else, even being certain part of the Rolling J herd wasn't being stolen. While he didn't know for certain, Mac suspected Weed and his gang made the trip up the Shawnee Trail, stealing cattle as they came. There might not even be a Lazy B ranch. He hadn't checked to see if the brand had been run, starting as something else and then being changed to the B on its side.

Before he reached the Lazy B camp, he heard a voice ringing out that he recognized immediately. Good sense told him to get the marshal. Let the law take care of Jimson Weed. Let Ready Reedy get his money back. He should have known any drover selling so cheaply had to be suspect. Or maybe he did know and thought to make a big profit from the rustled stock.

The only thought in Mac's brain was that Weed

had gut-shot Flagg. He had gotten away with severely injuring a man Mac thought highly of. Whether he counted Flagg as a friend or not didn't matter. He was a trail companion, and that bond was strong. They had looked after each other as well as the other cowboys and the Rolling J herd.

"You're supposed to be dead," Mac said as he walked past a pair of Lazy B drovers and stopped ten feet from Jimson Weed.

"Lookee here. The young snot from out on the prairie." Weed turned and pushed his duster back so he could reach his gun.

"You know what's another name for Jimson weed? Loco weed. A horse eats it and he goes plumb crazy. Have you been eating some jimson weed?"

"Why'd you say a thing like that?" Weed's eyes darted around.

Mac heard Weed's partners moving away to stay clear of stray lead. The fight was inevitable. He felt a calm settle on him. He had killed a man before. The reaction came afterward, when he realized what he had done.

"We're going to the marshal's office, where you can turn yourself in. I've got men cutting my cows from the others you stole. Then we can discuss how you shot Flagg, though that might count as a fair fight."

"Flagg? That ugly galoot? He's still alive? I'm slipping. I meant to kill him."

As Weed made his boast, he clawed at his gun. The rustler was trying to distract him, Mac knew, make him mad or make him think about anything other than the fight.

But instead, Mac's draw was swift, and his aim was sure. His S&W barked once. He fanned a second shot into Weed's chest as the rustler fell backward, then he spun and went into an even deeper crouch. The other Lazy B cowboys had yanked iron, too. Mac fanned off two more shots at a man standing to his right. Tumbling forward, he avoided a shot from the left.

Mac kicked up a cloud of dust, rolled to his knees, and fanned off the last two rounds in his gun. One missed. The other hit the cowboy in the forehead and went upward through the crown of his hat. He let out a tiny gasp and toppled onto his back, feet kicking feebly.

"Who else?" Mac swung his empty gun around, pointing it at three others from the Lazy B who came running up when the shooting started.

He bluffed them. They threw up their hands and backed away. When they got a safe distance, they turned and ran like jackrabbits with a coyote after them.

Mac stood and took his time reloading. Someone brought the marshal. By the time the lawman came huffing and puffing up, his gun out, Mac was ready with his story. He had to repeat it twice before the marshal agreed it was self-defense, three against one.

It took longer arguing with Reedy over who got the money from the Rolling J cattle that had been among those in the Lazy B herd. It took longer, but Mac finally convinced the cattle broker to pay up.

Then he set out to report to his boss what had happened.

CHAPTER 31

"I don't recommend trying to talk to him," the doctor said. "He's too weak."

"Will he make it?" Mac studied the doctor's face. The small twitches under the man's eyes and at the corners of his mouth told the real story. "Then there's no reason for me not to see him."

"You might be the last."

"There's nothing to lose. I'm about all he's got in the way of a friend." Mac pushed past the doctor and went into a small room off the main office.

Flagg lay propped up on a bed, sunlight filtering through blinds. The warmth must have kept him going because Mac had never seen a man who looked more like a corpse. Flagg was as white as bleached muslin and was more skeletal than human. Even so, he turned his head when Mac came in. The eyelids flickered up, and a hint of a smile came to the man's chapped lips. His eyes were sunken in deep, dark pits, and his face was gaunt with yellowed skin pulled tight over his cheekbones.

"Good of you to come, Mac. Thanks." Flagg's voice was just a whispered rasp.

"No need to talk." Mac pulled up a chair and sat close enough so he could hear Flagg's hoarse words. "The herd's sold for good money. I'll pay the men tomorrow."

"Good. Use mine to pay the doc. Any left over . . . is yours, Mac. You . . . earned it doing my job."

"You'll need it to get back to Waco. Carson's job is waiting for you there."

They both knew he was lying. Mac couldn't help trying to cheer Flagg up, and Flagg had to know by how he felt inside that he didn't have much time left.

"I killed him, Flagg. I put two bullets in him. Then I killed two more of the Lazy B gang for good measure."

"Weed?"

"I pulled him, and now they'll plant him—in a cemetery," Mac said, but the feeble joke fell on deaf ears. Flagg reached out and laid a bony hand on his arm and squeezed.

"Thank you. That means a lot to me."

Every time Flagg spoke, his voice got weaker.

"You rest up. I wanted you to know the herd's taken care of. Mr. Jefferson will have made about eight thousand in profit. That'll keep the Rolling J running for another year."

"Wait." Flagg squeezed down with impressive strength and pulled him closer to hear what he had to say. "You're a damned good man, Mac."

"I wish that were true."

"My coat pocket. Get it."

Mac picked up the tattered, filthy coat and reached

into a pocket. He froze when his fingers brushed across paper that had become all too familiar. The wanted poster was faded and almost impossible to read, but it carried his likeness.

He reached into his own pocket and took out the poster he had used to draw the Shawnee's map.

"You knew. How long?"

"Waco. General store."

"You could have fired me—or turned me in for the reward. This is almost as much as you were making as a cowboy."

"Wanted to see . . . what kind of man you are."

"I didn't do it. I was framed." Mac swallowed hard. "But I have killed men. Weed and his henchmen. The—"

"Don't. Don't dwell on the ones who . . . needed killing. I never did."

Mac started to ask if Flagg had a price on his head, then decided he didn't care to know. He held Flagg's hand and felt the life ebbing away. He held it even after it had gone limp.

He finally stood, crossed Flagg's hands on his chest, then tucked the wanted poster into his own pocket. That made another of them he had to burn.

"Good-bye, friend," he said softly. Then he left with only a nod to the doctor.

He stood outside the bank, a thick envelope filled with greenbacks in his hand. Mac squeezed it a couple times. He'd never seen this much money before, much less held it. All he had to do was climb on a horse and ride like the demons of hell chased him, and he would be richer than at any time in his life.

Had Evie figured out Leclerc wasn't what he claimed? That he had a mistress and only wanted her pa's money and influence? If he took this money back to New Orleans, he could offer her the life she deserved.

The only problem he saw was that she had chosen Leclerc over him. She hadn't had enough trust in him—in *them*—to ignore Leclerc.

And there was one more problem with that idea, he realized, an even bigger one. But he didn't really consider it a problem at all. He wasn't a thief. The men he had worked with for close to two months had earned this money.

He remembered Billy Duke and Huey Matthis. Whether Billy lied about having a family beaten down by hard times didn't matter. His share would be sent to Waco. The same with Huey Matthis's pay. Because Northrup and his gang had quit before collecting any money for their dubious work, everyone's share increased. That wasn't something Mr. Jefferson had authorized, but Mac didn't care.

He was trail boss. He made the decisions.

As he started toward the stock pens near the rail yard, he stopped by the doctor's office and paid him for his work.

"What about the body?" the doctor asked.

"Give him the best funeral you can with this." Mac counted out the balance of Flagg's pay. Keeping even a penny of it would make him feel he was stealing from a dead man. Flagg never expected a decent funeral. A shallow grave on the prairie stamped flat by a herd and marked with a crude wooden cross had been the most likely end to his life.

"You can get a good headstone with this. Marble."

"Thanks, Doc."

"You're not staying around for the funeral?"

"I have to be somewhere real soon."

"Where's that? I thought your job was done when you brought in the herd and sold it?"

Mac didn't answer the question. He just said, "Thanks, Doc," and left, thinking about his future.

He got to the stock pens filled with Rolling J cattle that had been fattened up for a couple days. Reedy's men were already moving the first of the longhorns to the corral at the rail yard, intending to load them and immediately send them to their fate in Chicago slaughterhouses.

As he climbed onto a crate, a cheer went up from the gathered Rolling J cowboys.

"It was a hard drive," Mac said. "We lost good men along the way. Too many good men."

Rattler crowded close. "What about Flagg? How's he doin'?"

"I'm a greenhorn when it comes to trail drives," Mac went on. "How many drives lose two trail bosses is a mystery to me." He took a deep breath. "Patrick Flagg's funeral will be in a day or two, if you want to pay your respects."

He saw the uneasiness this caused. Men who lived with death seldom celebrated it at funerals.

"I've got your pay, along with a generous bonus."

"The money owed all them who never finished the drive?" Rattler pressed even closer.

"Pay's been sent to families. The herd went for top dollar, and Mr. Jefferson is sharing his bounty with you and invites you all back for next year's drive. Thanks!"

He began paying out the money until only Rattler remained to receive his. The rest of the men went off, vowing to drink themselves blind and find other ways to celebrate. Mac knew better than to suggest they not get into trouble. They no longer worked for the Rolling J, and he wasn't trail boss anymore . . . as if he had ever been anything more than a second-hand replacement for Patrick Flagg.

"Where're you headin', Mac? You got somethin' in mind?" Rattler began rolling himself a cigarette as Mac hopped down from the crate. After Rattler had lit the smoke, Mac reached out and took the burning lucifer from the cowboy.

Before the flame reached his fingers, he held it to the wanted posters and waited for them to catch. As they flared up, he dropped them on the ground and watched them turn into a pile of ash.

"What were those?" Rattler puffed away. Then he said, "I don't want to know, do I?"

"You go on and join the boys. They were heading for the Son of a Gun Saloon."

"You be along, too?"

"I'm selling the chuckwagon and the horses in the remuda that weren't given to the men. Then I'll be along."

"It's been good knowin' you, Mac." Rattler shook hands, took a last deep puff, ground out the smoke, and walked away. He never looked back.

Mac thought Rattler might make a good trail boss.

He understood things without having to think real hard about them. Mac knew instinctively that their trails wouldn't cross again.

Mac sold the chuckwagon to Compass Jack Bennett, dickered a while and got a fair price for the Rolling J horses that had survived the drive, and then stood with more greenbacks clutched in his hand. Hurrying, he got to the bank and deposited the money in the Rolling J account.

His last chore done, he went to the livery, saddled, and rode away from Abilene. The bustle of the town as more herds arrived called to him. He knew he ought to turn his back on this life. It was hard, brutish, deadly. But he had found companionship and a sense of accomplishment cooking for drovers that amazed him.

"I can do better than just biscuits and custard pie," he said to himself as he left Abilene, heading west toward no particular destination. "There's apple and peach and chess pie. Definitely chess pie. And . . ."

He was still thinking about it as he rode out of sight.

Many thanks to cousin Agnes Jean of Sweet Home, Texas. Agnes Jean found these recipes in an old coffee tin in her attic. She's pretty sure they were written down by her great-grandfather, Cyrus Kendall Pippen, who was a real chuck-wagon cook and was, in part, the inspiration for Dewey "Mac" MacKenzie. We took the liberty of updating them for today's technology, but other than that, they are exactly as Cyrus wrote them—minus some cusswords.

—J. A. Johnstone

MAC'S GOLDEN BISCUITS

Here's what y'all are gonna need:

2 cups of flower
1 teaspoon baking powder—*if you ain't got none, them biscuits'll be flatter than a cow patty.*
1 teaspoon salt
1 teaspoon sugar
½ cup butter, softened
⅔ cup buttermilk

1. Preheat your over oven to 450 degrees F.
2. Grease down your flat pan (or a baking sheet).
3. Add baking powder and sugar to the flower. Cut in the softened butter. Stir in your buttermilk. Divide them little babies into balls and place on baking sheet or your flat pan.
4. Melt two tablespoons of butter and gently brush onto the top of biscuits (that's what makes 'em nice and golden brown).
5. Place in oven for 15 minutes, checking often. (Burnt biscuits can get a chuckwagon cook strung up faster than a horse or a wife thief.)

Remove from oven when top is golden brown and sides are good and firm.

CUSTARD PIE

2½ cups milk
3 *chicken* eggs—*if you got some laying hens handy, that is; if not, no need to read any more.*
Pinch of salt (¼ teaspoon)
¾ cup white sugar
1 teaspoon vanilla extract
¼ teaspoon cinnamon or to taste
¼ teaspoon ground nutmeg or to taste
1 9-inch unbaked piecrust
1 teaspoon powdered or confectioner's sugar, for garnish

1. Preheat oven to 400 degrees F.
2. Gently heat milk in saucepan until nearly boiling, then allow to cool. (Optional: Cooks in the Old West would scald the milk to be sure all the germs got killed; that is, if the germs hadn't died from overpopulation.)
3. Beat them eggs in a large bowl. Gently stir in the salt, sugar, and spices. Careful not to overbeat.
4. Add milk to the egg and spices mixture.
5. Pour mixture into piecrust and place in oven. Cook for approximately 30 minutes, checking often to make sure the pie ain't burning. Bake until top is golden brown and liquid is stiff. You can check 'er by sticking a knife in.
6. Cool pie on rack. Top with powdered sugar

for decoration, using sifter or fingers. (Keep that pie hid from the boys till suppertime. Something about a custard pie that drives men crazy enough to eat the devil with horns on.)

CHUCKWAGON BEANS

5 strips of bacon, cut into small pieces
A pound or two of dry beans—*depending on how many folks you gotta feed*
1 large onion, diced
Pinch of salt
Pinch of black pepper
1 23-ounce can of tomatoes
¼ cup brown sugar

1. Cook bacon first, then add all the rest to the pot.
2. Let simmer over a low fire for a good long while, stirring often, and tasting until all flavors are blended. Add more sugar for more sweet, if that's your pleasure. Or else some red chili, if it isn't. (And when you all bed down for the night, you'd be a mite smart to sleep way upwind of the others.)

A FINE COWBOY BREAKFAST

5 strips of bacon
1 large potato, cut into bite-size pieces—*cowboy-size bites, not them fussy little cubes*
1 medium onion, diced
1 green bell pepper, cut into bite-size pieces

1 clove garlic, peeled, smashed, and cut fine—*if you can find one; if not, might be for the best. Garlic gives some folks the trowser burps.*

7 eggs

Dash of milk (1 or 2 tablespoons)

1. First, fry the bacon in your skillet. When the pig strips are done, remove and put them aside to cool. Add the potatoes to the bacon fat. Cook until tender and golden brown, stirring often. Add in the onion, pepper, and garlic.
2. Beat eggs in separate bowl. Add milk, but not too much. What they call a "dash." Add mixture to the taters and such, then toss in the bacon, and scramble. Salt and pepper, if that's your pleasure. Serve with Mac's biscuits and you've got yourself one happy cowboy.

CHAPTER 1

It began with a rattlesnake in a glass jar and Chance Jensen's inability to pass up a bet he believed he could win.

A balding, beefy-faced bartender with curlicue mustaches reached under the bar, came up with the big glass jar, and set it on the hardwood with a solid thump.

The top of the jar had a board sitting across it. Somebody had drilled airholes in the board so the fat diamondback rattler coiled inside the jar wouldn't suffocate.

"Five bucks says no man can tap on the glass and hold his finger there when Chauncey here strikes at it," the bartender announced.

A cowboy standing a few feet down the bar with a beer in front of him looked at the jar and its deadly occupant and said, "Step aside, boys! This here is gonna be the easiest five dollars I ever earned!"

The men along the bar shifted so the cowboy could stand in front of the jar. Chance and his brother Ace had to move a little to their left, but they could still see the show.

The cowboy leaned closer and peered through the glass at the snake, which hadn't moved when the bartender set him down. "He's alive, ain't he?"

"Tap on the glass and find out," the bartender said.

The cowboy lifted a hand covered with rope calluses. He held up his index finger and thumped it three times against the glass, lightly.

Inside the jar, the snake's head raised slightly. Its tail began to vibrate, moving so fast that it was just a blur.

The saloon was quiet now as everyone looked on, and even through the glass, the men closest to the bar could hear the distinctive buzzing. That sound could strike fear into the stoutest-hearted man in Texas.

"Yeah, uh, he's alive, all right," the cowboy said. "What do I do now?"

"Show me that you actually have five bucks," the bartender said.

The cowboy reached in his pocket, pulled out a five-dollar gold piece, and slapped it down on the hardwood. Grinning, the bartender took an identical coin from the till and set it next to the cowboy's stake.

"All right. Tap on the glass a few more times to get Chauncey stirred up good and proper, and then hold your finger there. Then we wait. Shouldn't be too long."

Another man said, "Chauncey's a boy's name, ain't it?"

"Yeah, I suppose so," the bartender said with a frown. "What's your point?"

"I was just wonderin' how you know for sure that there snake is a male. Did you check?"

That brought a few hoots of laughter from the crowd. The bartender glared and said, "Never you mind about that. If I say he's a boy, then he's a boy. If you want to prove different, you reach in there and show me the evidence."

"No, no," the bystander said, holding his hands up in surrender. "I'm fine with whatever you say, Dugan."

The bartender looked at the cowboy and said, "Well? You gonna give it a try or not? You were mighty quick to brag about how you could do it. You decide you don't want to back that up with cold, hard cash after all?"

"I'm gonna, I'm gonna," the cowboy said. "Just hang on a minute."

He swallowed, then tapped three more times on the glass, harder this time.

"Hold your finger there," Dugan said.

From a few feet away, Chance watched with all his attention focused on the jar and the cowboy who was daring the snake to strike at him. Ace watched Chance and felt a stirring of concern at the expression he saw on his brother's face.

The cowboy rested his fingertip against the glass. Inside the jar, the snake's head was still up, its tiny forked tongue flickering as it darted in and out of his mouth. The buzzing from the rattles on the tip of its tail steadily grew louder.

Then, faster than the eye could follow, the snake

uncoiled and struck at the glass where the cowboy's finger was pressed.

"*Yeeeowww!*" the cowboy yelled as he jumped back. The rattler's sudden movement startled half a dozen other people in the Lucky Panther Saloon into shouting, too.

For a couple of seconds, the cowboy stared wide-eyed at the jar, where the snake had coiled up again, and then looked down at his hand. The index finger still stuck straight out, but it was nowhere near the glass anymore. Obviously disgusted, the cowboy said, "Well, hell."

Grinning, Dugan scooped up both five-dollar gold pieces and dropped them in the till.

"Told you," he said. "Nobody can do it. It just ain't natural for a man to be able to hold still when a rattler's fangs are comin' at him, whether there's glass in between or not."

Ace tried to catch Chance's eye and shake his head, but it was too late. Chance stepped closer to the spot on the bar where the jar rested and said, "I can do it."

People started to look around to see who had made that bold declaration. If not for what happened next, they would have seen a handsome, sandy-haired man in his early twenties, well dressed in a brown tweed suit, white shirt, and a dark brown cravat and hat.

But all their attention turned to the man who shouldered Chance aside, said, "Outta my way, kid," and stepped up to the bar. "I've never been afraid of a rattler in my life, and sure as hell not one penned up in a jar."

This man was tall and lean, dressed in black from head to foot, probably ten years older than Chance and Ace, who were fraternal twins. His smile had a cocky arrogance to it.

Ace was more interested in the gun holstered on the man's hip. In keeping with the rest of his outfit, that holster was black. The revolver was the only thing flashy about him. It was nickel plated and had ivory grips.

However, the gun wasn't just for show. Those grips showed the marks of a great deal of use. Maybe the man just practiced with it a lot—or maybe he actually *was* the gunslinger he obviously fancied himself to be.

The man in black held the edge of a coin against the bar and gave it a spin. It whirled there for a long moment, so fast it was just a blur, but finally ran out of momentum and clattered on the hardwood.

"I reckon my money's good, Dugan?"

"Sure, Shelby," the bartender said. "You're welcome to give it a try."

A spade-bearded man in a frock coat stepped up. He hooked his thumbs in the gold-brocaded vest he wore and said, "I have fifty dollars that says Lew can do it."

That wager was too rich for the blood of most of the patrons in this saloon in Fort Worth's notorious Hell's Half Acre, but the tinhorn gambler got a couple of takers. Coins and greenbacks were put on the bar for Dugan to hold while Shelby made his try.

Ace nudged a bearded old-timer who stood next to him and asked, "Who are those two?"

"The gun-hung feller in black is Lew Shelby," the

codger replied. "The one in the fancy vest is Henry Baylor."

"He looks like a card sharp."

"Good reason for that. He is. Or at least the rumor has it so. Nobody's ever caught him cheatin', though, as far as I know. Or if they have, they've had sense enough not to call him on it."

The old-timer licked his lips, tongue emerging from the shaggy white whiskers for a second.

"Baylor might be even slicker at handlin' shootin' irons than he is at cards," he went on. "Him and Shelby is two of a kind, and they run with a bunch just about as bad."

Ace nodded. Chance didn't look happy about Shelby pushing in ahead of him, but for the moment at least, he was keeping his annoyance under control.

Ace would say something to him if necessary, to keep him calmed down. They didn't need a gunfight in the middle of this saloon—or anywhere else, for that matter. The Jensen brothers were peaceable sorts.

That was what Ace aspired to, anyway. Oftentimes fate seemed to be plotting against them, however.

Lew Shelby stood in front of the bar, feet planted solidly, hands held out in front of him and slightly spread. He rubbed his thumbs over his fingertips and took deep breaths, as if he were working himself up to slap leather against the snake, not hold his finger against a glass jar.

The crowd began to stir restlessly.

Shelby must have sensed that impatience. He glanced over his shoulder, sneered, and said, "Hold your damn horses."

Then he reached out and tapped the glass several times, fast and hard. He pressed his finger against the jar as the snake reacted, coiling tighter in preparation to strike.

Everybody in the place knew it was coming. Nobody should have been surprised, least of all Shelby. But when the rattler struck with the same sort of blinding speed as before, Shelby jumped back a step and yelped, "Son of a bitch!"

Several men in the crowd cursed, too. Others laughed, which made Shelby's face flush.

Dugan picked up the gold piece that was all he'd had riding on the bet, but the other men who'd placed wagers moved quickly up to the bar to claim their winnings. Shelby and Baylor both looked startled and angry.

That anger deepened as Dugan smirked and said, "Told you so, boys. No man alive's got icy enough nerves to manage that little trick."

Ace tried to get hold of Chance's coat sleeve and pull him away, but Chance was a little too quick for him. He stepped forward and said, "I told you, I can do it."

Lew Shelby looked at him and scowled. "Run along, sonny. This business is for men, not boys."

Chance's voice held an edge as he said, "I'm full-grown, in case you hadn't noticed."

He moved his coat aside a little, revealing a .38 caliber Smith & Wesson Second Model revolver with ivory grips resting in a cross-draw rig on his left hip.

Shelby's dark eyes slitted, giving him a certain resemblance to the snake. He said, "You better walk soft, boy. I don't cotton to being challenged."

Ace stepped up next to his brother. He had been born a few minutes earlier than Chance, and he was slightly taller and heavier, too. Dark hair curled out from under a thumbed-back Stetson. He wore range clothes, denim trousers and a bib-front shirt, and his boots showed plenty of wear. He didn't take the time or trouble to polish them up, the way Chance did with his.

The walnut-butted Colt .45 Peacemaker leathered on Ace's right hip was strictly functional, too.

"Nobody's challenging anybody," he said. He had plenty of experience trying to head off trouble when Chance was in the middle of it.

"That's not true," Chance said. "I'm challenging that rattlesnake, as well as Mr. Dugan here. I can hold my finger on the glass without budging when the snake strikes at it."

"If I can't do it, kid, you sure as hell can't," Shelby snapped.

"The two hundred dollars in my pocket says I can."

Ace bit back a groan. Actually, the two hundred bucks was in his pocket, not Chance's, but they had that much, all right. They had worked for several months on a ranch north of Fort Worth to earn it, and now they were ready to take it easy and drift for a while, which was their usual pattern.

They couldn't do that, though, if Chance's reckless stubbornness caused them to lose their stake.

Things had gone too far to stop now. Chance had thrown the bet out there. Henry Baylor stroked his beard and said, "I'm down a hundred dollars tonight.

Winning two hundred from you would allow me to show a profit for the evening, son."

"I'm not your son," Chance said.

In truth, he and Ace didn't know whose sons they were. They had been raised by a drifting gambler named Ennis "Doc" Monday, after their mother died giving birth to them.

Once they were old enough to think about such things, they had speculated about whether Doc Monday was really their father, but there was no proof one way or the other and they had never worked up the nerve to ask Doc about it, since his health had grown bad over the years and he was living in a sanitarium. A big emotional upset wouldn't be good for him.

"If you actually have the money," Baylor said, "you have a wager."

"I've got it." Chance glanced around at his brother. "Ace?"

With a sigh, Ace dug out the roll of greenbacks and set it on the bar. He said to Dugan, "That's our whole poke. We don't have an extra five dollars to cover the bet with you."

The bartender laughed and waved a hand. "Hell, kid, I'll waive that for the occasion. In fact, I'm so sure your—brother, is it?—can't do it that if he does, I'll add a nice new double eagle to your payoff. How's that sound?"

Chance said, "We're obliged to you, Mr. Dugan. But get ready to pay up as soon as this fella"—he nodded toward Baylor—"proves that *he* can cover the bet."

Lew Shelby bristled at that. He tensed and started, "Why, you impudent little bas—"

Baylor stopped him. "That's all right, Lew," the gambler said with an easy but insincere smile. "It's fair enough for the lad to ask for proof, since I did."

He took a sheaf of bills from a pocket inside the frock coat and counted out two hundred dollars. He placed the money next to the Jensen brothers' roll.

"Satisfied?"

"Yes, sir, I am," Chance said. He turned to the bar and studied the snake in the glass jar. He asked Dugan, "His name's Chauncey, you said?"

"That's what I call him," the bartender replied. "Caught him in the alley out back earlier today. I started to kill him, then realized that maybe I could use him to make some money."

"All right, Chauncey." Chance leaned closer, putting his face almost on the glass as he peered at the rattler. "Get good and mad now, you scaly little varmint."

The snake stared back, as inscrutable as ever. The buzzing from its rattles sounded angry.

Three times, Chance thumped his fingertip against the glass. With the last thump, he left his finger there, pressed hard against the jar. The snake didn't waste any time. It uncoiled and struck furiously, jaws gaping wide to display wicked fangs dripping with venom.

CHAPTER 2

Just like the other two times, several men in the Lucky Panther let out involuntary shouts when the snake's head darted at the glass. One gaudily dressed saloon girl pressed her hands to rouged cheeks and trilled a little scream.

Then a few seconds of stunned silence ticked past before the place erupted in cheers.

Because Chance Jensen was still standing there in front of the bar with his finger pressed against the glass. He hadn't budged.

Nor did he move now, remaining where he was in the middle of the excited commotion, other than to turn his head and smile at Henry Baylor.

"I believe you owe me two hundred dollars, my friend," Chance said.

Baylor smiled in return, but his lips were tight and his eyes hooded. He said, "It appears that I do."

A few feet away, the bearded old-timer Ace had been talking to earlier tugged on his sleeve. Ace had to lean down to make out what the old man was saying.

"Better collect your winnin's and get outta here in a hurry, kid! And keep your eyes open! Baylor won't like losin' that money, and Lew Shelby sure as hell will be mad about your brother showin' him up."

Based on the expressions on the faces of Baylor and Shelby, Ace agreed with the old man. He reached out, scooped up their roll from the bar, and shoved the stack of greenbacks from Baylor into his pocket as well. Dugan grinned ruefully and handed him the double eagle he had promised as an extra payoff.

"Come on, Chance," Ace said. "Time for us to drift."

Chance still hadn't taken his finger away from the glass. He did it leisurely, mockingly, then lifted the finger to his lips and blew across the top of it, as if he were blowing away a curl of smoke from a gun muzzle.

"Wait just a damn minute," Shelby rasped.

"Why? You're not going to claim that I cheated, are you? That would have been hard to do with this many people watching me the whole time."

"But *were* they watching you the whole time?" Shelby turned to the bar. "Dugan! Did you have your eye on this kid? You didn't look away any?"

"I don't think so," the bartender said.

"You didn't even blink when the snake struck?"

"Well . . . I was trying to watch pretty close . . ."

Shelby glared as he jerked his gaze around the room.

"I'll bet everybody in here blinked just then! Nobody was watching the kid the whole time. He could've taken his finger off the glass for a split-second, and nobody would have noticed." When nobody spoke up to agree with him, he scowled even more and demanded, "Isn't that right?"

Shelby had a reputation here in Fort Worth as a gunman. Nobody wanted to disagree with him. Some men shuffled their feet and looked down at the floor in obvious discomfort. Others started edging toward the door, figuring it was better to leave than to wait and see how this played out.

But then one grizzled hombre who looked like a successful cattleman, the sort who didn't take any guff from anybody, said, "I was watching the whole time, and I didn't blink. The kid's finger didn't move."

Emboldened by that blunt declaration, several other men muttered agreement.

"You know I didn't move my finger," Chance said to Shelby. "You're just mad because I was able to do it and you couldn't."

A feral hatred came into Shelby's eyes as he said, "I can do it! By God, double or nothing! I'll show you."

"Lew, I'm not sure that's wise," Baylor cautioned. "We've already lost enough tonight."

"I'm not gonna let this damn kid think he can get the best of me!" Shelby's jaw jutted out as he said to Chance, "How about it? You willing to bet the four hundred that I can't do it?"

"Chance . . ." Ace said.

"Relax, Ace," Chance said with a smile. "If we lose, we're no worse off than we were before."

"Yeah, we are. Two hundred bucks worse!"

"Life would be mighty dull without a little risk now and then to spice it up." Chance nodded to Shelby.

"We'll take that bet, mister. Go ahead." He glanced at Baylor. "I won't even ask if you can cover it."

The gambler was grim-faced now. His friend had put him in a bad position. But he jerked his head in a nod, said, "Go ahead," and made a little gesture with his slender, long-fingered hand.

As Shelby faced the jar, Dugan said, "I don't know about this. Chauncey's been banging his head against the glass every time he strikes. He's liable to be gettin' a little addled by now. I don't want him to hurt himself."

"You gettin' soft on a rattlesnake, Dugan?" one of the customers asked with a jeering grin.

"No, but if he bashes his brains out, he can't win me any more bets, can he?"

"Does a snake even have a brain?" another man asked.

"Got to," his companion said. "Ever'thing that's alive has got a brain. Don't it?"

"Don't know. I never studied up on snakes. Just shot 'em or chopped their heads off with a Bowie knife."

Shelby snapped, "Shut your damn yammering! A man can't hear himself think."

Once again he went through the routine he had performed earlier. Silence descended on the saloon, broken only by the sound of men breathing. Even that seemed to die away as Shelby hunched his shoulders a little. He was ready.

His hand stabbed forward. His finger shoved hard against the jar. He didn't even have to tap on the glass this time. The snake was so keyed up it struck immediately.

Shelby's finger jerked back as the fangs hit the inside of the jar. He didn't flinch much, maybe half an inch, but his fingertip definitely left the glass and everybody who was watching saw that. Shelby tried to press his finger against the jar again, but it was too late.

"That'll be another four hundred dollars," Chance said into the awed hush that followed.

Shelby took a quick step back, away from the bar. A stream of obscenity poured from his mouth as his hand dropped to the fancy gun on his hip. Ace grabbed the back of his brother's coat collar and yanked Chance out of the way as he used his other hand to grab his Colt.

The gunman wasn't aiming to shoot either of the Jensen brothers, however. Instead, he was still facing the bar when his gun leaped up and spouted noise and flame.

The first bullet shattered the jar and sent glass shards flying through the air. The second swiftly triggered round whipped past Chauncey's weaving head and blew a bottle of busthead on the backbar to smithereens. The snake shot out of the wreckage, slithered across the bar, and dropped writhing to the sawdust-littered floor, the thick body landing with what must have been a thump.

Nobody could hear it, though, because the saloon still echoed from the reports of Shelby's gun. At least half the people in the Lucky Panther started yelling and screaming when they realized the big rattler was loose.

"Chauncey!" Dugan bellowed. "You bastard, you tried to kill my snake!"

Shelby snarled and shouted, "Get outta the way! I'm gonna blast the damn thing!"

Dugan reached under the bar, came up with a bungstarter, and raised it as he leaned across the hardwood. Another second and he would have brought the bungstarter down across the wrist of Shelby's gun hand, probably breaking the bone.

Before the blow could fall another pistol cracked, this one a small weapon that Henry Baylor had grabbed from concealment under his frock coat. The slug tore through Dugan's forearm and made him drop the bungstarter and howl in pain.

The Lucky Panther, which sat on the corner of Throckmorton and Second Streets, had two entrances, the bat-winged main one facing Throckmorton and a regular door on the side. The customers stampeded for both of them. The furious gunman and the equally agitated rattlesnake had everybody scrambling to get out of there before they caught a bullet or got bit.

Everybody except Ace and Chance Jensen. Ace knew Shelby was liable to hurt an innocent person if he kept flinging lead around like that.

Ace scooped up the beer mug he had emptied a few minutes earlier and heaved it at Shelby's head. The heavy glass mug struck the gunman a good enough lick to stagger him.

At the same time, Baylor swung his gun toward Ace. Acting instinctively to defend his brother, Chance tackled the gambler before he could fire.

The collision drove Baylor's back against the bar. He grunted and swiped at Chance's head with the pistol. The blow knocked off Chance's flat-crowned brown hat but missed otherwise.

Earlier, Shelby and Baylor had been sitting at a table with three other men, probably the bad bunch the old-timer had warned Ace about. Two of them charged into the fray now. The third man, an Indian by the looks of him, drew a knife from his belt and stalked across the room, ignoring the rapidly developing brawl.

Getting walloped by the beer mug had stunned Lew Shelby enough to leave him stumbling around in aimless circles. One of his friends took up the battle for him and went after Ace. The other man looped an arm around Chance's neck from behind and dragged him away from Baylor.

Ace ducked a roundhouse right that his attacker threw at him. He brushed his hat back off his head so it hung from its chin strap behind him. He crouched even lower and waded in, hooking punches to the man's soft-looking belly.

That paunch was deceptive. Hitting it was like hammering his fists against the wall of a log cabin, Ace discovered.

The man hit Ace a backhanded blow with his forearm. The impact knocked Ace halfway across the bar. He caught himself and managed not to slide all the way over. As his opponent charged in, he raised both legs and straightened them in a double kick to the chest.

That sent the man flying. He landed on a table that collapsed under him and dumped him among its shattered debris. He sat up and shook his head groggily.

Halfway along the bar, Baylor was slugging Chance in the belly while the other man hung on to him from behind. Chance was red in the face from the choking grip around his neck.

Ace swerved wide, picked up a chair, and crashed it down on the back of the man who had hold of Chance. That knocked him loose.

Chance twisted free, grabbed Baylor's arm as the gambler tried to hit him in the stomach again, and pivoted, throwing Baylor over his hip in a wrestling move he had learned during a rough-and-tumble childhood spent traveling with Doc Monday. Chance might look like a bit of a dandy, but he could handle himself just fine in a fight.

Baylor rolled across the floor, dirtying his nice frock coat. In the scuffle, he had lost the little pistol with which he had shot Dugan, but that wasn't the only weapon he carried. As Chance closed in on him, ready to continue the fight, Baylor came up slashing with a folding straight razor that he flicked open with a practiced twist of his wrist.

Chance had to jump back to avoid being cut. Baylor came after him, backing him against the bar.

At the same time, Ace was being hemmed in by Shelby and the man he had kicked in the chest, both of whom had recovered their wits and appeared to be ready to beat him to death.

The Jensen brothers found themselves standing side by side, backs against the bar, with no place to run as trouble closed in on them. Sadly, this wasn't the first time they had found themselves in such a perilous position.

Tonight, however, judging by the anger and hatred twisting the cruel faces of the men stalking toward them, they might not get out of it.

With no warning, the deafening roar of another shot slammed through the room and made everybody freeze.

Connect with Us

Visit us online at
KensingtonBooks.com
to read more from your favorite authors, see books
by series, view reading group guides, and more.

 Join us on social media

for sneak peeks, chances to win books and prize packs,
and to share your thoughts with other readers.

facebook.com/kensingtonpublishing
twitter.com/kensingtonbooks

Tell us what you think!

To share your thoughts, submit a review,
or sign up for our eNewsletters, please visit:
KensingtonBooks.com/TellUs.